PRAISE FOR GINNY YTTRUP

Writers and readers alike have been singing the praises of Ginny Yttrup since her debut novel *Words*. Now I understand what all the excitement is about! Her writing is fresh, winsome, and deeply spiritual. Faith isn't merely a thread woven through the story; faith is the fabric upon which *Invisible* is stitched with a loving hand. Healing and hope can be found among these pages—not only for each character, but for the reader as well. A fine effort from one of Christian fiction's brightest new voices.

—Liz Curtis Higgs, *New York Times*
best-selling author of *Mine is the Night*

Ginny Yttrup is one of the new luminous writing stars on the Christian fiction horizon. Her words inspire my spirit and grip my consciousness like few others do. She received the Christy award for her debut novel *Words*. *Publishers Weekly* described her second book *Lost and Found* as inspirational and entertaining. I have the happy privilege of commending her third book *Invisible* as yet another inspiring and riveting story of a woman who learns her dress size does not rule out romantic love. She can cook and eat but can she allow her heart to be fed as well? Her struggle with self-image and the ever-present inner voice of condemnation is a recognizable battle we all wage against the hurtful messages from our past. You will be encouraged, entertained and energized by the message of *Invisible*.

—Marilyn Meberg, speaker and writer with
Women of Faith and author of *Constantly Craving*

In *Lost and Found* by Ginny Yttrup, Jenna Bouvier used to have it all. Marriage to a wonderful man, wealth and a wealthy lifestyle, good health, and she had her freedom her life. She's not in good health and she feels like she's losing her husb

mother in law wishes to have total and complete control of every facet of Jenna's life.

As Jenna goes through some upheaval, she finds a true friend in a spiritual advisor named Matthew. He helps her learn how to walk the Christian walk with integrity. They have such a unique connection to each other that it's amazing to watch their friendship and spiritual advisement grow. But when Jenna's mother-in-law tries to intervene, Jenna has some weighty decisions to make. Will she continue to follow the path she believes God has put her onto? Or will she bow to the wishes of others as she has always done?

A deeply moving story that will hit each reader differently. It will bisect your own walk no matter where you are at in that walk with God. Be seeing the flaws of Jenna and other characters, such as Jenna's brother's girlfriend, Andee, we can recognize glimpses of ourselves. I was amazed at the twists and turns in the road and how one person's path would bisect another's road. I loved watching God map everything out to eventually bring glory to Him. I also appreciated the insight into the lives and thoughts of those who are abused or oppressed. Jenna faces a lot of mental and emotional abuse and hearing her inner thoughts helps give the reader a new understanding and sensitivity to those in an abusive relationship.

—One Upon a Romance

invisible

GINNY L. YTTRUP

invisible

B&H
PUBLISHING GROUP
Nashville, Tennessee

978-1-4336-7168-5

Published by B&H Publishing Group
Nashville, Tennessee

Dewey Decimal Classification: F
Subject Heading: SELF-ACCEPTANCE—FICTION \
SELF-ESTEEM—FICTION \ SELF-DESTRUCTIVE
BEHAVIOR—FICTION

Unless otherwise noted, Scripture quotations are from the Holy
Bible, New International Version, copyright © 1973, 1978, 1984 by
International Bible Society.

1 2 3 4 5 6 7 8 • 17 16 15 14 13

To my grandmother, Enid Virginia Foster

Thank you for the many times through the years that you've told me I'm beautiful. You've helped me to believe it's true. I love you.

ACKNOWLEDGMENTS

I SPENT A MONTH living in Mendocino, California, the setting of *Invisible*, as I wrote this book. It is a month of my life I will cherish forever. A few days of that month were spent with dear friends who came to visit, but the rest of the time I was alone. I sat in a soft leather chair, gazing out a picture window at the rugged coastline and always-changing sea and sky. Mesmerized by the beauty of God's artistry, I found writing difficult. I also struggled with nagging health issues that made writing a challenge. In fact, the emergency room scene in this book came directly from my own experience—I just changed the names and added a handsome doctor.

I returned home with an incomplete manuscript and an unmet deadline. So first, I want to thank my gracious fiction team at B&H Publishing Group for understanding my health needs and extending my deadline. I am so grateful for the work each of you does and the love with which you do it. Thank you also to Karen Ball, my fabulous editor and friend. You flexed your schedule several times for this manuscript and, as always, made it better than it was when you received it.

God's timing is always perfect, even when we believe we've failed, and my late manuscript was no exception. Because of the delay, I connected with two wonderful authors and speakers after my original deadline. They consulted with me, offering their expertise and experience as I finished the manuscript, and then gave their endorsements of *Invisible*. Thank you, Liz Curtis Higgs and Marilyn

Meberg—you are both delightful to work with and God blessed me through each of you.

I also want to thank my dear friend, Dr. Laurie Clark. Laurie, you offered your medical knowledge each time I asked a question either about Ellyn or about myself. You advised me to seek medical attention while I was in Mendocino, which was exactly what I needed. You are gracious, patient, lovely, and so dear. I love our friendship.

Thank you, Anna Rathbun, for the month of nutritional advice and research you offered while I was in Mendocino. I returned home stronger and a few pounds lighter. Thank you, too, for the tour of Corners of the Mouth and access to the store and you during that month. I am grateful for all I learned from you.

A special thank you to the writers who connected with me through the ACFW e-mail loop when I asked if anyone was willing to share their personal experience with anorexia nervosa. You know who you are. I appreciate your vulnerability and the information you shared with me.

I am especially grateful to my writers group who prayed me through this book along with a host of other dear friends. Your prayers were needed and appreciated. I also owe a debt of gratitude to Rebecca Qualls, who read this manuscript as I wrote and offered her insight and encouragement along the way.

James Warrick, you told me several times not to edit my life as I wrote this book. So, I didn't. Thank you. This is a work of fiction but there is a lot of me in these pages. And Laurie Breining, you are a great and patient cheerleader.

Beth Thompson, thank you for stepping away from your own writing one afternoon while we were in Mendocino together and brainstorming titles with me for this book. We landed on the perfect one.

I am awed, as always, by the depth of my Heavenly Father's love and His consistent provision for me. Lord, I will always remember the days we spent together in a little house in Mendocino overlooking the grandeur of Your creation. Thank you for that precious time.

So God created mankind in his own image, in the image of God
he created them; male and female he created them.

GENESIS 1:27

Men go abroad to wonder at the heights of mountains,
at the huge waves of the sea, at the long courses of the rivers,
at the vast compass of the ocean, at the circular motions of the
stars, and they pass by themselves without wondering.

SAINT AUGUSTINE

Now to the King eternal, immortal, invisible, the only God,
be honor and glory forever and ever. Amen.

1 TIMOTHY 1:17

Who will enable me to find rest in you? Who will grant me that you come to my heart and intoxicate it, so that I forget my evils and embrace my one and only good, yourself?

CHAPTER ONE

Ellyn

 I LOVE BUTTER.

If stranded on a deserted island, given the choice between a pound of butter and a man, Honey, you know I'd choose the butter. Any woman worth her weight can catch a fish and I'm worth every plentiful pound. I don't need a man to provide. But barbeque that fish over an open flame without a drizzle of liquid gold, and all you have is dandruff-dry flakes of flavorless flesh. With butter? That same flaky flesh becomes a gourmand's delight.

But do I love butter more than I love God?

That question nibbles at my peace, like I nibble at a cookie when others are watching.

I tap the rubber spatula I'm holding against the bowl on the mixer. It's a ridiculous question. I tap again. Butter and God can't be compared—that's like comparing baklava and broccoli.

But if it's so ridiculous then why does it leave dainty bites in my sense of serenity?

The Hobart HL600 mixer drones, but not loud enough to muffle the ongoing debate in my head. In my heart, I don't want to love anything or anyone more than I love God. But in my stomach . . .

Stop condemning yourself, Ellyn.

I set the spatula down, swipe my index finger across the pound of butter softening on a marble slab on the kitchen's stainless countertop, and then stick the finger into my mouth. My taste buds dance at the sweet cream and hint of salt. I lick my finger clean. "Mmm . . . heaven."

Paco, my sous chef, walks past and swats my upper arm with a towel. "Hey, Ellyn, you have a phone call. Time to stop flirting with the butter, Bella."

Doubt returns. See, even Paco knows where my loyalty lies—or at least my attraction. I grab a towel and use it to mop my forehead, then walk to the sink, wash my hands, and dry them on the apron tied around my waist. I remove the apron and toss it, along with the towel, in a basket for the laundry service. I run my hands over my black chef's coat, smoothing it over my hips.

I wouldn't be caught dead wearing beached-whale white.

Then I turn, sidestep through the entrance to the office, and pick up the receiver. "Hello, this is Ellyn."

"Ellyn, this is Dee at Dr. Becker's office calling to confirm your appointment. 9:00 a.m., Monday the 29th."

I lean back in the desk chair and look at the ceiling.

"Ellyn?"

"Um, yes, I'm here. What . . . what is the appointment for? I don't recall—"

"Your annual physical."

"Oh, right. You know, that date isn't great. I may need to resched—"

"You've rescheduled twice before." Dee's voice softens, but her admonishment is clear.

"Oh . . . well, okay, the 29th it is. I'll make it work. See you then." I hang up the phone and look at the calendar on the desk. I count the days until the appointment and mentally tally how many pounds I can lose before then. "Phooey."

"What phooey?"

I swivel in the office chair. Rosa, my dining-room manager, leans into the office. "Phooey! Who makes a doctor's appointment for a Monday morning? Women always weigh more on Mondays."

"Dat so? What phooey anyway? You fine."

"Yeah, right."

"*Si.*" Rosa smiles, her dark curls bouncing as she nods. "Napkins? We talk napkins now?"

I glance at the clock on the wall. "Later, okay?"

"Later? It's always later with you. *Camarón que se duerme, se lo lleva la corriente.*"

This is one of the times I'm grateful that I'm not fluent in Spanish. Though I keep trying to learn. It's survival in this area, especially inland where Mexican workers maintain the vineyards. The California wine community owes its success to the laborers.

And so do I.

I grab a pad of sticky notes and scrawl a reminder to discuss napkins with Rosa this afternoon. Then I heft myself out of the chair. As I stand, my knees creak and the arthritis in my feet accuses.

I sigh.

Stupid phone call.

Fatigue tempts me to sit back down. Instead, I walk out of the office. "Paco, I'll be in the garden." I shout this over my shoulder and then walk out the back door of the restaurant, letting the screen door slam behind me. I trade my kitchen clogs for my garden clogs and then limp my way across the patch of grass between the renovated Victorian house and the garden.

A physical? I shake my head. As much as I try to deny it, not having one annually would be irresponsible. There are employees, families, who depend on me for their livelihood. Keeling over in the kitchen won't do.

I stop at the edge of the garden—organic herbs and vegetables glisten in the morning sun, droplets of dew like prisms of crystals on the leaves. I sigh again.

I need to keep a grasp on my health.

Health? How about your weight? If you weren't so—

"Shut up, Earl." I do *not* want to hear another accusation from my inner critic.

The sensation washing over me because of that appointment reminder is as well known to me as Earl's voice. However, the sensation and I are not on a first-name basis. I simply call it what it is.

Shame.

That's what causes me to question my love for God, too.

I push the thought aside. I'll deal with it tomorrow.

Just like you'll eat healthier tomorrow?

Earl knows as well as I that tomorrow never comes.

Fine, so I'll see Dr. Miles Becker on Monday morning, the 29th. I wish, as I have many times before, that I could make an appointment with a female internal-medicine specialist, but with the lagging economy in Fort Bragg not many new doctors are setting up practice. Oh well, I'll step on the scale and don a paper dress for Dr. Becker—again.

I smile to myself. "*That*, Ellyn, is called a safe relationship. The man is married *and* he knows how much you weigh."

I turn my face to the sun and let it warm me, then reach for my hair and pull the clamp out of the back, letting the curls fall over my shoulders.

Those hair clamps induce more headaches than hormones.

But a day of sunshine on the Mendocino coastline will cure almost anything—maybe even my foul mood. I listen to the sounds of the village coming to life—bells ringing on shop doors, the grinding gears of delivery trucks, and the occasional conversation from the street outside the restaurant.

A lone gull squawks overhead.

"You single too?" I shrug. "Nothing wrong with that."

The scents of rosemary and basil growing in the herb section of the café's organic garden calm me. My shoulders relax and I draw in a deep breath of moist air. I look back down at the garden, a patchwork of colors. I eye the blue curled Scotch kale I planted two weeks ago. I use it for garnish in the restaurant—the blue-green foliage adds a pop of color on our white square dinner plates.

I reach for a basket on the potting shelf at the garden's edge and head for the herbs. Then an idea hits me and I look back at the kale. "Of course, a juice cleanse!" A juice cleanse has to be good for at least a pound a day—maybe more.

Seven pounds in seven days.

Perfect.

The weight on my shoulders lifts like a coastal fog.

I PUSH OPEN THE door of the old Baptist-church-turned-health-food-store, Corners of the Mouth, on Ukiah Street and brace for the smell of vitamins. *Good Lord, You could not have created that odor. That has to be something man conjured up after the fall.* But, as always, I'm surprised by the scent of fresh produce and the loaves of Café Beaujolais' bread they sell. There's a nutty warmth about the place.

I nose around the aisles for a while and land in front of the essential oils. I open small bottles and sniff the aromas. Lavender. Eucalyptus. Thyme. Then, I wander toward the refrigerated cases in the back.

"May I help you?"

I turn around and face . . . her nametag says *Twila*. The tattoo of—what? A branch of thorns?—across her right cheek says *I'm desperate for attention.* "Hi, Twila. Yes, I'm going to do a juice cleanse. You know, get all those disgusting toxins out of my body. Any suggestions?"

"Sure." Twila gives me the once-over, likely making her own judgments. "So, like, do you also want to lose weight or is it just a detox?"

I give twiggy Twila my most charming smile. "Well, if I lose a few pounds in the process that wouldn't be all bad, now would it?"

Twila shrugs. "It just means you'll do a different cleanse. No nut milks—just organic fruits and vegetables. Do you want something prepared or will you do the juicing yourself?" She looks at my chef's smock, pants, and clogs. "I bet you'll do the juicing yourself."

"Good call." I like her, despite her thin frame and cry-for-attention tattoo.

"Okay, so maybe a book with recipes and information about nutrients and antioxidants?"

"Great."

"The book section is in the choir loft with the herbs." She points me to the stairs. "You'll find several books on juicing. I recommend a three-day juice cleanse."

"Thanks, Twila." If three days is good—seven must be better.

"Sure. Come find me if, you know, you have questions or whatever."

I don't know that I've ever climbed the stairs to the choir loft—I've always thought of it as the area where they keep the voodoo stuff. Healing herbs? C'mon, herbs are meant to enhance the flavor of foods. Then I see all the loft has to offer, and my eyes widen. Jars filled with mixtures of dried herbs and teas line the shelves—each a delicious health aid—there are teas that energize, teas that calm, and teas and herbs that aid sleep. There's also a selection of teacups, pots, and infusers.

And not one voodoo remedy in sight.

After I've found a book I like, I head back downstairs, grab some organic Tuscan kale—or as they call it at Corners, dinosaur kale—and a bunch of organic carrots, and then find Twila behind the register. I hand her the book and vegetables and watch as she rings up my purchases.

"So . . . Twila, what's with the thorns? The tattoo?" Hey, if the girl has something tattooed on her face for the world to see, then it's open for discussion, right?

"Oh . . ." She raises her hand to her face and her fingers linger on the thorns. "It's a sign of solidarity with those who suffer, you know?"

My blank expression tells her I don't.

"Like, the sick, the hungry, the hurting."

The fat. "Wow."

"The greatest evil is physical pain." Sincerity shines in her wide, gray eyes.

"Really?"

"It's a quote. Augustine."

Lord, I'm such a dork for judging her. "Physical pain?" I look around the store at all the healing properties. "So is that why you work here?"

She shrugs one thin shoulder. "That's part of the reason."

"Are you new?"

"Sort of." She smiles and shrugs again. "I mean, I haven't worked here for that long, but my mom's worked here for like thirty years or something. I sort of grew up in the store."

"Oh, you're Nerissa Boaz's daughter?" I cock my head and look at Twila's features. "I haven't seen you in several years—I didn't recognize you."

She twirls a strand of her long, dark hair around one finger. "Yeah, I was gone for a long time. School and . . . you know, some other things." She places the receipt for the book inside its pages and hands it to me, along with the vegetables she's bagged.

"Welcome back." I drop the book and vegetables into the canvas bag I carried into the store. "It doesn't seem like many of the kids who've grown up here come back once they've left."

"Yeah, the town's kind of small. Not a lot of opportunities."

I nod. "So are you following in your mother's footsteps or is this"—I gesture to our surroundings—"just temporary?"

She shoves her hands into the pockets of the hooded sweatshirt she wears. "I guess I'm doing what she does, but we each do it in our own way. I plan to stay here, unless, like, I'm led somewhere else."

"Led?"

The sweet smile that crosses her face makes the tattooed thorns seem out of place. "Yeah, God. You know?"

"I do know."

"Nice."

"Well, thanks for your help, Twila. I'll see you around, I'm sure."

"Yeah. Hey, where do you work? Which restaurant?"

"Ellyn's on Main Street."

She looks back at the store's copy of my credit card receipt. "Like your name? You're the owner?"

"Owner and chef."

"Nice."

"You'll have to come by sometime." I realize as I say it that I'd like to get to know Twila. "Really."

"Yeah, maybe. Do you serve any vegan dishes?"

"Vegan?" *Seriously?* "No, I let Raven's up at the Stanford Inn handle the vegan stuff. But I could probably come up with something for you."

"Okay. Nice to meet you. Good luck with the cleanse."

"Thanks." I turn and wave as I go.

I can't wait to get home! I'll create recipes. Maybe even write my own juicing book. Add a juice bar to the café.

At the very least, I'm on the road to losing seven pounds in seven days and there's nothing better than that.

THE MORNING OF MY appointment with Dr. Becker, I step on my scale and gulp.

Maybe it's wrong.

I wander from the bathroom into my closet. The narrow space in the old water-tower-turned-home is flanked on either side by shelves cluttered with extra dishes, boxes, wrapping paper, whatever. I don't have enough clothes to fill the space, so I use it for storage, filling just one section of hanger space with my work smocks, elastic-waist pants in varying cotton prints, and a few other items. Another section of shelves holds the three or four pairs of sweats, long-sleeved T-shirts, and sweaters I wear at home or around town.

I reach for my one pair of dress slacks—black linen—and slip them on. I pull the waistband together and struggle with the zipper and then stretch the waistband even more to get the button into the buttonhole. I grab the black cotton sweater that I wear with the slacks and give thanks that it's long and baggy.

I don bronze leather flats I can slip out of and emerge from the closet dressed. "It's as good as it gets." I accessorize in anticipation of The Event and leave my watch and favorite bronze bracelet sitting on my dressing table and put small studs in my lobes rather than the hammered bronze hoops I usually wear with this outfit.

I didn't weigh the outfit, but once I lose the shoes, it has to come in under a pound, pound and a half, tops.

I sit at the dressing table in my room and turn the makeup mirror on. The light highlights each freckle across my nose. I dust my face with matte powder, then apply a little blush, mascara, and lipgloss. More makeup than I use most days.

My eyes, the color of green sea glass, stare back at me from the mirror. From the chin—or chins—up, I look okay. But from the chins down . . . Well, it evidences the occupational hazard that is my career. *Or my choices,* as Earl would say. Then I remember Twila. I rest my elbows on the dressing table and rest my chins on my hands.

"The greatest evil is physical pain."

Do I think that's true? I have my share of physical pain, but I assume it's just what God's allowed. So who am I to argue?

Get over it, Ellyn. You don't have real pain. You're just fat. There are people who really *suffer.*

For once, I agree with Earl.

I lean forward and eye my reflection in the mirror. "Suck it up, honey."

WHEN I REACH THE doctor's office, I walk in, register with the receptionist, and then take a seat. Magazines sporting cover models with long, narrow waists are scattered across a table between the chairs and there's an antiseptic smell to the air. The magazines repel me, but the woman sitting across from the chair I've chosen does look interesting. She's tall, slender, and her skin is the color of cocoa.

There's something exotic about her that I find intriguing, even if she is scrawny.

Her dark hair is cropped close to her head, accentuating her dark eyes and full lips. I notice the earrings dangling against her long neck—small turquoise stones hanging from chandelier-type drops. Those babies must weigh at least four ounces all on their own. But then, she doesn't need to worry about that, does she?

She must sense my stare because she looks up from the book she's reading and flashes a tight smile in my direction. I smile back and reach for a magazine, *Highlights*, my skin turning the color of a Big-Boy tomato, I'm sure.

"Sabina Jackson."

We both look up at the nurse's call.

"Dr. Norman will see you now."

The woman closes her book, drops it in her purse, and gets up.

Sabina. Her name is as exotic as she is. And it appears to be Sabina's lucky day—it's the pudgy nurse who will weigh her. The pudgy nurse never comments on my weight.

But who is Dr. Norman?

Camie calls my name—tanned, toned Camie, who, with my chart open in her hand, leads me to the scale. "Date of birth?"

"April 12."

Camie looks from the chart to me. "Year? Just to confirm . . ."

"Nineteen"—I swallow—"sixty-six."

"Okay, please step on the scale."

The Event.

I set my purse on the chair next to the scale and slip out of my shoes. I take a deep breath, step up onto the scale, and close my eyes. I hear Camie moving the little weight thingy.

Then I peek.

Big mistake.

"What? Wait. Are you sure? I mean, I know. But . . . I was hoping my scale at home was . . . wrong."

"You're up six pounds from last year."

Oh good. Chastisement. As if I don't feel bad enough already.

The juice cleanse did me no favors. That first morning of juicing kale, carrots, and apples left me holding a glass filled with green sludge. It looked like something scraped from the bottom of a stagnant pond. It smelled like it too. I pinched my nose closed and slammed the juice down. Oh, but the aftertaste . . . I chased the juice with a small bite of a buttery croissant I'd brought home from the café.

And, well, one bite led to another.

Failed diet plan number 1,358. Or something like that.

"Ah well, I'm a chef, you know."

She gets me settled, runs me through the usual routine, and then hands me the paper gown. "Doctor Becker will be with you in a few minutes."

I undress, stuff myself into the gown, climb up on the examining table, and wait.

A few minutes later I hear Doctor Becker's familiar *rat-a-tat-tat* on the door.

"Come in." I pull the gown tighter as he opens the door.

"Hey, gal, how are you?" He holds out his hand.

I reach for his hand, which swallows up mine, and we shake.

"How long have I been seeing you now?" He looks at the file. "Six years? So, may I call you Ellyn rather than Ms. DeMoss?"

"Sure. I mean, after all, you've seen all of me every year for the last half dozen." I smile while clenching my teeth. Why does everything that goes through my brain come out my mouth?

Dr. Becker laughs and I notice, as I have before, the sparkle in his blue eyes. The doctor is a large man—tall, broad, and, if not for that sparkle, imposing in the small space of the examining room.

He takes a seat on the rolling stool in front of the table I'm sitting on and stretches his long legs out in front of him. His feet, clad in running shoes, land just beneath mine, which hang over the edge of the table. He smiles up at me—my file sits on his lap. "How's the restaurant business?"

I cross my bare legs, and consider suggesting the good doctor don a pair of shades to avoid the glare coming from the white sheen of my shins. "It's good, considering the economy. The tourists keep us going."

He nods. "I'll have to come by for dinner soon. It's been awhile since I've meandered around the village."

"Well, it's still there." *Brilliant, Ellyn, like he thought it fell into the sea?* "So . . . um . . ." I look to the side and eye the blood-pressure cuff hanging on the wall. ". . . I guess blood pressure's first?" *Let's get this over with.*

Dr. Becker glances toward the wall and then looks down at my file, still unopened. He seems hesitant. He finally pats the file with his left hand and clears his throat. "Actually, Ellyn, I wanted to talk to you about something."

He looks at me, eyebrows raised.

"Okay." A knot begins to form in my stomach. Is he going to start with my weight? Did he look at my chart before he came in and see how much I've gained?

"I've taken on a partner. Dr. Courtney Norman? Maybe you'd heard?"

I shake my head. Thank heaven! No awkward discussion about my weight.

He looks from me to the floor, but before he does, I see a flash of emotion cross his face. Sadness? *What's up, Doc?* But the expression is gone when he looks back at me.

"It's time to live a little." He smiles and runs one hand through his salt-and-pepper hair. "And Dr. Norman was ready for small-town life after doing her internship in Chicago. She's excellent. Really." He waves one of his large paws in my direction. "And she's familiar with women's issues."

"So . . . you're . . ."

He waits for me to finish my sentence but I don't. Although I'd guess him to be in his early fifties, he still seems too young to retire and I don't want to offend him. But where is he going with his glowing report of Dr. Norman?

Once he realizes nothing else is coming out of my mouth, he begins again. "I'm lightening my case load—taking a day or two off each week to pursue other interests."

"Oh, great. I bet your wife is looking forward to that." He's always spoken of his wife and the time they spend together. I've met her at the café, they're regulars. Or were. I haven't seen them in some time.

He stares at me, and something clouds his expression again. I glance down at his left hand . . .

And see his bare ring finger.

Oh no. "Did I stick my foot in my mouth? It's the only acrobatic move I do well."

"No. No." He looks at the floor and doesn't even break a smile at my joke. "Anyway, I'd like to transfer you over to Dr. Norman. I think she'd be great for you and helpful with some of the issues you've struggled with. But I didn't want to do that without discussing it with you."

He's fidgeting with the corner of my file.

"Oh, okay. Sure, that's great. I've often thought a female would . . . I mean . . . you're great . . ."

He holds up one hand and smiles. "I understand."

He's dumping you, honey. Too much butter on your thighs. He's handing the fat girls off to the lady doctor.

He stands and reaches his hand toward me again, but this time when I shake his hand, he seems to hold mine for a moment or two longer than usual. "Ellyn, it's always good seeing you. I'll look forward, I hope, to seeing you at the café?"

"Sure. I'm always there."

"Great. Dr. Norman will be right in." He turns and leaves the examining room.

The warmth of his hand lingers on mine.

Well, at least it was a nice dumping. And you've wanted a female doctor, right?

"Right." I pull the paper drape closer around my ample stomach and chest as I wait for Dr. Norman, who I'm certain is young, skinny, and beautiful.

Maybe *she's* what happened to Dr. Becker's wedding ring.

See him at the café? Yeah, I bet. Nice way to soften the dumping, Doc. Although, maybe I deserve the dumping. Six more pounds? *Oh, Lord, I'm sorry I'm such a disappointment to You.*

Even more of a disappointment than I am to myself.

Grief darkened my heart (Lam. 5:17).
Everything on which I set my gaze was death.

SAINT AUGUSTINE

CHAPTER TWO

Sabina

I LEAVE THE DOCTOR'S office, prescription in hand. How often have I said to a client, "There is no shame in taking an antidepressant"? Yet I now understand that feeling firsthand. My mind knows the truth, but my psyche argues the point.

I'm a hypocrite.

I wouldn't even make an appointment with a psychiatrist. Instead, I scheduled a physical with an internist, explaining that I was spending some time in the village and wanted to establish with a doctor as a precaution. In case I encountered a need. And oh, by the way, I believe I'm fighting a mild depression . . .

Dr. Norman had paused and looked at my file, at the information sheet I'd completed. "You're a counselor?"

"Yes. Though I'm taking a sabbatical."

"How's life? Any cause you're aware of for the depression?"

"Just . . . stress. Hence the sabbatical. It may be hormonal. I'm about that age and, as you suggested, in the beginning stages of menopause." Not a total hypocrite though. It's true, the depression is the result of stress, of that I'm certain.

She nodded. "Well, I can prescribe something if you'd like."

As she wrote the prescription I recalled my momma's cure-all for every ailment: *It's nothing a plate of collard greens won't cure.* Usually, the collard greens were followed by a piece of her peach cobbler, which, I knew, was the true cure. But then came the opportunity to attend Stanford, and a bright new world: California. I left Georgia, the simplicity of youth, and the collard greens behind.

And moved up to sophistication, at least in my mind, a successful career, and a level of stress I hadn't imagined possible.

I thanked Dr. Norman when she handed me the prescription.

I CLICK THE BUTTON on my key fob and the doors unlock on my black BMW 550i. I stand in the parking lot of the doctors' office and peruse the sedan. I loved the car when Antwone surprised me with it. A gift to celebrate twenty-five years of a thriving counseling practice.

Now the car is a painful reminder of what was.

I sigh, get in, and head for the pharmacy.

After the pharmacy, I stop at Harvest Market in Fort Bragg, pick up a few necessities, and then make the ten-minute drive along Highway 1 to Mendocino. I've been here almost a week and I've barely noticed the grandeur of the rugged northern California coastline.

The house I've rented is at the north end of the village overlooking Agate Cove, where the crashing waves provide the resounding rhythm I hope will prove healing. But rather than take the exit that leads to the house, I take the second exit—into the heart of the village.

Just having the antidepressants infuses me with more hope than I've felt in weeks. And hope generates energy. For the first time since arriving in this place, I'm curious as to what's available. Heaven knows I'll die of starvation if I have to cook all my own meals, so it's time to find some alternatives to the frozen meals I've microwaved all week long.

It appears I can crisscross the grid of the village in less than five minutes. The narrow streets are lined with a combination of grand Victorians and simple, New England, saltbox homes. Miscellaneous other buildings—all housing businesses ranging from a corner bookstore, clothiers, jewelers, and art galleries—line the street. Scattered among the businesses are multiple restaurants and bed-and-breakfast inns.

There's a timeworn bohemian charm to the community. As I head two blocks west, the businesses give way to an eclectic array of houses. A few blocks further and I reach Mendocino Headlands State Park, which surrounds Mendocino on three sides. I only know it's a state park because of the research I did online before I arrived—otherwise, there is little to advertise that fact beyond a small sign at both entrances. The protected land includes trails on the bluffs with areas that overlook wave tunnels, blowholes, tide pools, and beaches, or so I read. A few people dot the landscape of the headlands—walking, or standing cliff-side mesmerized, it seems, by the swirling Pacific.

The headlands are only a few blocks from the house but I don't intend to spend much time there. I've barely ventured out of the house until today.

But girl, you will. You have to. You've let yourself languish in a state of melancholy too long.

I make a three-point turn where the street goes into the park, and turn back toward town and select a restaurant that looks interesting. Perhaps rather than slipping back into the robe I've worn all week, once back at the house I'll stay dressed and take myself out to dinner this evening.

Or not.

It will depend, I know, on whether or not this wave of energy wanes.

As I make the short drive back to the house, my cell phone rings and I start. I have a new number and the only people who have it are family. They're not scheduled to call, at least not yet. I glance at the screen of the phone sitting on the middle console . . .

Antwone.

We made a pact before I left Tiburon and headed north—well, *I* made a pact—he may call, but I won't answer until I'm ready. He's to leave a message if he has something to say. If it's an emergency, something with one of the girls, who are both away at college, then he'll text.

My hands clench the steering wheel. C'mon, baby, it's only been a week. Give me the break I need. But then reality intrudes. Antwone isn't the cause of my stress and there's no reason not to talk to him. I reach for the phone just as it stops ringing. I'll call him back once I'm at the rental.

But by the time I pull into the driveway, gravel crunching under my tires, the fatigue that's shadowed me the last two months has returned. I turn off the car and rest my forehead on the steering wheel.

I will give into it . . . again.

I lift my head, pull the keys from the ignition, grab the bag from the pharmacy off the passenger seat, and head inside. The leather purse I slung over my shoulder feels like it's filled with boulders as I climb the two shallow steps of the wooden deck leading to the front door.

I drop the purse on a shelf in the redwood paneled entry as I walk in, go straight to the kitchen, open the bag from the pharmacy, and pour myself a glass of water. I stare at the bottle of pills in my hand. I need them, I know. But instead of opening the bottle and taking the first dose, I set it on the tiled kitchen counter, along with the full glass of water, and answer the call beckoning me.

The respite of sleep.

I drag myself to the family room, close the blinds against the stunning ocean view, and then wrap myself in the shearling throw I brought from home. Thus enfolded, I curl up on the leather sofa in front of the fireplace.

And succumb.

To sleep.

That safe place, where reality is put to rest.

> If you understand, that isn't God.
>
> SAINT AUGUSTINE

CHAPTER THREE

Miles

THERE ARE PATIENTS I dread seeing and patients I look forward to seeing. Everyone else falls in the middle somewhere. I don't analyze each of them. The patients I dread aren't the hypochondriacs, or the lonely people who visit a doctor just to have a meaningful conversation. No. The patients I dread are the ones I can't fix.

I'm a healer. That's my job. So if I can't help you, I don't want to see you. That's about me. I don't like seeing my own limits.

Especially since Sarah . . .

I hate cancer.

My jaw clenches.

I look at the picture sitting on my desk—a picture of Sarah out on the headlands—the wind whipping her long, strawberry hair and laughter on her face. I can almost hear her laugh when I look at the photo.

Sarah was my wife for twenty-eight years. My wife, friend, lover, companion, and mother of our children. Was the marriage perfect? No. But it was good, solid. I loved her. Respected her. And I depended on her. I miss her wisdom, her strength, and the warmth of her pressed against me in bed at night.

And that's just the beginning of the list.

"Dr. Becker . . ."

Camie leans in the doorway of my office.

"Mr. Rohr is waiting in room two."

"Thanks."

I look back at the picture. When Sarah was diagnosed, I vowed I'd heal her. Well, not by myself, I had to admit. But I vowed she'd see the best oncologists in the field and I'd do everything I could to ensure she followed their treatment plan to the letter. And if that didn't work, I believe in a God who works miracles, so I also prayed—with purpose, patience, and faith. I prayed as I've never prayed before.

But she didn't heal.

God didn't perform a miracle.

I lost her—my gaze shifts from her picture to the calendar—two years ago today. Though I don't need a calendar to remember the date.

I trusted her to God's care and He chose not to save her. Bitterness was tempting. But I know God and I know He doesn't always respond in the way we want. I don't understand why. Nor do I want a God as small as my own understanding. But it took me awhile to get to that point. I've hashed through a lot with God in the last couple of years.

I look at the files on my desk—the patients I saw this morning. Ellyn DeMoss.

I've always looked forward to seeing her. Intelligent. Witty. Beautiful.

I've always wanted to know her outside of my practice. Sarah agreed. When we'd go to Ellyn's restaurant, Sarah always enjoyed Ellyn too.

So maybe it's time to get to know her.

I pick up the picture of Sarah. "After all, I have a promise to keep, don't I?" It's the most difficult promise to fulfill I've ever made. "You knew that, didn't you? That's why you made me promise." I swallow the lump in my throat as I run one finger across Sarah's photographed face.

Sarah saw something in Ellyn . . . Or a more accurate assessment is that she saw something in me when we were with Ellyn—those times Ellyn would make the rounds of the tables in the dining room of the café. She'd chat with patrons for a few minutes and because we knew one another, she'd stay at our table a little longer.

I open my desk drawer and put the framed picture inside. I push it to the back of the drawer where I won't see it every time I reach for a pen.

It was Sarah who . . . suggested Ellyn. When she asked me to make that promise. "You could ask out Ellyn DeMoss, Miles. You light up when you talk with her." There was no jealousy in her tone. We were secure in our love for one another.

"What? Sarah, I can't—I *won't* think about this now. God may still . . ."

But by then, we both knew.

I lost her a few days later.

Sarah will always be part of me—of who I am. I will never forget her nor will I ever love her any less. But she made me promise that I'd move on. That I wouldn't get stuck in my grief. That *I'd* continue living even if she didn't.

Easier said than done, my gal.

"Dr. Becker?"

"Coming, Camie."

I close the desk drawer and as I do I see my bare ring finger still indented from the band I wore there for almost thirty years.

I removed it this morning for the first time.

Just before my appointment with Ellyn DeMoss.

In seeking for you I followed not the intelligence of the mind,
by which you willed that I should surpass the beasts,
but the mind of the flesh.

SAINT AUGUSTINE

CHAPTER FOUR

Ellyn

I'D GONE FROM THE doctor's office straight to the lab for blood work, and from the lab to Cowlicks on Main Street in Fort Bragg. A woman deserves ice cream after a prodding physical and multiple pokes from a vampire disguised as a phlebotomist. A scoop of Black Forest and one of Candy-Cap Mushroom on a sugar cone took the edge off my post-appointment agitation. The pint of Blackberry Chocolate Chunk that I took home and ate for dinner settled me into a sugar coma that left me sprawled on the sofa, dozing in front of *American Idol.*

We Americans love our idols.

Earl woke me early this morning with the usual chatter. *What's wrong with you? Will you never learn? You know you're dragging this morning because of what you ate yesterday. You're worthless.*

"I know, I know!" I threw the covers back, stumbled from my bed to the bathroom—each aching step a reminder of what I know—I have to make changes in my diet. But by the time I reached the kitchen, my muscles and joints had loosened a bit and the half-and-half I poured into my coffee didn't seem all that bad.

It's just a few tablespoons.

The croissant slathered in butter and jam, my morning staple, shut Earl up.

I do need to make changes, but I won't know how much I need to change until Dr. Norman calls with the results of my blood work. So I might as well enjoy the next few days.

That being decided, I have a second croissant, shower, and dress for work—leopard print, elastic-waist pants, black chef's coat with three-quarter length sleeves, and black clogs. The leopard pants are my favorite—they go well with my coloring and are worn to just the right level of comfort. I pull my hair back into its standard ponytail.

I make the three-minute drive from home to the restaurant, then park along the opposite side of the street.

I sit there, fighting the desire to close my eyes for just a minute. Then I push my heavy limbs out of the car, and head into my day.

It turned out that Dr. Norman isn't all that young, skinny, or beautiful. I'd peg her at around thirty-five, a hundred-fiftyish pounds, and cute. Not pretty. Not beautiful. But cute. Bouncy bob haircut, button nose, and great teeth except for the front two uppers, which are just crooked enough to give her smile character.

And Dr. Becker was right—she's great. I learned so much in that appointment yesterday about women's bodies, how we're made, what happens with our hormones, and—of particular interest—how our estrogen levels can affect our appetites.

I also learned that Dr. Norman isn't the reason Dr. Becker's wedding ring is MIA.

I look at Rosa, who is sitting across from me at one of the tables in the dining room. The morning sun now streams in through the windows. We're folding black linen napkins—something she excels at and I don't. But I like to show my support. The black napkins were her idea. They don't leave white lint on black clothing—something she observed at a new restaurant in town. So now Rosa, or our servers, replace the white napkins with the black for those wearing darker colors.

I look across the table at Rosa. "You know Dr. Becker?"

She looks up from the napkin she's folding. "Dr. Miles Becker? Of course, everybody knows him. They used to come in here all de time."

"I know, Rosa. I know you know him. I just meant . . . Never mind. Do you know what happened to his wife?"

Rosa stops folding and looks at me.

"Don't tell me you din't know?" She shakes her head. "How you not know dat? You need to spend more time wid customers instead of wid your head in an oven."

"Someone has to cook, Rosa."

"You outta de loop, Ellyn."

"Okay, so include me in the loop when important news comes through the dining room. I can't believe you didn't tell me that she . . . died."

She shakes her head again.

"What happened to . . . her?"

"De cancer kill her."

"Oh . . ." I put my hand on my chest in an attempt to soothe the ache I feel for Dr. Becker. "I knew I hadn't seen them in a long time, but . . . They always seemed so happy when they'd come in."

"*Sí.*"

We continue folding in silence, Rosa folding three napkins to my one.

I recall my comment to Dr. Norman—and feel heat rise to my face again. "So where's Dr. Becker's wedding band?" I'd tossed her a grin. "I'm sure I'd have heard single women squealing all over the county if he was on the market."

She'd cocked her head and looked at me. "He's not wearing his ring any more?"

"Not today."

She looked back at my leg and tapped my knee with that thingy that tests reflexes. My leg gave a little kick in response.

"Hmm . . . he must have finally taken it off."

"Finally?"

She looked back up. "His wife died. About two years ago, I think."

"Oh . . ." I swallowed. "I didn't know."

I'm such a dork.

A day later and I still can't think about that conversation without embarrassment.

Rosa reaches for the last linen napkin and folds it in a triangle. "So, you interested?"

"In what?"

"In him. Doctor Becker." She folds the edges of the triangle together.

I sputter. "*What?* No, of course not. I was just curious."

"What wrong wid you? You ever gonna be interested in a man?"

"I don't need a man, Rosa." I push a loose curl behind one ear. "Anyway, look at me. No man is going to be interested in . . . this."

"Dat what you think? You just scared."

"Scared? I'm not scared. Rosa, there's nothing wrong with being single." I thrum my fingers on the table. "I love my life. I'm content. What do I need a man for?"

"You terrified."

I get up from the table. "Oh, hush. What do you know?" As I walk away, I hear Rosa chuckle. "Glad you find me so entertaining," I say over my shoulder on my way back to the kitchen. I remind myself, as I often do, about the apostle Paul's words: *"An unmarried woman is concerned about the Lord's affairs: Her aim is to be devoted to the Lord in both body and spirit. But a married woman is concerned about the affairs of this world—how she can please her husband."*

Do I use the verse as justification? Or am I as concerned about God's affairs as I profess? Sometimes . . . I'm not sure.

Terrified?

Oh, Lord, am I? I want Your will for me.

Honest.

I think.

> I found myself heavily weighed down by a sense of being tired of
> living and scared of dying.
>
> Saint Augustine

CHAPTER FIVE

Sabina

I LIFT ONE LEADEN leg to the seat of the wooden bench on the front porch and bend to tie the loosed laces of my walking shoe. Then I pull my sweatshirt on and tighten the batik scarf I've tied around my hair—or what's left of it. The week before I left Tiburon, I had Gloria, my hairstylist, remove the weave I've worn for years. Once she'd removed the extensions, I had her shear my hair close to my head so I could go natural.

When was the last time I went natural? Just before heading to Stanford at eighteen—thirty-four years ago. All those years, I've followed the hair trends of African American women. It's a cultural thing, those dos. I wasn't sure if I was punishing myself with the extreme cut or setting myself free. Either way, it was necessary. No self-respecting African American woman would pay that much for a do and then subject her hair to the damp, coastal elements.

When deciding where I'd spend a year, I knew I wanted solitude. A client spent a month in Mendocino County and declared it a place of healing—whole foods, holistic healing approaches, and fresh air. When I Googled information regarding the area, I saw that African Americans accounted for 0.9 percent of the population. Which means, among other things, that it's a good thing I don't have much hair left. No one in Mendocino County would know what to do with it.

When I came home from seeing Gloria, I saw the stunned look on Antwone's face. I hadn't prepared him, nor was there a need to. It was my choice. But, as always, he handled the change with grace.

"You're beautiful, baby." He leaned in to give me a kiss, but I avoided him.

He didn't know yet—didn't know what was going on inside me or that I was leaving. I couldn't take his love, his grace. I didn't deserve it.

I still don't.

I bend and stretch before I walk. After two weeks of almost complete inactivity, I already feel my muscles atrophying. I took my first dose of the antidepressant on Tuesday morning, the day after my appointment with Dr. Norman. This morning, I committed myself to a walk.

Not that anyone would know if I broke my commitment.

But I'm going. I have to. *It's time to get with it, girl.* God helps them who help themselves, right?

Wrong.

This has nothing to do with God.

I straighten and follow the curved driveway to the street. Lansing Street runs from the village out to Highway 1—it's the northern entrance and exit to Mendocino. On this Tuesday morning, the road is quiet. But there are no sidewalks, or even bike lanes—just two lanes without shoulders. I shimmy along the road's edge, past the Agate Cove Bed and Breakfast Inn, and the Sea Rock Inn, and then before the road curves, I cross the street and step over the guardrail and follow a narrow path between the guardrail and the cliff overlooking Agate Cove.

The morning dawned in pale shades of gray. The white foam of crashing waves is the exception in the palette. I slow my pace, and then stop to look down at the jagged rocks and roaring surf below. The small beach below is strewn with driftwood and what look like abalone shell halves and pieces. The only access to the beach is a steep trail on the other side of the cove. You'd have to be committed to your desire to reach the beach to try that trail.

As I look back down at the beach and the waves hugging the shore, I feel a pull. Almost magnetic. It would take just one step to lose myself in the stark vortex of white foam. I lean forward.

It would be so easy.

No.

I step back and reach for the guardrail to steady myself, my heart pounding like a grandioso movement.

We spent many evenings in our seats at Davies Symphony Hall, listening to the San Francisco Symphony's Classical Series. I am like the harsh dissonance—lacking harmony with myself.

I am the incomplete chord unwilling to resolve itself.

I turn and look back toward the house I've rented. Its warmth and safety woo me. But I turn back and trudge on, drawing not on feelings but rather on almost dormant determination. I crest the hill and follow the road back down to Heeser Drive, which turns toward Headlands State Park. I pass Hesser and follow the road into the village. When I see a couple walking toward me on the same side of the street, I turn, check for cars, and then cross to the other side. The last thing I want is a social interaction.

I look up at the gray, cloud-strewn sky and sense our kinship today.

A battering wind blows, its direction unchangeable. I thrust my hands inside the deep pockets of my jacket. Will I allow the wind to form and shape me as it does the surrounding cypress trees? Or will I break under the battering?

I walk into the wind, wanting to give in—to let it snap me in two.

I swallow my self-pity, sickened by my own weakness. I've never had patience with clients who wallow. Yet, here I am.

The hypocrite surfaces again.

I sigh and force myself to keep walking. Once I reach the edge of the village, I turn around and, with heavy steps, drag myself back toward the house. As I do, I catch a glimpse of a lighthouse jutting out on a distant point—charming, until its light winks at me as if it knows my secret.

I SPEND MOST OF the afternoon in one of the large leather chairs seated in front of the picture window, positioned now to face into the living room. I resist the urge to stretch out on the sofa. Though I'm not hungry, I fix myself a salad for lunch and make myself eat it. Then I place my iPod on its speaker dock and select Esa-Pekka Salonen and the Los Angeles Philharmonic playing orchestral arrangements of Bach. I set the iPod to repeat, then settle in the chair. I let the strains of Bach play over and through me. My eyes drift shut, and the music floods the aching void within, expressing with its lifts and falls what I am unable to express.

I sit for hours, lost in the music, until the rumbling in my stomach begins to compete with the Philharmonic. I haven't really been hungry in weeks and I expected the antidepressant might further suppress my appetite, but perhaps not.

I stand, stretch, and wander out to the kitchen. I stand in front of the open freezer and peruse the frozen entrees that all seem to taste the same. I close the freezer and stand in the shadowed kitchen. Through the window, I notice the sun lowering in the sky—a blaze of orange, coral, and purple streaks the horizon. I turn on the kitchen light and see its reflection in the window instead.

Only the whir of the refrigerator and the dull, annoying roar of the surf break the silence. For the first time since my arrival, I feel my aloneness.

I stand in the kitchen, opening and closing cupboards, looking for what, I'm not certain. What about the restaurant on Main Street that I'd thought looked interesting? Do I have the energy to dress and go out?

The clock on the microwave blinks the time: 5:11 p.m. I want something good to eat, the comfort of conversation murmuring around me—conversation in which I don't have to participate.

The walk this morning must have done its work and nudged my endorphins from their state of slumber.

So, tonight, I shall dine.

WHEN I STEP INTO the restaurant, it's as though I've stepped into a café in the south of France. The walls of the dining room are textured and faux-painted, and have the worn look of old-world plaster. Rough-hewn beams run across the ceiling, and the floors are distressed wood. The amber blown-glass light fixtures shed a warm glow over the linen-clad tables. An old bicycle with a basket leans against the hostess stand—the basket filled with fresh flowers. There are lit candles on each table, along with a vase of flowers matching the arrangement in the bicycle basket. I imagine the flowers are grown in the area.

Lovely. The restaurant may prove as healing as the antidepressant Dr. Norman prescribed.

"Reservation?"

The word is spoken in a thick, Hispanic accent—the only thing that reminds me I'm still in California.

"No."

"No problem. You early. You come and enjoy."

Glancing at my black pants, the hostess reaches for a black linen napkin along with the menu. She seats me at a corner table in front of the window that, if I could see, would look out over the street and another cove—the name of which I don't remember. But neither are visible now. Instead, the interior warmth and lighting reflect in the dark windows . . .

My lungs constrict with the memory of another time and place. Antwone and I took the twins to France to celebrate their high school graduations—

"You visiting de village?" The hostess picks up the white folded napkin from the table and replaces it with the black. She opens the menu and hands it to me and places a wine list on the table.

"In a way. I've rented a house here for the next year."

"Then we see you lots. Okay?"

I look around the dining room and offer my first genuine smile since arriving in Mendocino. "Yes, I think I'll see you often."

"Good. Enjoy."

A server comes to the table just after I've been seated. He places a glass of iced water at my setting, and a butter dish along with a cup filled with fragrant breadsticks on the table. I read the offerings on the menu and my mouth waters. The constant ache in my neck and shoulders relaxes a bit. And for the first time in many months . . .

I don't wish I no longer lived.

> The light . . . is obscured by a cloud, the truth is not perceived.
>
> SAINT AUGUSTINE

CHAPTER SIX

Ellyn

"GUESS WHO JEST MAKE a reservation for tonight?"

I shrug. "No idea, who?"

"De Doctor. Dr. Becker—6:00 p.m., party of three."

Three? I nod at Rosa. "Good." I look at the clock above the desk. 5:14 p.m. "Busy night." So Dr. Becker keeps his word. Not that it matters.

"*Si.*"

I walk back into the kitchen, Rosa on my heels. "Show time, Paco."

"Let's do it, Bella. Another Saturday night."

"I let you know when he get here so you can say hello." Rosa pushes through the swinging doors to the dining room before I can respond. Great.

"Paco, you've got to drop the *Bella.* Have some respect for my position as owner and executive chef. Your boss, remember?"

Paco laughs. "I know, Bella, I know."

I love the banter with Paco, a man who loves his wife and kids more than dessert. Just as it should be. We've worked together for eight years and settled into our routine early on.

As far as me being the boss, we all know it's Rosa who runs the place and keeps us in line.

"Hey, I'll be right back." I head back to the office, grab my purse out of the top filing cabinet drawer, and pull out my compact and lipstick. I open the compact, brush some of the matte powder across my nose, cheeks, and chin. It sounds like Rosa will have me make the rounds in the dining room tonight, so I might as well be ready. I don't take a second look into the small mirror. Instead, I reach for a clean apron and then head back to work.

THIRTY OR SO MINUTES later, Rosa pops back into the kitchen and tells me there's a new woman having dinner here.

"Okay, and that's unusual because?"

"Because she staying here for a year. She might become regular if you nice to her. You come say hello."

I look at Paco, eyebrows raised.

"Go ahead, everything's under control."

I look around the kitchen—he's right. It's the lull before the storm. I take off my apron, toss it over a stool, and follow Rosa to the dining room. Patrons are just beginning to come in. Rosa heads to a corner table near the window, where a woman sits alone. She seems familiar . . .

Ah yes. The woman I saw in Dr. Becker's waiting room on Monday.

"Dis is our executive chef and owner of Ellyn's—Ellyn DeMoss."

I hold out my hand. "Hello."

She looks at me, a question on her face, and then recognition. "Hello, I saw you in the doctor's office on Monday, right?"

"Right. Rosa tells me you're new to town?"

She reaches out her hand and clasps mine. "Yes, I've rented a house here for a year. After that, who knows?" Just like in the doctor's office, I see something in her eyes that I can't read, though her smile seems genuine this evening. "I'm Sabina Jackson."

"You two can be friends. Two single women alone in dis town. You need each other."

I shake my head. Rosa—the Queen of Relationships.

Sabina is quick to respond. "Oh, I'm not single, but I'm here alone. So it's good to get to know a few people."

I nod. "Well, please, come in any time. And if you need anything while you're here, just call."

"Thank you. I'll be back. I'm not much of a cook myself."

"I hope you enjoy your dinner."

I turn to go and see Dr. Becker and a woman walk in the front door.

Too late to hide. Oh, why can't I be invisible? Boy, he's dating a young one.

Then another woman comes in the door behind them—Nerissa Boaz.

"Hi, Ellyn." The young woman says.

Dr. Becker looks from me to the young woman at his side. "You two know one another?"

I look again and smile. Of course. The tattoo. "Twila, hi. I'm glad to see you." I smile at Dr. Becker. "Twila and I met at Corners of the Mouth recently."

"Great. That's where we met too." He turns and motions Nerissa forward and drapes an arm around her shoulders. "You two must also know each other." He looks down at Nerissa.

"Of course." Nerissa steps forward and gives me a hug. "Like many of the chefs in the village, Ellyn pops in from time to time to pick up some last-minute produce."

Well, aren't they a cozy little group. "I haven't seen you in the store in a while, Nerissa."

"I'm not there as often as I used to be. I'm doing more consulting with clients."

And consorting with doctors, it seems.

"When my wife, Sarah, was . . . sick, Nerissa helped me put together a diet to help treat her."

"Oh . . ." I exhale—something I don't think I've done since they walked in. "Twila, I'll see what kind of vegan dish I can put together for you."

"Thanks." She looks, wide-eyed, around the restaurant. "Wow, this is really cool. I love the vibe."

"Thanks." I laugh. "Come to think of it, I kind of like the *vibe* too." I look around the dining room and try to see it through Twila's eyes.

"I'll have whatever you make for Twila."

"Are you a vegan too, Dr. Becker?"

He smiles, "It's Miles, please. No, I don't follow a vegan diet as a rule, but I figure it's good for me once in awhile."

"Well, I hate to turn customers away, but maybe you should have gone up to Raven's."

"Raven's is good, but we wanted to come here. Just a salad will work for me, how about you, gal?" He looks down at Twila again.

"Sure, whatever."

Nerissa chimes in. "You know me, Ellyn, I'll eat anything you cook. I couldn't do it on a daily basis, but when I want to splurge, I want you to be the one doing the cooking."

"Well, thanks." I look back at Twila. "I'm sure I can come up with something besides a salad. Rosa will seat you and I'll head back to the kitchen. Nice to see you all again."

Rosa's been standing in the background. If she knew about Dr. Becker and Nerissa, she didn't mention it to me. Didn't I just tell her to keep me filled in on the local gossip?

Rosa comes forward with three menus in her hand. "Right dis way, Doctor."

I turn back to the kitchen and slip through the swinging doors. "Paco!" I hiss his name. "What can we put together for two vegan dishes?" I think through what's on our menu for this week. "What about the ravioli with the fresh tomatoes and crisp vegetables?"

It has to be good. No, it has to be great.

"They're cheese raviolis—asiago and romano."

"Yes, but we can use the tomatoes and vegetables on something else. Listen, Corners is open until 8:00. Run down there now, and I mean run! Get some polenta. I'll substitute the polenta for the ravioli and in the meantime, I'll make them a salad of greens and . . . something. Go, Paco, go!"

"*Sí,* Bella. I'll go. But who are we serving? The president?

"Just go!" I push him toward the back door. The president. Ridiculous. My heart races in my chest—as fast as I hope Paco races to Corners.

But then, that's silly. It isn't as if Dr. Becker hasn't eaten here before. I take a deep breath and look around for Rosa, but don't see her.

Good thing it was just Paco who noticed my . . . my what? My whatever. Rosa would never let me hear the end of it.

You have taught me that I should come to take food in the way I take medicines. But while I pass from the discomfort of need to the tranquility of satisfaction, the very transition contains for me an insidious trap of uncontrolled desire.

SAINT AUGUSTINE

CHAPTER SEVEN

Twila

WHEN I TOLD MY mom about meeting Ellyn at the store and wanting to try her restaurant, she seemed surprised. I don't eat out much. I told her it wasn't about the food, just that I thought Ellyn was sort of interesting. "Like, intriguing. You know?"

"She's engaging. I've always enjoyed her when she's come into the store. I love her restaurant." She didn't look up from the cutting board where she was cutting carrots into sticks.

"Engaging? Yeah, that's it. So do you want to go?"

"Of course. Miles mentioned wanting to eat at Ellyn's again."

That time she did look up at me.

"Mind if I invite him to join us?"

I did sort of mind. "Um . . . okay. He's for sure not my doctor anymore, right?"

"Right."

"Okay. Let me know when it works for both of you."

I met Dr. Becker when my mom was working with him at Corners, putting together a plant-based, cancer-fighting diet for his wife. I'd dropped out of school at that point and had been home for four or five months. He was the one who helped my mom get me diagnosed. Not that she didn't know what was going on with me—the diagnosis just had to be official to get me into a treatment program. Miles helped her choose the treatment center too.

I'd like to put that behind me, but I guess it will always be with me.

The thought of having dinner with Dr. Becker was sort of weird, but not because he was my doctor. The last time I had dinner with my mom and a man, the man was my dad. That was a long time ago. But still, it was hard not to make that connection.

"Any word from Dad?" She'd looked up again and I saw the concern in her eyes when I asked her.

"No, not since the last check he sent for your tuition. Did you hear from him when you graduated?"

She knew not to ask me about him unless I brought him up. "Yeah, the usual. He wrote *Happy Graduation* on the memo section of the check, so that was nice, I guess." I looked at the clock hanging on the wall in the small kitchen. "I've got to go. I open this morning."

"Did you have breakfast?" The concern was there again—in her eyes.

"Yeah, I did. Really."

"I believe you, Twila."

She did, I could tell.

She wiped her hands on a kitchen towel and then came over to put her hands on my face, so that I had to look at her. "I'm sorry about your dad. I wish I could love you enough for both of us—to make up for . . ."

"Mom, it's okay. I know."

She kissed my forehead. "I'll see you at the store later. And I'll give Miles a call and see when he's free for dinner, then we can compare calendars. Okay?"

"Okay."

As I walked out to my car, I thought about the check my dad sent for graduation. I used the money to get my tattoos. Maybe because I knew he wouldn't approve. Or maybe just because I knew what I wanted and he happened to provide the money.

It doesn't matter either way.

I don't look old enough to have tattoos or a degree, or so people tell me. My mom says I look twelve but have the maturity of a forty-year-old. She says I was born with wisdom in my eyes—an old soul.

But, she's my mom, so, you know.

When I tell people I'm twenty-six, they laugh and say things like No way or *That's not possible.* Someday, I'll be old enough to take their surprise as a compliment—but now, it makes it hard to do my job—for people to trust me with their health.

I grew up hanging around Corners of the Mouth and listening to my mom talk about the benefits of whole foods, herbs, minerals, and supplements. She quoted Hippocrates daily. *Let food be thy medicine . . .*

Kind of ironic, when I think about it.

Nutrition is part of my genetic makeup, I think. But I didn't follow my mom's path without exploring first. She believed that if she let me go, like a butterfly, I'd come back.

Which I did.

I left home after I graduated from high school and went to UCSC—University of California, Santa Cruz. It felt the most like home—but away from home. I fit there.

Even though there were similarities to where I came from—there were differences too. My mom wasn't there. I was free to explore other life paths, and other belief systems. I watched and listened and checked things out on my own.

I explored Paganism, a belief in gods other than the one true God. I had friends who worshipped the god of the moon—the god of the sea. I was drawn to worshipping creation because of its beauty, but each time I tried to put my mind on the god of the sea, all I could think of was the One I knew who created the sea.

So that year, I accepted, on my own, my mom's belief in Jesus and the truth of one God. But the Bible also was responsible for the personal philosophies I'm trying to live by now. Some of those philosophies are my own—rather than my mom's.

I'm not, like, big on limiting people with labels: evangelical, environmentalist, liberal, conservative, fat, thin, or . . . anorexic. Though it's taken me awhile to get past the fat and thin labels. But I began labeling myself as a vegan that year because it's a word people recognize. For me it's about a belief system, not a label.

Like when I read in Genesis that humans didn't begin eating meat until after the flood—I thought, whoa . . . we were originally created for a plant-based diet? Meat was God's provision for sure, but maybe not His original intent? I'm not sure.

Anyway, meat is hard for me to eat.

But then . . . a lot of things are hard for me to eat.

Funny thing is, since coming back, I've developed this . . . sense. I saw too many hurting people, especially when I did my stint at an in-house treatment facility. But a lot of hurting people come into Corners of the Mouth too. Usually after they've tried everything else. You know, when their doctor can't help them.

When they're desperate.

So . . . about this sense. I believe God's called me to help. He's given me a heart—and the experience—to help people in pain. I may not feel their physical pain in my body, but I feel their pain in my spirit. It's kind of hard to explain. But it's like it makes my heart bleed.

And I don't just sense their physical pain—I get their emotions too. Emotional pain and physical pain go together. One breeds the other. If you begin with emotional pain and don't resolve it, it manifests in the body.

That's what happened to me.

And if you suffer from physical pain, your emotions often follow along. But I find people are more willing to open up and talk about their physical pain. It's like a doorway to their emotional pain, right? That's why I reference the Augustine quote about physical pain being the greatest evil—people can relate to that and then, a lot of times, they'll open up. But they hold their emotional pain closer, keep it hidden longer.

If I've learned anything from my own experiences, it's that, most of the time, emotional pain is based in shame. And people don't want to go there.

I get that.

All too well.

It's like when I met Ellyn at Corners. She smiles, but she's in pain. She didn't say that. But I know. See . . . that's what I mean about it being hard to explain. I just know. Sometimes I even know it before they do.

Weird. But that's just how I'm wired. My mom says it's a gift.

I'm still deciding.

"Twila? Are you with us?"

My mom's question—and the hint of concern in her eyes—pulls my thoughts back to the table, where we're all sitting. I smile and nod. "Sure, Mom." But we both know . . .

For the most part, I'm just an observer here.

I eat all of my salad—organic greens, roasted beets, pistachios, and a dressing of olive oil and black fig balsamic vinegar—while listening to my mom and Dr. Becker catch up.

Dr. Becker tries to include me in the conversation, but I just want to listen. He seems to get that after the first several minutes.

I watched him watch Ellyn when she walked back to the kitchen. He ran his hand through his hair as he watched her. She's the reason he wanted to come here. Just one of those things I know—or at least suspect. I know him well enough to know that he only does that thing with his hair when he's uncertain.

My mom probably knew his reason for wanting to come, but she wouldn't tell me. She's a trustworthy friend.

She became friends with Dr. Becker during Mrs. Becker's illness. My mom already knew Mrs. Becker from the store, but she didn't meet Dr. Becker until he came to her seeking a nutritional plan for his wife. By that time, it was already too late, but maybe the diet made him feel like he was doing everything he could.

After Mrs. Becker died, I sort of hoped maybe Dr. Becker would ask my mom out, like when the time was right. But then I realized the time would never be right for my mom. She says God is her husband now. But that's okay. I respect her decision.

After our salads, Ellyn brings our dinners out to our table herself. She sets plates in front of each of us, and Dr. Becker and I look at each other and smile.

He looks from me to her. "Ellyn, this looks great."

I look up at her standing next to the table. Her face is flushed—from the heat of the kitchen, I'm guessing—and she looks, like, radiant. Her long red hair is pulled back but there are little ringlet curls around her face, and her light green eyes shine. I only sort of notice her size, which is another sign that I'm getting better.

I can see why Dr. Becker might, you know, be drawn to her even though she's large. Like my mom said, she is engaging. She's someone you just want to get to know. She's like that saying, *larger than life.* I can think of her that way and not let her size bother me. "Wow, Ellyn, this smells really good. Thanks for coming up with something vegan for me."

"No problem. You know, Twila, I've meant to get some vegan offerings on the menu. Maybe we could sit down sometime and you could help me create a few menu ideas."

"Really?"

"Of course, if that's something you're interested in doing."

I look at my plate and nod. "I'm not, I mean, I don't eat . . ." I hesitate. "I'm not like a foodie or anything, but I could give you ideas of ingredients to use. I'd like that."

"Then we'll do it soon."

"Nice."

I see my mom wink at Ellyn. My mom's just like that, always grateful and always ready to share her gratitude.

Dr. Becker picks up his fork and digs into polenta with what looks like a sauce of crushed tomatoes, fresh vegetables, and herbs.

"Mmm . . . Ellyn, this is fantastic! This is vegan? I knew I needed to come back here."

Ellyn smiles, her eyes shining at Dr. Becker.

"Thank you."

Then she seems to get serious. "Dr. Beck—I mean, Miles, I hadn't heard about your wife until recently. I'm so . . . sorry."

He sets his fork down. "Thank you, Ellyn. That means a lot. It's been two years now and, like I told you the last time I saw you, it's time to start living again."

She nods and smiles at him. Then she looks at all of us. "Well, I better get back to the kitchen. Enjoy your dinner. Thanks again for coming in."

"Thanks, Ellyn." My mom blows her a kiss.

I take the first bite of the dish Ellyn made, and my mouth savors the fresh flavors. The polenta is perfect—not too crisp on the outside, and creamy on the inside.

It is so good.

I mean it's really good.

So good that it scares me.

I set my fork down and look around the restaurant, trying to distract myself.

I notice an African American woman sitting at a table near a window. I loved the cultural diversity at UCSC. The woman looks up and sees me looking at her. She looks away without smiling back, like I made her think of something unpleasant. But all I can think about is the food in front of me. The scent makes my mouth water.

I turn back to my plate and take another small bite. And then—

I set my fork down and scoot back from the table. Just like a half inch or so, but enough that I see my mom notice. *Oh, please, don't say anything, please . . .*

Instead, she motions to someone behind me, and then the hostess appears next to our table. "Rosa, could we get a box to go—we'll never finish all of this."

"I be right back with boxes. No problem."

Once Rosa is gone, my mom glances at me and picks up her fork and continues eating. And then Dr. Becker puts his arm around my shoulders and gives me a squeeze. He doesn't say anything, just sits there with his arm around me and takes another bite of his dinner.

Something, whatever it is, makes it hard for me to swallow the lump in my throat.

And it has nothing to do with the food.

Enable me to love you with all my strength that I may clasp
your hand with all my heart.

SAINT AUGUSTINE

CHAPTER EIGHT

Miles

AFTER I DROP NERISSA and Twila off, I set off for the
twenty-minute drive home—Highway 1 through Fort Bragg, and
then about ten minutes north, where Sarah and I built our home
seven years ago. It was always Sarah's dream to have a house
overlooking the ocean. I'm grateful God allowed me to fulfill her
dream before she died.

We didn't buy the property or build the house on income from
my Fort Bragg practice. The money came from my practice in
Danville. I practiced there for nineteen years. That's where we lived
after we married, where we raised the boys. But once the boys left
home, we decided to make a change that suited us both.

Sarah got her house on the ocean, and I found a community
where I could practice medicine the way I wanted to—offering care
to the residents of a community whether they could pay for that care
or not.

In Danville, I was contracted with an HMO and I had to adhere
to their guidelines. It wasn't unusual for me to see twenty-five

patients in a single day, which meant no patient received more than about ten minutes of my time. That didn't suit me. I believe practicing medicine is as much about relationship as it is about treatment. But I knew what I was doing would facilitate what I wanted to do down the road.

And now, here I am. I love what I do, but I need some time—time to focus on what I want now. On my next step. Not professionally. But personally. That's why I brought in Courtney—Dr. Norman. It's time to build more friendships—male and female. I didn't take time to do that when I set up the new practice. Besides, I had Sarah. She was my best friend, I didn't feel the need for more. Which, in retrospect, wasn't fair to her.

Nerissa is about my only friend in Mendocino County. I appreciate her. Sure, I have acquaintances, but I want more than that.

As I drive the dark stretch of highway, my mind goes back to what I witnessed tonight. After we finished dinner, I asked Rosa if I could say a quick good-bye to Ellyn. Rosa took my arm and led me back to the kitchen, leaving Nerissa and Twila waiting at the table.

"You go on back." Rosa all but pushed me toward the kitchen. "She won't mind."

So I walked through the swinging doors into the kitchen—and stopped. No one noticed I was there, so I stood and watched.

Ellyn. In her element.

As witty and quick to speak as she is, I've noticed a reserve about her—when in my office, or when making the rounds in the dining room of the café. But in her kitchen—her place of comfort, I'd guess—that reserve was gone.

Though everyone in the kitchen hustled, Ellyn bantered back and forth with her staff. There was no tension in their busyness, just ease—the type of camaraderie you see between those who work together and enjoy what they do.

But then Ellyn spied me, and the shadow of reserve, at least that's what I thought it was, returned. I saw her sous chef notice the change in her, and then he looked my direction too. I raised my hand and waved at her. "I just wanted to say good night. Thanks for another great meal. It had been too long." I had to speak up to be heard over the clamor of the kitchen.

She'd smiled and nodded. "I'm glad you enjoyed it."

I turned to go, but I knew I'd kick myself later, so I turned back. She was still looking at me. "I wonder if . . ."

Her whole staff was listening in.

She must have sensed my discomfort because she set the knife she had in her hand on the countertop and walked toward me. I wiped my palms on my slacks as she made her way across the kitchen.

When she got to me, she looked at me, eyebrows raised, those green eyes curious. I felt my heart rate increase.

"I"—Good grief. My voice hadn't cracked like that since puberty!—"I wondered if I could buy you a cup of coffee sometime?"

"Oh . . ."

It was her turn to hesitate.

"Um . . . I—"

"—she *love* to have you buy her coffee. You jus' call her tomorrow."

Ellyn and I both turned to see Rosa, or at least what was visible of her on the other side of the swinging doors. Then she pushed her way in.

"You come now. She got work to do." And to Ellyn: "He call you tomorrow."

I looked back at her as Rosa led me out. "May I? Call?"

She looked blank—no expression on her face that I could read—but she gave a slow—and what? uncertain?—nod.

But it was enough. I smiled at Rosa on my way out. "Thanks." I gestured toward the kitchen.

"You make sure you call her. And you be nice to her. You want me on your side. *Sí?*"

"*Sí.*" I laughed, and then bent and dropped a kiss on Rosa's cheek. "I definitely want you on my side." She'd swatted at my arm and giggled. "You go. Go home, Mr. Doctor."

I smile now as I pull into the long, paved drive leading to the house. I reach for the remote on the center console and punch a button. The garage door rises and the lights in the house come on. I knew there would be nights when I'd be at the hospital and Sarah would be coming home from somewhere alone. I never wanted her to walk into a dark house.

When I enter the house, I hear chatter from the television in the great room. I set the TV to come on with the lights after Sarah was gone. I don't like walking into a silent house. But tonight, I go straight to the great room and turn the TV off. Then I head to the large kitchen and fill a mug with boiling water from the instant hot spigot on the kitchen sink, and take a tea bag from a canister on the granite kitchen countertop. I drop the bag into the water and watch it steep.

Nerissa's comment tonight, after Twila had gone into their house, passes through my mind: *"I think Sarah would approve of you getting to know Ellyn."*

I didn't tell Nerissa that I knew she was right, Sarah *would* approve—had given her approval, in fact.

Exploring a friendship with Ellyn is all I'm ready for. I chuckle as I take the tea bag out of my mug. "Then why'd you feel like a junior higher when you asked her out for a cup of coffee, ol' boy?"

I take my tea to my study and sit in the brown leather chair in the corner of the wood-paneled room. I put my feet up on the ottoman and then slurp the hot tea—a nighttime habit I picked up from Sarah.

The tea, not the slurping.

Now, in the still of the room, I consider the topic that's bothered me for awhile.

Ellyn's weight.

The issue isn't her looks. She's a beautiful woman. Period. My concern isn't whether or not I could find her attractive. Truth be told, I already do. Have since I first met her in my office. Of course, it wasn't something I dwelled on—it just was and is a fact. She's an attractive woman—inside and out.

So *am* I hoping for more than friendship? I don't know. The idea is still so new to me.

In our doctor/client relationship, Ellyn and I discussed her weight. Until the last year or so, her numbers were always good. Low cholesterol, low blood pressure, and normal blood sugar levels. The only time her weight came up was when she asked about it. Did it impact the arthritis developing in her feet and back? Did it affect the recent diagnosis of fibromyalgia?

I was honest with her—yes, her weight may exacerbate the symptoms of those diagnoses. Otherwise, her weight didn't seem like much of an issue.

But now . . .

I'm not looking at her from a medical standpoint anymore. If we become friends, or more—especially if we become more—how will I handle the issue of her weight? I set the mug on a coaster on the side table next to the chair and push the ottoman out of the way.

I get up from the chair and pace. Time to face the real question: Am I willing to risk my heart with a woman who might face potential serious health issues because of her weight?

Your heart is Mine, Miles.

Yes, Lord. But can I let myself care about her, if . . .

Could I talk to her about it? Ask her to consider the future ramifications of her weight? Why hadn't I done that as her doctor? Why hadn't I suggested she lose weight? Maybe I could talk to Courtney, she's her doctor now, and make certain she's having those conversations with her.

I sit in my desk chair and put my head in my hands. *Lord, how do I handle this?* I sit in silence, hoping for an answer. But nothing comes. I've learned enough through the years that when God is silent, it's my cue to hold tight. Do nothing. Wait on Him.

I sigh and lift my head. When I do, I see the family picture that sits on my desk—Sarah and me with the boys. It was taken the Christmas after we moved into the house and the kids were home for the holiday. I feel the familiar stab of grief. For myself. And for my sons.

I can't go through that again, Lord.

I stand, walk back to the corner of the room, and retrieve my mug. Then I walk out of the study, turning off the light as I go.

Trust Me.

I stop in the hallway outside my study, and an image of Ellyn, the way she looked in the kitchen tonight, comes back to me. There, in the dark hallway, in my quiet house, the answer to my earlier question comes to me. How do I handle Ellyn's weight and potential health issues?

Simple.

I don't.

Some would disagree. Friends speak truth in love, they'd say. I believe that too.

But, as a medical professional, I know that just because someone is overweight it doesn't always mean they're unhealthy.

Anyway, Ellyn belongs to God. She's not mine to fix. That was a hard-won lesson I had to learn with Sarah.

But I did learn it.

I trust You, Lord. Strengthen me for whatever You hold in store. I want to follow You with an undivided heart.

Your will be done on earth as it is in heaven.

Pride imitates what is lofty . . .

SAINT AUGUSTINE

CHAPTER NINE

Sabina

I WAKE ON SUNDAY morning after my evening out with pale sunlight streaming through the shutters I forgot to close last night. The room, bathed in gray, is cold. I reach for the robe draped across the foot of the bed, climb out from the warm swathe I've slept in, and step into the robe.

I close the shutters against the dull November sky and then debate: back to bed or to the kitchen for coffee? I look at the digital clock on the nightstand—9:33? Already? I'm sleeping my life away. Not that it matters. I have nothing pressing me to get out of bed. But I am accustomed to rising with the sun.

Coffee it is. I push my feet into my slippers and walk the few steps from the bedroom to the kitchen. I like the size and floor plan of the rental. The master bedroom, just off the kitchen, is separated from the other two bedrooms, and has a private entrance from the front deck. I could see living here and converting the bedroom into an office, where I could see clients.

But then my memory wakes and slaps me across the face. *I no longer see clients.* I work to push the memory back into its state of slumber as I watch a pot of coffee brew. Instead, I let thoughts of last night take over.

Getting out, I discovered, was a great distraction. Good food, listening to the conversations of others, and even entering conversations myself—with the hostess, whose name I learned is Rosa, and the owner of the café, Ellyn.

It gave me space to breathe in an environment where daunting memories had no place. The café, the people, were not connected to my former life.

My *former* life?

Is letting go really so simple?

No. But the escape was good. I will own it and call it what it was, because I'm too smart to fool myself. But sometimes there is a place for escapism—when it can be used as a tool to help transition one's thinking from an area of hyper-focus to something else. At least, that's what I tell myself.

One thing I know for certain is that isolation doesn't help depression. I need people, yet I've moved to a place where I know no one. Why? Because I want anonymity. I don't want to have to explain myself or answer questions. *Why aren't you practicing anymore? What are you doing with your time?* Or worse, *Rumor has it . . .*

I reach for one of the pottery mugs in the cabinet above the coffeemaker and then fill it. Back in the living room, I turn the iPod speakers on and click my iPod to play Yo-Yo Ma's *Bach: The Cello Suites*. I turn the volume low, so the strains of music are an accompaniment to my thoughts rather than the focal point. As I head for the sofa, I recall an article I read not long ago about Bach's compositions. The author felt there was an emotional detachment about Bach's music.

I shake my head at the ridiculous assertion. I wouldn't be drawn to Bach's work if I sensed an emotional detachment.

I settle on the sofa, cradling my coffee. Living here affords me new opportunities. I am free to embark on a new journey—to redefine myself rather than allowing my past to define me. I am still me, Sabina Louise Jackson, PhD. I'm proud of who I am. Those letters behind my name mean something. I worked hard for them. I won't hide. I'm not using an alias. Instead, I'm looking forward.

And allowing those I invite into my life to do the same, rather than be waylaid by my history.

Am I ready to invite others into my life? I don't know. But ready or not, it's time. Last night reminded me that I am a people person— one who needs the companionship and conversations of others to enhance my life experience.

I'll not only stay depressed if I remain alone, but I'll go crazy.

Maybe I'll call the restaurant this afternoon and see if I can reach Ellyn.

There's an ease about her. I noticed it in the doctor's office too as she spoke to the receptionist. It would be good to have a female friend. How long has it been since I've had one? Several colleagues come to mind, but friends?

I haven't had time.

Well, time is *all* I have now.

How many kinds of questions there are . . .

SAINT AUGUSTINE

CHAPTER TEN

Ellyn

I SIDLE INTO A pew in the Mendocino Baptist Church and plop down on the hard wood, so grateful to be where no one can reach me. I pull my cell phone out of my sweater pocket and turn it off, then drop it into my purse. I look around and recognize a few regulars, and what look like a handful of tourists. It's never a large congregation.

I settle in for the next hour.

I may just stay all day.

I wondered if I could buy you a cup of coffee sometime?

May I? Call?

No, you may not call. If you have something to say, say it now. Don't leave me hanging.

My part in this imagined conversation changes each time it plays. I say something, anything, rather than offering that nod. I'm a nodding bobblehead. Soon you'll see my bobbling figurines at drug stores everywhere. You'll buy them as stocking stuffers for your kids. *Bobblehead Ellyn.*

Why didn't I just say what I was thinking? Most of the time words flow out my mouth before ever going through that flimsy filter in my brain. But last night? No. They were trapped, deep inside. They're still there too. I didn't know what to say. Still don't. I keep turning the options over in my head as the conversation repeats, but I haven't landed on the response yet.

If you have something to say, say it now.

Has Dr. Norman sent you as the bearer of bad news? You don't have to buy me coffee to soften the blow.

My eyes widen. Is *that* it? Did something come back in my lab work that Dr. Norman asked Dr. Becker to tell me about? Did she think it would be easier for me to hear it from him because I was his patient for so long?

Others around me begin to shuffle. I look down at the end of the pew I'm sitting on and see the woman who was sitting there is now standing and holding a hymnal. Oh. I reach for the hymnal in front of me and stand too. I let it fall open rather than turning to whatever number hymn the pastor mentioned.

The church is so small that Pastor Cleveland wears all the hats—worship leader, preacher, treasurer, secretary . . .

I stare at the page of the hymnal while those around me raise their voices in worship.

No, Dr. Norman wouldn't do that. Neither would Dr. Becker. They're professionals.

I wondered if I could buy you a cup of coffee sometime?

Why does he want to buy me a cup of coffee?

My stomach clenches.

That's it. That's the question I want to ask.

Why? Why do you want to buy me a cup of coffee?

What possible reason could you have for wanting to buy me coffee?

Why?

His answers come back, rapid-fire.

Because I just discovered this great pyramid scheme.

Because Rosa paid me to ask you out.

Because Nerissa's not enough woman for me.

Ha! Yeah right.

Or . . .

Because while I was your doctor I forgot to tell you that you're fat!

What *is* it with men? They always make me feel like I'm in trouble.

I feel a tap on my back, and I turn and see a gray-haired woman motioning me to sit. Besides Pastor Cleveland, I'm the only one still standing in the sanctuary. *Oh.*

I sit down and slide the hymnal in its place on the back of the pew in front of me. Then I reach for the bulletin I'd tucked into my Bible. I want to at least look like I'm paying attention.

Because I find you irresistible.

"Good one, Earl."

"Shhh!"

The church lady pokes me in the back again.

Oops.

Well, at least now I know what I want to say when, or if, he calls. *Why? Why do you want to buy me coffee?*

Hey, at least I got it settled before the sermon. And that's what I'd like to say to the biddy behind me.

LAUGHTER FILLS THE KITCHEN, as it always does on Sunday afternoons as the staff and their families gather for our weekly Meal and Meet. No one works on Sunday mornings—that's my policy, but because we serve dinner on Sunday nights, early Sunday afternoon is the perfect time for the family to gather.

It's also the time I get to mother them—cook for them, try out new recipes, and spoil them with a scrumptious dessert. Rosa fills us in on new policies or practices, and everyone is free to make suggestions—whether for the menu, the dining room, or kitchen.

Paco's little ones have grown up at the rustic rectangular table in the back of the kitchen. And when Rosa's daughter, Pia, turned sixteen a couple of years ago, she asked to celebrate it at the table in the kitchen. With the family gathered.

The only thing we allow to disrupt our time is the ringing of the phone. Whoever is closest to it, answers. This is the time of day requests for reservations come in.

But today, I'm more observer than participant. I serve the food and try to listen and join in, but each time the phone rings, it's as though a starting pistol goes off and my heart takes off. After about the fourth call, I swear I'll have a heart attack before the day is over.

And then it happens.

"Auntie Ellyn, it's for you."

Rosa is training Pia, who is now eighteen, as a hostess, so she's answering most of the calls today. She looks at me, her hand over the mouthpiece.

"Take a message, Pia."

She gets the phone as far as her ear again before Rosa rips it out of her hand. Rosa then covers the mouthpiece and hisses, "You expecting a call today—you take it. Now!"

"You know I can fire you, right? You know I have that power. You do remember who I am, don't you?" But even as I'm hissing right back at her, I head for the phone. Otherwise, she'll make a scene. I shake my finger in her face, though, as I take the receiver from her hand.

I clear my throat. "Hello, this is Ellyn."

"Hello, Ellyn, this is Sabina Jackson. We met last night."

I sigh, my shoulders relax, and I drop onto the stool near the phone. Rosa, who is still standing next to me, shakes her head and walks away.

I'm not sure which of us is more disappointed.

I focus on the phone call. "Sabina, yes, hello."

"I wondered if I could buy you a cup of coffee sometime this week."

I hesitate. "Do I look caffeine deficient?"

"I beg your pardon?"

"Nothing. I'm sorry. Yes, I'd love to have coffee with you, but you don't need to buy. Why don't you just come here one afternoon before we open? We make a good cup of coffee."

"I'm sure you do. Coming there would be lovely as long as you wouldn't rather get away from work."

"No. I'm at home here and we won't have to fight the tourists for a table over at Thanksgiving's, which, besides Moody's Coffee Bar, where you have to stand and drink your coffee, is one of the few options."

"Perfect. My schedule is wide open. What day works best for you?"

We set a date and time and I hang up the phone. I glare at Rosa across the kitchen. "You meddling—" The phone rings again and I grab it. "Ellyn's."

"Ellyn? This is Miles Becker."

My heart shoots out of the gate again, only this time it seems it's jumping hurdles.

"Oh . . . hi." *Brilliant Ellyn, you're an astounding conversationalist.* I get up from where I'm sitting and stretch the phone cord as far around the corner, toward the office, as it will go. Someday I have to join the twenty-first century and invest in a cordless phone for the café.

"You said to call—" He pauses and chuckles. "Actually, Rosa said to call you today about getting together for coffee. But when I thought through the conversation, I thought I'd better give you an out, rather then let Rosa accept for you."

He thought through the conversation? He's giving me an out? I open my mouth to respond, but nothing comes out.

"What I'm saying is that now's your chance to tell me you don't drink coffee."

"Oh, um . . ." Wait, I know what to say! "I drink coffee. I do. But your invitation confused me. Would you mind telling me why you'd like to get together for coffee?" There. Well said. I wait for his response.

And wait.

"I'm sorry. Your question threw me."

Trying to come up with a good excuse to cover for the pyramid scheme?

He chuckles again. "I guess I'm out of practice. And, to be honest, I'm somewhat confused myself."

"Out of practice? I don't understand." Why is *he* confused?

He clears his throat. "Ellyn, it's been more than thirty years since I've asked a woman out. I'm rusty, I guess."

He's asking me *out*?

"I'd like to get to know you better. I've enjoyed our conversations through the years . . . and I'd like to spend some time with you. It may lead to an enjoyable friendship."

He just wants to be friends?

As he talked, I turned myself in circles, for some reason, and now the phone cord is wrapped around my knees. Which, might be good, as I think it's the only thing holding me upright.

"Ellyn? Are you still there?"

"Yes. Yes, I'm here. But, I'm . . . I'm sorry . . . I'm tangled—" I turn circles in the opposite direction and untwist the cord, and then step out of the last spiral. "I was tangled in the . . . cord." I'm stalling. I'm the one who's confused now.

"I'm . . . I'm flattered." I am? "But, what about Nerissa? I thought . . ." I don't give him a chance to answer, I keep rambling. "Anyway, I don't . . . date . . . I mean, not that you're asking—"

Rosa comes whirling around the corner mouthing something.

"What . . . Dr. Becker, excuse me for just a moment." I put my hand over the receiver. "Rosa, *what*? I'm on the phone."

"If you don't say yes to dat man, then I quit."

"You can't quit, Rosa. Save the drama for someone else."

"Oh, I can quit." She unties the apron she's wearing and pulls it over her head. "You jus' watch!" Then she throws the apron at my feet.

I jump back, more from her anger than her apron.

She stands there, all 5' 2" of her, with her hands on her hips and her black curls bouncing. "What's it going to be, Chica? It's your choice."

I sigh and shake my head, then put the phone back up to my ear. "I'm sorry, Dr. Becker—"

"Please, it's Miles."

"Miles . . ."

Rosa glares at me.

"As I was saying, I don't really date. But a cup of coffee with a friend would be nice." I stick my tongue out at Rosa.

I then have the same conversation with Dr. Beck—I mean, *Miles*—that I had with Sabina. I invite him to the café on Wednesday afternoon.

When I hang up, I'm so angry with Rosa that I want to put my hands around her little neck and . . .

"Whoa, you stop!" She turns and runs.

"Rosa!" I follow her back into the kitchen where I see her standing behind Paco. "How could you? You have no business—I need to set some boundaries with you. I can do that. I can set boundaries. I have a book on just that topic. Somewhere."

Paco holds up one hand. "Bella, she has your best interest at heart. We all do. Dr. Becker is a good man."

"You told Paco?" Then I turn and look at the rest of those gathered around the table. All eyes are on me. "You told them all? Rosa . . ." My anger starts to wane as Paco shakes his head.

"We love you, Bella. We want the best for you."

"What makes you all so sure a man is what's best for me? I know what's best for me. I'm free to make those decisions myself. Anyway, he just wants to be friends."

Right?

Rosa comes out from behind Paco—a look of contrition on her face. She comes toward me and then takes one of my hands in both of hers.

"I sorry, Ellyn. You right. You free to make choices yourself. I shouldn't meddle." She looks at the floor as she speaks.

"Look at me. Rosa, look at me." When she looks up, there's a sly smile on her face.

"Truly . . ." She drops my hand and crosses her heart. "I very sorry."

"You're not sorry at all. Anyway, it's too late. Now I'm stuck. Not with one coffee date, but two. Sabina and Miles."

Rosa nods. "Yes. Yes, you are." She smiles at Paco and then goes and sits back at her place at the table. I see she's served dessert while I was on the phone. I reach for a plate with a large slice of flourless chocolate-rum torte with lemon creme anglaise and then pick up a fork. I take a bite and my heart rate begins to slow.

By the time I take the last bite, and swipe my finger across the plate to get the last drop of lemon creme, I've calmed down.

So, okay . . .

It won't kill me to have coffee with the man just once.

At least, I don't think it will.

And Sabina? She's interesting. Coffee with her might just be fun.

So yes. I have two dates . . . no, appointments . . . um, *meetings* with friends.

Whatever!

You are God and Lord of all you have created.

SAINT AUGUSTINE

CHAPTER ELEVEN

Twila

WEDNESDAYS I'M AT CORNERS of the Mouth all day. The wind blows so hard today that the wood doors at the front of the store open a crack every few minutes and fill the entry with cold sea air. I turn the gas pot-bellied stove on to heat the place. The store is like, so quiet this morning. I guess most people are saving their errands until the wind dies down, though here, it could be spring before that happens.

I lean against the counter where the registers are and read a new pamphlet on the cancer-fighting properties of broccoli sprouts. I know most of the information, but make a note to order some of the pamphlets to keep in the choir loft/herb room next to the seeds for sprouting.

I hear one of the front doors bang again and move to shut it tight, but then I see Ellyn standing in front of the refrigerator case in the foyer. "Hi."

"Twila, hi, I was hoping you'd be here."

She's pulling long pieces of red curly hair off her face and then pulls a band out of her pocket and puts it all back in a ponytail. That's how I wore mine today too. "Pretty crazy wind, right?"

"No kidding. It came up off the headlands last night and battered my house all night long. I thought I'd find shingles on the lawn this morning, but the old thing is sturdy, I guess. It did keep me awake most of the night though, so now not only is my hair blown in a hundred different directions, but I also have bags under my eyes."

I look at her and shrug. "You look good to me. Which house do you live in?"

"It's the renovated water tower off of Little Lake. The one facing the headlands. It has natural cedar shingles and a widow's walk on top."

"I know the one. Cool. I love the old water towers around here. They have so much history."

"I like them too. When I moved here and saw that one, I knew I had to have it. It's unique—charming. I can say that because I just rent it. The owner refuses to sell it."

"So what made you leave it on a day like today?" The front door bangs again. "Hey, come in here by the stove."

We walk over to the stove, and Ellyn stands in front of it. "Oh, it feels so good. It makes me want to purr like a big orange cat."

I laugh. "Yeah, it's nice."

"Well, to answer your question, I have a couple of coffee dates today—people meeting me at the restaurant—and I'm out of cream. Since it's Wednesday and we're only open Thursday through Sunday, I don't get a delivery until tomorrow. So I thought I'd grab something here. Have any half-and-half?"

"No, you'd have to go to Harvest for that, but we offer some great alternatives—good but healthy, you know?"

"Twila, honey, do I look like I know?"

I shrug again and smile. "I don't know, I mean, you're a chef, so . . ."

"That I am. Le Cordon Bleu trained—in Paris, no less— which means heavy cream is a staple in my repertoire and healthy alternatives aren't a consideration." She grins. "So teach me something new."

"Sure. Follow me." I lead her to the refrigerator cases in the back of the store. "We have soy creamer, or you could use a nut milk, like almond milk."

"Soy?" She puts her hand to her throat like she's gagging.

I laugh. "I'll show you something else. C'mon." She follows me to the center aisle of the store where I reach for a can on a low shelf. "Organic coconut milk. It's rich and I hear it's good in coffee."

She takes the can from me and looks at the label. "Twila, do you know how many calories are in this stuff?"

"Sure. But it's still good for you—it's a good fat for your body. When you're eating what your body needs, you don't have to worry too much about calories. I mean, well, I know it's hard not to think about the calories. I do. But . . ."

"Really? Honey, look at you. You look like Twiggy."

"Who?"

She shakes her head. "Never mind. Are you sure about your information? Where'd you learn this stuff?"

"At UCSC. I have a masters in nutritional science."

She stares at me for a minute. "So you're a child prodigy? A girl with an Einstein IQ who graduated from college when you were, what, twelve, maybe?"

"No." I take the can of coconut milk from her and put it back on the shelf.

"Oh no, you don't, I want to try it." She reaches down and takes it off the shelf again.

"Okay. It's what Miles uses in his coffee."

She looks at me again and I watch as her neck and then her face blush the color of, like, a Pink Lady apple, or something.

"Oh . . . so, you know about that . . . coffee thing he wanted to do?"

"I'm sorry. I didn't mean to embarrass you." I'd asked my mom if Miles was interested in Ellyn after we went to dinner the other night. But I just guessed he might be one of her coffee dates today.

She looks back at the can in her hand and then bends to reach for a second one. I can tell bending isn't easy for her.

"Do you have back problems?"

"Honey, I have body problems." She sighs. "But back to the coffee thing. Don't you think it's odd that a man like Miles wants to have coffee with *me*?"

"Why?"

"Why? Because . . ."

She hesitates and looks, I don't know, like, uncomfortable, maybe.

"Because . . . look at me."

I shrug again. "Maybe others don't see you the way you see yourself, you know?"

She shakes her head. "All others have to do is look at me to see what I see in the mirror."

"It doesn't always work like that." I reach for the left sleeve of the sweater I'm wearing and pull it up. "See this?" I show Ellyn my wrist. She comes closer and takes my arm in her hands and turns her head so she can read what it says.

"*Imago Dei?* The image of God?"

"Right."

I look at her and smile. "You know that you're created in the image of God, right?"

She nods. "Sure, Genesis, chapter 1, but what's your point?"

"Just that we're each created in the image of God, but we're all different. You have red hair, mine is brown. You're tall, I'm not. But not only that, we all have different wiring on the inside too—things that make us unique. But all of us, in some way, reflect an image of God—of who He is. So who's to say what's right or what's wrong about how we look?"

Her forehead creases like she's thinking about what I'm saying.

"I mean, we're supposed to take care of our bodies, but I think the best way we do that is just to be close to God. Intimate, you know? Then everything else sort of falls into place."

"Huh. Pretty insightful. How old are you? Really?"

"Twenty-six."

"You must have great genes, girly." Then she looks at her watch. "Oh, I have to go!"

"I'll ring you up."

She follows me to the register where I key in her two cans of coconut milk.

"Twila, would you be willing to teach me some of what you know about nutrition—healthy nutrition?"

"Um, sure. But—"

"I have to run, but I'll call you or come by again, okay? We can work on creating those vegan dishes too."

"Okay."

As she turns to go and heads for the door, I remember something. "Hey, make sure you heat or froth the coconut milk, so it isn't chunky."

She turns back. "Chunky?"

"Yeah, the fat from the coconut solids coagulates."

"Right. Sounds . . . delicious?"

I laugh again. "Trust me."

"You know, Twila, I think I already do. Thanks."

After Ellyn leaves, I pull up the sleeve of my sweater again, and read the tattoo, something I do several times a day. Sometimes several times an hour. I need to remember why it's there and what led me to have it forever inked where I'd see it.

Imago Dei.

See how the human soul lies weak and prostrate when it is not yet attached to the solid rock of truth.

SAINT AUGUSTINE

CHAPTER TWELVE

Ellyn

I LEAVE THE CANS of coconut milk on the stainless countertop, along with a container of cookies I baked this morning. I flip the espresso maker on to heat, and then take my purse with me into the restroom to see if I can undo the damage the wind did to my hair. "Of all the days, Lord, to stir up the wind."

Like it's all about you, Ellyn.

I look in the mirror and see . . . myself.

You were expecting a super model?

I pull the band out of my hair and let it fall over my shoulders—a cascade of carrot-colored frizz. Ugh. I turn on the faucet, wet my hands, and run them through the frizz. I do this a few times until the frizz is damp and there's a slight hope of the natural curl making a comeback.

I pull a full makeup bag out of my purse, an anomaly, and swipe matte powder under my eyes and then apply peach-colored blush to my cheeks. I dust my eyelids with a neutral shade of shadow and then use a deep brown shadow above the creases of my lids.

I try to remember what the department store makeup sales woman who sold me all the makeup did to me the day she snagged me, sat me in a chair, and used me as her free makeover candidate. I haven't been back to the mall in Santa Rosa since.

I dig through the makeup bag until I find liquid brown eyeliner. "Steady." I follow the line of my lashes, applying a thin line on my upper lids. Then I use a brown pencil liner just under my bottom lashes. I reach for dark brown mascara and brush it through my light lashes.

I finish the job with a slash of coral-colored lipstick. I rub my lips together and then step back from the mirror to get the full effect.

A stranger looks back at me.

The brown eye makeup sets off my eyes, making them shine like wet sea glass. The matte powder, blush, and lipstick make my face glow.

My breath catches as I stare at the beautiful woman in the mirror.

You look like you're trying too hard.

"Shut up, Earl. Shut up."

He'll think you want more than coffee.

"Shut—"

Men always want more. He'll use you. You know men are like that.

"Who am I kidding?"

I reach for a paper towel and rub the lipstick off my lips. It leaves coral smudges around my mouth.

I turn the hot water on and let it run for a few seconds and then moisten the paper towel with warm water. I scrub my face until the paper shreds. I grab a handful of paper towels, wet them, and then pump soap onto them. I close my eyes and rub and rub until I'm sure the makeup is gone. I get more towels wet and wash the soap off my face.

When I open my eyes and look in the mirror, I see myself again. Red blotches cover my face where I scrubbed. Then my eyes fill and tears run down my cheeks.

Stupid soap.

I bend down and splash warm water on my face to wash the tears away. When I'm done, I reach for another paper towel, dry my face, and then stuff the makeup bag back into my purse.

I turn and head for the kitchen without looking in the mirror again.

I reach for a square dessert plate and begin putting the cookies on the plate. One on the plate, and one in my mouth, one on the plate, and one in my mouth—the small butter cookies melt in my mouth. I stuff two more cookies into my mouth and then put the lid on the container.

I garnish the plate with three blackberries and a sprig of mint.

When I swallow the last of the cookies, I want more. But I look at the clock and know he'll be here any minute. I get a glass of water and take a drink, swishing the water around in my mouth before spitting it into the big stainless steel sink, then I spray the sink down with hot water.

I open a can of coconut milk and pour it, chunks and all, into a pitcher and set it next to the espresso maker. Just as I'm filling two porcelain latte mugs with hot water to warm them, I hear a tap on the back door.

I told both Miles and Sabina to come around back since we aren't open. And I told Miles to come first, ninety minutes before Sabina. I look down at the sweater I'm wearing and brush crumbs off my chest. I take a deep breath and then go to open the back door.

I SEAT MILES AT a table for two near the kitchen and place the plate of cookies on the table.

"These look great."

"Well, it's what I do."

"You do it very well, Ellyn. Dinner the other night was incredible."

I nod. "I'll get our coffee."

"May I help?"

"No. No, just relax. I'll be right back." I go back to the kitchen, steam the pitcher of coconut milk, and then put the now-warm cups under the two espresso spigots on the machine. Two shots in each cup, and then I pour the coconut milk in—it doesn't froth as much as milk, but it's not bad. I top the lattes off with a sprinkle of grated fresh nutmeg.

When I return to the dining room, Miles is standing, looking at a print on the wall. "Is this a local artist?"

"Yes. I couldn't afford an original, so I settled for a print."

"I like it." He turns around and comes back to the table. "So, you like modern art?"

I shrug. "Some of it. I like the vibrant colors he uses and I like the texture—he layers paint on the canvas, so there's depth to his work. Though it's hard to see that on the print." I set the lattes on the table.

Miles comes around the table and pulls out my chair for me. I know this game. Always a gentlemen, until—

"Wow, the coffee smells great. What's on top?"

"Nutmeg. And the milk is coconut."

"Really? How did you know?"

I hesitate. Does he think I did it just for him? "I didn't know. I stopped by Corners to pick up some half-and-half. Twila seemed to know you were coming, so she suggested coconut milk. They didn't have half-and-half." I take a sip of the latte. "I think I'll stick with half-and-half in the future."

After my rude quip, I read a question in Miles's eyes. Ugh, I'm such a heel. I take another sip. "Well, maybe it just takes getting used to. It is pretty good. How'd you get started on coconut milk?"

He smiles. "Sarah."

"Ah . . ." I hate it when Earl is right. It *isn't* all about me. Miles has really suffered. "So . . . how . . ." I put my hand over my heart, which aches for his loss. "How are you . . . now?"

He leans back in his seat. "The last two years have been hard. Lonely. But the two years before that . . . watching her suffer. That was harder. I prayed for a miracle for her. For myself. But that wasn't God's plan."

"How did you deal with that? God's part in it, I mean."

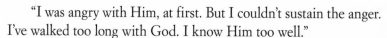

"I was angry with Him, at first. But I couldn't sustain the anger. I've walked too long with God. I know Him too well."

"Wow . . ."

"No, it wasn't as noble as it sounds. I struggled. I questioned. I . . . cried. I know God has the power to save—to heal. But He didn't. That was hard to swallow and I don't understand why He didn't heal Sarah. But, at the same time, He's unfathomable—beyond our understanding. That's part of faith—believing what we can't see or understand."

"I suppose."

"Haven't you ever questioned God?"

"Honestly?"

His blue eyes glitter as the afternoon sun streams into the café. "That's the only way to have a conversation."

I nod. "I lost my dad just before I was to leave for college." I shake my head at the stab of pain that still, all these years later, causes me to catch my breath "A senseless accident."

Compassion softens his features. "I'm sorry, Ellyn."

My throat catches at his gentle words. "It was a long time ago. But it did change the course of my life. I'd been accepted at Saint Mary's—away from home, but not far enough away after he was gone. My mother . . ." I sigh. "She's a story for another time. Anyway, I ran. I went to France—decided to cook. I did my culinary training at Le Cordon Bleu in Paris. I never took the time to question God." I shrug again. "The idea kind of scares me, I guess."

He leans forward, "Why?"

"Why?" I laugh, trying to lighten the conversation. "He might strike me with lightning!" Time to change the subject. I stand. "May I warm your coffee?"

He watches me for a moment. "Sure, if you'd like to."

As I reach for his cup, the muscles knotting in my neck and shoulders pull. Yes, I'd like to—I need to.

But why?

That's not a question I care to analyze.

In my somber state I did not consider from what fountain came
the flow of delightful conversation with friends . . .

SAINT AUGUSTINE

CHAPTER THIRTEEN

Sabina

I KNOW ON THE back door, as Ellyn instructed. It was good to have this on my calendar for today, otherwise I would have stayed in my bathrobe, hidden away in the house. Though the antidepressant is helping some, the dense fog of depression still looms most days. It will take time, I know, until I receive the full benefit of the meds. I may also need to convince Dr. Norman to increase the dosage.

I stand on the stoop waiting for Ellyn. When it's clear she isn't coming, I knock again—louder. This time my knock is followed by the sound of quick steps inside, heading for the door, which opens with a flourish.

"Oh, I'm so sorry. I lost track of time." She shakes her head. "I can't believe I did that."

She pushes on the screen door separating us and I step back. "No problem. I didn't stand here long."

"Good. Come in. Wow, look how gorgeous you are."

I smile at her. "Thank you."

"Really, you're stunning—so exotic. I thought the same thing when I saw you in the doctor's office." Ellyn's smile reaches her green eyes and lights up her face.

"You're too kind."

"No, I'm not. Listen, come into the dining room and I'll introduce you to . . . to . . . Well, just follow me."

We make our way across her kitchen—the stainless steel countertops and sinks shine, and the tile floors in the kitchen, covered in strategic places with thick rubber mats, are crumb-free. It is a kitchen, I'm happy to see, where the restaurant patrons could eat off the floor if they desired.

Ellyn pushes through the swinging doors leading to the dining room and then holds them open for me.

"Sabina, this is Miles Becker—Dr. Becker—Dr. Norman's partner."

Dr. Becker stands from his seat at the table, where it appears they were having coffee. I reach out my hand, "So nice to meet you, doctor."

"Please, call me Miles. Nice to meet you too."

I look down at the plate of cookies and the empty latte cups. "I hope I'm not interrupting . . ."

Ellyn's face blushes a charming shade of pink. "No. Not at all." Then to Dr. Becker, "Sabina is staying in the village for awhile. We'd planned to get together this afternoon too. I hope you don't mind. I guess I lost track of time."

Dr. Becker glances at his watch then back at me. "Sabina, enjoy your time with this lovely lady. And make sure you have one or two of her cookies."

I watch as he looks back at Ellyn.

"Well gal, thank you for great coffee, great cookies, and great conversation."

"You're welcome."

Then, after what feels to me like an awkward pause, Ellyn heads to the front door of the café with Dr. Becker in tow. I can't help but overhear their parting conversation in the intimate space of the restaurant.

"I'd like to do this again. Maybe dinner next time? We could go somewhere."

Ellyn hesitates. I look away and try not to eavesdrop.

"I don't—"

"Date. I remember. Friends?"

"Friends."

I imagine Dr. Becker holding out his hand to Ellyn as they make a pact of friendship. What's wrong with this woman? She must already have a significant other because that man is gorgeous. And he's a doctor. I remember what Antwone's mama told me after he'd proposed: *"I hoped one of the girls might marry a doctor, but I hadn't considered one for my son."*

She'd laughed at her own joke. I'd laughed along with her, relieved that she understood, as did Antwone, that I would finish the doctorate program, whether single or married.

Ellyn comes back to the table and begins clearing it. I help her.

"Sorry about that. I meant to have this done before you came."

"No problem. Like I said, I hope I didn't interrupt."

"Interrupt?" She laughs. "No, you saved me." She picks up the plate of cookies, the napkins, and spoons.

"How so? He seems like a nice man." I take the cups.

"I don't need a man. That's all. And for some warped reason, he's interested . . . or something. I don't know for sure."

I follow her back to the kitchen. "What's warped about that?"

She stops and turns and looks at me. "What do you mean? Isn't it obvious?"

"Obvious? No."

She sets the items she's holding on the counter and then makes a grand gesture—spreading her arms out, palms up.

"Oh, because you're a larger woman?"

"Thank you. Finally, someone who is truthful. Yes. What's wrong with a man that he'd be interested in someone who looks like me?"

I laugh. "Your perspective is skewed."

"Mine? What about his?"

"His is just fine. You're a beautiful woman."

"Ha! What do you know?"

I square my shoulders and lift my chin a bit. "What do you mean, what do I know?"

She takes the latte cups I'm holding and sets them on the counter. "You're gorgeous, tall, slender, elegant. What would you know about my perspective, or his for that matter?"

"I know plenty." I put my hands on my hips. "I have a PhD in psychology, I'll have you know."

"Oh." She puts her hands on her hips too. "Well, then, so you're *Dr.* Sabina . . ." She pauses. "Wait, what's your last name?"

I smile. And then I giggle. "Look at us, we're fighting like sisters and we don't even know each other's last name. Not only are you beautiful, you're feisty too." I point at her. "I like you."

"Yeah, well, there's probably something wrong with you too." She laughs. "You're going to be good for me, aren't you?"

"You bet I am—it's clear you need a therapist."

She shakes her head, still grinning. "Well, you might be right there."

Then I get serious. "And you'll be good for me. I need some laughter in my life."

"Why? What's your problem? C'mon, fess up, we've already established my problem."

I hesitate and then say as much as I can. "Depression."

"Oh." Concern clouds her eyes. "Well then, we'll make sure we laugh a lot when we're together. Deal?"

I smile again. "Deal. You know what I think?"

"What?"

"I think your hostess, Rosa, makes a good match. She's a wise woman."

"Rosa? Oh, don't get me started on Rosa."

"What's wrong with Rosa?"

"She's the one who matched me up with the good doctor."

"Like I said, she's a wise woman."

Ellyn holds one hand out flat and then waggles it up and down. "She's running about fifty-fifty right now. I suspect she was right on with us, but with him?" She gestures toward the dining room. "She's way off."

"Time will tell." I don't give her a chance to disagree. "So, are you going to give me a cup of coffee or am I going to have to walk over to Moody's?"

Ellyn reaches for two clean cups. "Coffee or latte?"

"Plain ol' black coffee, sister. And I think I'll help myself to a cookie too. They come highly recommended." I pick up the plate of cookies. "Want one?"

"Well, duh! I wasn't about to eat one in front of him."

We both laugh again.

By the time I leave Ellyn's the sun has already set and the wind has stilled. The cool, damp air refreshes me almost as much as our conversation and laughter did. I feel lighter as I walk to my car—as though, without asking, Ellyn lifted some of the burden I've opted to carry alone.

I get in the car and see my cell phone sitting on the passenger seat. I pick it up and look at the screen—no messages. Using my index finger, I key in a number and listen as the phone on the other end rings.

"Sabina?"

I hear home in Antwone's voice and all the comfort it *should* bring.

"Hi, baby. I thought it was time I checked in."

The decayed parts of you will receive a new flowering, and all your sicknesses will be healed (Matt. 4:23; Ps. 102:3).

SAINT AUGUSTINE

CHAPTER FOURTEEN

Ellyn

FOR THE SECOND NIGHT in a row, I lie awake, staring at my bedroom ceiling. But this time it has nothing to do with wind and everything to do with caffeine. What made me think I could drink two cups of coffee late in the afternoon?

There's the problem. I didn't think.

But, oh joy, I'm thinking now.

Sabina and I connected like long lost BFFs. We just dove right in. With the exception of my restaurant family, I'm everyone's acquaintance and no one's friend. This is a small community and I haven't pursued close friendships—I've put all my time into my business.

Miles and I connected too. But that doesn't matter.

I'm already grieving the day when Sabina returns home. She said she's here for a year, "more or less." When I asked her why she's here, she said she came to heal. I didn't press for more. I assume she's healing from her bout of depression. I guess if a counselor can struggle with depression, anyone can struggle with it. Maybe she'll share more when we're together again—which is already on the calendar for my next day off—Monday.

And Miles wants to get together for dinner. I sit up in bed and sigh. What do I do about that?

Don't worry about it. He'll tire of you soon enough. Probably right after you sleep with him.

Darkness covers me and I reach for my bedside lamp and pull the chain, filling the bedroom with light.

"Sorry to disappoint you, Earl. But I won't sleep with him." My voice sounds hollow in the empty house. I throw the covers back and ease my way out of bed and into my slippers. Then I make my way to the kitchen, my joints stiff and creaking. I set the teapot to boil and reach into a cupboard and pull out a box of chamomile tea bags. Maybe a cup of the herbal remedy will help me sleep.

A couple of cookies couldn't hurt either. I open the plastic container with the leftover cookies in it and take two out and set them on a napkin.

I eat the first one while waiting for the water to boil.

I eat the second one while waiting for the tea to steep.

I eat the rest of the cookies in the container between sips of tea.

Way to watch your weight, fat girl. Watch it increase, that is.

Somewhere in my head, I hear Earl's familiar laugh.

Food is my *go to.*

I turn to food, and I'm not talking celery sticks, when I'm happy, when I'm angry, when I'm hurting, when I'm bored. And when I'm hungry, of course, but that's a rare occasion.

A flaky, buttery croissant will heal any bad mood.

A dense butter cake with chocolate ganache is perfect when I'm angry. Or when I'm happy. Or depressed. Come to think of it, butter cake is the all-occasion food. The recipe is my mother's—the one positive thing I've received from her.

Butter cookies when I'm bored—or can't sleep, it appears.

Grilled filet mignon, rare, with a pat of butter flavored with lemon juice, shallots, and parsley when I'm hungry. Served with potatoes mashed with cream, fresh garlic, and butter, of course.

Along with tender asparagus drizzled with hollandaise sauce—my recipe calls for five ounces of unsalted butter.

I take the last sip of my tea, get up from the sofa in the living room where I've salivated for the last ten minutes while thinking about food, and go back to the kitchen. I set my teacup in the sink and then look out my kitchen window, to the dark headlands. What is it about the middle of the night that makes things seem worse than they are?

I love food.

Duh, big girl!

And my love of food led to a career I love.

So maybe making some changes in my diet wouldn't hurt. But, I feel my shoulders droop, how many times have I tried and failed?

Too many to count.

Well, maybe Twila can help me, although . . . I don't want to hope and then fail again, especially with tiny Twila watching. Or maybe I'm just like thorny old Paul who prayed three times asking God to remove the thorn in his side. But God chose not to. Heaven knows this weight issue pokes at me daily.

So it's a thorn? A license to sin?

"No, it's not a license to sin. Ugh. Earl, don't you ever shut up? Don't you sleep?"

It's just . . . I sigh. It's impossible. That's what it is.

I walk out of the kitchen, flipping off the light as I do. I am going back to bed and sleeping this time. But once under the covers, annoying thoughts ensure that sleep won't come any time soon. I might as well give into the thoughts and let them speak their mind.

Miles wants to see me again. Dinner. As friends.

I stare into the dark, listening to the sound of the surf, and feel an emotion of some sort crash over me. Great. So what is it?

Fear?

Well, sure, fear and men go together in my warped world. But that's not what I'm feeling now.

Just friends?

Disappointment? Is that it? Is that the suffocating emotion that came over me?

That's ridiculous.

It's relief, that's all. I'm sure of it.

Who knows, maybe having a male friend besides Paco will come in handy. Plus, I haven't visited any of the other local restaurants in awhile and it's good to keep tabs on the competition. Miles mentioned dinner, so maybe I'll suggest Cafe Beaujolais or 955 Ukiah. Both are also chef-owned and my strongest competitors.

Yep, I'm relieved.

I roll over and pull the covers close around me.

Now, it's time for sleep.

But it is still a long time in coming . . .

"WHA . . ." I reach out, batting the air, feeling . . . "What . . ." I roll over still feeling for . . . something.

The phone.

I close my fingers around it, lift it from the base. "Hel . . . um . . . Hello?" I try to sit up, but instead my head hits the pillow again. "Hel . . . lo?" My voice sounds like I have a throat full of gravel.

"Ellyn, are you sick?"

"Um . . . sick?"

"Bella, are you okay? We were supposed to meet early this morning with the new produce vendor, remember?"

"Oh no, no I . . . yes . . . but no."

"What? Bella, wake up."

Again, I try to sit up, but pain pushes me back down. "Paco?"

"Yes . . ."

"I'm not . . . feeling well. I'm sorry. You handle the vendor, okay?"

"No problem. Do you need anything?"

"No. Just . . . just give me some time. I'll call you in"—I turn my head and look at the neon blue numbers on the digital clock on my nightstand—"an hour." Then I hang up the phone.

I close my eyes again, still on my side after reaching for the phone. My legs ache. My hip burns, as do the arm and shoulder I'm lying on. The sheet and blanket weigh on the sunny-side-up part of my body, causing it to hurt too.

I think back to yesterday and last night. Coffee and cookies— caffeine and sugar. I lift my arm, which feels like a bag of cement mix, and put my palm on my forehead. How many cookies did I eat?

You know better.

I do know better. I'm so . . . lame.

I can't imagine getting out of bed, nor can I imagine staying in bed. There are no good options.

And there's no one to blame but myself.

I set myself up with the caffeine and sugar, which led to the lack of sleep, which only exacerbates the symptoms—or at least they do sometimes. There's no real pattern. But not even my memory-foam mattress can help me this morning.

Fibromyalgia.

The diagnosis I've tried to ignore. After all, if I deny it, it will go away. That's my theory. Or was my theory. I still think the pain just comes from the extra weight on my frame.

You're fat; therefore you deserve to hurt.

I scoot to the edge of the bed, each movement a chore, and then I sort of roll myself into a sitting position. I put my feet on the floor and stand, pushing myself up from the mattress, but my knees buckle under me and I fall back into a sitting position. I look down at my body, searching for the tread marks left behind by the eighteen-wheeler that must have run over me sometime after I fell asleep. Instead, I notice the rolls of fat making my pajama top protrude.

This morning, I relate to Sabina's depression.

I lie back on the bed and stare at the ceiling until I can no longer stand the pain in my back. Then I sit back up, reach for the phone, and call Paco back.

"Hey, I'll be there by noon."

"Don't push. Everything here is under control."

"I'm fine. I'll be there by 1:00 at the latest."

I won't give in to this. I hang up the phone and then push myself up, this time using the nightstand as leverage. Once standing, I wait until I feel steady and then edge my way along the bed, letting go only when I've run out of mattress to hold on to. I take halting steps to the bathroom, where I'll soak in a hot tub until the pain eases.

I hope.

I don't climb out of the tub until long after the water is tepid. My first step onto the bathmat tells me the bath didn't do the trick.

I sigh.

Maybe it's time to call Twila and set an appointment to meet.

Maybe?

Okay, okay. It is time to call.

She's my last hope.

What is more pitiable than a wretch without pity for himself who
weeps over death . . . but not weeping over himself dying for his
lack of love for you . . .

SAINT AUGUSTINE

CHAPTER FIFTEEN

Sabina

IT ISN'T THAT I don't love Antwone. I do. But I find it
difficult, at this juncture, to relate to him. I discussed this with Jana,
my therapist, before I left. I knew I owed it to myself and to my
family to seek help, after all that occurred. And I owed it to my
clients to take care of my own emotional health as I was transitioning
them into new counseling relationships.

I am, after all, a professional.

Jana was helpful, although, my own education and experience
far outweigh hers, but that doesn't mean she isn't effective. She asked
many questions about my relationship with Antwone, but that wasn't
really the issue I was there to address.

In simple terms, what Jana and I came up with was that, for a
time, I've lost track of myself, of who I am. Having done so makes
it difficult to engage with the person who knows me best—or who
thinks he knows me best. My need for distance from Antwone is a

symptom of the issue—not the issue itself. Although Jana wanted to unearth deeper reasons for our unsettled relationship, I assured her there is nothing more to uncover.

Once I heal from the core issue, the presenting symptoms will vanish. That is my professional opinion, not Jana's. But I haven't lost all of myself. I still know myself well enough to know what I need. I explained that to Antwone again last night when I called him. He may not understand, but the fact that I called and checked in soothed him. He is respectful of my need for space and wise enough to know it isn't about him.

Nor is it all about me.

I do recognize that as well now. But I lost sight of that in the haze of emotional pain. I also shared that with Antwone last night. He deserves more than I'm able to give him now. But time is a healer. I can't expect him to put his life on hold for a year while I wait and work toward healing. So my decision, my need for space, comes with risk.

But I see my shift in thinking—the new awareness that my isolation is keeping me focused on self rather than including others in my thinking and choices. The awareness came again after my long afternoon with Ellyn.

I take a sip from the mug of coffee I'm warming my hands around.

Not only are my hands warming, but my heart is thawing as well, I hope. Perhaps it was the laughter, or the natural way in which we connected, or maybe it was Ellyn herself—the warmth that radiates from her. Maybe just her presence broke through a layer of ice encapsulating my heart. My soul.

I look forward to spending more time with her.

I get up from the leather chair, my back to the view, and go into the kitchen and rinse my now-empty mug. As I finish rinsing and reach for a towel, something catches my attention outside the window over the sink. Something flits in the pine tree across the street. I stand for a moment trying to see it among the branches, whatever it was that caught my eye. Just as I'm ready to turn away, it darts from the branches, a silhouette against the gray afternoon sky. As it spreads its wings, snippets of a poem taunt me.

"Prophet!" said I, "thing of evil!—prophet still, if bird or devil!"

I turn from the sink, turn away from the raven outside the window, but the stanza repeats in my mind.

. . . bird or devil!

I stop in the doorway between the kitchen and the bedroom and close my eyes. I see the lines of poetry scrawled across my mind.

"On this home by horror haunted—tell me truly, I implore—
*   Is there—is there balm in Gilead?—tell me—tell me,*
I implore!"
*   Quoth the raven, "Nevermore."*

I open my eyes and walk to the bed, my vision blurs with tears.

Nevermore

Nevermore . . .

I rip the coverlet off the bed, and tear the blankets and sheet back before collapsing across the bed. Tears slip down my cheeks and soon turn to sobs, which rack my body. But the sobs go unheard. They are buried in a pillow.

They are mine alone.

There is no balm.

No comfort.

Nor will there ever be.

I am ruined.

[Friendship] is not possible unless you bond together those who cleave to one another by the love which is "poured into our hearts by the Holy Spirit who is given to us" (Rom. 5:5).

SAINT AUGUSTINE

CHAPTER SIXTEEN

Miles

"HOW WAS YOUR COFFEE date yesterday?"

I'm sitting across from Nerissa at a table next to the Living Light Café in the old Company Store building in Fort Bragg, where we each ordered a Green Giant, which Nerissa recommended. It's an acquired taste, I assume.

"It wasn't a date. She says she doesn't date. So it was two friends having coffee together."

"So how was your coffee klatch with your friend Ellyn?"

I chuckle. "It was good. I enjoyed the time." I lean back in my seat. "I enjoyed her."

Nerissa nods and then moves on.

"Thank you again for dinner the other night. I didn't intend for you to pay for it when I invited you. But I did appreciate it. I think Twila enjoyed it too."

I take another sip of the green drink, shake my head, and then set it aside. "Hold on a minute. Is that it? That's all you're going to ask me about the time with Ellyn? I thought female friends pried things out of their male counterparts."

Nerissa's smile reaches her gray eyes. "Ah, so that's how it is." She sets her cup on the table and leans forward. "So, Miles, what did your time with Ellyn evoke in you? How did you feel?" She winks.

"Thank you for asking, Nerissa." I smile and then turn serious. "It evoked . . . confusion."

Her smile fades and is replaced by a look of compassion.

"What confused you?"

I look past Nerissa. Sarah and I were together for so long it seemed she most always knew what I was feeling, most of the time she knew what I felt before I did. I'm rusty at putting words to feelings. But then it comes to me and I look back at Nerissa. "For the ninety minutes I was with Ellyn, Sarah only came to mind once or twice."

"Are you struggling with guilt?"

"Maybe. But I know that's not from God. I think it's more grief—the idea of moving on."

"Moving on won't diminish your love for Sarah."

"I guess not." I pick up my cup again and put the straw in my mouth and give the Giant one more try. "What is in this?"

"Greens, celery, ginger—"

I hold up my hand. "Never mind. It's good for me."

"Would I lead you astray, my friend?"

I laugh. "No." I lean forward again. "Look at us, *our* friendship is easy. I didn't feel that ease with Ellyn. I enjoyed her, but I don't think she was at ease."

"Our friendship developed naturally—you came into the store looking for help—I was there. And you were going through so much, Miles. You needed a friend. And besides that, our boundaries were clear."

"I was married."

She nods. "Right. I also needed a friend, someone to help me work through the issues with Twila. You were the natural person to do that. And after Sarah passed, we were and are content to remain friends."

I look across at Nerissa—long dark hair, steel-gray eyes, and milky complexion. No makeup. Simple clothing. She embodies Mendocino's organic and holistic culture. We didn't meet women like her in Danville when we lived there. As much as I appreciate her, I've never felt more than friendship for her.

But with Ellyn . . .

"What are you thinking?"

I reach across the table and give her hand a squeeze. "I'm thinking how much I appreciate you, gal, and your friendship." I pull my hand back. "I'm also thinking about Ellyn and what I want."

She cocks her head to one side. "What do you want?"

"I want to get to know her better—spend time with her."

"And?"

"And if we enjoy each other, I want the possibility of more. But, she's told me twice now that she doesn't date. She seemed to enjoy our time together too, but . . ."

"Maybe she's been hurt. Maybe she needs time."

"Maybe. I'm jumping the gun anyway, aren't I?"

She smiles and shrugs. "You're used to knowing what you want and going after it. But you can't always do that when others are involved. Relationships are best taken one step at a time. Let it unfold, Miles. Let God lead you."

I stare at her for a minute and digest her advice. "Thanks, gal, I needed your wisdom." I take another sip of the Green Giant but it's hard to get down. "I don't know how you drink this stuff."

She laughs. "I like it. Really."

"To each his own, or her own, in this case. About the other night, did you have something more to say about Twila? You thought she enjoyed the time?"

She seems to weigh her words. "I think she did enjoy it—maybe not having to eat—but the ambiance of Ellyn's, and getting to see her, and you. It made me think about something and I have a favor to ask of you . . ."

"You've got it, whatever it is."

She smiles. "Don't be so quick to agree. It's a bit unusual. I wonder if you'd spend some time with Twila—one-on-one?"

"Is she open to that?" I scoot back from the table and stretch my legs out.

"I haven't asked her. Is it dishonest if I just asked you to take an interest in her rather than talk to her about spending time with you?"

"I am interested in Twila, you know that. She's a special young woman. I'm happy to spend time with her, but tell me what you're thinking."

Nerissa sighs. "She mentioned her dad the other day—asked if I'd heard from him. I haven't, nor has she. He's paid his dues financially, plus some, but he isn't involved in Twila's life. I'd like her, before she gets involved with a man, to have a solid male role model in her life."

I see her shoulders drop.

"I want more for her. Someone besides me she can turn to, someone she can depend on. I want to know there's a wise man looking out for her, especially when she gets involved in a serious relationship, and that's bound to happen. What I want, is a surrogate dad for her. And I know, Miles, I know, that's a lot to ask."

"Twila already has all of that in her heavenly Father."

She nods. "She does. I know that. But how will she embrace those attributes of God—the maleness of God—unless she's had someone in her life to model those attributes? How can she relate to God as a Father? And how will she know what to look for in a husband?"

It's my turn to nod. "I'm honored that you'd ask me."

She smiles. "I don't know a more godly man. I mean that, Miles. I see Jesus' reflection in you every time we're together." She shakes her head. "I'm crazy not to go after you myself." She grins and winks.

I reach across the table again, this time taking her left hand in mine. I rub my thumb across the simple silver band on her ring finger. "You're already committed to Someone else. And I can't come close to competing with Him."

"Yes, and it's a commitment I've never regretted. After my divorce, God made it clear that He was my Husband. You may not be able to compete, but you come closer than any man I've ever met and that's why I'd like you more involved in my daughter's life."

I let go of her hand and lean back in my seat and consider her request. Though, there's really not much to consider. "I'll tell you what, I'll ask Twila to go out for lunch with me or for a walk or something. I'll see how she responds. But a wise woman told me once that relationships are best taken one step at a time. So I'll let it unfold. I'll follow God."

Nerissa laughs. "Ah, touché my friend, touché."

WHEN I STEP OUTSIDE the Company Store building and see the rain, I'm glad I drove today rather than walked the several blocks from my office to meet Nerissa. I have a full afternoon ahead of me—patients who'll need my complete attention—so I'm grateful for a few minutes to think about Nerissa's advice regarding Ellyn. *Take it one step at a time, let the relationship unfold, follow God.*

That was my original intent. But I was confused—am confused. Now I'm concerned I've confused Ellyn too. *Well, Lord, You know. I trust You to take even my confusion and mistakes and use them for Your purpose.* As I round the last corner and pull into the parking lot of the office, I find myself praying for Ellyn too. Something, I realize, I will continue to do whether or not our friendship progresses.

I go in the back door of the building and walk past the examining rooms and go straight to my office, where I put my lab coat on over the jeans and oxford shirt I'm wearing. Then I sit at my desk and check the phone messages that Dee, my receptionist, left on my desk.

I pick up the messages and read through them. The last message, I'm surprised to see, is from Twila. I chuckle. *Okay, Lord, I'm following You.* I glance at my watch to see if I have time to call her back before my next patient. Then I pick up the phone and punch in the number she left.

Little by little, Lord, with a most gentle and merciful hand you
touched and calmed my heart.

SAINT AUGUSTINE

CHAPTER SEVENTEEN

Twila

I SET MY CELL phone on the kitchen table and then go
to make myself lunch. As I walk toward the refrigerator, the same old
fears weigh in my empty stomach. Like, I can feel them there,
making me nauseous. Or making me think I'm nauseous. I stop in
front of the fridge.

What's the deal, God?

It started again at dinner the other night. The meal Ellyn made
for me and Miles was so good. The fear gnawed at me then, too.

I use one of the tools I learned in recovery and think through
things that might have triggered me. Because it's not about the food.

So was it the comment Ellyn made when she was in the store?
I still don't know who Twiggy is, but I know it was a reference
to my size. At one time, I'd have taken a comment like that as a
compliment and encouragement to keep losing weight, or I'd have
interpreted it in the opposite way and thought she meant I was fat.
Something only another anorexic would get.

But Ellyn's comment didn't bug me. It wasn't a trigger. I didn't even think about it again until now. So maybe it *was* the food this time. Was it just so good that I was afraid I'd lose control?

I open the fridge and take out the meat substitute I eat, it's soy-based so it's rich in protein. I scoop some out of the container I put it in last night after I cooked it with taco seasonings. I put it in a small saucepan and heat it on the stovetop.

I make a taco salad full of fresh, organic vegetables, baked tortilla chips, black beans, fresh salsa, and the taco "meat." I take the bowl of salad, set it on the table, and then grab a napkin and fork. When I sit down, I close my eyes.

"Thank You for this food, and the ability to eat this food. Thank You, God, for creating me in Your image."

I push my sleeve up and read: *Imago Dei.*

Then I pick up the fork.

Miles.

I hold the fork suspended above the salad. Oh . . . was he the trigger?

I set the fork back down. Things between my mom and dad started to get bad when I was like eleven or so. Maybe they were always bad and I just got old enough to notice. When I was twelve, he left. Things weren't all that different after he left—he was gone a lot before then anyway. And even when he was home, he didn't seem like he was really there, you know?

During my recovery, I worked with a couple of different counselors, one at the treatment center, and then another one in Fort Bragg when I came home. I still see the counselor in Fort Bragg when something comes up that I can't figure out, but I'm getting better at applying what I've learned. One of the things the counselors helped me figure out was how I felt about my dad. He's the same as hunger for me, you know?

When he still lived here, when I still saw him all the time, I wanted to make him happy—to make him like me. Or even love me a little. But it seemed like I could never make that happen. Like I could never get full enough of him.

Then when he left and I didn't see him anymore, I couldn't even try. How can you make someone love you when they don't even want to see you? I didn't have any control over it. I couldn't do anything to make it change. I couldn't even try to get full.

That's when my eating disorder—or ED, as we called it in treatment—took over. I could control what I ate or what I didn't eat. Fullness and emptiness.

But I preferred emptiness.

In my subconscious, I think it represented my dad. It felt like control, but at the same time, I lost control. Ed, as I came to call the disorder, controlled everything I did. But then, I didn't have to think about my dad anymore. All I thought of was Ed.

So Ed sort of served a purpose.

But now, I'm learning to let God fill the space my dad and Ed filled . . . or didn't fill. Instead of focusing on Ed, I'm practicing focusing on God instead.

Anyway, having dinner with Miles and my mom reminded me of my dad, which made me hungry—not in a stomach growling way—but in my soul. It made me desire what I can't have. It triggered Ed.

I take a deep breath and pick up the fork again and take a bite of the salad. My stomach protests, but that's okay. I eat one slow bite after another until the bowl is empty and my stomach is full.

Just as I'm getting up from the table, my cell phone rings. I look at the screen and recognize the number I called earlier. Before I answer, I take a deep breath and make a decision.

"Hello."

"Hey gal, it's Miles. I have a message that you called. This number must be your cell phone?"

My stomach cramps around the food it still holds. "Yeah, that's my cell number."

"What can I do for you?"

"Um, I have a customer from the store who told me she was diagnosed with fibromyalgia. I've done some research, but I was wondering if you could tell me more about it. Would you mind? I want to understand the condition."

"I wouldn't mind at all. I'm not an expert on the syndrome, typically fibromyalgia is treated by a rheumatologist or a neurologist, but I'm happy to share what I know. And if you'd like more information, I'll contact one of my colleagues who is a rheumatologist and we can meet with him together. How does that sound?"

"That would be great. I was thinking maybe you could just tell me what you know over the phone, but then today I decided I might want to talk to you about something else too." I pause. "So, maybe could we meet somewhere? I mean, if you're open to that?"

"I'm open to it. How does tomorrow afternoon work for you? I could come your way and meet you at Thanksgiving's, say 4:00?"

"That works. Thanks."

"I'll look forward to it, Twila. Do you mind if I put your cell number into my phone? I'll give you mine too, that way we can call or text if something changes."

"Um, sure." I grab a pen and scratch paper from a drawer in the kitchen and write down his number. "Okay, got it."

I hang up the phone. Talking to Miles in person, even though my stomach is still cramping at the thought, is a good decision. I learned in treatment that confronting my triggers is healthy. It takes the power out of the fear or trigger.

And I need them as powerless as possible.

WHAT WAS I THINKING?

By 3:00 p.m. on Friday, the emptiness inside me feels like a dark womb I could crawl into and hide. It's as bad as it was before I started treatment. I want the emptiness to grow, to engulf me.

It's hard to explain.

I can't meet Miles at Thanksgiving's. What if he offers to buy me a latte or something to eat? I don't want to eat—not with him. I need to face him, face the fear, and ignore the emptiness, but I can't do Thanksgiving's.

I make myself go to the kitchen and take a handful of raw almonds out of one of the canisters on the countertop. I count out ten of them and eat all of them, but each almond takes a huge effort.

I make a deal with myself: I can't change plans with Miles until I've eaten all the almonds.

I chew and chew and chew before I can swallow the last almond. But once it goes down and I'm sure it's not coming back up, I pull my phone out of the back pocket of my jeans and text him.

> Can we meet at the picnic tables by the cypress grove instead of Thnxgiving's?

I push *Send.* Within a few minutes he texts me back.

> Sure.

Good. That's better. Safer.

> Thnx. C u at 4.

MILES IS ALREADY SITTING at a picnic table when I get there. This is one of my favorite places on the headlands—a grove of cypress trees overlooking Agate Cove. If you walk inside the grove, there's a large clearing and one picnic bench out on the point on the edge of the cliff. When you're out there, it feels like you're on the edge of the world.

But today, even though the sky is crisp and clear, the damp breeze goes right through me. I pull my jacket out of my car and put it on over the long-sleeve T-shirt, sweater, and hoodie I'm already wearing. Even though I've gained some weight back, I'm still always cold.

I walk over to the table, hands stuffed into the pockets of my jacket. Just before I'm there, I hear his usual greeting.

"Hi, gal."

"Hey." I sit on the bench across the table from him. "Thanks for meeting me here."

"Sure. Are you warm enough."

I nod. "How about you?"

"I am. I came a few minutes early and took a brisk walk. Sarah and I used to walk out here. There's no place like it."

"I like it here. I come here a lot, but on warmer days." I look around me. The huge cypress trees remind me of mythic creatures—bent, with sharp edges, silhouetted against the blue sky. The prairie grass waves in the breeze. You can't see the ocean from the picnic tables, but you know it's there—you hear it crashing.

"So, um—" I know what I need to say, but . . . I push myself to keep going. "Before we talk about medical stuff, I have something else I want to get out of the way, you know?"

"Sure. Shoot."

"Okay, well, I hope you'll get that this isn't about you, because, it's not. It's me." The lump in my throat catches me by surprise. I clear my throat.

"So it's the old 'it's me, not you' line." He chuckles.

I just nod, afraid that if I smile or talk, he'll see what I'm feeling. Whatever that is. I turn and look around again until I sort of get hold of myself. When I turn back toward him, he's watching me. His blue eyes shine in the sun, and the wrinkles around his eyes make him look wise, and kind.

"Twila . . ." His voice is serious. "Whatever you have to say is okay. I'm listening."

I nod and swallow. "Okay . . . so, um, the other night . . . at dinner?"

He nods.

Tears prick my eyes and I turn away again. I should have done this over the phone, where he couldn't see me. I don't want him to see me. I want to go into the dark empty space. I take a deep breath and then I notice him standing next to me. He's gotten up and come to my side of the table.

"I'm going to sit on this side with you, down here on this end."

He sits on the other end of the bench, but before he does he puts one of his big hands on my shoulder and gives it a quick squeeze. "Take your time . . ."

I nod, still looking away from him.

> Entrust to the truth whatever has come to you from the truth.
> You will lose nothing.
>
> SAINT AUGUSTINE

CHAPTER EIGHTEEN

Miles

I WATCH TWILA, HER gray eyes the size of silver dollars in her thin face. Her long, dark hair is pulled back, and the tattoo of thorns is black against her pale skin. Her frame is hidden beneath layers of clothes.

But her emotions are bare.

My training as a physician has taught me patience, to wait and encourage when a patient is struggling to tell me something. But this afternoon . . . I'm not a doctor.

It's my training as a man of God I rely on today. Though she's twenty-six, Twila is just a girl. She spent her teenage and college years battling a disorder that separated her from her peers. Her suffering has given her wisdom beyond her years. But socially, she's still a kid.

It's the kid sitting with me today.

So I wait. I pray. I let her gather herself. I am here to offer mercy and love. I pray she will sense Christ, through me.

I reach out again and put my hand on her shoulder and give her another gentle squeeze. "Your tears are okay, Twila."

She turns on me, almost fierce, her eyes now like molten metal. "Stop! Just *stop* it!"

I pull my hand back from her shoulder, slow so I don't startle her, and wait. *Lord, comfort her . . .*

Her tears flow now.

"Stop being so . . . so . . . *nice* to me. It just . . . makes this harder."

I shift on the bench. "Whatever you have to say to me, Twila, just say it."

"Okay . . . okay." She takes a deep breath and wipes her eyes on the sleeve of her jacket. "The other night . . . at dinner, um, I got triggered. You know? The eating disorder." She takes a deep breath. "I figured out . . . why. I learned those triggers are fears—fears, I have to face. So I'm facing it now. I'm talking to you, because I need you to know that you were the trigger. It's not your fault. It just is what it is. So, I can't eat with you again, you know? With you and my mom. I can't do that again."

Her words come out fast now, though she doesn't look at me as she talks. I think a moment, waiting for the Holy Spirit to give me His words. "Twila, thank you for your courage and your honesty. I respect it. I respect you."

She glances at me, her dark lashes wet. Then she looks back down at her lap.

"May I ask you a question?"

She nods, still looking at her lap.

"Is part of facing the fear also working through the fear?"

She glances at me again, a question in her large gray eyes. She dips her head in a hesitant nod. "Yeah, that's what I'm doing by telling you."

"What if we took it a step further—you and me—what if we worked to overcome the fear? Do you think that's possible?"

"What do you mean? How?"

"I'm not sure. I don't understand how I triggered you, so I'm not sure what the best plan is. But it seems important to not only face your fear but also work through it—beyond it. Maybe together we can come up with a way to do that." I have her full attention now. Her eyes are wide—focused on me.

"You'd . . . do that? For . . . me?"

"You bet." I stretch out my legs. "Do you have any thoughts on what might help?"

She shrugs.

"Well, what if we eat together again? We could talk . . . and eat. Just give it a try. Maybe before we do that though, you could run it by your counselor. See what she thinks."

"Yeah, I can call her. That's a good idea. I don't know about the eating part, but . . . Can I, you know, think about it?"

"Sure. There's no pressure. How about this, let's both pray about it and you give your counselor a call and then get back to me. Deal?"

She smiles and takes her right hand out of her pocket and sticks it out toward me. I take her hand and shake it.

"Deal."

"Great. Now, do you want to talk about your customer's condition?"

ON MONDAY, ONE OF my patients doesn't show up. I use the time at my desk to chart some information and then decide to give Ellyn a call. I know the restaurant is closed on Mondays, but that's the only number I have. I could pull her patient file and find her home phone number, but that would be a breach of privacy. So I look up the number of the café and call there and leave a message for her.

If divine providence is on my side, Rosa will pick up the message.

Four patients later, when I check my messages again, Dee has written a note that Rosa called and left the number I need. I smile. Probably Ellyn's home phone number. God bless Rosa.

I pick up the phone and punch in the number.

"Hello."

"Ellyn, it's Miles Becker."

"Oh."

"Is this your home number?"

"Yes, it is."

"I hope you don't mind me calling you at home. I left a message for you at the restaurant and—"

"And Rosa called and gave you my number?"

"Right."

"Ah . . . Rosa. Well, no problem, I suppose. It's not like you're an ax murderer, right?"

"Not the last time I checked." I hesitate. Do I dare ask? "I . . . wondered if you'd given any thought to having dinner together?"

"Oh, well, yes, I mean, I haven't dwelled on it or anything, but sure, dinner as friends would be fine. It's good for me to get out and check in on the competition every now and then."

I chuckle. "Well, glad I can help then. So dinner as friends it is. Are you free tomorrow evening?"

"Oh. Well, yes, I am. Let's see, tomorrow is Tuesday . . . Café Beaujolias serves on Tuesdays, would that work?"

"You bet. May I pick you up?"

She's quiet on the other end, but I don't jump in. I give her time to think.

"I can just meet you there."

"Sure, though there's not a lot of parking—just the spaces along the street."

"Oh, right."

"Whatever you're comfortable with."

"Okay, well then . . . let's go together."

She gives me directions to her house, but as soon as she describes it, I know which one it is. We agree on a time and I tell her I'll make a reservation. "All right, gal, I'm looking forward to it. I'll see you tomorrow."

"Yes, tomorrow. Great. And thank you."

"You bet."

I hang up the phone and lean back in my desk chair. *Am I pushing this, Lord?*

I don't sense a red light from God. So until then, as Nerissa advised, I'll take it one step at a time—and the next step is dinner tomorrow evening.

With a woman who couldn't seem less enthused.

The lost life of those who die becomes the death
of those still living.

SAINT AUGUSTINE

CHAPTER NINETEEN

Sabina

ON MONDAY MORNING, I crawl from bed, where I've
spent the weekend, wearing the same pajamas I slipped into late
Thursday afternoon. I can no longer stand myself.

Time to at least shower and change.

And to call Ellyn and cancel our plan to get together this
afternoon.

Just the thought of those three tasks has me turning back toward
the bed. But no, I will at least make myself shower.

One thing at a time, girl.

After I shower, I dress in sweat pants and a sweatshirt, and then
dig through my purse in search of my cell phone. Once I find it, I
see the battery is dead, so I plug it in by the bed and climb back
under the covers. I search the contacts list for Ellyn's number—we
exchanged cell phone numbers when we met on Wednesday. I
punch in the number.

Don't answer. Please, Ellyn, don't answer.

When her voice mail sounds in my ear, I exhale the breath I was holding. I leave a message, then end the call. I also need to call Dr. Norman and let her know the medication isn't working. But I can't deal with that right now. Instead, I slide from my sitting position on the bed and lie flat again. I pull the sheet and blankets up under my chin, wanting nothing more than to drift back to the depths of slumber.

My phone rings.

I reach for it, pick it up, and see Ellyn's name on the screen. I set the phone back down and let it go to voicemail. I told her I needed to reschedule our time. I can do that later.

Then I succumb to sleep—that place where, for a time, I vanish and cease to exist.

I BOLT UPRIGHT, HEART pounding.

What woke me?

I hear the pounding again. It's . . . someone is pounding on the door. The door between the bedroom and the front deck. I look up and see the outline of someone outside the frosted glass door, just beyond my bed.

Have they seen me?

I sigh. No one knows I'm here except the woman from the rental agency, who gave me the key to the house.

I sigh and throw the covers back, get out of bed, and then pull the covers back up so it isn't obvious I was in bed. Then I take the short walk to the door, unlock the deadbolt, and open it.

"There you are. Are you okay?"

I blink at the smiling woman before me. "Ellyn?"

"Who else would it be? You don't know anyone else here, do you?" She stands at the door, arms laden with shopping bags.

"How . . . how did you know which house I'd rented?"

She blows a red curl off her face. "May I come in and set these down?"

"O . . . kay. Do I have a choice?"

"Not really."

I swing the door open wide and point in the direction of the kitchen. Ellyn struggles to get herself and all the bags through the door and then rounds the corner into the kitchen. "Wow, this is great. Makes midnight snacking easy."

"Ellyn, how did you know where I was?"

She sets the bags on the counter and then turns. "It's a small village. If a house is for rent and someone new moves in, it's news—or at least gossip. Besides, you said it overlooked Agate Cove, so unless you're living in one of the B&Bs for a year, I knew it had to be this house. I know the people who own the other houses on the street."

"So much for remaining anonymous."

Her tone becomes serious. "Listen, Sabina, you didn't sound good on the message you left. You didn't answer when I called back, and you told me you're struggling with depression, so I was concerned." She shrugs. "I'm sorry if I'm intruding."

I can't decide if she is or not—or if I should feel angry or grateful. "What's in the bags?"

"You also said you don't cook, so I brought a few things." She begins unpacking items from the bags. As she does, she talks over her shoulder. "If *I* was depressed, I'd want to eat, so . . ."

She stops and turns around and looks back at me. She looks me up and down. "Oh, am I projecting?"

"Very good. Where'd you learn the psychobabble?" Then my stomach growls loud enough that we both hear it.

"Ha! You *do* need to eat. When did you eat last?"

I stare at her and try to remember. I go to the counter and look at the containers she's setting out. "Wow, this looks amazing."

"C'mon, tell me, what did you eat?"

I look at the floor, and then back at her. "I had the cookies you made, and . . ." I try to remember. ". . . after that, on Thursday, I microwaved a frozen entrée."

"And?"

"And that's it."

"Are you kidding me?"

I shake my head.

"What are you trying to do to yourself? You don't have enough body fat to live like that. You'll starve to death. You know that, right? Right?"

"I . . . I didn't think—"

She shakes her head again. "You go sit." She looks through the kitchen, out to the dining and living room area. "Go sit out there, at the table. I'll bring you a plate."

I start to protest.

"Go. Now!"

"Girl, you can't boss me." I put one hand on my hip.

She looks at me and laughs. "Wanna bet? I'm bigger than you."

I shake my head and sigh. "Okay, I give. Bring me a plate. I don't have the energy to fight you." I go and sit at the table, my back to the window, and listen as a pan bangs and the coffeemaker dings. I thumb through an issue of last week's local paper and wait . . .

Then scents waft from the kitchen. And, against my will, my mouth starts to water.

In less than ten minutes, Ellyn sets not one, but two plates in front of me. Then she goes back to the kitchen and comes back with coffee and cream.

I'm almost drooling. "Look at this—it looks wonderful. I'll never eat all of this."

She looks down at me. "You haven't eaten in days. Trust me, you can eat it all, and you're *going* to eat it all. And I'm going to sit here and watch you eat it all. Just to make sure."

She goes around to the other side of the table and then gasps. "Oh, Sabina, look at the view you have. It's gorgeous. Oh, I will never tire of the beauty here—especially these sunsets." Her voice drops to almost a whisper. "They're so magnificent."

Ellyn looks back at me, and her forehead creases. "Why in the world would you sit with your back to it?"

I glance over my shoulder. "I . . . wanted you to sit there, where you could enjoy it."

She stares at me a moment and then takes a seat.

I look down at the plate and my stomach growls again. "So an omelet, and bread, and salad."

She looks across at my plate. "It's a French omelet made with chervil, tarragon, chives, and parsley. Very simple. A baguette with butter. And salade verte—or as it's otherwise known—green salad dressed with olive oil and lemon. I put most of it together at home in case you weren't here. I was going to leave it on your front porch, but when I saw your car . . ."

I smile at her. "Thank you for this and for your concern." I take a bite of the omelette and it's like none I've ever had. "Oh my goodness, it's so . . . so light, and creamy, and good." I don't say another word until the egg dish is gone.

Ellyn stares past me at the view. As I'm finishing the omelette, she looks back at me. "Sabina, are you taking an antidepressant?"

I nod.

"Is it helping?"

I shrug, take the last bite, and set the fork down. "I thought it was, but . . . no, not really. I need to give it another week or so to know for certain."

"What if I hadn't come by today? How long would you have gone without eating? How long would you have stayed here without leaving?"

I set the fork down. Who does she think she is? "Who made you my caretaker?"

"I did. You need one."

"You know, we just met . . . You can't come in here and take over my life. I told you, I'm a doctor, a psychologist, I know what to do. I can take care of myself."

Ellyn looks down at the table and falls silent for a moment. "You're right, I can't take over your life, but I can care, even if you don't. Did Dr. Norman prescribe the antidepressant?"

"I'm not accustomed to being spoken to this way."

"Oh, I'm sorry, Doctor, does my concern offend you?" She looks at me around the centerpiece on the table. "Eat your salad."

I pick up my fork like a scolded child. "No . . ." The word comes out on a whisper. I clear my throat. "Your concern doesn't offend me. It's just . . . it's just that . . . I'm used to having a semblance of control—over myself and others, actually. Or at least, I believed I did."

"I'm sorry if I was harsh." She tucks a long curl behind one ear. "I'm used to being the one in charge too—although not of myself, I will admit." She smiles.

And I, for the first time since I saw her last Wednesday, laugh.

AFTER I FINISH EATING—AND yes, I cleaned my plates—Ellyn takes the plates back to the kitchen and returns with two pieces of cake.

"Butter cake with chocolate ganache."

She sets one piece in front of me and sets the other on the table where she was sitting. "More coffee?"

"No, thank you. This looks delicious, but I don't think I can—"

"You can. It's the best remedy for depression or anything else that ails you. Trust me."

I take a bite and my taste buds explode—rich, buttery, dense cake, with the lightest, creamiest, chocolate frosting. "Mmm . . . just something you whipped up?"

She smiles. "It's a standby. I keep the ingredients stocked at home."

We eat our cake in silence, until I think my stomach will burst. I push the plate away leaving at least a third of the piece on the plate. "I can't, I just can't, eat another bite."

"Wimp." She takes another bite of hers. "So . . ." She swallows, picks the napkin up from her lap, and wipes her mouth. "Why not call Dr. Norman and tell her the medication isn't working?"

I shrug. "I don't have the energy."

"But, you can't just do what you're doing. Or not doing. I mean, you're the expert and all, but . . . really?"

I shrug again.

"What if I call her for you? Now, while I'm here with you?" She reaches for her phone. "Wait, would that be codependent?"

I laugh in spite of myself. "Borderline."

She looks at her watch and then hands me her phone. "Go ahead, call. The office will be closed, you can leave a message with the answering service and she'll call you back. Easy."

"I don't have the number."

She takes the phone back from me, scrolls through her contacts, and pushes buttons. When she hands it back to me, it's already ringing on the other end. When someone from the answering service picks up, I explain my issue and ask for a returned call.

Ellyn smiles. "There. Done. Now . . . can we talk about me?"

I shake my head and smile. "Go for it." I'm done talking about me, that's for sure.

"Well, since we're talking about doctors . . . I'm having dinner with Dr. Becker tomorrow evening. Just as friends. But I don't have anything to wear."

I shake my head. "Girl, what's with you and the *just friends* thing? This is a good-looking, and from what I understand, well-respected doctor we're talking about. Why *just friends*?"

"There's nothing wrong with being friends."

"What's wrong with being *more* than friends?"

She flips her long red curls over her shoulder and looks past me again.

I pick up my fork and tap it on the side of my plate. "*Hello!* I believe you wanted to talk about yourself? So talk. What's wrong with being more than friends?"

She makes eye contact. "I don't want to get involved, nor do I plan to ever marry, so what's the point?"

"Is it the institution of marriage or an intimate relationship with a man that you're opposed to?"

"All I wanted was a female opinion on what to wear to dinner with a male friend. I don't get out much. I work a lot. What's appropriate to wear?"

I put my elbows on the table and clasp my hands under my chin. "Hmm . . . avoiding the question?"

"No. You're the one avoiding the question. What do I wear?"

"Fine. What do you *have* to wear?"

"One pair of linen slacks, which I wore to my last appointment with him."

I lean back in my chair. "Well, then you need to shop tomorrow."

"Ha! You haven't lived here long, have you? My choices are two or three boutiques that don't carry my size, or I can order something online, but it won't arrive in time."

"So drive to wherever you'd drive to shop, or wear the outfit you have. He's *just a friend*, right? So what does it matter?" My cell phone rings and I pick it up. "Hello."

"Sabina Jackson?"

"Yes."

"This is Dr. Becker, I'm on call for Dr. Norman this evening."

"Hello, Dr. Becker." I raise my eyebrows and look at Ellyn. "Actually, I'm sitting here with our mutual *friend*, Ellyn DeMoss." I watch as Ellyn's head shakes like a rag doll in the teeth of a dog. "She says to tell you hello." I smile as Ellyn puts her face in her hands.

I go on to explain the issue with the antidepressant to Dr. Becker, who tells me he'll get back to me within the hour. I hang up the phone. "Ellyn"—I smile again. I can't help it—"you're good for me. I'm already feeling better."

"You're"—she points her finger at me—"you're *trouble*, that's what you are." But then she giggles. "How could you do that to me?"

"Hey, just one *friend* saying hello to another." I raise one eyebrow. "Now, did we settle your wardrobe issue?"

My hunger was internal, deprived of inward food,
that is of you yourself, my God.

SAINT AUGUSTINE

CHAPTER TWENTY

Ellyn

I STAND IN MY closet trying to figure out how to make
something from nothing—or at least something from nothing much.
With food, it's easy. You might have sugar, flour, salt and yeast—
none of which are much on their own. But mix those ingredients
with water, work some magic, and a while later you're taking a
fragrant loaf of warm French bread out of the oven. Cut, slather with
butter, and you've created a slice of heaven.

I look at my linen slacks. It's November, but even in Mendocino,
where almost anything goes, I don't want to wear linen. October was
a push for linen, so November is out of the question. I'm certain an
alarm would sound in my mother's head all the way in San Francisco,
and she'd call to inquire as to what I'd done wrong now.

I must have something else.

Twila is meeting me here at 4:00, and Miles is picking me up
at 6:30. I'd prefer not to have to change in between. I don't know
how long Twila will stay, but since she'd expressed an interest in the

history of the water towers, I thought I'd show her mine. Plus, it's more relaxed here than in the store or at the café.

A meeting with a nutritionist and dinner with a man? It's almost a journal-worthy day. Well, if I owned a journal.

Don't get excited—you'll fail the nutritionist and repulse the man. Or repulse the nutritionist and fail the man. Whatever.

I attempt to ignore Earl's bullying, but my heart rate accelerates nonetheless.

After searching my closet, I finally come up with what could almost be called an outfit. Black elastic-waist, wide-leg pants that don't look too much like sweats, a russet colored cardigan, and a cream-colored long-sleeve T-shirt. When I come out of my closet, I realize the russet sweater is more burnt orange, and with the black pants I resemble a jack-o-lantern.

You're shaped like one.

I dig through a drawer of accessories and come up with a patterned scarf in autumn hues that, once tied around my neck will, with any luck, distract from the pumpkin get-up. It also dresses up the T-shirt.

What was I thinking when I said yes to dinner with Dr. Miles Becker?

TWILA ARRIVES JUST AFTER 4:00, and when I invite her in, I do what is natural for me and give her a hug. As I put my arms around her, I feel her body go rigid and her arms remain at her sides.

Note to self: Twila's not a hugger.

What's more, hugging her feels like hugging a comfort-top mattress. How many layers is she wearing? "May I take your coat?"

She scrunches up her shoulders and puts her hands in her pockets. "Um, I'll keep it on for now."

"Oh. Is it cold in here? My body gauge runs hot. I have a thermal blanket of fat to keep me warm." I cross the living room to where the thermostat is on the wall and turn up the heat.

"It's okay, it's just me."

"Put some meat on those bones, honey, and you'll warm right up."

Twila looks at the floor.

"Oh, honey, I'm sorry. You're beautiful just as you are. I'm just sensitive about weight—and you're so thin. I make it about me."

Twila's beautiful gray eyes seem to shine with understanding when she looks back at me. "I get it."

I stare at her for a minute and then shake my head. "You do?"

"Yeah." She looks around the living room. "Wow, your place is awesome." She walks over to the west-facing windows. "Look at your view. I love the headlands, don't you?"

I follow her to the windows and look out with her. "I do. They're beautiful and so peaceful. From the deck upstairs, I can see the white water breaking too." I look at her. "Want a tour?"

"Sure."

We walk through the cozy living/dining room, which is the base of the tower, and into the kitchen and nook area. Our shoes tap against the rustic hardwood floors.

"This part of the place is an addition—added, I'd guess, when the tower was renovated and made into a residence. I don't know much of the history about this tower, only that it was one of the larger, working water towers in its day."

"This is so great. But the vibe is totally different than your café."

"You have a good eye. The café represents my years in Paris and some of the French fare on the menu. But my home is pure comfort—warm colors, soft textures, plush, down comforters and pillows. That kind of thing."

Twila nods. "So it reflects you. You're comfortable."

"Am I?" I smile.

She nods again.

"So what kind of décor reflects you?"

She shrugs. "I still live with my mom, but I guess if, like, I ever have my own place, I'd want cool colors—restful, you know? Grays and neutrals, organic cotton, natural stuff."

"I can see that. You exude peace, Twila."

She smiles. "That's not me, that's God. I'm a mess inside."

"Really?" Maybe she'll elaborate.

"So what's back here?"

"That's the downstairs bathroom and the mudroom. At least that's what I like to call it. It's technically a laundry room, but it has a door to the outside, so I call it a mudroom. That sounds more charming, don't you think?"

"Yeah, for sure."

We take the narrow stairs to the second floor, which consists of the master bedroom, bath, and a hallway. More stairs lead to the third floor. We breeze through my bedroom. "Sorry, it's a mess."

"Looks like mine."

I take her up to the guestroom/office. My favorite room in the house.

Twila's eyes shine. "Wow, this is amazing."

"You like it?"

"Yeah, it's great. I'd stay here."

"You're welcome anytime."

I keep a pod coffeemaker up here with handmade pottery mugs. There's a desk, where I pay personal bills, and shelves of books I don't take the time to read. But it does feel like a small sanctuary.

"The best part is out here." I open the single French door leading to a small balcony and the outdoor staircase, which goes up to the platform deck on top of the tower. We climb the stairs to the deck.

The wind coming off the sea is cold on this sunless afternoon. I glance at Twila. "Good thing you kept your coat on."

She goes to the rail and stares out at the ocean, and then does a slow 360-degree turn. "You can see, like, everything from up here. Do you come up here much?"

"Not as much as I'd like."

"What's this?" She walks to one corner of the deck.

"It's an outdoor heater. I keep it and the table and chairs under cover during the winter months."

"Oh, so you can eat up here or . . . whatever?"

"I can, but I don't very often. I got the heater thinking I would."

We make our way back downstairs to the kitchen. "Would you like some coffee or hot tea?"

"Is the tea herbal?"

"I have both. You want herbal?"

"Sure. Thanks."

I fix a cup of herbal tea for both of us and then set a plate of butter cookies, a fresh batch I made this morning, on the kitchen table where we settle. I watch Twila watch the cookies. "Help yourself."

"No, thanks."

Oh, I'm such a dork! "Oh, Twila, I'm sorry. I forgot. They have butter in them. They're not vegan."

"No, it's okay. I don't eat . . . cookies." She takes off her coat and lets it drape over the chair back.

"No cookies? Aren't there vegan cookies? Although, what's a cookie without butter?"

She shrugs.

"You know, I think I may try the vegan thing for awhile myself. It must be a good, healthy way to lose weight, right?"

"It depends. Every body is unique and everyone responds different."

"Really? But if I cut out . . ." I sigh and roll my eyes as I tick things off on my fingers: "Butter and other dairy, and meat, what else is there to eat? How could I not lose weight?"

You give up butter? Yeah right, fat girl.

"You can try it. There are still a lot of choices—legumes, grains, all fruits and vegetables, vegan breads. You could even gain weight if you ate enough."

I take a sip of my tea and grab a cookie. "What if I cut out sugar too?" I take a bite of the cookie.

"Cutting out sugar is always good—refined sugar anyway. It's, like, one of the worst things for us. Especially high fructose corn syrup, you know?"

I nod.

"You said you have osteoarthritis and fibromyalgia, right? So, like, an anti-inflammatory eating plan would be great for you. Inflammation screws up a lot of stuff in the body—it's tied in with pain, right? So if you can limit inflammation, you can help relieve pain."

"Really?"

She nods and then glances at the cookies again.

"Honey, are the cookies bothering you?" I reach for the plate and slide them my way.

She doesn't respond, but her gray eyes look like storm clouds—there's something there I can't read. In my usual fashion, I start to fill in the silence, but something holds me back. Divine intervention is about the only thing that stops my mouth, so I wait out the silence.

"Um . . . remember that day in the store when you said that all people have to do is look at you to see what you see in the mirror?"

I nod.

"And I said it doesn't always work that way?"

"Right, which, to tell you the truth, I didn't really understand. How can it not work that way? I'm fat. I see it in the mirror. Others have to see it too. Oh, is that why the cookies bother you? You're afraid you'll end up looking like . . . me?"

That's what she's thinking, Tubby.

"No . . . that's not what I meant. It's just that . . . well, you think I'm thin or twiggy or whatever, but . . . when I take my clothes off and look into a mirror? I see fat. Like, that's all I can see, is fat on my body. So . . . then the cookies sort of scare me. Like what if I ate one and then got fatter, you know?"

The weight of Twila's confession sits on my chest. "Twila, I do know. I understand that feeling. Unlike you, I gave into it long ago and I guess I eat too much now." I have to force those last few words past the lump shame has planted in my throat. But if admitting that will help Twila, it's worth it. "But, honey, how can you look in the mirror and see anything but a petite, lovely, young woman?"

She shrugs. "I don't look in the mirror much anymore. But maybe it's the same with you. Like, you look into a mirror and see someone who's overweight, but I look at you and I think you're great. You're pretty and smart and funny. All of that makes up what you look like to other people."

I feel heat rising from my neck to my face, and I'm tempted to look away, but I work to maintain eye contact with Twila. I want to respect and even return her level of vulnerability, if I can. "Thank . . . you. But you really are thin, and you see fat. I really am fat, and I see fat. So . . ."

"But maybe like me, that's all you see?"

I shift in my chair. "Oh."

"And there's, like, so much more to you than that. Just like there's more to me than what I see."

"How'd you get so wise, girly?"

She smiles. "Therapy. Lots of it. I was in an in-house treatment center for a while too. I saw a counselor every day there."

"Really? Wow." I smile too. "Well, I guess it worked."

"Sort of. I still have work to do. I'm applying what I've learned, but like, sometimes it's still so hard. The whole eating thing."

"So you have an . . . eating disorder?"

"Yeah, anorexia. But I'm not big on labels, especially that one, but . . . yeah. I'm getting better though. Especially about telling people so they'll understand me. And better about confronting fears. Like, I mean, who's afraid of cookies? That's just weird, right? But if I don't tell you, then it makes the fear feel bigger."

"Huh . . . you're so brave. I wish I had your courage." My admiration for Twila grows each time we're together.

"I'm just learning how to live a healthy life. I did the same thing with Miles this week, too. I had to tell him about a fear. Now, he wants to help me."

At the mention of Miles's name, I sense my face coloring again. I lift the mug of tea to my lips, hoping Twila won't notice the feelings I'm wearing on my face. Although if she could identify the feelings for me, it might help. I take a sip. "How does he want to help?"

"He wants to help me overcome one of my triggers. I figured out that having dinner with him at your place the other night sort of triggered my eating disorder. It reminded me of . . . my dad. Which, I don't know, just sort of set things off. So he asked if maybe I'd eat with him again and we could, you know, like work through it or something. He's just like that—he cares about people."

I tuck away what she says and know I'll think about it later. "So are you going to do it—eat with him again?"

"I don't know. It's hard. It brings up stuff I don't really want to deal with. I told him I'd pray about it. And he's doing the same thing. So I guess I'll let God, like, weigh in on it." She smiles. "No pun intended. I just mean if I feel like that's what God wants me to do, then I'll do it. He's the one healing me, you know?"

I nod like I know because I do—in theory at least.

"Wow, sorry, I didn't mean to talk all about me. I just wanted you to know that I sort of get some of what you feel. It's different. But it's sort of the same too."

Tears fill my eyes. "Thank you for sharing that with me. You're so . . . honest, and . . . vulnerable, and wise, and brave. You really are. Do you know that?"

It's her turn to blush. "I don't know. I'm just . . . me."

"Well, just you is pretty great."

"Thanks."

We go on to talk more about health issues, and a specific eating plan, and her work at Corners, and my work at the café. We talk and talk and talk, and as we do, my heart opens and creates a spot just for Twila.

"So, you think the vegan thing is okay for me to try?"

"Sure, if you want to."

I hear a knock on the front door and look at my watch and gasp. "Oh, I can't believe it's so late! I didn't even notice the sun setting."

"Me either."

I hop up from the table. "It's . . ." I swallow. ". . . Miles."

Twila follows me toward the living room and front door. "Nice. So you're seeing him again?"

"Well, sort of, I mean, we're just friends."

"Friends are good."

I stop just short of the front door and look back at Twila. "You know what, girly? Friends *are* good. And I feel like I made a new one today. Thank you."

She smiles. "Yeah, me too. Thank you for . . . like . . . everything."

Miles knocks again. "Oh, I better—" I point to the door, and then take the last two steps and open it.

I was violently overcome by a fearful sense of shame . . .
SAINT AUGUSTINE

CHAPTER TWENTY-ONE

Ellyn

As I REACH FOR the door, I notice my hand shaking. Oh my. I open the door and there stands Miles. His French-blue dress shirt matches his eyes, and his salt-and-pepper hair looks mussed, as though he's just run his hand through it. My heart betrays me as it flutters in my chest.

"Miles . . . hi. Come in. Twila's here—we weren't paying attention to the time." I turn to Twila. "We didn't even talk about recipes. We need to do that still, so another time?" I'm rambling. I know it, but I can't seem to stop. I look back at Miles. "You know how it is when women get together, we just talk and talk. Twila's a sweetheart, isn't she? So it's cold out there. Twila, do you have your coat? I better grab a coat for myself, although, really, I'm fine without one. But . . ."

I stop to take a breath, and then notice Miles is holding a small gift bag stuffed with pale green tissue.

Miles has stood there, watching me talk, a crooked smile on his face. Now that I'm taking a breath, he walks over to Twila and puts an arm around her shoulder and gives her a squeeze. He hangs onto the gift bag in his other hand. "Hey gal, good to see you. Sounds like you've had a nice afternoon together."

He looks from Twila to me.

"Yeah, we did. Isn't her place great?"

Miles looks around the living room and then to me. "It looks like you—warm."

"Thank you." I am warmer than he knows—I feel like a peri-menopausal hot flash has me by the throat. I loosen the scarf around my neck. A coat? Who am I kidding?

"Well, I better head out." Twila puts her coat on.

Oh, how I wish she'd stay. "No rush, honey."

She shrugs. "You guys have plans and my mom's expecting me for dinner." Then she turns to Miles. "Um, I'm still praying, you know?"

He nods. "Me too."

"So, like, I'll call you soon, if that's okay?"

Miles puts his arm around her again and smiles. "I'll look forward to hearing from you."

Twila heads toward the front door, then stops and turns back to me. "Hey, thanks for everything." Then she gives me a hug. *Wow.* It's quick, but I know it's significant.

"I'll call you. We have unfinished business."

She smiles at me and her face lights up, making the dark thorns look out of place. "Yeah, we do. Call anytime."

She grins at Miles. "Have fun tonight."

"We will. You take care."

I close the door behind Twila and wish I could just stand there with my face to the door and my back to Miles, but how dorky would that look? I turn back to him and smile.

He holds the bag out to me. "Here, I brought you something."

I'm certain a flock of fowl have taken up residence in my chest. I picture feathers flying as I take the gift bag. "Oh, you didn't . . . you shouldn't . . ."

"Open it."

I look at him. "Oh. Okay." I pull the pale tissue out of the bag and reach inside and take out a small box that's heavier than it looks.

I set the bag and tissue aside and take the lid off the box. "Oh . . ." I smile at him.

"It's the color of your eyes." His voice is low. "Sea-glass green."

I swallow and try to respond, but I'm sure there's a feather stuck in my throat. Instead, I pick up the piece of sea glass that's shaped like a rock, and focus on the word etched into the glass: *Friends*. I will myself to look back at Miles. "Thank you." I nod. "Really."

"You bet. So, are you hungry?"

"Hungry? Well, look at me? What do you think?"

Brilliant, Ellyn.

"Me, too. I'm starved. Shall we go?"

I shake my head. "Just give me a minute, okay? I want to . . ." I point to the stairs. "I'll be right back. Make yourself at home."

"Sure. Take your time."

I take the piece of sea glass and set it on the coffee table in the living room, and then tuck the box back into the bag with the tissue and take it with me. I climb the stairs to my room, praying he isn't watching my big back end as I go. Once up the stairs, I drop the bag and box on my nightstand and then go to the bathroom where I brush my teeth, dust my face with powder, and touch up my lip-gloss. I do the powder and gloss by braille, avoiding the mirror.

My hands shake as I try to screw the lid back on the lip-gloss.

I swish some mouthwash around in my mouth, spit into the sink—and then I take a deep breath and go back downstairs.

Miles's eyes shine as he talks.

We're seated at the corner table in the Garden Dining Room, overlooking Café Beaujolais's garden. It's lit on this dark night with soft, white lights along the garden pathways. I listen as he tells me about his sons, whom I picture as younger versions of him. While I listen, I also notice how thick his hair still is and how he has permanent smile lines near his eyes and mouth—noticeable only when he's serious. I also take note of how well his shirt fits and, again, how the color sets off those blue eyes of his.

Smitten, big girl?

I pick up my menu and glance at the offerings. My stomach, usually growling, is knotted and silent. I run through the *House Apertifs, Appetizers, Entrees,* and *Desserts.*

"What do you recommend, Chef Ellyn?"

"Oh." Nothing registered as I read the menu—I was too caught up in thoughts of him. But then, I check the menu online often to make certain my seasonal offerings are unique, so I should be able to come up with something. "Well"—I do a fast search—"the braised beet salad is always good, if you like beets, and for an entrée, how about the escargot gratin or the seared fois gras?"

He clears his throat. "Those sound . . ." He looks up at me and his eyes crease into a smile. "Horrible. Sorry."

I laugh. "I set you up. And you don't have to apologize, I'm not the one cooking tonight."

"Do you enjoy either of those?"

The disgust on his face makes me laugh again. "They're an acquired taste. I had escargot for the first time when I was in school, in Paris, and they really are good. But then how can anything swimming in garlic butter be bad?"

"It's a *snail* swimming in garlic butter."

We both laugh again. We chat over the menu and make our choices. After the waiter leaves, Miles leans back in his chair. He seems so relaxed that he almost puts me at ease.

"It was great to see Twila with you today."

"Really? Why?" I take a sip of my water.

He looks at me and cocks his head to one side as though he's sizing me up.

She's a size jumbo.

I shake my head.

"You okay?"

"Oh, yes . . . it's just. Nothing. I'm sorry. Go ahead."

He leans forward. "You're special, Ellyn. You're warm, accepting, funny."

I pull the scarf loose around my neck again and take another sip of my water.

"Twila needs good people in her life."

"Oh, well, thank you. But, you're the one who is really good for her. She told me about her struggle, and your offer to help her work through some things."

"I'm glad she told you about the anorexia."

"You know"—I put my hand over my heart—"she's so dear. I learned a lot from her today. Not just about nutrition." I wave my hand. "That was the least of it."

"What else?"

I pause as I search for the right words. "I learned some things about myself. Funny, but . . . we have more in common than you might think."

He waits for me to elaborate.

"We look like polar opposites. She's young, I'm not. She's brunette, I'm not. She's skin and bones. I'm . . . not. Which is no surprise to you, Dr. Becker, after all, you know how much I weigh." I have a strong desire to pull the tablecloth up and over my head. Why do I remind him?

You think he's forgotten? C'mon, Chubs, all he has to do is look at you.

I look around. When will our order arrive? I need to stick a steak in my mouth to shut myself up.

"Ellyn . . ."

I look back at him.

"I'm not your doctor anymore. I'm your friend. But I'm also a man. One who thinks you're beautiful."

"I . . . I . . ." Forget the steak, his comment shuts me up. He must be kidding, right?

"Here are your salads. Madame." The waiter sets the braised beet salad in front of me and the same in front of Miles. "May I get you anything else?"

I shake my head, pick up my fork, and dig in. Before I take my first bite, I look at Miles and smile. "Saved by the salads."

WHEN MILES PULLS INTO my driveway after dinner, the flock of nervous chickens in my chest take up their fluttering again, though

I don't know why. This doesn't happen when Sabina drops me off, and Miles is a friend just like Sabina. There's no difference. Friends. That's all. Nothing more.

Really.

"Ellyn?"

"Oh. What? Did you say something?"

He chuckles. "I said maybe next time we can check out 955 Ukiah or Raven's."

"Next time?" He wants to do this again? Oh, no. Oh, yes. Oh, no. Oh, dear. "Raven's doesn't use butter in any of their dishes."

He laughs. "So Raven's is out?"

"Definitely."

"I enjoyed the evening, Ellyn. Thanks for joining me."

"I enjoyed it too." As I say it, I realize it's true. I had a wonderful time—and I'm not sure what to make of that. "Thank you for dinner. You didn't have to . . ."

He holds up one hand. "It was my pleasure."

Miles reaches for the door handle and gets out of the car. It appears he'll walk me to the door. Do I invite him in? I open my car door and by the time I do, he's there. I get out and he closes the door behind me.

Ever the gentleman.

We walk in silence to my front door.

"Well, gal, thank you again."

I hesitate. "Would you . . . I mean . . ."

He watches me, then seems to understand. "Oh, thanks, no. I have an early morning." He comes close and gives me a hug.

Quick. Appropriate. Like friends do.

"I'll see you soon."

"Okay. Thanks again for dinner." I watch as he turns and goes to his car. Once there, he looks back and waves. I put the key in the lock and open the door, then wave back before closing the door. Once inside, I flip on the entry hall light and then lean back against the front door.

My heart hasn't returned to its normal rhythm. I take a deep breath. And then another. What is *wrong* with me? It was a nice evening with a friend. Nothing to get in a tizzy about. I put my hand over my chest and feel the pounding of my heart.

But there's something more than the pounding. Something deeper calling for attention. Is it . . . disappointment?

"Disappointment? Good grief, no. Not at all. Why would I feel disappointed?" I converse with myself as I walk to the kitchen and open the refrigerator. "It was a nice evening. He's a good conversationalist. The food was enjoyable." I rummage through the offerings and then close the fridge door. "Nothing to feel disappointed about."

Maybe it's just indigestion. I turn off the kitchen light and make my way upstairs to my bedroom.

Later, when I climb into bed, Earl crawls in with me.

So how'd that hug feel? You kind of liked that, didn't you? You better watch yourself. Watch your heart. You know how men are—he'll only hurt you.

Is it possible that Rosa and Sabina are right, and that Miles Becker is a good man? A different kind of man?

Earl cackles. *He's just like the rest of them. He'll only want one thing. He made his first move tonight—telling you you're beautiful. Really? You?*

I turn out the bedside lamp and pull a pillow over my head, but Earl's assault continues.

I reach out from under the covers, leaving the pillow over my head, and feel around on the nightstand for the box of tissue I keep there. Instead, my hand lands on the gift bag that held the piece of sea glass. I lift the pillow off my head, turn the light back on, and reach for a tissue. I blow my nose and wipe the tears from my eyes and cheeks. Then I sit up and think of the gift from Miles.

Friends.

He's respecting my boundary.

Ha! You're so gullible. Respect? You don't deserve respect.

I turn the lamp off again, and pull the covers tight around me. I fall asleep to Earl's litany of insults.

Our heart is restless until it rests in you.

SAINT AUGUSTINE

CHAPTER TWENTY-TWO

Miles

I CLICK THE REMOTE and turn off the 11:00 p.m. news after catching the lead stories. As the flat screen fades to black, so does the bedroom. I roll my pillow into a ball and put it under my head and settle on my back.

Saved by the salads.

I smile. She deflected my comment about her beauty. Maybe it made her uncomfortable—crossed the bounds of friendship between a man and a woman. I don't know. But it was truth.

Father God, I pray she will see herself as You see her—as You created her. I pray she recognizes herself as one knit together by You, fearfully and wonderfully made.

I stare into the dark. *Lord, inform my prayers for Ellyn.* I listen to the silence and wait. *Heal her, Lord, whatever her brokenness. You know her needs. I lift her to You.*

Eyes closed, I wait as an invisible Spirit intervenes and prays for Ellyn in a way I can't understand.

I hear the whir of the refrigerator going on downstairs and the familiar creaks and groans of the house.

I wait.

Then I pray again.

Lord, You know my needs. Nothing hides from You. I turn to You in times of loneliness, but in my humanness, I'm tempted to turn to others. I pray I never let anyone take Your place. You also know what's taking place in my heart regarding Ellyn. Father, I want to follow You. If this growing desire is not from You, I pray that becomes clear.

I stop. Is God making it clear through Ellyn's insistence that she doesn't date? Or is that, as Nerissa suggested, fear on Ellyn's part?

Lord, I ask for eyes to see and ears to hear You.

I sigh. *Lord, You know I'm afraid. I don't want to hurt again. Not after already losing so much.*

I open my eyes and stare into the dark. Is it foolish to build a friendship with someone I suspect I'm already falling in love with? Or is friendship enough?

I roll onto my side and pull the blanket up over my shoulders. *Your will be done on earth as it is in heaven . . .*

I found no calmness, no capacity for deliberation. I carried my lacerated and bloody soul when it was unwilling to be carried by me. I found no place where I could put it down.

Saint Augustine

CHAPTER TWENTY-THREE

Sabina

"So how did your apparel crisis work out for the big dinner date last week?" I switch my cell phone from my right hand to my left, and then pick up my mug of coffee.

"It wasn't a date."

"Oh right. So what did you wear to dinner with your *friend*?"

"My bathrobe and fuzzy slippers."

I laugh. "Ah, a classic. Well done."

"You sound like you're feeling better?"

The concern in her voice warms me. "I do feel a bit better this morning. Dr. Becker spoke with Dr. Norman and increased the dosage on the antidepressant. He called a new prescription into the pharmacy the evening you were here, and I picked it up the next day. I think it will help."

"Good, I'm so glad. What are you up to today? Do you feel like getting together?"

I smile. "That's why I'm calling. I'm thinking of forcing myself to take a walk—get some endorphins flowing. Would you like to join me?"

"A walk? Endorphins? You're suggesting we exercise together?"

"I'm not suggesting a marathon, girl. Just a walk. If you'd like to keep it simple, we could walk around the village. Wander through a few shops, and stop for coffee too. How does that sound?"

"Coffee is always good. What time?"

I DRIVE THE SEVERAL blocks into the village and turn right on Ukiah. Ellyn suggested we meet in front of a co-op she frequents—a large red building across from the post office. I pull into a parking space in front of what looks like an old church painted red, just as Ellyn drives in from the opposite direction. We park side by side.

I get out of my car and walk over to the driver's side of Ellyn's car, where she's just gotten out.

"Hi, there. Have your walking shoes on?" I give her a hug and then look down at her feet.

"Walking shoes are all I own. Can you see me trying to balance on heels?"

"Yes, I can. However . . ." I look around. ". . . I doubt there's much need for them here."

She laughs. "You're figuring the place out. No, heels aren't a requirement here. In fact, you're even a bit overdressed. What is this?"

She tugs on the collar of my jacket. "What's wrong with this? It's just a sweatshirt."

"Oh, yeah? Probably some designer thing from the big city, right?" She smiles.

"Ralph Lauren."

"Right, *now* who's classic?" She stands back and looks at me. "It suits you. That cream color with your skin is gorgeous. Makes me want vanilla ice cream with hot fudge."

I swat at her and smile. "So, what is this place?" I look up at the red steeple with the rainbow stripes. "Health food?"

"Healthy foods housed in an old Baptist church."

"I bet some of those old Baptists are rolling over in their graves."

Ellyn laughs. "I bet you're right. Mind if we save it until the end? I need to pick up a few things for home."

"Fine with me."

Ellyn points up the street. "This way."

I nod and we start up the street. I shorten my stride and slow my pace to match Ellyn's.

"Speaking of . . . Baptists, do you go . . . to church?"

We've only walked a couple hundred yards and Ellyn is already winded. "I go with Antwone occasionally. I was raised in Georgia, the Bible Belt, where there's a church on every corner, so I went as a child. It's part of my family heritage, but it isn't something I've felt I need."

"But Antwone goes?"

"Yes, he finds it meaningful. What about you?"

She nods. "I . . . go. But, it's . . . less about . . . church . . ." She stops to catch her breath. ". . . and more about a . . . relationship with God. Which is something I need . . . and want."

"The other day you said you're used to being in charge. So how does that fit with needing or wanting God?" I stand on the sidewalk with Ellyn, waiting for her to recover.

"I run my own business . . . and others depend on me. But I'm not the boss. God is. That doesn't mean I always . . . acknowledge Him as the One in control, or that I don't try to wrestle that control away from Him, but I'm so grateful that I don't make all the decisions alone." She takes a deep breath and wipes her forehead with her palm. "And I need God because I need Jesus. I need a Savior."

"Well, you and Antwone will become fast friends. Ready?"

She nods and then points across Lansing Street. "There's Thanksgiving's. You said we'd have coffee."

"We haven't even walked two blocks yet." I look at her and notice how flushed her face is and that the curls that have come loose from her ponytail are damp. "But exercise is overrated—coffee sounds great." I put my hand on Ellyn's arm. "Are you all right?"

She pushes a curl back behind her ear. "Just out of shape, I guess. But I didn't know I was *this* out of shape." She puts her hand on her chest. "My heart's doing the rumba. Good thing I'm dieting, huh?"

We head across the street and into Thanksgiving's. The aroma of fresh-brewed coffee feels like a familiar embrace. "So what kind of diet?"

Ellyn holds up one finger and then orders a soy latte. "Ugh. A diet that restricts dairy and includes soy. I'm trying veganism for a while. I need to get some weight off."

I nod. Good for her. "I'll have a mocha with whip." Then I look at Ellyn. "Sorry."

"You skinny girls have all the fun."

AFTER COFFEE, WE WANDER through a couple of shops and then take a slow stroll back down Ukiah Street to the co-op. "Corners of the Mouth? What kind of name is that?"

Ellyn laughs. "I don't know." She pulls open the heavy front door. "After you."

I walk into the store, half-expecting pews and a pulpit, but instead I'm met with a refrigerator case filled with juices, energy drinks, and the like. The wood floors look original and the eclectic array of foods, gifts, essential oils, and supplements, all housed in a church, seem to embody the essence of Mendocino. I notice two women behind the registers—the younger woman is the one I noticed at Ellyn's the first night I had dinner there. Following Ellyn's example, my heart does, if not the rumba, at least a fast two-step.

I make a quick left down the first aisle and stand looking at breakfast cereals as I hear Ellyn greeting the girl.

She looks so much like—

No. Don't go there, Sabina. I pull a package of gluten-free steel-cut oats off the shelf and try to read the label. *I can't believe how similar . . .*

Ellyn comes around the corner. "Sabina, I want you to meet a friend of mine."

I look at her, and she must read something on my face.

"Or . . . not. Are you okay?"

I replace the oatmeal on the shelf and turn back to Ellyn. "I'm fine. Why? Who do you want me to meet?" I *am* fine. It's not like the girl is a ghost.

"A friend who works here. C'mon."

I follow Ellyn to the registers and watch as the young woman answers a question for a customer. The tattoo is different, but otherwise . . .

"Twila, this is my friend, Sabina. Sabina, this is Twila."

I put my hand out and she shakes it. I struggle to make eye contact with her.

"It's nice to meet you, Sabina. Ellyn says you're here for, like, a year or something?"

I shrug. "We'll see. Nice to meet you too. What's upstairs?" I look to my left toward the stairs I noticed when we came in.

"That's the choir loft—herbs and teas, mostly."

"Great. I think I'll head up." I wave at Twila without looking at her again. I also avoid looking at Ellyn. As I take the few steps to the stairs, I hear Ellyn continue to chat with Twila. Thank goodness she isn't following me.

I need a moment.

Once upstairs, I stare at a shelf of boxed teas. I take a deep breath in, and exhale, breathe in, exhale, breathe in, exhale. The exercise brings me back to the present and calms me.

I collect myself, but it won't last long if I go back down there. So the solution is easy.

I will remain upstairs until Ellyn comes looking for me.

AFTER ELLYN AND I part ways, I drive through the village, up to Highway 1, and head north. I drive the short distance to Lansing Street, and turn in, and drive the block or so to the rental, thus avoiding Agate Cove. It takes a few more minutes to return this way, but the day posed enough challenges without also having to ignore the view of the cove one more time.

I walk into the house, go to the living room still darkened by the closed shades, flip on the gas fireplace, and then turn on my iPod and speakers. I turn up the music as loud as my ears can stand. The whining, moaning cello reverberates through the room. Yo-Yo Ma playing Bach's Suite No. 2. I sit in the dark, lights off, staring at the flames of the fire.

The music is a dirge, carrying me to that place of haunting.

When I close my eyes, the flames play on the insides of my eyelids, obscured only by the face of the young woman I met in the store today—or is it Ashley's face? Or maybe it's the other young girl, blood of my blood, lost to me so long ago?

I'm not certain, nor does it matter.

Ellyn's words come back to me: *I need a Savior.*

Jesus?

He's never saved anyone I care about.

How does it come about that out of the
bitterness of life sweet fruit is picked by
groaning and weeping and sighing and mourning?

SAINT AUGUSTINE

CHAPTER TWENTY-FOUR

Twila

ROSA GREETS US AS we walk into Ellyn's. "Ah, you two
came back. Where your mama at, Chica?"

"She's at a conference for a few days."

"Good for her. You keep the doctor company, *Sí?*"

I nod.

"Rosa, we don't have a reservation. Is that a problem?"

"No, Doctor, not for you. We busy, but not too busy. Only on
Friday and Saturday are we too busy. Sunday, all the tourists already
go home."

We follow Rosa to a corner table near the window. Once we're
seated, Rosa leans in close to Miles. "I tell Ellyn you here."

He smiles. "Thank you, Rosa."

When I called and told Miles I'd like to try eating together
again, I also told him I'd like to go to Ellyn's again too, if that was

okay. "I know her and I like it there. It feels sort of safe, you know?" I doubted he would mind.

I was right.

I look at the menu. "Hey, look! Ellyn added one of the vegan recipes we talked about a few days ago."

"Great. I'll try it. What about you?"

I pretend to read the rest of the menu. "Maybe."

"Twila, we're not here just to eat. I'm here to listen too."

I look back at him. "Yeah. Thanks. It's just . . . like, hard." I swallow the lump in my throat. "After I said I'd do this, it . . . triggered Ed, my eating disorder, again." I close the menu. "It's like, I'm getting better, but then sometimes I'm not. But I saw my counselor and we talked about it."

"Was that helpful?"

"Sort of."

He nods.

I see Ellyn come out of the kitchen and look over at us. She starts to come our way, but then she stops. Miles has his back to her so he can't see her. I wave her over and she starts our way again.

"Hi, I don't want to interrupt."

"You're not. We wanted to see you."

Miles stands up and puts his arm around Ellyn's shoulders and gives her a squeeze—just like he does with me. Then he stands back and smiles at her. "How are things in the kitchen?"

"They're good."

"It smells great, as always."

"Thanks. You two are a nice surprise." Ellyn looks at me. "Did you notice the new vegan dish on the menu?"

I nod. "Yeah, you did it."

"With your help, girly. It's necessary in this area, I realize. Even Patterson's Pub has a veggie burger on their menu."

I nod.

"So, honey, are you . . . okay here?"

"Yeah, I'm okay. I'll probably order the new dish, but . . . you know, I might take it home and eat it."

"You do whatever's best for you."

Ellyn turns back to Miles. "And how are you?"

"No complaints. I have a lovely dinner companion and one of the area's best chefs in the kitchen."

Ellyn smiles at him and I see something in the way she looks at him that's different than the way she looks at other people.

"I need to get back to the kitchen." She bends down and gives me a hug and then smiles again at Miles before going back to work.

Miles sits back down after watching her walk away.

"So, you really like her, right?"

Miles looks toward the kitchen again and then he runs his hand through his hair. "Well, gal . . . yes, I really like her."

"She's pretty likeable."

AFTER THE WAITER BRINGS our meals, Miles looks at me and holds out his hand across the table. "Let me pray over this."

I hesitate, but then I reach out and take his hand.

"Heavenly Father, I thank You for the gift of the food that sustains us. Thank You for Your presence at the table with us. Lord, I also thank You for Twila and her heart for You. May Your will be done here as it is in heaven. In Jesus' name I pray, amen."

I bowed my head while he prayed, and when he's done I open my eyes but keep my head down.

"Twila?"

I nod without looking up. "I . . . I wish . . ." I take a deep breath and then wipe my eyes with my napkin. "I wish my . . . dad . . . loved God. Like, you know . . . the way . . . you do." I glance up at Miles and then look back down.

"Gal . . ."

I look up again.

"I'm sorry for what you've gone through with your dad. Your mom has shared some of it. I know I can never replace him, but I want you to know that I'm here for you—for whatever you need."

I wipe my eyes again. And again.

"I care about you, Twila."

I nod. That's all I can do. I wipe my eyes yet again. "Um . . ." I stand up. "I'm going . . ." I point toward the restroom. I walk across the café with my head down and go into the restroom and then into a stall. I can't stop the tears. I mean, I really can't stop them. I stand in the stall with the door closed. I pull paper from the roll and wipe my eyes and blow my nose. And I cry some more.

The emotions come . . . things I haven't let myself feel. Feelings I've starved. The feelings Ed helped me avoid. The emptiness is huge and black and aches, but like, now . . .

It aches to be filled.

For the first time ever . . . I get that. Instead of starving it, I can . . . risk . . . *filling* it. Like, with food, but also with love.

God's love.

His love through the people who are in my life—my mom, Miles, Ellyn.

They don't replace my dad, but I'm beginning to understand that God . . . well, He's enough.

More than enough.

And that makes me cry even more.

The house of my soul is too small for You to come to it.
May it be enlarged by You. It is in ruins: restore it.

SAINT AUGUSTINE

CHAPTER TWENTY-FIVE

Ellyn

 "ELLYN. ELLYN!"

I look up from the sauce I'm stirring and see Miles standing just inside the swinging doors of the kitchen. The look on his face tells me something's wrong.

"Paco, come finish this."

Paco looks from me to Miles and then takes the spoon from me. "Go, Bella, whatever it is. I can handle things here."

I untie my apron and go to where Miles is waiting. "What's wrong?"

"It's Twila. She's upset. She left the table crying and went to the ladies' room. Will you check on her?"

I put my hand on Miles's arm. "Oh, of course." Before I turn to go, I see the creases in his forehead and the concern in his blue eyes. "She'll be okay, Miles. She will." I head out of the kitchen and to the restroom. *Oh Lord, comfort Twila and give me wisdom. And let there be no one else in the restroom.*

I push open the door and then look under the doors of the two stalls. In the second stall, I recognize Twila's khaki cargo pants. Once I coax her out, I see the pain in her expression and the tears on her cheeks. The black tattooed thorns glisten.

"Oh, honey . . ." I put my arms around her and pull her close. It's the only thing I know to do. At first she stiffens, but then her body goes limp against mine and she rests her head on my shoulder.

"It's okay, just let it out. Let it out, honey." As she wets my chef's coat with her tears, my heart breaks for her. I hear the restroom door open behind me and I turn my head toward the door. "Occupied! Use the men's room."

I hold Twila tight until she stills. Then I pull back from her and push long strands of her dark hair away from her face. "Hold on . . ." I go back into the stall and get toilet paper for her to wipe her nose and eyes on.

She dabs at her eyes, blows her nose, and hiccups. "I'm . . . sorry."

"Honey, you have nothing to apologize for. Can you tell me what's going on?"

"It's . . . it's Miles. And my dad. It's . . . grief. My counselor said spending time with Miles might stir up some grief, you know?"

I hug her again and then I step back and look at her. "Twila, you're the strongest, most courageous young woman I know."

She looks down at the floor, and I sense she can't take in what I say. I reach out and put my hand under her chin and lift it so she has to look at me again. "I mean that. Even knowing what kind of feelings Miles might stir up in you, you still met with him."

"I . . . I needed to work through this. Like, I had to. Even though this is hard, there's hope too. I mean, I'm understanding new things, you know? I get now how God provides for me through other people and how much He loves me."

Twila's insight silences me for a moment. "You're amazing. Really." I take the used paper from her and put it in the trash. "Oh, look, I could have handed you tissue." I point to the box of tissue on the granite countertop in the restroom. "Oops, sorry."

She smiles for the first time since I came in the restroom. "Whatever."

We both stand at the sinks and wash our hands, and Twila wets a paper towel and presses it against her eyes.

"So now what? Do you want me to take you home, or are you okay to go with Miles?"

She looks at her feet again.

"Honey, is your mom home?"

She shakes her head. "No, she left today for a conference in Santa Rosa."

"Oh."

"It's okay. I'll be okay."

"You're okay alone?"

She shrugs.

"What about my guest room? Maybe, for my sake, you could spend the night at my place so I know you're all right?"

She looks up and her eyes meet mine. "Really?"

"Really. Do you feel okay having Miles drive you over there?"

"Yeah."

"Okay, I'll give you my key, you can go by your house and get a few things, and then go to my house. I don't know what Miles has planned, but if you'd rather not be alone, maybe he can stay there with you until I get home."

"Okay."

"I'll be here a few more hours, but you can get settled. The sheets on the bed are clean and there are towels and things in the guest bath."

She sighs. "Thanks, Ellyn."

I wave off her thanks. I can't explain it, but I feel as though this is more a favor to me than it is to her.

IT'S NEAR 11:00 P.M. by the time I close up the kitchen and café. As I get in my car, my phone dings, indicating I have a text. I pull the phone from my purse.

I stayed with T. Front door unlocked. Didn't want to startle you.

I smile at the text from Miles, but the smile doesn't last long.

Twila's courage—her willingness to face and work through something that causes her such pain—unnerves me. She's half my age and twice as mature. I reach for the bag of croissants on the passenger seat that I brought to send home with Miles. I need one. I pull one of the fresh rolls out of the bag, lift it to my mouth, and then remember—

This foray into veganism might do me in! The buttery scent of the roll makes my mouth water. What difference would just one make?

Yeah, you'll fail anyway. It's just a matter of time.

I lift the croissant back to my mouth, but . . .

Oh Lord, I want it so much. Help me.

Almost shaking with desire, I put the croissant back into the bag. I step on the accelerator and speed through the sleepy streets toward home. When I pull into the driveway and turn off the engine, I reach into my purse for a breath mint. The beauty of living alone is that you don't have to worry about this kind of thing. Who needs to come home after a long night worried about how fresh their breath is? Not me, that's for sure.

I reach for the bag of croissants and still think about having one before bed.

You'll never change.

The downstairs lights are on inside, making the house glow with warmth. The upstairs is dark. Gravel crunches under my feet as I make my way from the driveway to the stone walkway leading to the front door. Once there, I stand on the threshold, take a deep breath, and open the door.

Miles waits inside somewhere.

All is quiet. I see Miles, his long legs stretched out in front of him, sitting in one of the overstuffed chairs in my living room. His head is tilted back, his eyes closed. It seems he fell asleep between the time he sent his text and the few minutes it took me to get home.

I stand still and watch him. He looks vulnerable. Tenderness rises in me. I want to go over and cover him with a blanket, brush his hair off his forehead, and kiss the furrows in his brow.

All of which surprises me . . . but not in an unpleasant way.

What I *don't* want is to get caught watching him.

"Hey . . ." I close the front door with a bang and see him jump. "I'm here."

Duh, big girl.

Miles gives me a slow, sleepy smile. "Hi. How—" He covers his mouth and yawns. "Sorry. How was the rest of your evening?"

I put on a bright face. "More interesting than yours, from the looks of it."

He sits up and puts his hands on his knees. "Mine was quiet—after dinner, that is."

"Is she okay?" I point to the stairs.

He stands up and stretches. "She is. She's a brave one."

"I know. I told her that." I cross the living room and set the bag of croissants and my purse on the dining room table. "So she talked to you?"

He nods. "She shared some of what she's learning and how I fit into the picture of her life—not as a replacement for her dad, but as 'God's provision,' she said. We began a good dialogue. One I pray will continue. I raised sons. Girls are . . ." He shakes his head and smiles. "Girls are a different world. But nice."

As he talks, my heart melts like a pound of butter over a hot flame. His concern for Twila—his willingness to engage with her, to give of himself—gets to me. His reference to prayer and his love for God, so evident whenever we talk . . . and those gorgeous, sleepy, blue eyes.

Is it possible? Is this man as good as he seems?

Careful, Tubby. If he seems too good to be true, then he is.

I walk toward him and stop just short of where he stands. He watches me but doesn't move. I take one step closer and then stand on my toes, intending to give him a quick kiss on the cheek and thank him for his goodness to Twila. But as I do, he puts his arms around me and pulls me close. The warmth of him against me both soothes and ignites me.

"Mmm . . . you smell wonderful—like everything good: garlic, cream, herbs, and butter."

"Eau de chef." I start to pull away from him. I need to pull away from him. But as I do, he reaches up and places his hands on my face. He holds me there, staring down at me, those deep blue eyes serious.

And then his lips are on mine.

His kiss is tender and undemanding.

My mind screams a warning, but I ignore it and let my other senses take over. His breath is warm and the stubble on his chin brushes against my face. The spicy scent of his aftershave swirls. The sound of my own heart beating in my ears drowns out everything, including my common sense.

I surrender.

I reach my arms up around his neck and let one hand rest in his hair.

And I kiss him back—a long, lingering kiss.

A moment I've dreamt of most of my life.

Breathless, I lean my head back, still in his embrace.

"Ellyn . . ." His voice is thick. "You have to know I'm falling for you."

He's good. Using that line already. You know where this is going. I hate to say 'I told you so,' but I did.

I look at him and know my eyes mirror the desire I read in his. Oh, what am I *doing*?

You might as well lead him upstairs right now. You know that's what he's expecting.

I shake my head. *No.* "No . . ." I drop my arms back to my sides and take a step back. "No . . . I can't . . . I can't do this." I try to catch my breath and hope he can't hear my heart pounding.

"Ellyn?"

I turn my back on him now and take a few more steps away. Then I turn back. "I can't do this. I won't do this. I won't. I told you from the beginning . . . I told you. I . . . don't want this."

I see the hurt in his eyes, but the armor shielding my heart snaps back into place. "I'm sorry, Miles. I . . . need you to . . . leave. Now." I walk toward the front door and open it when I get there. I turn and look at him still rooted where we'd stood together just moments before.

He walks toward the door and then stops at the coffee table. He reaches down and picks something up off the table and drops it in the pocket of his slacks. His keys, maybe? When he gets to me, he stops and looks at me. "Ellyn, I—"

"Please, just go."

He shakes his head and, again, I see the pain in his eyes. But he says nothing else. He walks out my front door.

And I close the door behind him.

Then I turn and lean against it.

He will not get in again.

Not into my house.

Not into my heart.

I stand there until I hear his car, him, pull out of the gravel driveway.

When he does, I let the tears come.

I walk back to the dining room table, pick up the bag of croissants, and take one out of the bag. I go to the kitchen, set the bag on the counter, and open a drawer and take out a paper napkin. I wipe my eyes and nose with the napkin and then take a bite of the croissant. The lump in my throat makes swallowing a struggle, but I work at it until the bite goes down.

Then I take another bite.

And another . . .

With the last bite of the last croissant in the bag, a small voice whispers in my mind. Or maybe in my heart.

You don't love food more than you love Me, Ellyn. You trust food more than you trust Me.

I swallow.

Then the whisper comes again.

Will you trust Me?

There are no caresses tenderer than your charity,
and no object of love is more healthy than your truth,
beautiful and luminous beyond all things.

SAINT AUGUSTINE

CHAPTER TWENTY-SIX

Miles

GRAVEL SPRAYS BEHIND ME as I put my foot to the accelerator leaving Ellyn's driveway. When I reach the end of her street, I turn right toward the water rather than left toward the highway. I round the curve of Headlands State Park and pull into the first parking space—the beams of my headlights bounce across the lot and land on the dark expanse of water. I turn the lights off, put the car into park, and open the door.

Once out, I turn and look behind me and see the lights shining from Ellyn's tower flick off one by one. I imagine her climbing the stairs to her bedroom. That was an intense end to an evening.

For both of us, I'd guess.

That intensity presses on my chest from the inside out. Or . . . is it anger?

I turn and look back at the water.

Anger at myself for my lack of self-control, for ignoring the boundary Ellyn set.

I let my eyes adjust to the dark, and then walk to one of the trails leading from the parking lot out to the cliffs.

I thought I saw her soften tonight—read something more in her face. But I was wrong. So wrong.

An owl swoops down on its prey in front of me.

Or was I? Didn't she return my kiss?

My throat tightens. "Ah Sarah, it was so easy with you." A void inside me cracks wide and the trail, lit only by a slice of moon, blurs in front of me. I step up my pace needing an outlet for my anger, my grief.

The anger of rejection.

The grief of loss.

Again.

A crisp wind blows now, carrying spray from the surf below. I jam my cold hands into my pants pockets as I walk. When I do, I feel the smooth edges of the piece of sea glass I took from Ellyn's coffee table. I wrap my hand around it and clench it in my fist.

I knew, from the beginning, that I felt more for Ellyn than friendship.

Felt more. And wanted more.

She made herself clear from the beginning, so I have no one but myself to blame for her rejection.

I see Ellyn in my mind—the emotion in her green eyes tonight— or at least the emotion I imagined I saw there. But it's Twila I think of—what she shared with me tonight. The void her father left in her life. In her heart.

My anger boils again. Will Twila's father ever know the damage he's caused?

I think of my sons, Will and Alex, each named after a grand- father. I can't imagine not having a relationship with them. Not being involved in their lives. I talk to them every chance I get. I love them. I miss them.

Twila's pain was so visible. When I met her, just after she came home from school, too weak to continue her education, I wondered if her shrinking body was her way of disappearing. If you don't exist, you can't hurt.

Well, maybe she had the right idea—maybe disappearing is the answer. If I disappear from Ellyn's life, maybe I'll save her some hurt.

Her . . . and myself.

I pull my hand from my pockets, the piece of sea glass still in my grip. I veer off the path and trudge through the prairie grass until I'm standing as close to the edge of the cliff as I dare. I pull my right arm back and then hurl the piece of glass, the color of Ellyn's eyes, into the sea. As I release it, it catches the light of that slice of moon, and then it disappears into the inky water.

It disappears.

It becomes *invisible*.

Lord?

Ellyn's words, spoken a couple of weeks ago when talking about Twila, come back to me now: *"Funny, but we have more in common than you might think."* She'd kept talking—contrasting herself with Twila. I heard the contrasts, but she never got to their similarities. Why hadn't I asked?

What do they share in common?

I wait, asking God to help me understand. I think of Twila again—how her body manifested her pain. Could she and Ellyn share that in common? Is Ellyn's weight a manifestation of her pain? Is the root cause similar for both of them, but the outcome different?

Twila confirmed tonight that she'd wanted to disappear. To hide from her pain by shrinking away. I triggered that pain in Twila. Is it possible Ellyn also wants to hide? Has she disappeared behind the weight she carries? Is she covering her pain?

I shake my head.

I hear these types of stories from patients. I've learned some of the root causes of eating disorders. Though they may manifest in different ways, the underlying issue is often similar.

Is that it, Lord? Two women longing for invisibility—to hide from the pain they've experienced?

But what is Ellyn's pain? Do I trigger her pain in some way too?

I recall our conversation about death. I lost Sarah, Ellyn lost her father. But I sensed she'd grieved her father and moved on. And I'm certainly not a father figure for Ellyn. But Nerissa had wondered, too, if Ellyn was afraid of getting involved with a man.

Someone hurt her.

If I let myself, I can still feel the warmth of Ellyn's kiss. But more than that, I feel my heart constrict at the thought of her hurting. And I choose to focus on the latter.

Lord, thank You for Your forgiveness. I didn't want to hurt Ellyn, yet I disrespected the boundary she set. But Lord, You know my heart—my intent—I don't want to hurt her. Comfort her tonight, Lord.

My throat tightens again.

I don't know how to pray for her. I don't know what's gone on in her past. But . . . You know. Lead me, Lord.

Rain drizzles now and I head back to the car. The smell of damp earth rises as I walk. I get in the car, turn on the engine, heater, and wipers, and then back out of the parking space.

Lord, show me how to pray for Ellyn . . .

The screeching of the wipers against the windshield is the only sound in the car. But inside me, I sense, more than hear the answer.

Pray for Ellyn as you would Twila.

An image of the tattoo on Twila's wrist comes to mind.

Imago Dei.

Father, I pray that both Twila and Ellyn will recognize themselves as being created in Your divine image. May they live into that image, and embrace their value as being made by You and like You, Father. Heal the wounds others have inflicted on them. Restore them.

God, may they know Your love, Your mercy, Your grace. May they fall more in love with You day by day.

Father, I pray I will reflect Your image to each of them. I pray my own wounds don't blur the wonder of who You are, but rather that they will see wholeness that comes only from You.

I stare at the road ahead, and new resolve grows within me. To reflect God's attributes in a way that pleases Him—in a way that reflects His truth instead of the lies others have portrayed. To do what He calls me to do that these two hurting women may recognize God as Father, Savior, and Lover . . .

As All.

I prayed for another chance to cast a picture of God for Ellyn. As for what I longed for . . .

Father, I trust my heart to You. You are enough. May Your will be done on earth as it is in heaven.

In the name of Jesus, I pray.

Amen.

> The greatest source of repair was the solace of . . . friends.
>
> SAINT AUGUSTINE

CHAPTER TWENTY-SEVEN

Ellyn

SABINA LOOKS BACK. "YOU'RE quiet this morning."

My heart is hammering as I try to keep up with her long strides—her legs are twice as long as mine. No exaggeration. We agreed a couple of weeks ago that we'd start walking together on a regular basis and we also agreed that we'd each go our own pace.

"Just going my own pace. Hard to talk when you're up there and I'm back here."

We're walking up Ukiah toward 955 Ukiah and Café Beaujolais. Why we can't walk on the headlands, I still don't know.

"You sure that's it, or is something more going on with you?"

Strands of my long hair, which I've pulled back for our walk, come loose in the wind and blow across my face. Frustration wells as I try to secure my hair again. "I'm *fine*." We've both stopped walking and I stare at her—now just in front of me.

"What?"

"I'm drenched, but there's not a drop of condensation on your skin."

"Condensation? I'm not a glass of iced tea."

I wave her comment away. "You know what I mean."

She gives me that counselor look of hers. "Girl, what is up with you this morning?"

"I'm fine. I told you."

"I know what you said, now I'm asking for the truth."

"Don't analyze me. I'm not one of your clients."

"Well, at least that's *something* to give thanks for." She puts her hands on her hips. "No, but you are my friend and something's off. That's what real friends are for, or has it been so long since you've let your guard down for anyone that you've forgotten?"

"Oh, good one, Counselor."

She looks down at her feet—hands still on her hips. When she looks up, I see what looks like a flash of anger, or at least irritation, cross her features. "Listen, Ellyn, I am who I am—take it or leave it." She turns and starts walking again.

"Okay. Wait. Wait! I can't keep up." I start walking toward her but she outpaces me again, which I think is her intention this time. Then she stops and turns back toward me—her movements brisk.

"Can't or won't?"

Can't or won't? "Now you sound like Earl."

"Who? I sound like who?"

"No one."

"It didn't sound like no one. It sounded like you said *Earl.* Who's Earl?"

"Never mind." I lift my shoulders and paste a smile on my face. "Hey, are we arguing?" Maybe my attempt at levity will put an end to this conversation.

No such luck.

"No. What I hope we're having, or what I hope we're going to have, is our first *real* conversation." Her eyes soften along with the tone of her voice. "Are you game?"

"Real? What do you mean by—"

She holds up one hand and stops me midsentence. "I don't need your defensiveness." She turns and begins walking away again.

I stand there and debate with myself for a minute, and then I shout to her over the wind, which has begun howling. I wrestle another curl behind my ear. "Okay! I weighed myself this morning and . . ."

She stops and walks back to me again.

"And?" she encourages.

"And I wanted to pick up the scale and slam it against the bathroom mirror until both were as shattered as . . . as . . ." I wipe the tears now dripping down my face.

"As you felt?"

I sniff. "Something like that."

Sabina reaches out and puts her hand on my arm. "I'm sorry the number wasn't what you wanted to see."

"Not even close."

"Girl, a number doesn't define you."

"Oh, no? Which galaxy do you come from? First there's the number on the scale, which defines me as overweight, then there's the BMI number, which defines me as obese, then there's those blood pressure numbers, which are getting close to defining me as hypertensive. Then there are the numbers for . . ." I choke back a sob.

"Ellyn . . ." She pulls a tissue out of the pocket of her Windbreaker and hands it to me. "Those numbers don't even begin to tell the story of who you are. Are the numbers important? Sure they are. In terms of your health, for those of us who care about you, they're important. But they don't define you."

"You don't *get* it!" I kick the dirt with the toe of my shoe.

Nobody as skinny as she is can understand what you're feeling.

"Maybe it's you who doesn't get it." She pins me with her stare.

"I can't lose weight. Do you get that? I can't do it!"

"Who told you that?"

"No one had to tell me. I've tried every diet in the book! I can't do it!"

"Well, sister, as long as you're listening to the *can't* voice, you're right, it's not gonna happen. You just go ahead and keep hiding away in that kitchen and eat yourself to death." Again, she turns and heads down the trail.

I stand there, mouth agape. *What?* "Hiding? Really?" I shout over the wind. And then I sprint toward her. Okay, sprint is a little strong, but I do my version. By the time I reach her, I'm gulping for air. I come up behind her and grab the back of her Windbreaker and jerk her to a stop.

"Hide . . ." I gasp. "Hiding? Me?" I bend at the waist and put my hands on my knees, fearing I may pass out as the landscape around me begins spinning. "Who . . . who's hiding?" I stand again. I lean my head back, close my eyes, and wait while the spinning stops and I catch my breath—or some of it anyway. I wait for her to respond, but she just stares at me.

"Who's hiding? What . . . are you doing here, Sabina?" I make a grand gesture with one arm taking in the village. "Huh? Tell me. You want a real conversation? Okay, *your* turn."

She begins to turn away again, but I grab her jacket and hang on this time. "Is this how you deal with your clients—just walk away when a conversation takes a turn you don't like? Huh?" My voice is sharp as a knife, even to my own ears. But come on, who does she think she is? "Answer the question, Sabina. Who or what are you hiding from? You say you have a husband who loves you and . . . and daughters. What are you doing here?"

"You're changing the subject, Ellyn. We were talking about you."

I hold her gaze with my own and lift my chin just a bit.

"Let go of me." She pulls away, but I keep my grip on her Windbreaker.

"No. I have—" I take a deep breath, my hair whipping in the wind now. "I have something more to say. You're right. I hide in the kitchen—or I hide behind this layer of . . . of . . . you know."

She raises one eyebrow.

"There. Satisfied?"

She puts her hands out, palms up. Like she doesn't know what I mean, but we both know she does.

"But I think your question was projection." I see a brief look of surprise in her eyes. "I think you're hiding as much, if not more than, I am, and I want to know why." My voice has softened along with my heart. I know the words I just spoke were not my own.

She looks from me to her feet. When she looks back up—her sable eyes are swimming with tears.

"Sabina?" I let go of her jacket and put my hand on her shoulder.

She shakes her head and turns away from me, but I can see she's wiping the tears away. When she turns back to face me, a fresh sheen of tears covers her cheeks. I reach in my pocket and hand her the tissue she gave me. Only now it's used and crumpled.

She smiles and then we both laugh—her through her tears.

She reaches in her own pocket and pulls out a fresh tissue and then wipes her eyes and nose. She takes a deep breath. "I came here to . . . heal, I told you that. But . . . you're right, I've done more hiding than healing."

"What happened?"

Sabina's gaze leaves my face and she looks at her feet. Her tears flow again.

I wait.

Her chest rises and falls. She talks to the ground. "I . . . I had a client, a teenager still—just seventeen. Her name was . . . Ashley." She looks at me and takes a deep breath. "She was gifted—so talented—so much potential. But she was different, unique. She was an artist." She looks past me back toward the village. "She would have loved it here. She belonged in a colony of artists, using her gift among those who'd have understood her . . ." Her voice softens to a whisper.

I wait, but finally have to ask, "What happened to her?"

Sabina swallows. "Like I said, she was different—had her own way of doing things, her own style. She didn't fit in. Ever. By the time she reached high school she was bullied, sometimes daily—at school and through social media. She was an outcast, but she resolved to be true to herself. A lovely combination of strength and tenderness. At least that's how I saw her and how I tried to help her see herself.

"I had one of her paintings, an abstract. She gave it to me after I'd helped her process a difficult"—she wrings her hands—"dirty event. I brought it with me—her painting, that is. It's in one of the galleries here. The gallery owner was so impressed with her work that he wanted to show more." She stops and stares at nothing for a moment. "But that's impossible. When it sells, I'll forward the money to her family."

She starts walking again. The wind has calmed some and so have we. I wait for her to continue—to tell me what happened to the young artist. But she's quiet.

"Sabina, *what happened*?"

She looks at me and her eyes seem to glaze over, like she's gone somewhere else in her mind. She is silent for too long.

"Sabina?"

She stops walking and turns on me. "Fine! You want to know what happened? She hung herself." Her eyes fill with tears again, this time she makes no attempt to wipe them away. "She walked out of my office one afternoon and later hung herself from a pull-up bar on her high-school campus."

"Oh, Sabina . . ." I cover my mouth with my hand.

"You want to know what I'm hiding from? I'm hiding from reality! I'm hiding from myself! Satisfied?"

As she shouts at me, her anger is palpable—like I could reach out and feel the heat of it. Though I'd no more attempt to do so than I would reach out and touch the gas flame of one of the burners on the kitchen range.

Sabina turns and walks away. After several paces, she begins to run.

And this time, I let her go.

I FILL THE CLAW foot tub in my bathroom with hot, almost scalding, water. I strip off the sweats I wore for our walk, toss them onto the bathroom floor, and then sprinkle lavender bath salts into the water.

I called Paco when I got home and told him not to expect me for a few hours. It will set his schedule behind a bit, but I'll make up for it this afternoon.

I climb into the steaming water, sit, and then stretch my legs out and let myself sink up to my chin. While the water warms my chilled body, my heart remains cold.

Twila left soon after getting up this morning, and for that, I was grateful. I had little energy left after the encounter with Miles last night. And Twila seemed okay. Maybe she sensed my fatigue, or my mood, I'm not sure. But she said we'd talk later, after she'd had time to think about her conversation with Miles.

I splash hot, scented water on my face and rub my eyes. I have a few things to process about Miles myself. I lean back in the tub and hope the hot water will soothe some of my tension.

You kind of overreacted last night, don't you think?

"Shut up, Earl. I'm sick of you." What is wrong with me that I still listen to you?"

I didn't overreact.

I reach up and turn the hot water back on. No, what I did was . . .

Hurt Miles.

Hurt him? He'll find someone else before you can blink, big girl. It's not like he was telling you the truth. It's not like he's really attracted to you or falling in love with you. I mean, look at you.

I draw my knees to my chest and wrap my arms around myself. The last thing I want is to look at myself like this. Then I lean forward, turn off the water, and lift the plug from the drain. The number I saw on the scale this morning continues to taunt me.

Lord, is that it? I trust food more than I trust You? But . . . I don't understand what that means.

I stand. It will take more than warm water to soothe me. I reach for a bath sheet and wrap it around myself—a regular-sized towel wouldn't begin to cover me. I glance down at my body and know . . .

That's why I pushed Miles away.

Duh! The only man who'd want you is a desperate man.

As sick as I am of Earl, there is truth in that statement. I climb out of the tub.

Here I am feeling sorry for myself when Sabina has something real to grieve. What must she have felt when she'd heard her client took her own life? What is she still feeling? I can't imagine.

Lord, only You could have healed her client. Does she know that? Is she blaming herself? Though I can't imagine what she's feeling, it seems clear based on what she said that she's angry with herself and with God.

I trade the towel for my bathrobe, and then get ready to go.

Mercy cannot exist apart from suffering. Is that the sole
reason why agonies are an object of love? The feeling flows
from the stream of friendship.

SAINT AUGUSTINE

CHAPTER TWENTY-EIGHT

Sabina

I RECOGNIZE THE INSISTENT knock on the front door.
Great. I turn down the music and go to answer the door.

"Come on in." I swing the door wide.

"I wanted to give you some time. But I also wanted to check on
you."

"Ellyn, I don't need your pity." We stand in the tight entry, with
the door still open.

"Good, because I'm not doling out pity. So, are we just going to
stand here?"

"Do I have a choice?"

Ellyn smiles. "What do you think?"

I swing the door closed and follow her to the kitchen, where she
sets the teapot to boil.

"Make yourself at home," I say to her back as she turns on the
range.

"I hear the sarcasm in your voice."

"Good." I go to the cupboard and take out two mugs. "Listen, Ellyn, I appreciate your concern, but I don't want to talk about . . . about what I shared with you. I had no intent of ever discussing it, but you pressured me."

Ellyn leans against the counter next to the stove. "Sabina, if one of your clients went through something as traumatic as what you've experienced, would you let them get away with saying they don't want to talk about it and blaming you for pressuring them?"

"I can't own my client's responses or reactions."

"But you *can* own their choices?"

The tenderness in her voice is like an arrow through my heart. "I told you, I don't want to talk about this."

She reaches over and turns the range off just as the teapot begins to whistle.

"Just tell me this. Are you talking to someone? A counselor?"

"Yes. I did." I drop tea bags in the mugs and set them on the counter so she can fill them.

"You did?"

"Yes."

"And now?" She pours the boiling water into the cups.

"And now I'm here."

"Hiding."

"Ellyn, I don't expect you to understand. There's more to it than you can imagine. I'm healing. End of story." I take my mug and head to the living room.

"Why is it so dark in here?"

"Here, let me turn on the lamps." I see Ellyn look at the closed blinds and at the leather chairs I moved so they face into the living room rather than toward the picture window.

"Honey, you have one of the most beautiful views in the world . . ." She looks at me and cocks her head to one side, as though she's thinking. "You . . . avoid the view. That's why you always want to walk around the village rather than the headlands. Right?"

"I don't avoid it. I'm a city girl. I like the village."

"No, there's more to it than that."

"Ellyn, not everyone loves the ocean as much as you do. I'm not a big nature lover. If you want to see the view, we'll open the blinds." I set my mug down and walk to the window and pull on the cord that pulls the blinds open. Then I walk to the other wall and do the same. The early afternoon sunlight streams into the living room. "There, better?" I turn, face Ellyn, and then move and sit in one of the leather chairs in front of the window.

"Have a seat."

"Why won't you look out? Why won't you look at the ocean?"

"Girl, let it go. I mean it. Unless you're ready to talk about yourself, you might as well leave." I raise one hand. "I'm done."

She stands in the middle of the living room and stares at me for a moment, then she looks past me, at the *spectacular* view. I see the questions in her eyes, but she doesn't ask anything more.

She comes over, sets her mug next to mine, and then sits in the other leather chair. As she does, I see her demeanor change—her shoulders droop and I notice, for the first time today, the dark circles under her eyes.

"Ellyn, are you all right? Is it just the number on the scale?"

She takes a deep breath, "It's something else too. I might . . . you know . . . want to talk about it."

"But?"

"But . . . I don't . . . I don't want to . . . kiss and tell."

I raise one eyebrow. "Girl, if you kissed someone, you'd better tell."

"I didn't exactly. It was more him. He kissed me."

"Paco?"

"What? Paco? He's married."

I cross one leg over the other and lean back in the chair and smile. "Well, there are only two men in your life that I know of, and if it wasn't Paco, then it had to be the doctor, which makes this a fascinating conversation. So how do you feel?"

She looks from me to the floor. "Fat."

It's the first time I've heard her use that word, and condemnation rings loud and clear in her tone.

"So Miles kissed you and now you feel fat?" I'm gentle with the word.

"No, Counselor. I am fat and Miles kissed me."

"And when you weighed yourself this morning, you felt the scale confirmed your feelings?" My eyes narrow as they have a thousand times before as I've sat across from a client and tried to understand what they're feeling.

She nods. "I don't get it, Sabina. I mean, when a man kisses a woman it's because he's attracted to her."

"Yes."

"There has to be something wrong with him, right?"

"Why?"

"Because . . ." She looks down at her body. ". . . look at me."

I watch her face color and see the pain in her eyes. "Ah, because you're large, you think you're unattractive?"

"No, I'm large and, therefore, unattractive. What man is attracted to a woman who . . . who . . ." She looks at me, her question hanging between us.

"Ellyn, anyone who's in the same room with you and Miles knows he cares about you, enjoys you, and yes, is attracted to you. Beauty is more than a number on a scale. It comes from the soul. You're one of the most beautiful women I know, inside and out."

"Give me a break. He's just playing with me, Sabina. He's not attracted. He's probably just desperate."

I take that one in. "Wow, you don't give yourself much credit, do you? Or Miles, for that matter."

She crosses her arms over her chest. "It isn't just about . . . the weight. I set a clear boundary with him. I told him I didn't want anything more than friendship. And he crossed that boundary. I let him cross that boundary." She rubs her forehead as though our conversation is making her head ache. "I . . . I . . . didn't resist . . . at all. But afterward . . ."

She lifts her chin and looks me in the eyes. "Afterward, I told him to leave. I told him I don't want that type of relationship." She stands up and walks to the fireplace. "I'm done with him."

I watch her for a moment, then I nod. "That's your right—you don't have to see him again." I watch as her shoulders relax just a bit. "You made it clear that you only wanted friendship. You know, I've teased you about that. I'm sorry. It's your choice, Ellyn. It's your prerogative."

She nods.

"So you're comfortable with the black-and-white nature of the decision. You've let him know the friendship is over. How do you feel now?"

I see tears well in her eyes and then she looks away.

I consider my next question and instinct tells me it's the right one to ask. "Ellyn, who's Earl?"

She wipes away her tears. The vulnerability I witnessed is gone, replaced with a resolute set of her chin. The conversation, I'm certain, is finished.

"I . . . I don't want to talk about this. I thought I did, but I don't."

I start to encourage her to talk and then stop. How can I expect her to do what I refuse to do myself? The hypocrite appears again. I look down at the floor. Will I let the hypocrite rule or will I do the right thing? Will I sacrifice myself, my desires, for another?

"I better go. Paco's alone—"

"Ellyn, wait." I get up and walk over to where she's standing by the fireplace. "I understand not wanting to talk. I do. But . . ." I take a deep breath. "I'll make a deal with you."

She looks at me with a question in her eyes.

"I'll talk if you will."

Most high . . . deeply hidden yet intimately present, perfection
of both beauty and strength, stable and incomprehensible,
immutable and yet changing all things.

SAINT AUGUSTINE

CHAPTER TWENTY-NINE

Twila

"HOW WERE THINGS AT the store?"

I set my backpack down on a chair in the kitchen. "The usual. How was your morning?"

My mom is sitting at the kitchen table taking notes from a book on healing foods that she picked up at the conference.

"The usual." She smiles and winks. "I called Ellyn and thanked her for letting you stay at her place the other night."

"Nice." I walk into the kitchen, grab an apple, wash it, and then take it, a knife, and a small cutting board back to the table. I sit across from my mom and begin slicing the apple into paper-thin slices. "Want some?"

"No, thanks." She smiles. "I'm glad you're home. I've wanted to talk to you since my conversation with Ellyn."

"Why?" I nibble one of the apple slices.

"Because she said some kind things about you. She's an insightful lady. Also, as I've pondered some of what she said this morning, I've wanted to ask you something."

I set the knife and the rest of the apple on the cutting board so I can focus on my mom. "Okay, what?"

She sets her pen down and looks past me for a minute like she's thinking about what she wants to say. "I'm wondering if you see a specific purpose in your friendship with Ellyn?"

"Um . . ." I pick up the slice of apple again and take another tiny bite. My mom and I are tight, like friends, you know? So I know what she's getting at. "So you think there's a specific purpose and you're wondering if I've figured it out or not?"

"I didn't say that."

I smile at her. "Yeah, right." I take another bite and think while I chew. "The first time I met Ellyn at the store, I knew she was in pain—physically—but also emotionally. You know how sometimes I just know?"

She nods.

"It wasn't hard to figure out because she's the same as me, only opposite."

"What do you mean?"

"We're opposites. Like, we have similar issues but they look different. I'm . . ." I swallow. "I'm . . . sm . . . small." My mom nods her encouragement. "And Ellyn's large. But on the inside, I think we're more alike than different. But, I don't know why. I mean, I don't know what her emotional pain is about."

"You've come a long way, Twila. I'm so proud of you—of your courage and strength."

I don't feel courageous or strong. "I want to get better—like finally, I want that. You know?"

She nods and I see the tears she's trying to hold back.

"Anyway, I'm not sure if there's a specific reason Ellyn and I are becoming friends. But if there is, I think it has something to do with the body image stuff." I finish eating the slice of apple I've been working on and then pick up another slice. "So do you think there's more to it than that?"

She seems to think for a minute. "Maybe."

"Like maybe there is but you want me to figure it out on my own, or like maybe you don't know."

She laughs. "You're on to me. Really, it's just a hunch. But I'm not the only one who's noticed your courage, honey. Ellyn's noticed it too and commented on it more than once this morning." She leans forward. "Here's what I think I know—God's put you in Ellyn's life for a purpose. I think you're meant to lead Ellyn to health. I don't know if that's physical health, emotional health, or spiritual health." She laughs again. "And, it's *possible* I'm wrong."

"Yeah, right." I smile. "But wait, how could I lead Ellyn? I mean, I'm so much younger."

"Age has nothing to do with it. It's who you are, Twila—who God made you to be, the gifts He's given you."

"The same gifts He's given you?"

"Yes, but you use them in your own way." She leans across the table and takes my free hand in one of hers. "Sometimes God allows those He'll use for His purposes to suffer. You know what it is to suffer and you share, in your soul, the sufferings of others. It's what that tattoo on your face is all about, right?"

I nod.

"But more than that, you share in the sufferings of Christ. He wants you for Himself, Twila. He wants to enjoy you, lavish you with His love, and complete the good works He's begun in you."

I LEAVE THE HOUSE, hop on my bike, and turn toward the headlands. I ride down Lansing and turn on Hesser and stop at the cypress grove. I lock my bike to a picnic table and walk from there.

I go through the grove to the trail that runs along the cliff and out to the point, where I zip up my hoodie and sit on a mound of prairie grass and stare out at the waves tumbling against the rocks.

This is my place—where I come to think and pray. Only, I don't pray with words. I just sort of open myself up to God and let Him search me. I sit with legs crossed and hands in my pockets. The rhythm of the waves is like a mantra focusing my concentration on God. As all the other stuff in my mind drifts away, I'm aware of a growling emptiness—not in my stomach, but more in my soul. It's the void that begs me to leave it empty—to starve it to death.

Until I no longer exist.

It's that part of myself, that void, I'm learning to open to God.

A cold wind blows around me, but I'm like a caterpillar cocooned in the layers I'm wearing. As I stare at the bright blues of the sea and sky, at the sun lowering on the horizon, my eyes water. Soon, I can't tell the difference between the tears that come from the sun and the tears that come from the Son. My breath catches. They are like one in a way, filled with the mystique of God.

I pull my now-warm hands out of my pockets and rest them, palms up and open, on my knees. I close my eyes against the brightness, but tears still drip. I wait. I mean, I don't know what I'm waiting for, but because this is my ritual—my experience—I'll recognize it when it comes.

The mantra plays, reverberating through me now. I feel the pounding surf in each pounding beat of my heart. The beats reminding me that I am here, visible, exposed. But I am not here alone.

There is nothing to fear, there is nothing to fear, there is nothing to fear . . .

The growling void settles.

When the sun is hovering just above that horizontal line between sea and sky and the blue tones are washed with yellow, orange, red, lavender, and purple, I stretch out my legs and stand again. My back end is numb from sitting on cold, hard earth. I walk to the edge of the cliff, and stretch my arms high—palms still open.

I close my eyes. "Thank You, thank You, thank You . . ." I whisper it over and over.

When I head back through the grove to my bike, I understand my purpose with Ellyn—the purpose my mom asked about. It's not like I understand what to do or how to do it. It's more like a knowing, an assurance—that God is doing it.

Through me.

I just have to show up.

Before I get on my bike, I push the sleeve of my hoodie back and look at my wrist.

Imago Dei.

Then I hop on my bike and head to Ellyn's café.

While I pass from the discomfort of need to the tranquility of
satisfaction, the very transition contains for me the
insidious trap of uncontrolled desire.

SAINT AUGUSTINE

CHAPTER THIRTY

Ellyn

I LOOK UP FROM the steaming pot and see Twila
peeking into the kitchen. I wave her in. "Hi, there. What's up?" I
wipe my hands on my apron and meet her just past the swinging
doors into the kitchen.

"Hey, I thought I'd come by and say hi, but I know you're busy."

I give her a hug—she's wrapped in her usual layers. "Wow,
you're cold."

"I've been out on the headlands and then rode my bike here."

"Ah . . . did you watch the sun set?"

She nods.

"Good. Well, it's the busy time of the evening, but I'm always
happy to see you. Want to just hang out, or do you have other plans?"

"Hang out?"

"Sure. Pull up a stool and watch the action."

"Really? Nice."

I go to the back of the kitchen and take the tall stool we keep by the phone. I set it where it's out of the way, but where Twila can see what's going on and we can talk a bit. I look back at her. "Are you . . . hungry?"

Does it bother her that I ask?

She puts her hand over her tummy and nods. "Yeah."

Her smile warms my heart. "Well then, I'll make you a plate of something."

"Um, I don't have any . . . you know . . . money with me."

"Oh, no. You don't have to pay for it. You're practically an employee now—you help me develop the vegan dishes." I smile and wave her concern away. "Anyway, I love feeding my friends."

"Thanks. So, can I have the polenta dish again?"

I nod. "Sure. That's what I had for my dinner earlier. Give me a few minutes." I plate a few orders, making certain they're perfect down to the last garnish. Then I prepare an order of the polenta with the sauce of fresh herbed vegetables for Twila. The dish I came up with under duress the first night she came in for dinner with Nerissa and . . . Miles.

"Twila, go grab yourself a napkin and utensils while I plate this."

Once it's finished, I set it on the table in the back of the kitchen and Twila takes a seat.

"It smells so good. Thanks, Ellyn."

"Anytime. So, have you seen or talked to Miles?"

She puts the napkin on her lap and picks up her fork. "Not since the other night at your place. Why?"

"No reason."

"Have you seen him?" Her gray eyes stare up at me through her dark lashes.

"Me? Oh, no. I've had lots going on." I watch as she moves the food around on her plate and then takes a tiny bite. She looks up and smiles.

"It's so good."

"Well, enjoy it, Honey. I need to get back to work."

"Okay."

I watch as she takes another bite, if it can even be called a bite, it's more of a bit. But as I see her push herself to eat and push herself to let go of whatever fear or wound drove her to the extreme of anorexia, I'm reminded again of her strength.

I admire Twila.

Almost as much as I envy her.

I TURN THE JUICER off, look at the green sludge in the glass beneath the spout, and remind myself that it's good for me. Before drinking it, I open the fridge, take out a container of fresh blackberries, and wash four or five. I set them on a folded paper towel, and then, holding my breath, I down the juice. I reach for the berries and pop them in my mouth and chew them before letting myself breathe again.

The berries, or whatever fruit I choose, were Twila's solution to my resistance to the taste of my morning kale and carrot juice. Bless her. I'm drinking the juice for the nutrients now rather than as an end-all weight loss plan, as I'd attempted before.

I look at the scum left around the edges of the juice glass. "You've come a long way, baby." I never expected I'd come to enjoy the morning pond-sludge ritual—but, though I may not enjoy the taste, I'm sensing the benefits. I'm not sure what they are exactly, but I feel better about myself when I drink it.

For now, that's enough.

I wander out to the living room and sit on the sofa for a few minutes. The sun is just peeking over the mountains. I put my slipper-clad feet up on the coffee table and that's when I notice it—or rather, notice it missing—the piece of sea glass Miles gave me. That's what he picked up and put in his pocket the other night?

Friends.

A weight lodges itself in my chest and sits there like a five-pound bag of flour. I don't know if it's loss or anger, but I feel something.

Maybe Earl was right. Maybe Miles's offer of friendship was just a means to an end. But no. That makes no sense. There are plenty of beautiful women he could take to bed if that were his goal. He wouldn't choose me.

Like it matters anyway.

I get up and go back to the kitchen, where I consider my breakfast options and put Miles out of my mind. I settle on steel-cut oatmeal with the "granola" topping I created with Twila's help: flaxseeds, hemp seeds, sunflower seeds, slivered raw almonds, and an assortment of dried berries. Do I miss my morning croissant? Yes! But like the kale juice, I'm finding satisfaction in the oatmeal and other natural, vegan meals I've created.

Mid-morning, at the café, I'll make a protein shake with berries, a few banana slices, a plant-based protein powder, and flaxseed oil.

I haven't lost weight.

Yet.

But the pounds have to start dropping soon.

I mean, with the exception of my croissant binge the other night, I haven't eaten anything good in weeks. I've also noticed that my cravings are waning. Who'd have thought? I haven't wanted butter cookies or butter cake in, well, at least a couple of hours.

Though, now that they've come to mind, my taste buds beg me for them.

What I'm not noticing is an increase in my energy level.

I set the oats to boil and then sit down at the kitchen table for a few minutes until the oats need stirring.

I'm pooped.

Sure the café was busy last night—but that's nothing new. And okay, maybe I did lose some sleep over the way I treated Miles last week. I guess he had every right to take his gift back. But . . . I did what I had to do.

I see steam rising from the pot on the stove and get up to stir the oatmeal, but as I do, the room begins spinning around me. I reach for the kitchen chair I was sitting in and steady myself before I plop down in the chair again.

"Wow, what's *that* about?" I take a couple of deep breaths and then stand again, but slower this time. The spinning continues, but it's less pronounced and I'm able to make my way to the range and stir the oats to completion.

Maybe hunger got the best of me this morning? I spoon some extra oatmeal into my bowl, hoping it will fill me and alleviate the dizziness.

After I eat, I trudge upstairs to dress for the morning and church later. But by the time I reach the small landing, I'm winded, clammy, and dizzy again. When I make it to my bedroom, all I want to do is go back to bed. Instead, I make myself shower, dress, and then drag myself to the café.

It is, I fear, going to be a long day.

By the time I reach the café, I notice I have a message on my cell phone from Sabina. "Ellyn, I thought we were going to set a time to talk. Call me." I sigh. Yes, we need to talk—or, I suspect, Sabina needs to talk and God's using me to draw her out. Or, okay, maybe vice versa. But the thought of it is exhausting. I make a mental note to call her later.

Lord, help me. I need Your strength today.

If you weren't so fat you'd have more energy.

I put my hands up and cover my ears. And please, Lord, Shut. Earl. Up.

Nice try, Tubby.

I take my hands off my ears. It does no good trying to block the sound of a voice that comes from within. Instead, I turn on the radio in the kitchen and listen to the eclectic pop selections ranging several decades on KUNK FM—The Skunk—a Fort Bragg station I've grown to love. Listening to everyone from The Bee Gees' "Stayin Alive" to Lady Gaga's "Paparazzi" has me be-bopping in no time—well, okay, if not be-bopping, at least moving through the kitchen with more energy.

And it shuts Earl up. For the moment, anyway.

After a couple hours of work, I feel rejuvenated. I pick up the phone and call Sabina.

"Ellyn?"

"Hi there, how are you?"

"Good. Where've you been hiding?"

"In the kitchen—work. Hey, are you free tomorrow afternoon for a walk and talk?"

"Walk and talk?"

"Yes. I think I need the exercise and I think you need to talk."

She laughs. "I need the exercise too, but I thought you were the one who needed to talk."

"Nah, that was just a ruse to get you to talk. So how about it—1:00?"

"Sounds good. Monday at 1:00. Meeting at the usual spot?"

"Yep."

"See you then, girl."

I hang up. All I need is a little more exercise and I'll feel better.

You never abandon what you have begun.
Make perfect my imperfections.
SAINT AUGUSTINE

CHAPTER THIRTY-ONE

Miles

AFTER THE EARLY CHURCH service, I glance at my watch. 9:45. In the time it will take me to drive over to the village, the shops will be open. I hit Highway 1—I have an errand to take care of. When I reach Mendocino, I park near the Gallery Bookshop. Once inside, I go to the gift section, where I bought Ellyn's piece of sea glass. I look at the pieces of glass in a basket and turn them over looking for another one engraved with the word *Friend*. But after looking at each one, I don't find what I want.

I go to the counter. "Do you have any more of the sea glass in the back—the ones in the basket over there?"

"Let me check." The clerk gets up and sets the book she was reading on the counter next to the register. Then she makes her way to the back of the store. I wander through the aisles looking at book covers, but not really seeing them as I wait.

I'm still ashamed by my behavior—taking the glass I gave Ellyn and then throwing it into the water. *I'm sorry, Lord.*

I see the clerk coming back carrying what look like several pieces of the glass. I follow her back to the counter. "Here's the rest of what we had in the back." She spreads five more pieces of the glass out on the counter. But *Friend* isn't there. Then I read a word on another piece of glass. I pick it up and rub my thumb over the word. "This one is perfect."

I hand it to the clerk and she reads the word engraved on the glass. Then she smiles. "I take it this is a gift?"

I give her my best *I'm-in-the-doghouse* smile. "Yes."

"I'll wrap it for you."

I leave the store as I did last time, with a gift bag holding a piece of green sea glass the color of Ellyn's eyes. As I think of her eyes—and all she allowed me to see in them—I feel a stab at my heart. But . . .

This isn't about me.

I walk up the street just a block or so and turn left down an alleyway planted with ferns and blooms. I go around to the back of Ellyn's Café and knock on the back door. I hope someone will be here even though it's still early. Just as I'm ready to knock again, the door opens.

"Hola, Doctor."

"Morning, Rosa."

She eyes the gift bag I'm holding.

"I keep telling her you a good man." She points to the bag. "She not here yet. You come back later."

"No, Rosa. I'd like to leave it for her. Could you give it to her, please?"

"Ah, a surprise? I take care of it."

She reaches for the bag and takes it from me.

"Thank you, Rosa."

"I still on your side, you know."

"Good. I need you." I wave at her as I leave.

> You do not cease to rescue me.
>
> SAINT AUGUSTINE

CHAPTER THIRTY-TWO

Ellyn

AFTER PREPPING FOR THE Sunday evening crowd and the afternoon family Meal and Meet, calling Sabina, and making my protein shake, I leave the café for church. Sundays are my longest day. No wonder I was dragging this morning. It would exhaust anyone just thinking about it.

But now, my energy renewed, I look forward to the rest of the day. Sunday—church, the family gathering, and even the Sunday night crowd, usually comprised of locals—is my favorite day of the week.

Since the dizziness I experienced earlier has subsided, I consider walking to church, but then I think better of it. As much as I love Sundays, I better conserve my energy.

After the service, I decide to make a quick stop at home before going back to the café. I check my watch. I have plenty of time with all I accomplished this morning. I keep a change of clothes at the café for Sundays, but today I'll change at home and take the vitamins I forgot to take this morning.

By the time I arrive at the café, Rosa, Pia, and Paco's family are already there. The kitchen is abuzz with conversation as the others trickle in. Soon, we're all seated around the table, elbow to elbow, and heart to heart. Paco blesses the meal and then Rosa and I get up and serve the family.

I take my place at the head of the table, but before Rosa sits, she instructs us all to wait and then she disappears. She comes back a minute later holding a gift bag. She stands by me and picks up my knife and clanks it on my water glass—calling everyone to attention.

Then, with great ceremony, she hands the gift bag to me. "A gift for Ellyn from"—no one does a dramatic pause like Rosa—"de good doctor."

My heart leaps from my chest to my throat. "No!"

"Yes. He bring it himself earlier. You open it."

I look around the table—expectant faces, all. Okay, let's get this over with. I reach in the bag, pull out the tissue, and see the familiar box. I pull the box out and open it, expecting that he's replaced the piece of glass he took from me.

I open the box, pull the tissue paper aside, and pull out another piece of sea glass. Then I read the word engraved on the glass and feel my face color.

Sorry.

Rosa, who's peering over my shoulder, reads it out loud. "Sorry? What he sorry for? What he do? If he hurt you, he have to answer to me—to us. Right?"

The group at the table murmurs agreement.

"Bella?"

I look up and see the concern on Paco's face and on the faces of the others.

"Oh, no, it was nothing. Really." The color I felt rush to my face deepens. I'm certain I'm now the color of the rhubarb tart I'm serving for dessert. "Just a . . . misunderstanding."

That would have to suffice. Because there was no way in the world I was going to explain further.

I WAKE ON MONDAY morning to blue skies and blue water. A great day for late November. I climb out of bed, bracing for the usual ache in my feet and overall stiffness. But when I take my first steps, nothing . . . hurts.

Honey, that just doesn't happen.

Maybe Twila's on to something with this vegan thing. Is it possible this new way of eating will help alleviate some of my aches and pains? She talked about avoiding foods that cause inflammation in the body—especially sugar. Well, that's easy. What's the appeal of sugar unless it's paired with butter?

"Hot dog!" Or whatever it is a vegan would say to celebrate. "Carrot sticks!" I make my way to the kitchen and brew myself a cup of half-caf. Giving up half my morning caffeine is all I'm willing to sacrifice.

A girl has to have a few vices.

I stand at my kitchen window while I wait for the coffee and look out over the headlands. It's a perfect day for a walk, but then I remember Twila's suggestion that because I already spend so much time on my feet, I should consider riding a bike, a non-weight-bearing exercise. I'd written off her suggestion—I don't have a bike and didn't think I had time to ride one anyway. Plus, I'm walking with Sabina. Isn't that enough exercise?

But this morning, the thought of a bike appeals. I haven't ridden in years. Maybe, I could ride it to work. It is only a few blocks to the café. For that matter, it's only a few blocks to anywhere in Mendocino.

You'd look ridiculous on a bike. You'll make a fool of yourself.

I reach for an apple from the bowl of fruit on my counter, wash it, and then bite into it. As I chew, the crunching drowns out Earl's voice, which was my plan. In fact, I'll do more than that.

I climb the stairs to the guest bedroom, sit at the desk, and flip on my computer. Then I Google bike shops in Mendocino County— it seems like there's a shop at one of the local inns. Ah . . . The Stanford Inn, mecca for the ultra-healthy, of course that's where it is. I click on the link for *Catch A Canoe And Bicycles Too!* In addition to rentals, their site says they sell bikes.

In your face, Earl!

After breakfast, I head over to The Stanford Inn and find the bike shop at the bottom of the hill, along the bank of Big River. I walk down the stairs leading into the shop and then stare at an array of bikes.

"Hey, I'm Adam, what can I do you for?" Adam, a throwback to another era, puts out his hand.

I shake his hand. "Hi, um, I want a bike." I look around at the different styles.

"Okay. What kind of riding do you do?"

"What kind? Oh, well, just riding around, you know."

"Riding around town? Riding around on trails? Riding around on roads?"

Really? "Around town, I guess. Maybe out on the headlands—on the road."

Adam smiles. "So you're not a mountain biker or road racer?"

"Right." I work hard to keep the sarcasm out of my voice. Do I look like a mountain biker or road racer?

"So how about a comfort bike—nice seat, keeps your posture upright, a few gears to make things easy? Something like this?" He pulls a shiny white bike off the rack.

"Perfect. I'll take it."

"Whoa . . . Try it out. Take it for a spin. See how it fits and if you like it." Adam leans the bike against a wall and then walks behind the counter and pulls a helmet off a shelf. "Here, put this on and take 'er for a ride."

Adam is out the door with the bike before I can say no. So I follow him while attempting to stuff my mass of curls into the helmet. When I go to click the strap closed around my chin, it comes up short, so I leave it dangling.

By the time Adam has carried the bike back up the stairs to the parking lot, and I've climbed the stairs behind him, I'm already winded, but I do my best to hide it as Adam gives me the "lowdown" on the bike. He points up the hill I drove down to reach the shop.

"So you can either ride it up the hill or walk it, whatever suits you, then turn right onto the road with the white house at the end. That's Inn property too, and it's a nice flat road where you can get a feel for the bike. Okey dokey?"

I nod. "Great."

"Okay, hop on. Get 'er done."

I take the handlebars of the bike from Adam's hands and swing my leg over the bike. Well, *swing* is a relative term. Then I look at Adam. "I've got it from here." I'm hoping he'll leave me alone rather than watch.

But no, he just takes a step back and points at the hill. "It's hard to start on a hill. Sure ya don't want to walk 'er up?"

Now that I'm on the bike, I shake my head. "No problem." I put my foot on the pedal, push down, and attempt to balance. I make a few false starts before I get going. I weave back and forth, fearing I'll fall, and push the peddles with all I've got. But, Adam was right, starting on a hill proves challenging. The steep incline takes everything I've got. By the time I'm steady on the bike, I'm already perspiring and breathing hard. I shift the gears, like Adam showed me, hoping to the make the climb easier.

The gears clunk and I lose my balance. I put my feet down and catch myself, and the bike. I stand there for a few seconds and assess the situation: it's me against Mount Everest. I get off the bike. I don't look back to see if Adam is still watching. Instead, I tell myself he's gone back down to the shop. I begin the arduous task of pushing the bike up the hill.

On my ascent to the top, my heart begins flip-flopping like a fish out of water and I'm gasping for each breath. I stop and start. Stop and start. Stop and start. When I reach the top, at least a full hundred yards from where I began at the bottom, I'm certain I'll die. But it seems I value my pride more than my life, because when a gardener doing work at the top looks at me with concern, I get back on the bike and ride it on the flat road Adam suggested. As I pedal an ache settles in my right leg. Did I pull a muscle? I ride to the end of the road—another hundred or so yards—and ride back. I see nothing except black spots bouncing in front of my eyes. *Oh, God, please don't let me faint—please don't let me faint.*

I ride past the gardener again and then turn and coast down the hill, where I see Adam waiting for me. Great. I stop in front of him, get off the bike, and turn my back to him so he won't see how hard I'm breathing. I take the helmet off and feel damp curls stuck to my face and neck. I'm sure my face is cherry red.

"Whaddaya think?"

"Nice," I gasp. "Good," I say over my shoulder.

"I'll take 'er back inside."

Oh, thank You, God, he's not going to stand here and talk. I consider getting in my car right now and leaving, but then remember that my purse and car keys are down in the shop. So instead, I wipe my wet brow, and try to catch my breath before following Adam down the stairs. As I make my way down, I grip the railing, fearing I may still faint. I'm drenched, dizzy, and nauseous.

I'm having a heart attack.

I know I am.

A dull pain settles in my chest. I feel it all the way through my back. And my world is spinning, spinning, spinning.

I need to get out of here.

Now.

I mumble something to Adam. Grab my purse. And then . . . *Oh Lord* . . . I climb back up the stairs to the parking lot.

Glib satisfaction must shut Earl up because I hear nothing but the pommeling of my heart.

When I reach my car, I bend at the waist, hands on my knees, sure I'll be sick. After several minutes, the wave of nausea passes and the dizziness wanes some. I dig in my purse, find my cell phone, and dial the café, where I know Rosa will be sitting in the office.

"Ellyn's."

"It's . . . me."

Rosa is quiet for a moment. "Ellyn? What wrong wid you?"

"I . . . I don't . . . feel well. Can you . . . come get . . . me?"

"Where? Where you at?"

"I'm . . . fine. Just come to . . . The Stanford . . . Inn." I tell her where I'll be waiting for her.

"You don't sound fine. Where's your car? You can't drive?"

"No. Just . . . come. Now."

I hang up, get in my car, and wait. I don't want to go to the hospital. I don't. But if I am having a heart attack, then . . . I lean my head back on the headrest and close my eyes.

I'll let Rosa figure it out.

I don't know if I black out or fall asleep, but within what seems like seconds, I hear a tapping on the window of my car and then a rush of cool air washes over me as someone opens the door.

"Ellyn?"

I feel a hand on my shoulder. I turn my head without lifting it from the headrest and open my eyes. Before I can say anything, he's holding my hand with one of his and has two fingers on my wrist. Then he moves the fingers to my neck, which I know is slick with sweat.

"No . . . no. Don't."

"Shh . . ."

"I'm . . . don't. I'm . . . fine." I lift my head and wipe the damp curls off my forehead. "Where's . . . Rosa?"

"She called me." Miles fumbles in his back pocket and pulls out his cell phone.

"She . . . she . . ." I try to get out of the car.

But he holds me back while he punches keys on his phone with one hand.

"I'll . . . shoot her." Then I hear what he's saying. "No . . . oh, please. No."

Miles has called for an ambulance.

So much for my pride.

Pride? You're nothing but a fat slob. I always knew you'd die of a heart attack.

Yeah? Well, you know what, Earl? If I do, at least I won't have to listen to you anymore.

For wherever the human soul turns itself, other than to you,
it is fixed in sorrows.

SAINT AUGUSTINE

CHAPTER THIRTY-THREE

Miles

WHILE I WAIT FOR the ambulance, I try to get Ellyn's pulse again, but it's still weak and her breathing is shallow. Her symptoms are indicative of several issues, one or two of them serious, which is why I called for an ambulance rather than risk moving her myself.

"Shh . . . You're not fine, but you will be." I try to quiet her again. I also attempt to stay in a professional mode of operation rather than personal.

She *will* be fine.

She has to be.

Although . . .

What if Ellyn's rejection of me was actually God's way of protecting me? Protecting my heart? The thought evokes fear rather than relief. But I push all that aside for now. "C'mon. Where's the ambulance?"

"What?" Her voice sounds as weak as her heartbeat.

I reach down for Ellyn's hand and clasp it in my own, giving it a gentle squeeze. "Just watching for the ambulance." I hear the siren up above on Highway 1. "They're on their way. You'll feel better soon, gal. You will." I squeeze her hand again.

When the ambulance arrives, I step back and let the EMTs do their job. I follow them to the hospital, park in the doctors' lot, and meet Ellyn in the hallway of the ER. I'm not there as a doctor though—just as a friend. I can't treat her.

"I'm here if you need me. Do you want me to come with you when they take you back?"

She looks up at me—more alert now. I read the fear in her eyes, but then she looks away.

"I'm . . . fine. I've taken enough of your time already."

I nod. This isn't about me right now. "Would you like me to call someone to come? Rosa or Sabina?"

"No. Oh, but I'm supposed to meet Sabina at 1:00. Can you . . . just tell her I can't meet today?"

"You bet."

I stand back as a nurse comes and wheels Ellyn's gurney back to one of the curtained cubicles.

"I'll have them keep me posted. And I'll call Sabina."

She lifts her hand and waves her thanks.

AFTER I CALL MY office and fill Courtney in on what's going on, I have Dee pull Sabina's file and give me her phone number—this time it's an appropriate use of the information we have on file.

Once I've talked with Sabina, I take a seat in the ER waiting room. I am more comfortable treating patients than waiting for them. I don't sit still long. I get up, wander the ground floor of the small hospital, stand in front of a vending machine for several minutes, and then go back to my seat. As I do, I see Sabina walk into the waiting room from the parking lot.

I wave at her and she comes my way.

"Hello, Dr. Becker."

"Please, it's Miles." I motion to the seat next to mine. "You didn't need to come."

"I wanted to. Any more news?"

"Not yet. It may take awhile."

She nods. "Well, if you don't mind, I'll wait with you."

We sit in silence for a few minutes. "Would you like a magazine?" I point to a rack on the wall.

"No, thank you." She shifts in her seat. "Were you with Ellyn when this happened?"

"No. She was alone. She called Rosa to pick her up. Rosa called me."

Sabina smiles. "Good for Rosa. Although, Ellyn will certainly have a few words for her when all is said and done, won't she?"

I smile. "I imagine so."

"Just for the record, Ellyn is the only one who doesn't realize how good you are for her."

"Well, thank you." I get up. I don't want to talk about my relationship with Ellyn. "I'm going to see if there's anything new to report." I go to the reception desk and ask for a report. Though I'm not treating Ellyn, and rarely spend time in the hospital, the receptionists know I'm a local doctor.

"Just a moment, Dr. Becker, let me go check." She tells the other receptionist that she'll be right back.

A few minutes later, she comes back to the desk with the latest information. "Her blood pressure is low and there's an abnormality on her EKG. They've ordered an ultrasound. Dr. Nguyen will come out and talk to you when he has a minute."

"Thank you."

I go back and tell Sabina the little I know, but not what I suspect. I sit back down beside her and run my hand through my hair.

"You're . . ." She clears her throat. "You're sure she'll be . . . okay?"

I nod. "Yes." Though I speak with more confidence than I feel.

"May I ask you a question? It's personal."

I nod, but hope it isn't about Ellyn. "Sure."

"Ellyn shared that you lost your wife a couple of years ago." She looks around and then looks back at me. "I'm sorry."

"Thank you."

"I'm wondering how . . . you handled that . . . as a doctor, a healer?"

"That's an insightful question. Are you in medicine?"

"Not exactly. I have my PhD in psychology and have . . . or had . . . a clinical practice for many years."

"I see. To answer your question, it was frustrating. As you can imagine, working as a healer yourself. I felt like I had no control. Like I was impotent, as a doctor. And . . ." I shrug. "I was angry."

"Did you deal with depression?"

"Not clinically. My faith helped." She looks away and I notice her body tense. "Did something I say offend you?"

She looks back at me. "No. I just don't put much weight in *faith*, as you call it."

I let her comment pass for now. "Have you lost someone recently?"

She raises her eyebrows. "Ah, turnabout is fair play?"

I smile and nod.

"Yes, I lost a client."

"I'm sorry."

She shifts in her seat again. "She committed suicide."

Her tone is curt, as though she's daring me to accuse her.

"So you understand then . . . some of what I may have felt?" I see I've caught her off guard. She doesn't respond for a moment.

"Well . . . as much as I cared about . . ." She twists her wedding ring around her finger. "I recognize it isn't as difficult as . . . losing a . . . spouse. Though, I admit, I haven't thought of that until now. I am . . . sorry for your loss."

"Death is a painful experience whenever we lose someone—especially if it's someone we care about or someone we cared for professionally. Death wasn't part of God's plan. It's jarring—painful."

"What do you mean it wasn't part of God's plan?"

"Death came with sin."

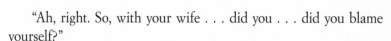

"Ah, right. So, with your wife . . . did you . . . did you blame yourself?"

I think about her question. "No, but doing so was tempting."

"Tempting?"

"It wasn't about me. To blame myself would mean that I consider myself on the same plane as God. That I see myself as omnipotent." I stretch my legs out. "But I don't believe that. And as a doctor, I can't believe that. God is the only One who holds life and death in His grasp." I see tears come to her eyes before she looks away again.

"I see."

She still isn't looking at me. I put my hand on her forearm. "Do you, Doctor?"

She turns back to me and lets her tears fall. "I'm beginning to." She rests her hand on top of mine. "Thank you, Doctor." She pulls her hand back. "Now, let's hope, for both our sakes, that Ellyn is just fine."

All that is ebbing away from you will be given fresh form
and renewed, bound tightly to you.

SAINT AUGUSTINE

CHAPTER THIRTY-FOUR

Ellyn

I AM AWAKE AND feeling better now, my heart is no longer flopping, nor do I feel like I'm strapped to a merry-go-round instead of a gurney. The only thing pressing on my chest is the strong desire to throttle Rosa.

I can't believe she called Miles. I can't believe Miles is standing next to me. I can't believe he saw me like . . . this: hair matted, sweating, and sick.

And I can't believe how grateful I am that he's here.

The double doors of the inner sanctum open and a nurse, dressed in raspberry-colored scrubs, emerges. She wheels me through the doors and into a curtained cubicle she refers to as Room #5. I wave to Miles as I go.

Norton's brother is in Room #6. I know this because an older man on the other side of the curtain is wailing, "I want to see Norton. Norton? Where's my brother, Norton? I just want to see my brother."

The raspberry nurse nods toward the curtain. "I'm sorry. He's altered."

Altered, as in neutered? Altered, as in transgendered? Altered, as in chemically? This is Mendocino County. It could be any of the above.

"Where's my brother? I just want to see Norton."

How about altered, as in psychologically? I'm going to believe the best about Norton's brother and choose the psychologically altered option. After all, I'm feeling a bit altered myself this morning.

Raspberry spreads a warmed blanket over me, and I experience my first moment of comfort since getting on that stupid bike. She takes my blood pressure and my temperature and records the results on my chart. "Do you know your weight?"

Do I know my weight? What woman doesn't know how much she weighs? Anyway, I weighed myself when I got out of bed this morning. "I'm not sure."

"Okay, we'll get it later."

She jots something more on my chart and then begins wiring me for sound. She places sticky *electrodes*, as she calls them, to my ankles, arms, chest, and who knows where else. I lose track. Then she hooks wires to the electrodes and tells me to hold still. All wired up, I imagine I look like Frankenstein. Our body types aren't too dissimilar.

"Norton?"

"Mr. Romano, Norton's not here," Raspberry says through the curtain.

"Where is Norton? I just want to see my brother. Norton?"

I begin praying for Norton's brother, Mr. Romano. *Oh Lord, may he experience Your peace. Comfort him, Lord. Heal him, as only You can.* He quiets for a few moments, and then begins wailing again.

The nurse smiles. "Just another day in the ER."

I hold still for the minute or so required for her to complete the EKG.

"All done."

She starts ripping sticky electrodes off my skin. Ouch! How much of my skin is going with those patches? Enough to make a difference when she weighs me, I hope.

After the EKG, I'm left alone in the curtained cubicle and the tears well. When Miles asked if he could call anyone for me, I thought of my mom. Odd. She'd still be in her silk robe, sipping coffee at this hour. But what could she do? It's a three-and-a-half-hour drive from San Francisco to Fort Bragg. Anyway, I know what she would do. I'd get the "I told you so . . ." speech.

No, the hospital can notify her if I croak.

An attendant comes to take Mr. Romano to his room.

For almost sixty seconds the ER is quiet, until I hear Raspberry in the hallway. "I'll take full responsibility for the mental-health patient. Just put him in #6. Now!"

Busy day at the ER. Tension levels seem high.

Wait, they're putting the mental-health patient in Mr. Romano's room? Next to me? Now I wish I'd had Miles stay.

Did he leave? Or did he say he'd wait? I can't remember. I shift on the gurney and the dull ache I felt in my chest earlier returns and settles between my shoulder blades and the merry-go-round takes off again. I close my eyes, but that makes the spinning pick up speed. I open my eyes and take a deep breath—at least as deep as my aching chest will allow.

Another nurse pokes her head through the curtains. "Have they done an ultrasound or chest X-ray yet?"

"An ultrasound or X-ray? No." The words come out in a hoarse whisper. I put my hand on my chest.

"Are you okay?"

"I . . . I don't think so."

The nurse comes into my cubicle. "I'm Nita, what are your symptoms?" She glances at the computerized screen that registers my blood pressure and blood oxygen levels.

"Pain between my shoulder blades. Chest heavy. And I'm so dizzy."

"When did the dizziness start? That's new."

"It's not new."

Nita moves behind my bed and rustles around a bit, and then she comes back and puts tubing into my nostrils to administer oxygen and puts a clip thingy on my index finger that registers . . . something to do with oxygen levels.

Nita looks toward the curtain. "Mel, I need you in here."

It sounds as though Mel is getting the mental-health patient settled, but in a few moments she comes around and sticks her head through the opening in the curtain from the hallway. "What's up?"

"She needs that ultrasound now."

Melanie, aka Raspberry, disappears again.

My chest tightens and each breath I take becomes a chore.

Lord, is this really happening?

A snicker from Room #6 breaks into my thoughts. Then a low rumble of laughter that rises in pitch to the point of hysteria sends a shiver through me.

My new neighbor.

The mental-health patient.

"Really? That's awesome!" His laughter is interrupted only by his own comments.

"Hey, Diego, keep it down in there." Melanie's voice, from the hallway.

Nita is decorating me with electrodes again, but my skin, dampened again with sweat, isn't cooperating.

A wave of nausea comes over me and I roll my head to the side. The sudden movement causes the gurney and curtained cubicle to move round and round and round. Spinning faster and faster. I grab the side rails and hold on. All the while Diego laughs, hyena-like.

Black spots begin dotting the curtains and then my vision blurs. I try to sit up—to stop the spinning. Please, let me get up.

"Mel!"

Nita's voice seems distant. Did she leave? I look around, careful this time. No she's still here, putting electrodes on my ankles.

The hyena cackles.

Then just as everything begins to go black again, Diego stops laughing.

"What? Dude, really? The secret of life has changed? What's the new secret?"

Who's voice is he listening to? Who does he hear in his head? Is it Earl?

A dark curtain closes around me.

"That's the new secret? Dude, that is so cool!"

Maybe he's listening to God.

The curtain suffocates.

I can't see. Can't breathe. Can't feel.

Diego ushers me into a place of silence. But I try to speak, "Wait . . ."

"Don't try to talk." A voice from afar instructs. "Just relax."

"But—" As the laughter fades, I try again. "Wait—" I . . . I need to . . . know.

What's the . . . new . . . secret?

What . . . is it?

I have to . . . know.

The laughter stops.

And finally.

Finally.

As all goes black . . .

I'm at peace.

My groaning is witness that I am displeased with myself.

SAINT AUGUSTINE

CHAPTER THIRTY-FIVE

Sabina

I PONDER MILES'S WORDS about putting himself on the same plane as God. Is that what I've done with Ashley's death? By allowing the burden of her choice to rest on my shoulders, have I put myself in God's place?

No.

I put myself in God's place long before Ashley's death . . .

It was after Jazzy died.

I stand up—a sudden flourish of movement. I look down at Miles. "I'm sorry. I don't wait well. I'm going to walk around. May I bring you something? Coffee or a soda?"

"No, thank you."

"May I give you my cell phone number, that way if you hear something you could let me know?"

"Sure."

We exchange numbers, and then I turn and walk back toward the doors that lead to the parking lot—the ones I came in not long ago. I need the slap of the cold wind against my face, but as I exit the building I see the sun is still shining.

How dare it.

I walk through the parking lot to the street and then through the neighborhood surrounding the hospital. *If You let anything happen to Ellyn, I swear . . .* I leave my threat dangling. What good would it do? *You do what You want, regardless of my prayers.*

A lump of emotion lodges in my throat. I wish I'd brought my iPod with me so I could listen to music as I walk. I need a distraction.

I do not want to consider God.

Nor do I want to think about Ashley.

I slow my pace.

And Jazzy. A tear slips down my cheek. Oh, Jazzy.

No. I can't—I won't let those memories control me. I turn back toward the hospital, but then I stop. A scream rises in my chest. I want to shake my fist at God and demand answers. Jazzy, Ashley, and now possibly Ellyn?

Why?

Ellyn. The first friend I've allowed myself in years. And now she's lying in a hospital.

Hot tears fall. I reach in my purse for a tissue and wipe my eyes and nose. As I do, a car passes by. How must I look walking down the street, crying? I look like the fool I am. A fool who's demanding answers from a God she no longer believes in.

Antwone, Ellyn, and Miles can have their God.

But something nags. Antwone, Ellyn, and Miles are intelligent people—people I respect. And my mama believed in God more than in the air she breathed. She was a woman to reckon with. If she'd ever heard me denounce my belief in God, she'd . . . well, she'd have walloped me. Such a choice from me would have wounded her in the deepest part of her soul.

So how do I reconcile my respect for others who believe? Maybe they just don't get it. But my mama? Oh, she got it. And Miles? He seemed to understand. Why is it they've moved on with their lives and I'm stuck?

The answer seems obvious.

And that makes me even more angry.

> Miracles are not contrary to nature, but only contrary
> to what we know about nature.
>
> SAINT AUGUSTINE

CHAPTER THIRTY-SIX

Miles

AFTER SABINA COMES BACK, we sit in silence.

I check in with the receptionist again, but learn nothing new. I pace the waiting room and the parking lot, and then sit again. After almost three hours, Dr. Nguyen comes looking for me. When I see him coming, I stand and meet him across the waiting room. I want a medical report without Sabina next to me.

I shake Dr. Nguyen's hand. "So?"

"Her potassium level is low—2.7."

I nod. "That accounts for some of her symptoms."

"Yes, and the flattened T waves on the second EKG concur with the low potassium. But take a look at this. This is the first EKG."

He hands me a piece of paper from the file he holds. It reads like a seismic encounter with its peaks and valleys. I look at the waves and now understand his hesitation. "Pulmonary embolism? That's consistent with her symptoms."

"Exactly. But the ultrasound was negative. As was the chest X-ray. Her blood oxygen level has returned to 9.8, and the dizziness and chest pains have subsided, as has the ache in her leg."

"Huh, interesting. Maybe the first was a false reading?"

"Maybe."

"But her symptoms . . ." I stop.

"One of those medical mysteries, I guess." Dr. Nguyen takes the EKG results back. "I won't keep her. We gave her some potassium and she's feeling better. I told her not to take the HCTZ she's been taking for her blood pressure and to call Dr. Norman tomorrow to schedule a follow-up appointment."

I nod and listen as he looks at her charts and repeats her current stats. "She says she lives alone. I'd like someone with her for the rest of today and tonight, just in case."

"Good. Thank you." I put out my hand to shake his again and then he turns to go, but stops.

"Oh, Dr. Becker, she'd like to see you. Go on back."

She'd like to see me? His words or hers? Oh, I hope they were hers.

"Thanks."

"Hi." The curtain is open and Ellyn is sitting up. "I hear you're feeling better?"

She nods. "What . . . happened? Dr. Nguyen explained it, but I don't understand."

"He doesn't really understand either." Her color has returned. That's good.

"What do you mean?"

I motion to a chair. "May I?"

"Oh. Sure."

I scoot the chair to the side of the gurney and sit, stretch my legs out, and run my hand through my hair. "Well, the symptoms you were experiencing when I met you at the bike shop were indicative of a couple of things, but one of them is what's called a pulmonary embolism—a blood clot that's dislodged and moved to the lungs.

The first EKG reading substantiated that diagnosis, which is why the ultrasound and chest X-ray were ordered."

"I have a blood clot?"

I lean forward to reach for her hand, but stop myself. "No. Nothing showed up on the tests." I see her chest rise and fall. "Your labs showed a low potassium level, but nothing else. The second EKG reading concurred with the low level of potassium."

"Did he read the first EKG wrong?"

"No, I saw it myself."

"So it just was wrong?"

"We don't know if it was wrong. It was consistent with your symptoms—"

"Miles! Just tell me what happened." She takes a deep breath and exhales. "I'm sorry. I'm just . . . I'm tired."

"I know, gal. I'm not sure what happened. But the end result is this: Your potassium level was low, most likely from the HCTZ you take for your blood pressure. It's a diuretic, and low potassium can be one of the side effects. Some of your symptoms were consistent with a low level of potassium." I lift my hands, palms up. "The rest, we're not sure. Dr. Nguyen called it a medical mystery."

She hesitates. "What . . . do you call it?"

"God's intervention."

She tilts her head to one side and I see the doubt on her face.

"Not only did Rosa call me to pick you up, but when I let her know you were here, she let others know and asked for their prayers—Pia, Paco, your pastor. I called and asked Nerissa to pray and to ask Twila to do the same. And Sabina, though I don't know that she's praying, is sitting vigil in the waiting room."

"She's here?"

I nod. "In fact, I should go and let her come back and see you—if you're up to it?" I stand.

"Sure. But Miles, wait . . ." Her voice softens. "I . . . I want to apologize for . . . you know, what happened the other night. I over-reacted. I'm . . . so sorry for the way I treated you. I didn't mean to . . . I don't want to hurt you. I'm just not cut out for *that* type of relationship."

The façade I've worked to keep in place cracks. I clear my throat. "Ellyn, I overstepped a boundary you set. You were clear with me from the beginning. I'm the one who needs to apologize. I'm sorry."

"It wasn't just you." She takes a deep breath. "I overstepped my own boundary."

"Ellyn . . ." I hesitate, but I'm not sure I want the answer to the question I'm about to pose. "Is it . . . just me? You're not drawn to me?"

She opens her mouth to respond, but nothing comes out. I watch as tears fill her eyes and then she looks away. When she looks back, the tears are gone. "No, it isn't just you. If I were ever . . . I mean, Miles, you're a great guy, a wonderful man, I'm sure. It's me. It's my issue."

I nod. "Okay. I can't say that I understand, but I respect you and I won't cross that boundary again, I promise." Do I say more to her? Or leave it as is? *Lord?*

"Thank you. And thank you for all you did today—for being here."

I turn to go but when I reach the edge of the curtained cubicle, I turn back. "I'm available for you, Ellyn, as a friend. If there's ever anything you need, you know how to reach me."

Then I leave to find Sabina.

After I talk to Sabina, and she tells me she'll drive Ellyn home and stay the night with her, I leave the hospital. The late afternoon sun is low in the sky and there's a chill to the air, but instead of going home, I turn left onto Highway 1 and head for the Little River Inn Golf Course—the only course on the Mendocino Coast. I keep my clubs in the trunk of my car for days like these.

I want to hit a bucket of balls—to hear the smack of the club against the ball—to release some of the day's tension.

As I make the fifteen- or twenty-minute drive down the highway, I consider Ellyn's condition when I found her this morning compared to how I left her this afternoon. As I do, I also consider the feelings I suppressed all day.

I can't afford to let fear intrude when I'm treating a patient—especially in an emergency. But when I found Ellyn in her car this morning, I was just a man looking at the woman I care about, and—I exhale—she gave me a scare.

Like with Sarah, I knew too much.

But today didn't end the way it ended with Sarah.

Sure the circumstances were different, but the symptoms Ellyn exhibited this morning were, or could have been, life-threatening.

And then, all of a sudden, they weren't.

Thank You, Lord, for healing Ellyn. As I pray, a question darts through my mind . . .

Why Ellyn and not Sarah?

I don't pose the question to God though. *Father, I take this thought captive to the obedience of Jesus Christ. Though I don't understand Your ways, I choose to trust You. I won't dwell on doubt, instead, I'll walk in faith—I'll walk in the unknown.*

The unknown?

Not a comfortable place. I felt the uncertainty of the unknown this morning in that moment when I found Ellyn sitting lifeless in her car. It intruded again during the hours of waiting at the hospital. And again as Ellyn reiterated her stance on not becoming involved "in that type of relationship."

But today, through it all, I discovered a few things:

I am in love with Ellyn DeMoss.

Loving her will hurt me.

And God's calling me to sacrifice. To love her in the way He loves. Though I'm not sure what that means on a day-to-day basis.

I trust He'll show me.

WHEN I REACH THE golf course, I park, pull my driver out of my golf bag, and buy a bucket of balls. I tee up on the driving range and take a few practice swings before aiming at the ball.

I roll my shoulders back and feel the tension in my neck.

Then I step up to the tee, pull the driver back over my shoulder, and swing. Hard. The head of the driver connects with the ball and sends it sailing. I bend, grab another ball out of the bucket, and repeat the action.

I do it again.

And again.

And again.

Until, with the final smack of club against ball, I've exhausted all emotion.

May I know you, who know me. May I "know as I also
am known" (1 Cor. 13:12). Power of my soul, enter into it
and fit it for yourself . . .

SAINT AUGUSTINE

CHAPTER THIRTY-SEVEN

Twila

I KNOW ON THE door, knowing Ellyn is home. I called
before I came. I set the bag I brought on the porch and shove my
hands into my pockets to keep them warm while I wait for her to
answer.

But it's Ellyn's friend, Sabina, who opens the door.

"Um, hi. I'm here to see Ellyn."

"She didn't tell me you were coming."

Sabina stares at me and doesn't open the door any wider. "I
called and talked to her a little while ago—she's expecting me." I
smile, hoping she'll warm to me, but she doesn't.

"Wait here."

She starts to close the front door and leave me on the porch.
"Hey, I'll wait inside. It's cold out here."

"Suit yourself. I'll tell her you're here."

"Thanks." I pick up the bag, and step inside. I wait in the small foyer with my back against the front door. I don't have to wait long.

"Hi, honey, you're so sweet to check on me." Ellyn comes around the corner from the kitchen and through the dining and living room. She gives me one of her big hugs, which I'm kind of starting to like. Her hair is damp, and she's wearing a fluffy green bathrobe.

"Hi. Hey, you look good—not like you were in the hospital all day."

"Yeah? Well, go figure. To tell you the truth, I feel good too. Much better than I did this morning. I just showered and came downstairs for a cup of tea. Would you like one?"

"Um, I don't know. I don't want to, like, intrude. I mean, Sabina's here so I can just leave this . . ." I lift up the bag I'm holding. ". . . and then go."

"Go? No. You're not intruding. I love that you came by."

She puts an arm around me and guides me out to the kitchen. "Sabina won't mind. She's just babysitting me because the doctor didn't want me alone tonight." We round the corner into the kitchen. "Right, Sabina? Twila isn't intruding. I asked her to have a cup of tea with us."

Sabina says nothing, instead she just reaches for another mug. Yeah. She thinks I'm intruding. She glances over her shoulder at me. "Herbal or regular?"

"Herbal, please."

"So what's in the bag, girly?"

"I made you some soup. Curried butternut squash. It's vegan."

"Sounds great. Thank you."

"Well, you know, it's not like what you'd make. But I didn't know if you'd feel like cooking. There's enough for you too, Sabina. There's also a salad with vegetables and greens."

"You are so thoughtful. Look, Sabina, saved by Twila. You don't have to cook."

Sabina turns from the counter, where she's making our tea, and faces us. "Lucky for you," she says to Ellyn. She hesitates then looks at me. "Thank you, Twila. It was nice of you to think of Ellyn." Her smile is tight.

Maybe it's the tattoo on my face that's off-putting to her. It makes some people think I'm weird or something.

"No problem. My mom helped. We were praying for you today, Ellyn. I'm so glad you're, you know, okay. When Miles called and talked to my mom, it sounded kind of serious."

"Yeah, I guess it was."

We sit with our tea at Ellyn's kitchen table. "Sabina, stop wiping off my counters, they're clean. Come join us."

While Ellyn tells me about what happened to her this morning, Sabina rinses the sponge, washes her hands, dries them, and then puts some sugar in her tea, and uses the bathroom . . .

All before she joins us.

After Ellyn tells us about the mental-health patient next to her in the ER, she stops and reaches for my hand. She pushes up the sleeve of my sweatshirt. "Huh."

I watch her and see an emotion I don't recognize. "What?"

"I'm not sure." She turns her head to one side, but keeps her eyes on my tattoo.

"What does it say?" Sabina leans forward.

"*Imago Dei.*"

"Why did you choose that—what significance does it have?"

I feel my face color. Her question—or her tone, I guess—is curt. "Um, it means image of God."

"I know what it means."

Ellyn lets go of my wrist and looks first at me, and then at Sabina. She's noticed Sabina's tone.

"It's a reminder to me that I'm created in the image of God. It helps me remember that I have value as a person. And that I have purpose."

Sabina squints her eyes. "What's your purpose?"

"To be in relationship with God. That's why He created us. That's each person's purpose." I don't mind explaining, but I guess she just intimidates me.

She motions to my cheek. "What about that one?"

Ellyn sits back in her chair.

I reach up and run my finger over the area of the tattoo. I can no longer feel the ridges of it as I could at first. It's just become a part of me now. "The thorns are a symbol of suffering—a sign of solidarity with those who suffer."

She doesn't respond right away. She seems to think about what I said. Then her tone changes, as does the look on her face. Both seem to sort of soften—but just a little. "You know what it means to suffer?"

"Sort of. I mean, I've had challenges—things in my life that have hurt me, but I haven't suffered to the extent that many others have and do, you know?"

"Yes, as a matter of fact, I do know."

And then I get it. The look I've seen on her face when she's seen me. Her attitude when she speaks to me. In that knowing way, I just get it. "Do I remind you of someone who's caused you to suffer?"

Sabina leans back in her chair—fast—like she wants to get away from me, and I hear Ellyn shift in her seat. I watch Sabina. She looks away from me, looks around the room, then opens her mouth . . . but closes it before she says anything.

"Sabina?" Ellyn's voice is almost a whisper.

She stands up and turns her back to us. Ellyn starts to get up, but I hold up one hand and she stops. When Sabina turns back around, she's crying. She says just one word: "Yes."

Then she walks out of the kitchen and out the front door.

Ellyn's eyes follow Sabina, but she lets her go. Then she looks back at me. "How did you know?"

"I just knew. That happens sometimes. It's kind of weird, I guess."

"It isn't weird, Twila. It's God."

"So, you understand?"

"Not exactly. But you seem to, and that's the important thing."

IT'S AFTER 6:00 AND already dark by the time Sabina comes back to Ellyn's. She knocks on the front door and then lets herself in. I'm sitting in the living room with Ellyn where we watched the sun set over the water.

"Hey, it's cold out there." Sabina's just wearing a thin sweater.

Ellyn gets up from the chair near the window. "Did you walk the village?"

Sabina nods. Then she looks at me. "Twila, I owe you an apology. I'm . . . so sorry for the way I've treated you. It wasn't about you, yet I . . . Well, I'm just sorry."

"Thanks. Are you okay?"

Ellyn leaves us and goes into the kitchen, coming back a minute later with a mug of tea. "Here, drink this. I kept the water simmering so it would be hot when you came back. It'll warm you up."

"Thank you." Sabina takes the mug. "I'm not okay, but . . . I think I will be. Your question made me look at myself—my behavior." Still standing, she looks down into the mug she's holding. When she looks back at me, her emotions are easy to see. She takes a deep breath. "You remind me of someone I cared about and someone I cared for professionally—a client. She took her own life not long ago. But that's no excuse for treating you as I have. I am sorry."

"I forgive you." I don't say anything else because I don't think she's done talking.

She looks at Ellyn, as though to include her in the conversation. "As I walked, I realized something. I've given myself over to guilt. Rather than grieve, I've allowed myself to languish in grief. I've lost myself in it—lost who I am, personally and professionally. I came here to heal and it's time I work at healing rather than hiding." She looks at Ellyn again. "Thank you for speaking truth to me. That's what real friends do."

Ellyn nods and wipes tears from the corners of her eyes, and then she goes to Sabina and gives her a hug. "I'm here for whatever you need, you know that, right? I don't know if I can help your healing process, but I'm here."

"Thank you."

"Hey, I'm going to take off now that you're back, Sabina." I smile at her. "I was just babysitting her while you were gone." They both smile at me.

"Why don't you have some soup and salad with us before you go?" This time it's Sabina who invites me.

"Of course, eat with us first, then we'll let you go."

"Um, okay." I don't really want to go anyway.

> I have hidden you from myself, not myself from you.
>
> SAINT AUGUSTINE

CHAPTER THIRTY-EIGHT

Sabina

"WHEN WAS THE LAST time you had a sleepover?"

Ellyn's green bathrobe accentuates her eyes. She smiles. "The last time I had a girlfriend stay the night? Gosh, with the exception of Twila staying here the other night, probably high school." She giggles.

"Ah, so there have been sleepovers with boyfriends?"

"Oh. Well, actually . . . no. I haven't . . . I never . . . I'm still . . . I mean, no."

I shake my head and laugh. "What?" But then I see the look on her face and realize what began, at least in my mind, as a simple question about sleepovers, has taken a serious turn.

"No, I've never had a boyfriend sleep over. I don't date."

"I know, but . . . ever?" My question is quiet—serious—to match her change in mood.

"Never."

"Never ever? Or never again?"

She hesitates and then takes a deep breath. "Never ever. I've never . . . dated or, you know, had a relationship with a man. Except, almost, with Miles."

We're sitting on opposite ends of Ellyn's sofa, facing one another, both wearing pajamas and bathrobes, and playing a game, as young girls might, of truth or dare.

Only, it isn't a game.

And we aren't young girls.

We're middle-aged women and one of us, I suspect, is speaking a truth long left unspoken. As I look at Ellyn, I see what I interpret as shame on her face—it's a look I know all too well from years of counseling others.

"Never ever is a long time. How do you feel about that?"

"Is that a counseling question?"

"Just a question from one friend to another."

She's quiet for a few moments as though she's debating whether or not to answer me. "Do I need to feel one way or another about it?"

"I suppose it depends on whether you made an intentional decision never to date or whether, for one reason or another, it just worked out that way. Is not dating a personal choice?"

She stares at me for another moment. Then she shakes her head in a slow, deliberate movement. "Not exactly. Not at first, anyway. Now, it's just . . ." She leans back against the arm of the sofa. "I . . . don't know."

"Why Miles? I mean, why now?"

"I told him from the beginning that I didn't date. But he was my doctor, I trusted him. I thought a friendship with him might be . . . nice. He seemed different, you know?"

"Different than Earl?" I watch for her reaction.

She leans forward. "Earl? Earl's not . . ." She leans back again. "I'm . . . exhausted. It was a long, crazy day. I think I'll head to bed."

"Sure. You need to rest and take care of yourself. You gave us a scare today."

She nods. "Thanks for being here."

"I can't think of any place I'd rather be." And I mean it.

Ellyn stands and comes to my end of the sofa and leans down to give me a hug. "Do you have everything you need? Towels are in the bathroom."

"Yes, I have everything. Thanks. I'll stay up a while longer."

"Okay. Good night."

I watch as she walks to the stairs, her gait sure, and then climbs the stairs to her room.

Why has she never dated? And who is Earl? I hoped Ellyn might let her guard down tonight. But she's right, it was a long day, especially for her. She'll talk when and if she's ready.

I stretch my legs out on Ellyn's sofa, lean back against the armrest, and close my eyes. It was a long day for me too, beginning with the call from Miles this morning. A knot forms in my stomach at the memory.

I take a deep breath and exhale.

The day didn't end as I feared it might.

But it was still long . . . Miles's call, rushing to the hospital, the conversation with Miles, bringing Ellyn home, and . . . Twila coming to the door and the fool I made of myself with her. Embarrassment warms my face as I consider it again.

But it was a valuable day. A day where the past and present collided—my fears based on past circumstances triggered by Ellyn's incident and my grief, my guilt, triggered by Twila's resemblance to Ashley.

The realization that I've lost who I am to fear and guilt was powerful.

Will I allow that collision and realization to impact my future behavior? Will I allow it to heal and transform me? A deep weariness settles over me—a familiar lethargy. I open my eyes and shift on the sofa so that my feet are on the floor again. I push myself up and switch off the lamps in the living room. Then I climb the two flights of stairs to Ellyn's guest room.

Upon entering the room, I walk to each of the two windows and pull the shades down. Then I cross the room to the French door that leads to the small balcony and the stairs to the upper deck. Before I pull the shade on the door, I crack the door open and peek outside.

The crisp night air lures me, so I open the door wide and step out onto the dark balcony. I rest my hands on the railing and close my eyes. The sound of the battering surf is like nails screeching against a chalkboard. But I will myself to stand still and if not listen, at least endure the sound.

The conundrum of earlier today comes back to me now. How do I reconcile my respect for others who believe in God? Eyes still closed, I shake my head. "I'm surrounded by people who believe in You."

How can I talk to someone or something I don't believe exists?

The question nags and a shiver runs up my spine. "It's cold out here."

I turn to go, but before I do, I open my eyes. The screeching has stopped. In its place, the rhythm of the waves becomes a melodious concerto rivaling that of any of the great classical composers. It accompanies the dance of a multitude of stars overhead.

Tears prick my eyes. I turn and walk back into Ellyn's guest room. I shut the door to the balcony and pull the shade to the bottom of the door. Then I stand and catch my breath. I place one hand over my pulsing heart. The melody of the sea beyond the closed door plays on, tempting me, wooing me, to . . .

Believe.

And for a few seconds, a moment in time, I almost feel I can believe once again.

But heaven and earth and everything in them on all sides tell me
to love you. Nor do they cease to tell everyone that
"they are without excuse" (Rom. 1:20).

SAINT AUGUSTINE

CHAPTER THIRTY-NINE

Ellyn

I WAKE TO THE dark gray of early morning, having
slept straight through the night. I sit up in bed, glance out the
window, and then assess how I feel after yesterday's hospital
escapade.

I feel . . . great!

I swing my legs over the side of the bed, stand up, and make my
way to the bathroom without even a limp.

You were fine yesterday. You made a big deal out of nothing.

"Shut up, Earl."

Once I've taken care of business, including brushing my teeth
and running a brush through my mane, I go to my closet and
exchange the pajamas I'm wearing for sweats and a jacket. I slip my
socked feet into my tennis shoes, bend and tie the shoes, and then
stand to make sure I really feel as well as I think I do.

And . . . I do.

I won't let Earl dampen my spirits.

I emerge from the closet, check the clock—7:05 a.m—and hope Sabina will sleep in. I'm not familiar with her morning habits, but she seems like one who might linger in bed. I make my way downstairs, set a pot of coffee to brew, and leave Sabina a note on the counter under a mug next to the coffeemaker.

Then I go out the back door, tread through the dew-dampened grass, and out the gate that opens onto a path on the headlands.

Better take it slow, big girl. You don't need to cause a stir again today.

"I thought you said I was fine?"

Well, that heart of yours can't last under the weight of you forever, you know.

As I walk, I put my fingers in my ears and sing "The Star Spangled Banner" until I'm sure *you know who* has fled my squawking rendition of our nation's anthem. However, I do heed Earl's advice and amble toward the cliffs rather than sprint.

As if you could really sprint.

"'Oh, say can you seeeee . . .'"

By the time I reach the cliffs, I'm winded, but nothing like I was yesterday, or even like I've felt when walking with Sabina the last few weeks. I turn and look back at my house, the sun just peeking up over the mountains that set the backdrop for the water tower and the village. The morning is still. Silent, except for the surf and the occasional squall of a seagull.

I leave the trail and walk to the edge of the cliff to look out over the vast expanse. With the exception of sleeping last night, these are the first minutes I've had to myself since Miles rode in on his white horse yesterday—or white Jeep Grand Cherokee, as was the case.

While I watch the motion of the sea, the events of yesterday replay. *Lord, what happened?* As I ask, Earl's accusation that I made a big deal out of nothing repeats. Somewhere, deep inside, I believe him.

Why didn't I just get into my car and drive home yesterday? I just needed rest. I'm just out of shape. What's wrong with me?

Tears of shame sting my eyes. "I'm sorry." I whisper my apology to God. What I'm apologizing for, I'm not sure. Just for being, I think. I look down and kick at a rock imbedded in dirt until it loosens and goes over the side of the cliff. As I do, memories return of the wonder and awe I felt yesterday when Miles suggested that God interceded and healed me.

Confusion fogs my pathetic red head. Things don't add up.

My symptoms.

The differing EKGs and diagnoses.

Dr. Ngyuen's conclusion that the opposing diagnoses were a *medical mystery.*

Part of me wants to believe a miracle took place—that God healed me.

But . . .

Why would God waste a miracle on me?

As doubt intrudes, I watch cotton-candy clouds drift on the horizon followed by dark, angry billows. Fear settles in my chest, somewhere near my heart—the heart Earl assures me is failing.

But it's not your everyday, yikes-there's-a-spider kind of fear.

No.

It's reverent fear.

I step back from the cliff.

"I'm sorry." This time, I know what I'm apologizing for. I remain standing, but my soul is prostrate, humbled before God. Confusion passes. Cognition returns. And my *failing* heart beats strong and steady.

So there, Earl!

God healed me.

How dare I doubt Him, or worse, accuse Him of wasting a miracle on me. Me. The one He sacrificed His own Son to save.

Tears flow now.

There is no condemnation in my clarity.

No condemnation!

Only conviction.

Here you go, making a mountain out of a molehill again.

The voice in my head interrupts, but is it Earl, or . . .

My mother.

Yes, it's her voice. After all, how many times did I hear her say those words as I grew up.

Too many to count.

I smile. "Yeah, yeah, Mom, it's me, the drama queen again. But that's okay—this is how God wired me." I smile. *Oh Lord, thank You.*

Thank You.

Thank You for healing me.

WHEN I WALK BACK into my kitchen, Sabina is sitting at the table, the note I left is on the table in front of her, and she's sipping a mug of coffee.

"There you are. I was going to give you five more minutes and if you weren't back I was going to call Dr. Charming to gather a search party."

"Dr. Charming?"

She smiles. "How do you feel?"

"Great."

She tilts her head to one side and looks at me for a minute. "You know . . . I think you look better than you have since we met. There's a glow about you. It seems you made an amazing recovery, my friend."

"Not amazing. Miraculous."

She raises one eyebrow. "You're serious?"

I nod. "I am serious." Although I know Sabina doesn't share my love for God, I tell her of my revelation this morning. I can't keep it to myself. She listens, and I can see she's considering what I say.

"I don't mean to discount what you believe, and no one is more thrilled than I that you pulled through whatever it was that happened yesterday. But . . . why you? I mean, if this miracle is from God rather than a fluke, then why doesn't He do the same for others? For Miles's wife, for . . ." She leaves her sentence hanging. "I don't understand."

"I don't understand either. As I walked back here, the same question occurred to me. You grew up in church—remember the Bible story of Jesus cooking breakfast on the shore for John and Peter and some of the other disciples after His resurrection?" Sabina nods. "Later, in that same story, after Jesus told Peter to feed His sheep, to care for His followers, He also tells Peter that one day he'll be led where he doesn't want to go."

Sabina nods. I can tell I'm pushing her patience, but I continue anyway.

"It was a reference to Peter's death—that he'd die a martyr—which he did. He was also crucified. So Peter says to Jesus, 'What about him?' and points to John. And Jesus says to Peter, 'What is that to you?' In other words, what's chosen for John is none of your concern. This is about you and Me."

Sabina takes a sip of her coffee and then raises her eyebrows. "So?" Her tone is sarcastic.

"So . . . that's how God responded to my question this morning. I felt like He said to me, 'What are they to you?' The others who've died or fought terminal illnesses, like Miles's wife. I . . . I don't mean that to sound callous. It's just that I felt like God said, 'What happened yesterday wasn't about them, it was about you. You and Me.'" I look down at Sabina, who's still seated at the table. "It's really humbling and I don't understand it all. But there are a lot of things about God that I don't understand. That's . . . all I can tell you."

"Ellyn, do you really believe God responded to your question this morning? You remembered a Bible story. Big deal."

"No, it's more than that . . ." I walk to the counter, fill a mug with coffee, and then go sit across from her at the table. "It's hard to explain, but it's a combination of things. I asked God a specific question, then a story from the Bible I hadn't thought of for a long time comes to mind and answers my question. With the answer came a sense of peace."

I put my hand on my chest. "Right here. I felt it. Plus, I was outside where everything, I mean *everything*, around me speaks of the power of God. All I have to do is look out the window to see

God in the beauty of His creation. There's even a verse about that somewhere, about how people who don't believe have no excuse because of everything that God made surrounding them—they see Him through His creation."

"It's in Romans."

"What?"

"The verse you're talking about, it's Romans 1:20. Believe me, I know. Antwone quotes it to me all the time."

"Oh, well, anyway, I know—" I stare at Sabina for a second. "Wait a minute. That's it. That's why you keep the blinds closed and why you turned the chairs in your rental away from the window. That's why you won't walk on the headlands, but insist on walking in the village. That's it, isn't it?"

"What are you talking about?" Sabina gets up and goes to the sink to rinse her mug.

Her back is to me, so I get up and go to the sink. I put my hand on her shoulder. "Sabina, turn around—look at me." My tone is gentle. She ignores me and keeps rinsing her already clean cup. "Sabina?"

She turns off the water, sets her mug in the sink, and turns around. *"What?"*

Oh Lord, help me here. "You suffered a deep loss when Ashley took her life. I can't . . . I can't even imagine how that must have hit you. You're angry with God. I think that's natural. You're right, He could have intervened with Ashley in some way, just as He intervened with me yesterday. I don't know . . . I don't know why He didn't."

She takes a deep breath. "What's your point, Ellyn?"

"I think you're so angry with God that you've denied He exists at all. But . . . if you look around you, especially here"—I wave toward the outside—"then your denial is broken. You can't help but see Him. And you don't want to see Him. Right?"

"You don't know what you're talking about. How can I be angry with a God I don't believe exists? Anyway, Ashley's just part of it. You don't know—you have no idea." She takes a deep breath and exhales. "Listen, I respect your beliefs in the same way I respect Antwone's beliefs. I just don't agree. So let's agree to disagree and move on. All right?"

"I'd like to say one more thing."

"Go ahead, get it out of your system."

I look her in the eyes. "It isn't just Antwone's belief, or my belief, it's also Miles's and Twila's and Rosa's and Paco's belief. And a whole lot of others. God's surrounded you, Sabina. He loves you too much to let you walk away from Him, so He's surrounded you with others who believe in Him."

"Now, you've said what you wanted to say, can we agree to disagree?"

Lord, give her eyes to see. "There are things we can agree to disagree on, but I won't compromise truth."

"So what, if I don't agree with your truth, we can't be friends?"

"That's not what I'm saying. I can't force you to believe, nor would I want to."

"Good. So, what do you eat for breakfast? I'm starved."

This conversation is over, for now. "Me too. I'll make us some juice to start with." I smile to myself as I head to the refrigerator for kale and carrots.

Maybe some pond sludge will improve Sabina's sight.

It is not the impurity of food I fear but that of uncontrolled desire.

Saint Augustine

CHAPTER FORTY

Twila

When I walk out of Corners after my shift on Friday evening, there's a black Mercedes sedan parked in front of the store. A tourist. The car looks sort of out of place in the village—like it should be parked in front of a five-star resort instead. As I walk past the front of the car, the driver's-side door opens and a man gets out.

"Twila?"

I stop, like, frozen.

"I've been waiting for you."

I try to breathe but it's like all the air got sucked out of me and I can't get anymore in.

"You look good. I thought we could get some dinner and catch up." He looks around. "Are there any decent restaurants here?"

He walks toward me and then stops. "What have you done to yourself?" He gestures toward the tattoo on my cheek, a look of disgust on his face.

I straighten to my full 5' 2" and square my shoulders. "It's a tattoo. I have another one too." I show him my wrist. "I got them with the money you sent me for graduation."

"Huh, figures. Kids. I guess now I'll have to pay to have them removed. Well, come on, what kind of greeting is this? Give me a hug and let's go get some dinner. You don't have plans, do you? There can't be anything to do in this town."

"No, I . . . don't have plans." I don't hug him and he seems to forget he even mentioned it.

"Good. What's the best restaurant?"

"Um . . . Ellyn's."

"Okay, get in. Let's go." He walks back to his car.

I just stand there.

"Twila, hello? Get in."

I shake my head. "No."

"No?"

"We can . . . um, walk. It's through there." I point to the alley that runs alongside Corners.

He looks around again. "Is my car safe here?"

A bubble of anger, like acid, rises from my chest to my throat, but I'm not sure why. I just nod.

"So, let's go."

His tone is familiar—like when I was a kid—but I hadn't remembered it until now. Then he smiles and . . . I don't know . . .

"Here, give me that backpack over your shoulder. I'll carry it for you. You know, you really do look good except for that thing on your face. Well, that and you're too skinny, but hey, better than too fat, right?" He laughs at what I guess he means as a joke.

I hand him my backpack, turn toward the alley, and start walking. He follows me. Most of the narrow alleys in Mendocino are just walkways cut through the blocks—many are landscaped with plants and flowers. Flowers grow here all year long. I look down and count the red and white cyclamen blooms as we walk and he talks. I can count, but I can't listen. I can't take in what he's saying.

We reach the street, cross, and then I lead him down the street to the alley that comes to Ellyn's garden and then around the side of the café. As we reach the café, the scent of cooking food causes my stomach to lurch. I take a deep breath to keep from gagging. I look back. "I'm not . . . hungry. I had a late lunch."

"Well, I didn't and I'm starved. Have a drink or a salad or something. I just want to spend some time with you."

Another bubble pushes from my stomach to my throat.

As we walk in the front entrance, I pray there's a table available so we don't have to go somewhere else.

"Ah, Chica, you here for dinner?" Rosa greets me and then looks over my shoulder. "Two?"

"We don't have a reservation."

Rosa grabs two menus and puts her arm around me and leads us to a table. "You early, it's okay. We not crowded yet." Then she leans close to me and whispers in my ear. "You okay? You don't look okay."

I smile, sort of, and nod.

"Okay, here, you sit here."

Rosa pulls out a chair for me and once we're both seated she opens the menus and hands one to each of us. "I have de chef and owner come say hello." Without waiting for a response from my dad, she turns and walks toward the kitchen.

As he looks at his menu, I look at him. It's sort of surreal. His dark hair is graying around his temples and he has a goatee now, which is also turning gray. He's not as tall as I remember, or as handsome.

"So, what's good?" He looks over the menu at me.

"The vegan dishes are great."

"Vegan?" He shakes his head. "You're just like your mother."

He doesn't mean that as a compliment.

"Hello."

Ellyn comes up from behind me and gives my shoulder a squeeze before coming around to the side of the table. She puts her hand out toward my dad. "I'm Ellyn—owner and executive chef." Her voice sounds different, more formal than usual. When I look up at her, I see she isn't smiling when my dad shakes her hand.

"So owner and executive chef, what's your specialty?"

His tone is condescending and I feel my cheeks burn. "Ellyn's a friend of mine."

He looks up at her again and then back at me. "Have any friends your own age?"

I look down at the table, unable to look at Ellyn again.

"My specialties are the vegan dishes. But if you're a *carnivore*"— she pauses—"and I'm guessing you are, then the Beef Bourguignon is good." Then, before he can respond, she puts her hand on my shoulder again. "Twila, may I see you in the kitchen for a moment, Paco has a question about the new dish we created."

My dad looks at me. "*We* created?"

"Um, yeah, I help Ellyn create some of the . . . never mind . . . I'll be right back." I get up and follow Ellyn through the swinging doors into the kitchen.

As soon as we're out of sight of the dining room, she turns. "Who *is* that?" She sounds, like, fierce or something. "You're not out with him on a date, are you?"

"What? No. That's my . . ." I turn back toward the dining room, still stuck in that surreal place, where I can't quite believe what's happening. "He's my father."

"Your father? Oh. I didn't know he was visiting. Not that I needed to know. But Rosa thought you looked upset."

I look at her and swallow the ache in my throat. "I . . . I didn't know he was coming. He just showed up at the store. He was waiting."

"Does your mom know he's here?"

"I don't know. I don't think so. She would have told me."

"Do you want to call her?"

"No. Not now."

"Honey, are you okay?"

I see the concern on Ellyn's face and for some reason, that makes me want to cry. But instead, I take a deep breath and nod my head. "I'm . . . okay."

Ellyn hesitates. "Well, I'm here if you need me. And you know Rosa will be watching every move he makes." She smiles.

I nod again. "Thanks." I turn to go back to the dining room, but then stop and turn back and give Ellyn a hug. "Really, thanks."

WHEN I GET HOME, I'm alone. My mom is out with a friend. I walk through the dark house straight to the bathroom, where I turn on the light, close the door, and lock it. Then I lean over the toilet and make myself throw up.

Something I haven't done in over a year.

Because I've eaten almost nothing today, there's little to get rid of except the water I drank at dinner. But even that has to go. All of it. I gag over and over and over, until I'm heaving nothing but shame. With my stomach still cramping, I flush the toilet and then curl into a ball on the floor—the tile cool against my hot, tear-stained cheek.

I WAKE TO THE sound of knocking—then I hear my mom.

"Twila? Are you in there? Open the door."

I sit up, my body aching, and then get up off the floor and unlock and open the bathroom door. I just stand there and look at her.

"Oh, sweet girl, what happened?" She wraps her arms around me and holds me in a tight hug.

And the tears start all over again. "I'm . . . sorry . . ." I hiccup. "He came . . . back . . . and then . . . I had to . . . I—"

"Shh, baby, shh."

She holds me tight and lets me cry. When I stop, she leans back and looks at me. She doesn't ask me questions, instead she turns on the sink and lets the water run for a minute. Then she steps away, takes a washcloth out from the cabinet under the sink, wets it in the warm water, and then picks up the bar of almond soap from the dish on the counter. She washes my face—wipes the tears away. The almond smell, like, calms my freaked-out nerves.

"It's late. Why don't you go get into your pajamas and I'll come in and say good night."

I go to my room, strip off the clothes I wore to work this morning, and find my favorite old flannel PJ bottoms and faded UCSC sweatshirt. I put them on and then pull the comforter back on my bed and climb in. When my mom comes in she hands me a cup of hot tea. I don't have to ask what it is, I can tell by the smell—valerian, chamomile, and lemon balm, all grown in her garden. She sits on the edge of my bed and straightens the covers around me and tucks them under me.

"Do you want to tell me what happened?"

I nod. I hold the mug of tea close to my face and breathe in the scented steam, but I don't drink it. "Dad's here." I watch her expression change to one of control. She doesn't say anything so I keep going. "When I came out of the store after work he was out front . . . waiting for me. He said he wanted to go to dinner and . . . catch up."

"Did you have dinner with him?"

I nod.

"How did it go?"

I shrug. "We went to Ellyn's." I watch her face. "He's . . . different than I remember." She doesn't say anything but I watch as she licks her lips and then begins to chew on her bottom lip.

"He's not as tall . . . or . . . as . . . I don't know. He's just different."

"Is he staying here? In town?"

"He checked into the Mendocino Hotel."

"How long is he staying?"

"I don't know."

She points at the cup I'm holding. "You need to drink that or you'll be . . . dehydrated."

She knows what I did. I look down into the cup. "I'm sorry."

"You don't need to apologize to me, Twila. I'm just concerned. Can you drink some of the tea?"

I lift the cup to my lips and take a small sip.

She stands up and leans down and kisses my forehead and then tucks the covers around me again. She smiles. "It's been a long time since I've tucked you in. Get some sleep."

"Okay."

After she leaves, I set the cup of tea on my nightstand. I don't want it.

I turn off the lamp next to my bed and stare into the dark. If my dad isn't as tall or as handsome as I remember, are, like, any of my memories of him even real? Or does he just seem different because I was a kid the last time I saw him?

He says he wants to spend time with me.

Isn't that what I've always wanted?

The dark has no answers for me.

> You are certainly not our physical shape. Yet you made
> humanity in your image . . .
>
> SAINT AUGUSTINE

CHAPTER FORTY-ONE

Ellyn

ON SUNDAY, LONG BEFORE dawn, I wake to a roar of wind and the spatter of rain pinging against the windows. In the distance an angry ocean roars. Great. I roll over, pull the sheets and blankets up around my ears, and close my eyes. I will my brain to remain inactive by focusing on the dark interiors of my closed eyelids.

I *will* go back to sleep.

But just as my brain is headed back to dreamland, it triggers my olfactory system. Unmoving, eyes still closed, I inhale through my nose. I sniff—once—twice. I pull the blankets tighter around my face and breathe the air from the warm pocket the blanket creates.

I'm imagining the scent, right?

I sigh. No, something smells.

Stinks, actually.

Shoot! I throw the covers back and sit up. What in the world? I swing my legs over the side of the bed, slip my sock-clad feet into my slippers, and then head to my closet for my robe. I wander through the dark house, flipping lights on as I go. I follow my nose to the kitchen, where I stand sniffing.

"Ugh." The stench fills the kitchen. I turn in circles trying to detect where the smell is coming from.

Something is rotting. Or rotten.

Food?

I shake my head. Food could never smell that bad.

I head toward the kitchen sink and the smell seems to get stronger. I bend down and place my face near the garbage disposal. I breathe deep and then lift my head so fast that it bangs against the faucet.

"Oh, Lord . . . what *is* that?" I back out of the kitchen while rubbing the lump on my head. I turn in the living room and go to the front door. I open the door and gulp breaths of clean, damp air. Standing in my small foyer, I close my eyes and listen to the rain as the cold wind blows around me and into the house. I stand there until my heart rate and breathing become normal again and consider my options. Then I turn and head back to the kitchen.

You can do this, Ellyn.

First, I go to the fridge, grab a lemon, and quarter it. I toss it into the sink, and turn on the faucet and garbage disposal. "Oh Lord, let it be this simple."

You should know better by now.

"Shut *up*, Earl!" I'm really getting tired of the nagging.

I step back from the sink and sniff. The fresh scent of lemon intermingles with the scent of—I sigh again—death. It's the smell of roadkill that lingers in my kitchen. There's no denying it. But what died and where? The smell is stronger near the sink, but it's not coming from there.

I slam my hand against the faucet, turning it off, then turn on my heel and leave the kitchen again. I need coffee, but there's no eating or drinking anything in there. My gag reflex threatens a revolt. I make my way upstairs to the guest room, flip the light switch, and then eye the small single-serving coffeemaker I keep in the room. *Yes!* I choose a pod from the small wooden box next to the brewer, slip a pottery mug under the spigot, and put the pod into the machine. As I wait, the scent of fresh coffee soothes me and I feel my shoulders relax, but just a bit.

"Lord, I need a simple solution to a pointless problem." I wait, hoping for divine inspiration but nothing comes to mind. "Fine."

I take the cup of coffee and reach for some of the powdered creamer I keep on the tray with the coffeemaker. Then I stop. The creamer is full of high fructose corn syrup. Sugar. My hand hovers over the creamer for a few seconds. Since my episode at the hospital last week and the recognition of God's intervention, I haven't struggled at all with sticking with my vegan, no-sugar, diet. But now . . .

Oh, phooey! I dump a couple of heaping teaspoons into my coffee. I take the mug and sit in the natural-colored linen upholstered chair in the corner of the room and sip my coffee. I start to apologize to God for my weakness, but something stops me. Instead, I whisper, "Thank You." I hold the cup close to my nose and breathe in the rich aroma. So much better than the stench downstairs.

Then I make a plan.

"Hi."

I sit on the front step, letting the wind and rain batter my overheated body. I hold the phone in one hand and wipe my damp brow with another.

"Hey, you, happy Sunday."

"Yeah, not so much."

Sabina laughs. "Uh-oh, what's wrong?"

"This is serious."

"Oh, I'm sorry. What happened?"

"Well, I mean, it's not *that* serious." As I talk some of my frustration diminishes. "In the grand scheme of life, I guess it's not a huge deal. But I woke up several hours ago to a horrible smell. I mean, Sabina, it's bad." I hear her chuckle. "Okay, you get your scrawny behind over here and smell it. That will stop your laughing."

"Oh, you are funny. Okay, so what's the smell?"

"It's . . . I think it's . . ." A smile comes to my face and I begin laughing as well. "Really . . . it isn't funny . . . it's just that I . . ." I catch my breath. "I thought I could handle it. I thought I could take care of it myself. But then I saw fur . . . and . . ." I stop laughing as the reality hits me again. "I don't know what to do. I just can't . . . I can't."

"Fur?" Now she's serious.

"It's a rodent, of some sort. Rat, maybe. Or squirrel. It died in one of the walls in the kitchen. Oh, it stinks!"

"At the café? Can't Paco—"

"No, at my house."

"So call an exterminator. They'll figure it out for you."

"It's Sunday. I called. No answer. I left a message—told them it was an emergency. But—"

"Ellyn, I don't know if you can call it an emergency."

"Oh, yeah? Easy for you to say. Again, come smell it."

"You know, I've got a lot to do today." She laughs again.

"Listen, I've almost got it. Really. I traced the smell to a cabinet in my kitchen. You know that wall that juts out from the bank of cabinets around the sink? It's under there—behind one of those cabinets."

By now, I'm standing back inside the house just near the front door so I can hear Sabina better. I keep opening and closing the door so I can take breaths of fresh air.

"Are you sure?"

"Yes. Remember the fur?"

"Oh . . ."

"I took everything out of the cabinet and bashed in the sheet-rock with a hammer. I thought if I could do it inside the cabinet rather than on the other side of the wall, I wouldn't have to have someone repair the sheetrock. I could just patch it myself with ply-wood or something."

"But?"

"But then I took a little gardening shovel and was digging out the insulation and stuff and I found . . . droppings." I take another breath of clean air. "Oh, Sabina, in my kitchen! Anyway, I found the droppings and then the next shovelful I pulled out had a clump of fur in it. So . . . I knew. But now . . . I can't . . . I can't make myself . . ."

"Well, girl, of course you can't. That's a man's job. Call Paco."

I begin pacing back and forth in the foyer. "No. No, I don't need Paco. I just need . . . well, you know . . . moral support. I thought if you could come over and just . . . be here to encourage me. Cheer me on."

Sabina begins laughing again.

"Seriously, I know I could do it then."

"I'm not coming within fifty feet of any rat, dead or alive. Not doing it. Either you call a man or you're on your own." She pauses. "You know, Ellyn, there are some things men are good for."

"Yeah, okay, I'll take care of it myself."

"Ellyn, stop it. Call Paco or someone."

"I don't want to take him away from his family on a Sunday morning."

"Then call Miles."

"No. He did enough for me last week. Anyway, you know, I can't just call him for something like this. I don't want him to feel like I'm using him."

"He's a friend, Ellyn. You told me he said if you needed anything to call him."

I consider it. "No, I'm not calling him."

"Oh give me a break. He'd love to help you. In fact, God probably let that big ol' rodent die in your wall just so you'd have to humble yourself and ask a man for help—good man, by the way."

"So *now* you believe in God?"

"Whatever. Just call Miles."

"Okay, okay." I hold up one hand like she can see me. "I have to go. I smell a rat!"

As I'm pushing *End* on my phone I hear Sabina say, "Call him, Ellyn."

Some friend she is.

I drop the phone into the pocket of my robe and turn and face the direction of the kitchen again. I can do this—I can. I will! I cover my nose with one hand and walk back into the kitchen. Bits of sheetrock and pink insulation are strewn over the floor in front of the open lower cabinet. And next to the small shovel is the clump of . . . fur.

"Oh, Lord. I can't!"

You're such a wimp, Ellyn. It's just a dead rat. Just get down on your hands and knees and dig it out.

I bend down, pick up the gardening gloves I was wearing before calling Sabina, and put them back on. I get back down on my hands and knees, grab the shovel, take a deep breath, hold it, and put my head back inside the cabinet. I reach toward the area in the open sheetrock where the fur came from and I dip the shovel back inside and begin to dig again. As I pull out more of the pink fluff, some of it brushes against my wrist just above one of the gloves.

I scream.

I'm back on my feet so fast it's a miracle.

I run from the kitchen back to the front door and out to the step. I throw the shovel down, rip the gloves off my hands, and choke back a sob. "I can't. I can't do it." Defeated, I plop down on the step again.

I can think of nothing else to do.

I bury my head in my hands and bang a fist against my knee.

I sit there a few minutes, then I get up and storm back into the house, slamming the door as I go. I climb the stairs to my bedroom, rip my damp robe off, and toss it across the foot of my bed. Then I go to the bathroom to blow my nose. As I do, I catch a glimpse of myself in the mirror.

My hair is a mass of chaotic red frizz, my green eyes are bloodshot, and my eyelids swollen and as red as my nose. I look down at the loose yellow flannel pajamas I'm wearing. The back bottoms of the legs are tucked into my socks and on my feet are my fuzzy slippers.

Call Miles? Looking like this? Yeah, right.

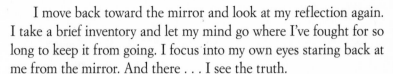

I move back toward the mirror and look at my reflection again. I take a brief inventory and let my mind go where I've fought for so long to keep it from going. I focus into my own eyes staring back at me from the mirror. And there . . . I see the truth.

I am afraid.

Afraid of men. Just as Rosa said.

But why?

Shivering now, I wrap my arms around myself.

As I look at myself—I see me. Not me, the chef. Not me, the friend. Just me, and me alone.

Alone.

Fat.

Ugly.

"No, Earl. You're wrong." The words come out on a whisper. "I'm created in the image of God."

The words embarrass me. They are foreign—not something I've applied to myself before. But I swallow my fear—or try to. I look in the mirror again and still see just me. But there is determination shining in my green eyes.

That's when I make a decision.

I shut the bathroom door, turn the shower on, undress, and step inside the steaming stall. I lather my hair with floral shampoo and stand long enough to allow the hot water to ease the tension in my shoulders.

After I shower, I blow-dry my long hair. I use product. I even dig out and plug in a long-ignored straightening iron. And then, I put on a little of the department store makeup.

That done, I head for my closet.

I pull the pair of black sweat pants off the shelf and reach for an olive sweater that I know sets off the color of my eyes. I put on shoes and earrings. I glance at myself in the full-length mirror—but just glance. If I look too long or think too much, I'll change my mind.

Then I go to the bed, take my phone out of the pocket of my robe, and I call. "Hello, Miles? It's Ellyn."

> Yet let us seek more diligently and not lose heart.
>
> Saint Augustine

CHAPTER FORTY-TWO

Miles

"ELLYN? ARE YOU FEELING all right?" I assume she's calling with a medical issue.

"Yes, I'm fine. I've been fine, good actually, since last Monday."

"No more problems?"

"Not at all."

I relax. "Good. What can I do for you?"

"Well, I have another type of problem and I was wondering if . . . well, I could use some help. I mean, if you're free."

I hesitate. There's a part of me that wants to tell her to call someone else, but I know that's not what God would have me do. "I was going to head to church, but tell me what's going on."

After she's explained her predicament, I chuckle. "I bet it smells bad."

"Really bad."

"I'll come on over."

"Do you want to go to church and then come? It can . . . wait."

I smile. "It can?"

"Oh. Well, sure."

I laugh. "I'm on my way."

I make a quick change from church clothes to jeans and a sweatshirt. As I do, I remind myself that God's asked me to love Ellyn in the way He loves her, which also means sacrificing for her. Not that getting a rat out of her wall is a big deal. The sacrifice will come with the tug on my heart when I see her.

I grab my car keys and go.

WHEN ELLYN OPENS HER front door, I'm struck by two things: her—and a reeking stench. "Wow . . ."

"I told you it was bad. I can't believe I didn't notice it when I came in last night, but it was late and I went straight up to bed without even turning on a light down here. I didn't even go into the kitchen. Then I woke up around 4:00 and something smelled, so I got up and . . ."

She's nervous. Why? And what did she do to her hair? It looks so soft. I jam my hands into my pockets to keep myself from reaching out and touching her hair. Oh Lord, help me.

"I'm babbling. Sorry. Here, come in out of that weather."

I step inside. Her house is cold—all the windows open, though it's not helping the smell much. I follow her into the kitchen, where she covers her nose and mouth with her hand and points to an open cabinet with a mess in front of it.

I look from the mess to her. "Do you have a plastic garbage bag?"

"Sure."

She goes to her sink, and grabs a bag out from the cabinet underneath, and hands it to me. "Great. I've got this, you go back outside."

"No. I can . . . help or . . . wait."

"Out!" I smile and point back toward her front door. Once she's gone, I take a deep breath, hold it, and pick up the gardening shovel she left on the floor near the cabinet. I dig in the wall until I feel the problem, then shovel out the dead rat. I drop it in the open garbage bag, tie the top of the bag in a knot, and then run to the front door. I do it all in one breath.

"Got it." I hold up the bag and then join her out on her front step. "Where's your garbage can?"

"That was fast. You're amazing! It's on the side of the house on the other side of the driveway."

I run through the rain, dispose of the rat, and then run back. I shake the water off and go back inside, leaving the front door open so the house can continue to air out. I find Ellyn in the kitchen, sweeping the mess out of the cabinet and off the floor. I get another garbage bag out from under her sink and hold it open as she, using a dustpan, fills it with bits of insulation, droppings, and sheetrock.

"Do you have any rat poison?"

"No. I've never needed it."

"I'm surprised—seems like mice and rats would come with living on the headlands. You've been lucky."

"I guess so." She empties the dustpan one more time.

"I can pick some up, and then come back and patch the wall. I can just screw a piece of plywood against the hole since it's inside the cabinet—that's easier than patching the sheetrock. I'll drop some poison in first."

"Really? You don't . . . mind?"

"No." Her smile makes it worth it.

"Miles, thank you so much. I tried to do it myself. I should have been able to, but . . ." She shakes her head.

"Don't be so hard on yourself. You did an amazing job. How did you pinpoint exactly where the rat was?"

She laughs. "I have a great nose."

"Evidently." I chuckle.

She empties the last of the debris into the bag. "I need to disinfect the floor and cabinet." She looks up at me. "Have you had breakfast?"

"Not yet."

"This will only take me a few minutes. Why don't you come over to the café and I'll make you breakfast? It's Sunday, so I need to get over there. If you'd like, you could even stay . . ."

I watch as her face colors, the freckles on her cheeks almost disappearing with the color.

"I mean, if you want to, you could stay for lunch. It's our Sunday tradition—the staff and their families."

Her invitation entices me. I think a minute. "Thanks, Ellyn. It sounds great, but I have some things I need to get done today. Why don't you leave your key under your mat and I'll go get the rat poison and a piece of plywood. I'll get this patched up and then head home."

"Oh. If you're sure . . ." She looks down at the cabinet—away from me.

"Yes, thanks for the invitation. Maybe another time."

"Okay."

AFTER I FINISH, I put Ellyn's key back under her mat. I get in my car and turn toward the headlands. I'll take Hesser Drive around the loop. The rain has let up and the sun is breaking through the clouds. I glance out at the water and sky as I go. I round the corner, heading toward Lansing, and see someone, hood up, hands in pockets, walking the trail out to the point. I slow to a stop and watch her.

Then, as if she knows she's being watched, she turns and looks at me. I pull into the nearby parking area, get out of the car, and wave at her. She doesn't wave back, but she starts walking toward me. I step over the log between the parking lot and trail and go to meet her.

"Hey, gal. Good to see you."

"Hi."

"Taking advantage of a break in the weather?" She doesn't look well.

She nods. "What are you doing out here?"

"I just came from Ellyn's. She had a dead rat in her wall." I smile. "I got it out for her and patched up her wall."

"Yuck."

"That's how she felt."

She doesn't say any more. Something isn't right with her. "How are you doing?"

"Okay."

"You sure?"

Her thin shoulders lift and then drop.

"I don't want to interrupt your walk, but how about joining me for a cup of coffee or lunch. I could use the company."

"Why?"

I hesitate. "Because I'm hungry?"

"No, I mean, why could you use the company?"

I run my hand through my hair and look out at the changing clouds. Twila deserves my honesty. I look back at her. "Guess I'm a little lonely."

"Things aren't going well with Ellyn?"

Because Twila still looks and talks like a teenager, I often forget she's twenty-six and quite astute. "Well, we're friends. And that's good."

"But you wanted more, right?"

"Right."

"She doesn't, like, see herself the way others see her or the way God sees her."

"I think you're right. So, what about lunch?"

Twila looks at the ground. "I can't . . . eat." She looks back at me.

That explains the gaunt look and the circles under her eyes. "What's going on, gal?"

"My dad . . . he showed up here on Friday."

"I see. So you're experiencing a setback?"

"Yeah, I guess."

As she's talked, I've noted her mouth is dry. "It seems to me like we could both use some company today. Why don't you come with me to Thanksgiving's, and I'll grab a sandwich for myself and a bottle of water and a smoothie for you."

"No, but thanks."

"Twila, when's the last time you ate or had anything to drink?"

She twists a piece of her long hair, sticking out from under her hood, around one finger. "I left a message for my counselor, I'm going to see her tomorrow."

"Good. When's the last time you ate or had anything to drink?"

She sighs. "It hasn't been that long."

"How long?"

"Lunch on Friday—I had a salad. I drank a glass of water on Friday night."

"Did you keep it down?" I read the shame on her face.

"I thought . . . I always thought . . ."

I see tears in her eyes. One slips down her cheek, which alleviates some of my concern. She's not as dehydrated as I suspected.

". . . that if he came back, it would be different . . . you know?"

"Different in what way?" I take a few slow steps toward the parking lot hoping she'll follow me.

"I guess I thought he was . . . different, or that he'd be different. I figured out that my memories of him are sort of warped."

She's in step with me as I head to the car. "I don't think that's unusual. When we care about someone, we remember the best about them. Since Sarah died, I've recreated her in my mind—recalling only the good things about her. She wasn't perfect, but you'd have a hard time convincing me of that now."

"But at least Sarah really loved you, right?"

"Right."

"I don't think my dad cares about me."

I put my arm around her shoulders as we walk. "That's his loss. Do you know why he's here?"

"I don't know. I think it's just so he can feel good about himself."

We reach the car. "Thanksgiving's?"

"Nah, I'm going home."

"Twila . . ." I measure my words. "In different ways, we're both feeling rejected and maybe a little fragile emotionally. This is when we need to rely on God. Let His strength work through our weakness."

"Sometimes, I don't, like, know how to do that—to let Him be strong."

"Just remember who you are." I reach for her wrist and pull up the sleeve of her hoodie. I turn her wrist so we can both see the tattoo there.

"Never forget that. Your dad can't take your identity from you—no one can. There are many of us who love you and appreciate who you are. We don't want to see you waste away. Don't let him defeat you."

She looks at her wrist a moment longer, then looks at me, her eyes wide. She nods her head. "Okay."

"Okay?"

"Yeah."

"So, Thanksgiving's?"

She nods again and opens the passenger side door of my car and gets in.

My error was my god . . .

SAINT AUGUSTINE

CHAPTER FORTY-THREE

Sabina

I OPEN MY MOUTH, but nothing comes out. *Oh, God, please. Please make the music stop.* I want to beg, to plead with Jesus to make it stop, but the words are lost to me—my voice nonexistent. Beethoven's Sontata for the Piano, No. 12, plays in A-flat. The chords drowning out my cries.

Stop! No more!

But still, only the strains of the dirge fill the candlelit chamber—wisps of smoke from the candles in the tall candelabras twist heavenward.

I look up—following the spirals of smoke—and then I see her. Her braids dangling, her neck at an awkward angle. *Jazzy! Jazzy!* One of her knee socks is scrunched around her ankle, the other still covering her calf. *Jazzy!* Her eyes, open, are without expression.

Help! Someone help! I struggle, I fight to force the words from my mind to my mouth, but—nothing. Frustration heaves in my chest. My temples pound with the deafening strains of the sonata.

I run to get help, but my legs won't carry me. I run, but I don't move. Quicksand, or so it seems.

Jazzy! I have to help Jazzy!

"Sabina! Sabina! Where's Jazzy? Where?" My mamma shakes me, but I can say nothing. Instead, I lift a leaden arm, the movement slow, oh so slow. I point up—up to the branches of the climbing tree—the one in the backyard—the one now transplanted in the chamber.

There's Jazzy, Mamma. She hangs from a branch, her neon-pink rubber jump rope—the one with the neon-green handles—tangled around the branch . . . and her neck.

Her braids dangle.

There's Jazzy, Mamma. There!

"Oh, Sweet Jesus, oh my Jesus . . . You've taken my baby. Jazzy! Oh, my Lord . . ." Mamma wails. "You've taken her home."

Mamma drops to her knees in the dirt beneath the tree. The candles flicker and then go out. The smoke swirls. And Mamma cries.

"Jazz . . . y. Jazz . . . Jazz . . . y!" My tongue is thick as I thrash back and forth in bed. I pull at the tangled sheets, tying me down. I try to kick them off, but to no avail. Then I bolt upright—Beethoven's sonata ringing in my ears. I cover my face with my hands.

I gasp for breath. "Oh . . . oh, no. No. Please, not again. Never again."

My temples still pound.

The nightmare has haunted me off and on for almost forty years. Since that fateful day when my mamma asked me to watch my little sister while she went next door to take a cake to the neighbors.

She'd stayed and visited a bit.

I was fifteen. Jazzy was eight.

One minute she was skipping rope in the backyard. The next minute, she was hanging, dead, from the climbing tree.

An unfortunate accident.

That's what the authorities said. Mamma said it was God's sovereign will. And later, days and even years later, Mamma would say, "Jazzy's jumpin' rope with Jesus now." Then she'd shake her head. "Good Lord, I can't wait to see that," she'd say to the ceiling.

My aunt Athena, an accomplished pianist, played Sonata for Piano No. 12 in A-flat, by Ludwig van Beethoven, at Jazzy's funeral. I've not listened to Beethoven since, at least not by choice.

I lean forward and untwist the sheet from around my legs. I get out of bed and go straight to the steam shower. I turn the water as hot as it will go and set the steam temperature to 115 degrees. I drop my nightgown on the floor and step into the shower. I will, as I have so many times before, attempt to wash the memories away.

For several years, the nightmare stopped. As part of the requirements for my degrees, I had to go through my own extensive therapy. I worked through my feelings of responsibility for Jazzy's death. And my grief.

But then . . . the twins were born.

Being responsible for the girls' little lives overwhelmed me. And the nightmare returned.

Needless to say, I never allowed the girls to learn how to jump rope. And it wasn't until they left for college, when they weren't under my roof, or my control—or at least, my sense of control—that the fear subsided.

A bit.

Then Ashley hung herself from one of the pull-up bars on her high-school campus. Another girl I was supposed to watch . . .

Dead.

I reach for the shampoo, lather it into the little hair I have. As I do, I breathe in hot, almost scorching, steam.

I let burning, pulsating water batter me.

I punish my body.

As I punish my soul.

AFTER I SHOWER, I sit in front of the fireplace with a cup of coffee. The emotions of the nightmare lead me to reflection. I recognize there is a dichotomy between what I say I believe, or don't believe, and what's intrinsic to who I am.

God, who I cease to believe exists, is always a part of the nightmare. A part of Jazzy's death. I recognize His presence, though I construe it as negative. All the times I've woken from that same nightmare, I've never analyzed it. I've never given conscious thought to God and His role in the dream. Until now. I'm certain, as Ellyn pointed out, it's because I'm surrounded by believers. Happenstance, though Ellyn asserts otherwise. But with all the God-talk going on around me, it's no wonder I'm more aware now of God's role in the nightmare. I beg Him, plead with Him . . . all to no avail.

But it's more than that. Like it or not, God is woven into my being. He is present in my earliest recollections. Mama made sure of that. And there was a time, before Jazzy, that I loved Jesus. Or thought I did.

When I went through those years of required therapy, I vented my anger. I decided then that not only did I not believe in God, but that He in fact, does not exist. So what, now I'm saying I believe He exists, but it's impossible to know Him? Agnosticism versus atheism? Semantics, really. Of course, there are those who'd argue otherwise, but in the scheme of things, what difference does it make?

The Bible is clear: there is one way—and only one—to eternal salvation and relationship with God—through belief in Jesus, as part of the divine Trinity, belief in His death on the cross and His resurrection.

Oh, Ellyn was right, I was raised in church. I may refuse to acknowledge God, but I'm familiar with the teachings of the Bible. Those early lessons taught in Sunday school stayed with me.

I set my mug down, stand up, and pace the living room. I stop in front of the entertainment cabinet and turn on my iPod. A little Bach will soothe me. With Yo-Yo Ma manipulating the strings of his cello in the background, I turn toward the windows.

The blinds remain drawn.

I walk to the window in front of the leather chairs and reach for the cord, then pull up the blind. I will prove Ellyn and her theory wrong. I stand at the window and focus my gaze on the large cypress tree across the street.

It's a tree. So what? It's supposed to prove God's existence? Then a raven takes flight from somewhere deep within the branches. It flits around the tree and then lands on a branch at the very top. It sits facing me.

Staring at me.

Mocking me.

That is all the proof I need.

There is no reliable security except in You.

SAINT AUGUSTINE

CHAPTER FORTY-FOUR

Ellyn

I SLIP OUT OF my pajamas and step onto the scale. For once, I'm looking forward to seeing the number. After living on vegetables and odd sources of protein, the number can only be lower. But when I look down, my countenance drops.

The number is the same.

The same as it was last week.

And the week before.

Get used to it. You're a failure at weight loss, you know that.

I roll my eyes. "Yeah, yeah. I've heard it all before, Earl. Get some new material."

I look down at the scale again. While Earl's snide comments don't wound like they used to, I still can't believe what the scale says. I've made major changes in my diet, cut out everything good, how is it possible I haven't lost even a pound? How? I step off the scale . . .

And then kick it.

"Ouch!" Not a good move with bare feet.

Pajamas back on, I walk out of the bathroom, slamming the door behind me, and head downstairs to the kitchen. Just as I get there, the phone rings.

"Hello?"

"Did Miles save you from the rat?"

That's Sabina's greeting. I sigh. "Yes, as a matter of fact, he did."

"You're still irritated that you needed a man, aren't you?"

"Oh, hush. How are you?"

"I'm good. Are we walking this morning?"

"If we have to."

"Your enthusiasm is overwhelming."

"I'd rather sit, drink coffee, and eat buttery croissants."

"Wouldn't we all?" She laughs. "Same time, same place?"

"Sure. Well . . ." Wait a minute. "I'd really prefer walking on the headlands today. I could use a good dose of sea air. If you want to join me, great. If not, that's fine too."

She hesitates. "O . . . kay. You don't think it's too cold out there?"

"Have you looked outside? The sun is shining. It's gorgeous. Wear one of those designer workout jackets of yours. You'll be fine."

"Where do you want to meet?"

"I'll park in the lot by the cypress grove, just down from Hesser and Lansing. See you there in thirty minutes."

"Fine."

I hang up the phone. *Oh Lord, open her eyes. Give her eyes to see You.*

I'm in no mood to exert myself, or drink pond sludge, or eat a breakfast better suited for a squirrel. I look at the nut mixture in a container on my countertop. I sigh again and glance at the hot cereal I made before I went upstairs to weigh myself. I spoon a serving of the steel-cut oatmeal from the pan on the range into a bowl. It looks no more appealing in the bowl than it did in the pan. I sprinkle a handful of the nut mixture onto the cooked oats.

I shake my head. "I am so over veganism."

Of course you are. You're a woman, not a rabbit. You need real food. You deserve it.

"Why thank you, Earl. I agree." But even as I agree with Earl, something nags at me. Is it the tone of the voice I hear in my head? Or the words themselves that bother me? I cock my head to one side, like a dog who's heard a familiar voice. "Huh . . ."

Something about Earl is different. Or . . .

Maybe it's me who's different.

Changing.

I'm not sure.

I reach into the freezer and take out the pound of butter that I couldn't bear throwing away when I ventured into my little vegan experiment. I put a cube of the butter into the microwave for a few seconds. Then I pop two pieces of cinnamon swirl bread, also from the freezer, into the toaster. As I wait for the bread to toast, I attempt to ignore the red flag waving in my brain.

Agreeing with Earl, I've learned, is never wise. But just this once can't hurt. Right? I'll get back on track tomorrow.

I take the toast out of the toaster, slather it in butter, and take a breathless bite, like a woman about to receive a long-anticipated kiss. Mmm . . . heaven. Nothing has tasted this good since . . .

I sigh. Miles's kiss.

I pull a paper towel off the roll and set the piece of toast on it.

It's not often I'm shocked by my own thoughts, but I feel my face go pink . . . I'm caught off-guard by what just went through my mind—and heart.

Miles's kiss.

So tender.

Gentle.

And safe.

S.A.F.E.

In an alluring, exciting, and adventurous sort of way.

"Get hold of yourself, Ellyn." I walk away from the toast—no longer interested in what it offers.

Or doesn't offer.

I pad my way back upstairs to brush my teeth, wash my face, and dress for our walk. I give the scale dirty looks each time I pass it.

Then I recall something Twila said about the scale that makes a lot of sense this morning, so before I go back downstairs, I pick up the scale from the bathroom floor and carry it down with me. I set it on the counter in the mudroom until I'm ready to go.

I go back to the kitchen, throw the now-cold oatmeal out, and do up the dishes. Then I fill my aluminum water bottle, cap it, and stand it up in my purse. I grab my car keys, and go back to the mudroom and pick up the scale.

Once in the driveway, I leave my purse and water bottle in the car and then walk to the end of the gravel drive. I lift the scale above my head and throw it, as hard as I can, onto the asphalt street. It makes a satisfying crunching sound—like a car wreck—as it lands. Metal and plastic parts fly in opposite directions.

There! Take that!

I retrieve the pieces of the scale, large and small, from the street and put them into the garbage can. Then, smiling, I leave to meet Sabina.

BY THE TIME I reach the cypress grove, I'm several minutes late. I pull into the lot and park next to Sabina's BMW. She's sitting in the car, head down, looking at something. Of course, she wouldn't get out of the car and enjoy the fresh air and scenery.

I get out of my car and walk to the driver's-side door of her car and tap on the window. She jumps. Then she opens the door. I see she's holding her cell phone.

"Oops, sorry. I didn't mean to startle you."

"That's okay. I didn't see you. Solitaire." She holds up her phone and I see tiny playing cards lined up on the screen.

She gets out of the car and gives me a hug. "How are you?"

I smile. "Well, I just smashed my scale into multiple pieces. So, I'd say, I'm better than usual."

Sabina smiles, her eyes shine in the morning sun. She holds up one hand. "High five, girl."

I slap her hand.

"What precipitated that act of emotional health?"

"Emotional health? Ha! It was *precipitated* by frustration and distress."

"Well, taking out your frustration on an inanimate object isn't always bad—especially, if, as I guess is the case, that object was the source of your frustration."

"It was. C'mon, let's go."

"I'll follow you."

"Have you seen the cathedral?"

"Do you never stop talking about church and God?"

I ignore her quip. I take the trail toward the restrooms and then veer to the left and follow the trail into the middle of the grove of trees, which opens up onto a wide clearing. The old-growth trees surrounding the clearing form a canopy high overhead. "This is what is known as the cathedral. It's a favorite place for local and destination weddings."

Sabina takes a quick look around. "Nice."

"Nice?"

She nods. "Ready to walk?"

"Wait. Look out there. Isn't that incredible?" I point to the picnic table at the end of the clearing, where it opens onto the cliff overlooking the ragged coastline.

"Beautiful. Can we go? I'm cold. I need to move."

My heart is heavy for her. *Lord, she refuses to see You.* "You need some body fat to keep you warm. I'm happy to share."

"Very funny."

"I thought so."

We make our way back to the parking lot and then to the street. I keep to the street rather than taking one of the many trails out toward the cliffs. I'm grateful to walk out here this morning—I won't push Sabina any further. We fall into a companionable stride, which is unusual. "You're taking it slow this morning."

"I want to hear what happened with the rat. It's nice to talk when we walk too."

Talking probably keeps her from noticing the grandeur of her surroundings. I don't know if that's intentional on her part or not, but I welcome the chance to talk this morning and take the walk at a slower pace.

"I'll tell you about the rat, but may I ask you a question first?" She raises her eyebrows. "Sure."

"Do you think I . . . sabotaged my friendship with Miles?" Her pace slows and she looks at me. "I'm not sure. It's possible."

I look out at the morning sun gleaming on the water and consider the thought that occurred to me earlier. "I think maybe I did. Not intentionally, but maybe out of habit, or something. Rosa says I'm terrified of becoming involved with a man."

Sabina stops walking. "Is she right?"

"I don't know. I may be. It just never seemed like an option for me."

"Why?"

"Are we going to walk or just stand here?" I take off at a clip this time, although it isn't like I can outwalk Sabina's long stride.

"Why doesn't it seem like an option for you? I want to understand."

"I'll tell you what, when I understand it, I'll fill you in."

"Ellyn, have you considered talking with a counselor? Talking things through with someone experienced could help you understand."

Sabina walks a few paces beyond me before she realizes I've stopped again. "A counselor? *You're* a counselor."

"Yes, I am. I was. But not yours. I'm your friend."

"What's the difference?"

"The difference is that I'm not doing therapy with you. We have a mutual give-and-take friendship. It's just different."

"Oh. No, I haven't considered a counselor. It's not that big a deal."

"Girl, it's *your life.* How is that not a big deal?"

The same reverent fear or awe I felt the morning after my hospitalization returns. *Lord?* My life, in my mind, never meant much. I'm grateful for life, but most often it seems I've failed the exams. Haven't passed some elusive course where others excelled. My life isn't a big deal because I am a disappointment to God, or so I've let myself believe.

"Huh, I've never thought of it that way." I take a few steps and Sabina falls in stride with me again. "I'll think about it. Okay?"

"Whatever you decide. It was just a suggestion."

"So do you want to hear about the rat now?"

She laughs. "I thought you'd never ask."

Look into my heart, my God, look within. See this, I remember it, my hope; for you cleanse me from these flawed emotions. You direct my eyes towards you and "rescue my feet from the trap."

CHAPTER FORTY-FIVE

Sabina

I RETURN TO THE rental after my walk with Ellyn and make myself a cup of coffee. As I wait for it to brew, a mental image of the cypress grove returns—bringing with it the question I asked of myself soon after arriving here: *Will I allow the winds of suffering to form and shape me as it does the cypress trees? Or will I break under the battering?*

Didn't I answer that question for myself that evening at Ellyn's, after the realization that I'd lost myself to fear and guilt? Didn't I determine then that it was time to work at healing?

But then came the nightmare . . . and a new measure of guilt. And with it, I toppled, like one of the dead trees I noticed lying in the grove today. Or, I think I noticed. I can see the grove in my mind, but there are no trunks or logs.

Maybe I made them up.

Not that it matters.

Restless, I walk out to the living room. Another entire afternoon and evening lie ahead of me, and I have nothing to do. My self-imposed exile is becoming wearisome. I miss the activity of a purposeful life. It is the first time I've acknowledged this since arriving in Mendocino. Perhaps the antidepressants are finally doing their job.

And the exercise. And the friendship with Ellyn. I know she is a significant part of why I'm feeling better—especially today. I would never jeopardize our friendship by attempting to analyze her or drifting into a therapeutic relationship with her. The boundaries are clear. Yet, I see her processing—beginning to look at her life and wonder about the choices she's made—and it stirs the counselor within me.

I loved what I did.

I'd made something of myself.

I wander to the bookshelf in the hallway and choose one of the owners' books to read. Before sitting in one of the leather chairs in the living room, I open all of the blinds in the living and dining areas. The chairs are still turned inward, away from the view, but the sunlight streaming into the house makes for a lighter atmosphere.

I've wallowed in guilt and grief for too long. It's time to push myself to make some changes.

I open the novel and read the prologue, but my mind doesn't focus. I read the pages more than once, but to no avail. The words on the pages can't keep my mind from the cypress grove. I set the book aside and stand, going to the window behind the chairs to look out. The large tree that the ravens favor is just across the street, and beyond the tree is the water. This is the first time I've really looked at the view. The swirling expanse is so close—so vast. There's something almost frightening about the power of it.

I leave the window and open the door off the dining area that leads to an outside deck. I haven't stepped out here since I arrived. I walk to the edge of the deck, which is dappled with sunlight. I close my eyes, lift my face, and feel the warmth of the sun and the gentle sea breeze on my skin. I breathe deep of the salty air.

I open my eyes and lean a bit, looking for the grove. Can I see it from here? Yes.

The cluster of large trees is a dark silhouette against the sunny backdrop.

Why does the grove call to me?

I shake my head. *Call to me?* Ridiculous.

I go back inside, turn on some music, and pick up the book again—

And spend the next thirty or so minutes staring at the same page.

I PULL INTO THE spot where I parked this morning. *What am I doing?* I have no idea. I only know that I had to come—felt compelled to come. I wipe my damp palms on the pants of the same workout outfit I was wearing when I met Ellyn earlier.

Am I here because I have a point to prove to Ellyn? And perhaps to myself? Maybe. But there's something deeper that I can't pinpoint. I open the car door and get out.

Let's get this over with.

I walk the trail cut through the prairie grass leading into the grove. It's a short walk from the parking lot, but before even entering the grove, I see what my subconscious registered earlier when I was working so hard to ignore my surroundings. Several fallen cypress lie on the ground—trunks bare of bark and white-washed by the sun. They've fallen away from the others that make up the grove. I stop and look at one of the trunks on the ground—the outside is smooth, beautiful. But the inside, where the tree broke, is rotted, hollowed.

The tree died from the inside out.

The thought resonates.

A recollection surfaces of one of the twins, home from college for a few days, talking about the Monterey Cypress trees that dot the California coastal regions. Since earning a degree in arboriculture, Shauna's always talking about tree diseases and the like. I have no reference for, nor interest in, much of what she tells me, so I don't retain it. But the counselor in me related to the thought of dying from the inside out. It's what so many people do, if not in a literal sense, then a figurative one.

It is what I'm doing.

Or have done?

I've been losing myself, dying bit by bit as a person, as a professional, by wallowing in guilt. But it's more than that.

I'm dying an eternal death.

My person, my soul, who I was—I swallow—*created* to be.

Imago Dei.

I was created in the image of God, for God. As Twila put it, for relationship with Him. By rejecting God—rejecting Jesus—I've condemned myself.

For eternity.

And I've missed my life purpose.

I recoil at the thought. My life has been *filled* with purpose. I healed people.

No, Sabina. I healed them.

The thought is not my own.

A shiver runs up my spine and the hairs on the back of my neck stand at attention.

Miles's words in the ER, his answer when I asked if he blamed himself when his wife died, return to me now.

"To blame myself would mean that I consider myself on the same plane as God. That I see myself as omnipotent. God is the only One who holds life and death in His grasp."

I leave the dead trees and walk a few more paces into the edge of the grove—the clearing Ellyn called the cathedral.

A breeze rustles the foliage of the cypress trees, far overhead.

These trees . . .

Move.

Breathe.

Live.

The surf crashes on jagged rocks below the cliffs. The sound I've worked so hard to ignore since my arrival here. The irritant that, for a moment in time, turned to serenade on Ellyn's balcony.

I walk into the center of the clearing, though it feels more like I'm pushed there.

I am not alone. A recognition that, oddly enough, brings peace rather than fear. I have been, I know now, called here.

Summoned.

I look up at the canopy of branches—shafts of sunlight filter in through the foliage, the breeze sends patches of sunlight dancing on the earthen floor. I stand in one of the patches of light and watch as the breeze stills and one shaft of light from above seems to encircle me.

My heart swells.

I smile. It's as though Mozart's "Magic Flute" is the song of the surf as joy fills my empty soul. I turn in a slow circle, arms out, face upturned. The scents of salt, seaweed, and the pungent aroma of cedar waft around me. Somewhere deep within I know that what's taking place in my spirit has little to do with me.

God, yes, *God,* the creator of the universe, of the magnificence surrounding me, has called me to Himself. Ellyn was right. I couldn't see His creation, *can't* see His creation, without seeing Him. I was, I am, without excuse.

I will resist no longer.

I can resist no longer.

He invades my opening soul.

The months, maybe years, of anger—my fist clenched and shaking in the face of God, and then the years spent denying His existence—melt away as I glimpse, for the first time, His mercy and grace—an inkling of more to come. So much more.

I pull my arms in and cross them over my chest, and my eyes close. I am awash in the wind, in the very breath of the Creator. It embraces me, caresses my cheek like a Father calming a frightened babe.

Shame is no more.

Guilt is replaced by grace.

"Yes, Lord. Yes." I whisper my surrender into the breeze as it stirs again. And then I hear my mamma's sweet soprano in my mind, singing the words of her favorite hymn:

"Come home, come home,
"Ye who are weary, come home;
"Earnestly, tenderly, Jesus is calling,
"Calling, O sinner, come home!"

Mamma said the hymn was sung at Martin Luther King's memorial service back home. She said Jesus had called Martin home to rest. Just like years later she'd say Jesus had called Jazzy home. The song, I see now, was her comfort.

Today, God has called me home. Not to eternity—not yet—but home to His lap, where my mother prayed I'd stay for all my years. Instead, I wandered. But today . . .

I've come home.

I walk out to the end of the clearing, to the picnic table that seems to hang on the edge of the cliff. I sit on the bench nearest the water and let the wind wash over me. As it does, tears come. I don't stop them, as I've done for so long. Tears for Jazzy, and for Ashley. Tears for my mamma. Cleansing tears mixed with tears of gratitude.

I sit for hours watching the constant motion of the sea and wiping away tears now and then. The seascape changes moment by moment—the surf rolls in, crashes, and then returns from whence it came. Over and over. As constant and dependable as the love of God. As the sun moves lower in the sky, the water changes from aqua to sea foam to a dark gray-blue. Finally, as the sun drops to the horizon, the water reflects back the colors of the sky—the brilliant orange and peach and lavender of a perfect sunset.

I've grown cold, but I can't take my eyes off the display in front of me. I've missed so much. The time has come to pick up the threads of my life, to reengage, to complete the work with a counselor that I began so long ago. But this time, I will leave nothing to chance. It is time to return to the roles I've known: wife, mother, and perhaps, one day, counselor.

But first, I will live my purpose. The purpose Twila spoke of . . . I will engage, fully, in a relationship with God. I will get to know Him. I will rest in, or at least try to rest in, the role my mama claimed for herself and her girls: daughter of the King.

I breathe contentment out on a sigh, and then reach into the pocket of my sweatshirt jacket and take out my cell phone. There are few places in the area where I have cell coverage, but maybe here, on the edge of the world, I can make a call. I turn on the phone, see a few bars, and then dial.

Antwone answers after the first ring.

"Sabina?"

When I hear his deep baritone, the tears begin again. "Hi, baby."

"Are you all right?"

I nod and choke back a sob. "I'm . . . better than all right. Really. I've . . . I've come home, baby. God brought me back. To Himself." What I was so certain of just moments ago now feels foolish when I hear myself say it out loud. "Antwone?"

"I'm here."

"Do I . . . sound crazy?" I look around me—the evidence remains. God is who He says He is. I am not crazy.

"No, baby. You sound"—he clears his throat—"good. You sound good."

A hush comes between us—a silence of reverence—a oneness we've not experienced together, ever. Yet, it also feels familiar.

It is the Spirit within us, connecting us.

I close my eyes. "I want to see you—I want you to come here. There's so . . . much. So much to say, so much time to make up for. I want to experience this"—I make a sweeping gesture with one arm—"with you. I want to experience God, with you."

"I'll come soon. Soon, Sabina. I have some things to take care of, and then I'll come. But baby, now, while you're alone, He wants you to Himself. Okay?"

"Yes, I understand." My words are hurried, breathless. As strong as my desire was for Antwone's presence, just moments ago, my desire, my hunger now is for God.

And Him alone.

There are also acts which resemble a vicious or injurious act but are not sins, because they do not offend you, Lord our God . . .

SAINT AUGUSTINE

CHAPTER FORTY-SIX

Twila

I LOVE EARLY MORNINGS in the store, before the doors open and customers arrive. I wander the aisles making sure the shelves are stocked and check the refrigerator cases one last time. I hang out in the produce section for a few minutes just looking at the colors and textures of the fruits and vegetables. I'm always awed by the way God packed so many nutrients into the coolest colors and shapes.

It isn't my usual day to work, but I covered for Anna this morning, who had a dental appointment. Because Corners of the Mouth is a co-op, we're all part owners of the store. Most of the proceeds go back into the store and the community. We're also like family. This may seem like a small job to some, but, like, for me, it has meaning. I'm contributing to something important.

The time here helps me forget the other stuff going on in life right now—like my dad. He's been here several days, but I still don't get why. After spending some time with Miles, talking to my mom, and my counselor, I'm feeling sort of better and eating a little bit. I still have to work through my feelings though . . . and talk to my dad. But for now, while I'm here, it's sort of like a reprieve. When Anna comes in, I'll have to get back to the rest of my life.

I SIT ACROSS THE kitchen table from my dad, who seems uncomfortable. "Where's your mother?"

"She's around."

My counselor suggested I have this conversation someplace where I feel safe. Not because she thinks my dad will flip, but because I'll feel, like, more confident or in control if we meet on my terms. So when he called and asked me to go to lunch with him, I said no. When he said he wanted to see me, I told him he'd have to come here.

I could tell he didn't like that. But for some reason he came anyway.

"So let's go somewhere. Do something." He moves to stand.

"No, wait. I want to ask you something." He settles back in his seat but I can hear his foot tapping against the wood floor. "Why are you here?"

He looks at me like I'm stupid. "Because you didn't want to go to lunch and said to come—"

"No. Why are you in Mendocino? Why did you come here?"

"To see you. Believe me, there's nothing else to do here."

I sit up straighter. "You never cared about seeing me before."

"Listen, Twila, I may not win any father-of-the-year awards, but I've always provided for you, and provided well. You can't deny that. But my life took a different turn. After I remarried, I had other responsibilities."

"And now?"

He's quiet for a moment and then he smiles. His gray eyes shine. For a moment I see the daddy whose love I clamored for. The "charmer," as I've heard my mother call him.

"I was going to wait to tell you this, wait until we'd spent more time together, but since you're pushing me, I'll tell you now. I have a business opportunity, the one I've worked my whole life for—it's finally come through—and I want you to come with me to New York. You can leave Hippyville behind and get a taste of the real world. It's time you begin acting like the adult you are, Twila. I'll set you up in your own place, an apartment near my penthouse. In turn, you can help me—act as hostess when I have business dinners or associates over for drinks. You can take care of things for me. It's a generous offer, and you certainly don't have anything going on here."

I try to ignore his barbs and focus on the point. "But why? Can't your wife do that?"

He shrugs. "I'm not taking her with me. I filed for divorce last month."

I ball my hands into fists under the table. "What about your kids?"

"They'll be fine."

"Just like I was fine?"

"You're great. Look at you."

Tears fill my eyes. "You . . . don't know. You don't know what I . . . went through."

"C'mon. It's all in the past. We can start fresh. Share an adventure together."

I shake my head. The charm he exudes is replaced by manipulation.

"Twila." His voice is firm now. "I've supported you all these years—made sure you had everything you needed. The best schools, medical care, whatever you needed. Now it's your chance to support me."

I choke back my tears and ask the question I've wanted to ask since I was a child. "Do you . . . love me?"

His foot starts tapping under the table again. He blows out a breath through his teeth. "Of course I love you, I'm your father. Now, why don't you go pack a bag and we can send for the rest of your things later. Now that you know the plan, there's no reason to hang around here any longer."

As I've watched him and listened to him, my stomach has clenched and unclenched over and over. Bile rises in my throat. I take a deep breath, praying I won't be sick right here, right now.

"No." I take another breath. "I won't go." Then I speak the truth I've always known but denied. "You don't love me. You never have." Tears blur my vision again. "But for some reason, now you need me, or think you need me. It's never been about me. Like, all you can see, all you can love, is yourself." As I speak and accept the truth, my stomach relaxes. "You . . . starved me. I was so hungry for your—"

"Listen, young lady, I don't need your—"

"No! *You* listen." I stand up. "I was so hungry for your love. I just wanted to please you, to make you love me. But now . . . now I get it. You won't . . . you won't ever love anyone but yourself."

His face reddens and I see the vein in his neck throb.

"Twila?"

I turn and see my mom standing in the opening between the kitchen and living room.

"I'm okay." I turn back to my father. "I want you to leave now. I don't want to see you and I don't want your money. I can support myself. Please, just go." Tears stream down my face. I sniff and point to the back door. "Go."

He stands and looks at my mother. "Nerissa, are you going to talk some sense into her? I make her a generous offer and this is how she acts?"

My mom steps into the kitchen. "I believe she asked you to leave. Please go."

He shakes his head. "You two are a pair. You've made a big mistake, Twila."

His eyes, steel now, bore through me. But I stand still, firm. I have some of his steel in me too and I will use it now. I will stand strong. No, I take that back. I have nothing of him in me except his chromosomes. It's my heavenly Father's strength that sustains me. "If you don't leave now, I will call 911 and tell them I've asked you to leave and you won't. Go!" I point to the door again.

He hesitates just a few seconds longer, then he slams his hand against the kitchen chair, shoving it into the table. The metal chair hits the edge of the old metal and Formica table and sends it skipping against the floor.

I jump at the clamor.

Then . . . he turns and walks out.

It's not the first time he's walked out on me. But it will be the last.

I have forgiven him and I will forgive him again. But I won't allow him to use me or mistreat me.

Or the Spirit within me.

I know who I am.

As the back door slams, I let out my breath and wipe the tears from my cheeks with the back of my hand. Then I feel my mother's arms around me—hugging me—loving me.

"I'm so sorry," she whispers. "And I'm so proud of you. So proud of your strength, and dignity, and self-respect."

I lean into her. "I know who I am. You taught me." I pull back from her and lift up my arm so she can see the words forever inked on my wrist.

"Yes, you reflect His image for all to see." She pulls me close again. "Twila, I'm so proud of who you are—of who you've become. I love you so much."

I quiet in her arms. The tears stop and peace engulfs me. As she continues to hug me, my stomach rumbles.

She leans back. "Was that your stomach growling?"

I giggle. "Yeah, I'm hungry. Like really hungry."

She pats me on the back and wipes the tears from her own cheeks. "Well, that's good news. What would you like? Anything. Name it and I'll make it."

My mouth begins to water at the thought of eating something delicious. But not just eating it . . .

Maybe even enjoying it.

There are no caresses tenderer than your charity,
and no object of love is more healthy than your truth,
beautiful and luminous beyond all things.

SAINT AUGUSTINE

CHAPTER FORTY-SEVEN

Miles

I HAVEN'T SEEN OR spoken to Ellyn since helping her with the dead rat last Sunday. I thought earlier today of calling to say hello, but just as I did on Sunday when she offered to make breakfast for me and invited me to stay for lunch with her staff, I know I need to set and maintain some boundaries with her for my own emotional well-being.

That doesn't mean I won't continue our friendship, just that I need to also care for myself in the process. I will be intentional in seeking God. I am willing to sacrifice myself, my heart, if that's how He leads—but I must know it's His leading.

Instead, I pick up the phone and call Nerissa and ask her if she'd like to meet for lunch. "I'll come your way. I have a light caseload today. How about Mendocino Café at noon?"

"Sounds lovely. Perfect timing too."

"Why's that?"

"I have something I want to share with you."

"Great. I'll see you soon, gal." I hang up the phone and thank God again for Nerissa. I also resolve that it's time to find a golfing buddy—before spring if possible.

I arrive at the café a few minutes early and decide I'll get a table and have a cup of coffee while I wait. I'm shown to a corner table and sit with my back to the window so I can see Nerissa when she comes in. I look at the menu, though I already know what I'll order. Then I hear a familiar sound.

Laughter.

Ellyn's.

I look around until I see her. She sits with her back to me—across the table from her is Sabina. I watch their animated conversation for a moment, then get up from the table and walk toward them.

No reason not to say hello to two friends.

Ellyn

"Thanks for meeting me spur of the moment." Sabina takes a sip of the water the waiter placed in front of her.

"Spur of the moment seems like our best plan. So what's up? I'm as curious as a cat. And you look like you swallowed the canary."

Sabina's eyes shine and I see something new there—something I don't recognize.

"Who came up with that saying? Do you ever wonder who created some of the idioms we use?"

I don't take my eyes from her face. "No, I don't. Would you please tell me what's going on with you."

She leans back. She seems so relaxed. "Okay. Well, first I want to apologize. You were right about something—"

"Whoa, hold on. Let me just savor this moment. You're apologizing *and* saying I was right about something? This is too good." I let out an exaggerated sigh and then wait several seconds. "Okay, go ahead."

Sabina raises one of her perfectly tweezed eyebrows. "You better savor the moment because this isn't likely to ever happen again. You know I'm rarely wrong."

"Okay, c'mon. Give it to me. What was I right about?"

She's quiet for a moment. "You were right about the view."

Her voice has dropped to almost a whisper and I lean forward to hear her. "The view? I was right about the view?"

"Yes."

"That you avoid it?" This conversation is no longer a laughing matter.

"I did."

"You did. But . . . you don't anymore?" Then it strikes me. What I see in her eyes, the expression on her face.

Peace.

For the first time since I met her, she is at peace.

"Sabina, what *happened*?"

Just as she opens her mouth to tell me, I feel a presence next to me. I look up—and my heart leaps.

Miles. He's standing right beside me.

And I'm almost knocked over by how happy I am to see him. "Miles! Hello."

Miles

When Ellyn turns and looks at me she is unguarded. Her face radiates pleasure. Is she happy to see me? Or is it the conversation I've interrupted that's made her so happy? But the gasp she let out when she saw me and the way she said my name . . . I want to believe the reactions are to me. But the hand of caution seems to hold me back. *Take it slow, Miles.* "Looks like great minds think alike."

Ellyn's smile is open and genuine. "Looks like it. Can you join us?"

"Please, join us, Doctor." Sabina reaches over and pulls out a chair from their table.

"Thank you, but I don't want to interrupt your conversation. I'm meeting Nerissa."

"Oh."

Is that disappointment I hear in Ellyn's tone?

"Well, thank you again for your help on Sunday. I still can't believe I couldn't take care of it myself. And thank you for patching up the wall too. You went above and beyond, Miles."

She puts her hand on my arm as she speaks.

"Anytime. You know I'm available if you need anything."

"I'd love to repay you in some way."

I hold up my hand. "Not necessary." Ellyn takes her hand off my arm and glances at the floor, then looks back at Sabina. Did my refusal hurt her? Or am I imagining her disappointment? Wistful thinking? Confusion settles in.

Ellyn looks back up at me. "Well, thank you. I really did appreciate it." But the happiness I read on her face earlier is gone now.

I put my hand on Ellyn's shoulder, but as natural as it seems for me to touch her, I feel her tense. "I just wanted to say hello, I'll let you get back to your lunch. Good to see you again, Dr. Jackson." I smile at Sabina.

"Nice to see you too, Dr. Becker."

Ellyn raises her eyebrows at our exchange, maybe sensing that Sabina and I know one another better than she realized. Who knows what she's thinking? I sure don't.

"Enjoy your lunch." I walk back to my table, trying not to let my tangled emotions frustrate me.

Why didn't I chose another restaurant?

As soon as I'm seated again, I see Nerissa come in. I wave and she sees me. Then she sees Ellyn. She stops at their table, and I watch as Ellyn introduces Nerissa to Sabina. They all chat for a few minutes, then Nerissa makes her way to where I'm sitting.

"Hello, my friend."

I stand and greet her with a brief hug. "Sit here." I motion to the chair where I was sitting. I'd rather have my back to Ellyn.

We settle in and Nerissa pushes the menu aside and then looks across the table at me. "How are you, Miles?" Her question is sincere, not a pleasantry.

I put my hands, palms down, on the table. "Well, I'm okay. I've been better and I've been worse. How about you?"

"I'm fine. You're okay here? With Ellyn?"

I lift my hands from the table and reach for the napkin next to my plate. "Sure. I can't say seeing her doesn't affect me, but I'm committed to remaining her friend. I went over and said hello when I saw them here."

"She looks well. She hasn't had any problems since her hospitalization?"

"She does look well and no, I saw her briefly on Sunday and she's fine."

The look of concern remains in Nerissa's eyes. She hesitates. "Well . . . good. I'm glad she's okay. But it's you I'm worried about."

I wave off her concern as the waiter comes and takes our orders. I order the steak and Brie melt on a French roll—a favorite when I'm here for lunch. Nerissa orders her usual—the Healing Bowl, soba noodles in miso broth with kale, mushrooms, and tofu. I'm glad that, unlike the Green Giant—that ghastly green juice she claims to like—she's never asked me to try the Healing Bowl.

"You said you had something to tell me?"

Nerissa unwraps her flatware from the linen napkin and places the napkin on her lap. "Yes, it's about Twila."

"Is she okay?"

Her eyes crease at the corners as she grins. "Yes. Better than okay. I asked her if I could tell you and she said to go ahead. You know her father was here—"

"Was? He's gone?"

"Yes!"

"Good."

"He's gone because Twila told him to leave. She confronted him, and it was such a step of healing for her. Oh, Miles, it was so good for her."

Nerissa fills me in on the details including Twila's renewed appetite.

"She's an amazing little gal."

"She really is, Miles. I can't help but think God will use her in powerful ways."

"No doubt."

The waiter brings the iced herbal tea Nerissa ordered.

"Thank you for the time you've spent with her."

"No need to thank me. I care for her. And I enjoy her. I was concerned when I saw her on Sunday. Good to know she's doing better. How about you?"

As Nerissa and I catch up, I start to relax. This is good. Conversation with a friend, but without any underlying currents and confusion. And I am so happy for Twila.

But as I listen to Nerissa talk, one thought nags at the back of my mind . . .

I'd rather have currents and confusion with Ellyn than a calm conversation with anyone else.

Indeed, Lord, to your eyes, the abyss
of human consciousness is naked.

SAINT AUGUSTINE

CHAPTER FORTY-EIGHT

Ellyn

"THAT WAS NICE OF Miles, to stop by and say hello."

I look at Sabina, refusing to take the bait. "What was with all the *doctor* talk?"

"It has to do with what I'm going to tell you."

"Well, get to it! So you're no longer avoiding the view . . ."

"Right. I went back to the cypress grove after our walk the other day. I felt drawn there—pulled there." She shakes her head. "I felt like there was something I needed to see or figure out or . . . Anyway, I went back and while I was there, I realized you were right. I have avoided things. Everything." She makes a sweeping gesture with one hand. "The view from the house, the headlands, the ocean, the trees . . . all of it. I couldn't . . . I couldn't take it in and ignore God at the same time. I couldn't deny His existence when everything around me spoke of Him."

I swallow and tears prick my eyes. "Oh."

"When you were in the ER, I was afraid"—she looks down at the table and then back up—"I was afraid I'd lose you too, and all the guilt I felt over Ashley's suicide and . . . my sister's death. It all came crashing in around me."

"Your sister?"

"Yes. Her name was Jazzy. She died when I was fifteen—while I was babysitting her. It was an . . . accident. A horrible accident. But I blamed myself."

"Oh, Sabina. I'm so sorry. I had no idea." As I express my grief for what Sabina's suffered, I see her in a different way. Instead of saccharine, she's sugar. Instead of whipped topping, she's heavy cream. Instead of margarine, honey, she is butter. She's *real*. And while my heart aches for her wounds, she finally makes sense to me.

"It's not something I . . . talk about much. But that day, when you were in the ER, I asked Miles if he blamed himself for his wife's death. And some of what he said impacted me. He spoke to me as one doctor to another and it helped me realize my arrogance in blaming myself for something only God has the power to control. So that afternoon, back at the cypress grove, I . . . surrendered. I acknowledged God—His presence and omnipotence. And I felt His forgiveness. His grace. And His love for me. Isn't that amazing?"

I just stare at Sabina for a moment and then the tears begin to flow. "I kept praying . . ." I sniff. "Praying that God would give you eyes to see Him. Yes, it's amazing—He's amazing."

"He answered your prayers, Ellyn. Thank you. Thank you so much for caring enough to pray for me and for speaking truth to me. You are a true friend."

I wave her compliment away. "I'm just so happy for you."

"Thank you. I would have called you that evening, but I spent a long time on the phone with Antwone. I needed to explain what I'd gone through, and to tell him what I'd discovered. I also needed to ask his forgiveness."

"How did that go?"

"He's an extraordinary man, Ellyn. Much too good for me. A gift, really. But I've been so busy all these years proving how good I am, that I didn't really take the time to appreciate what I have in him."

Regret permeates her tone.

"I'm just lucky, or blessed, that he's remained with me—stood by his commitment to our marriage. After I talked with him. I spent the rest of the night and the next two days getting reacquainted with God and His Word. There was a Bible on one of the shelves in the rental. I've just soaked in it—rested in the truths. It's all so meaningful now."

I swallow the lump in my throat, unable to say anything.

"What's wrong?" Sabina leans forward.

"Oh. Nothing. No, I'm just awed, really."

"But?"

I shrug. "Nothing."

"Ellyn . . ."

"I don't want to make this about me, it's just that . . . Does this mean you'll leave now? Go back home?" I wipe my eyes with the linen napkin.

She reaches across the table and takes my hand in hers.

"Oh, no. Not yet. I signed a one-year lease on the house. And I think this is where I'm supposed to be. I need friends. I need you, Ellyn. I need to spend time with people like you and Miles and Twila—people who walk with God."

"What about your husband?"

She gives my hand a squeeze, then lets go and leans back in her seat.

"Yes, I need him too. More than that, I *want* to spend time with him. He's coming here. He's taking this week to wrap some things up at work and then he's coming to stay through New Year's. After that, we'll see . . ."

I let out the breath I've held since it occurred to me she might leave. "Oh, I'm so glad. I'm not ready for you to go yet."

"Thank you, my friend. That means a lot to me."

I put my hand on my chest, across my heart. "Well, as much as we poke and prod at each other"—I grin at her—"you've sort of grown on me." I wink and then we laugh together.

When we've finished lunch and paid the bill, Sabina says she wants to tell Miles something. I start to follow her but then hear my name. I turn and see the owner of Mendocino Café. I wave at him and then turn back toward Miles's table. But when the owner calls my name again, I stop and turn back again. It's clear he wants to talk to me—to talk shop. I take a step toward the kitchen and then turn back and take a step toward the table where Sabina stands talking to Miles and Nerissa.

Miles is like a magnet.

And I'm a flimsy paperclip.

Oh. No. I'm in trouble.

I turn back and walk straight to the kitchen. Discussing produce vendors and new recipes is the safe bet.

Even though my heart years to, just this once, jump into unsafe. With both feet.

Miles

Just as I finish my sandwich, Sabina comes by our table.

"Dr. Becker, Miles . . ." She seems so much more at ease today. "I want to thank you for some things you shared with me during our conversation at the hospital. They proved significant."

"I'm glad."

Sabina glances at Nerissa and then looks back to me. "I've reestablished my relationship with God—I'm getting to know Him again. Between you and Ellyn and Twila"—she looks at Nerissa again—"well, He got my attention. Nerissa, you have an extraordinary daughter."

"Oh, Sabina, thank you."

"I'll let you get back to your lunch. I just wanted to say thank you."

I stand as she turns to go. "Doctor . . ." I put out my hand to shake hers. Once her hand is in mine, I grin and pull her into a hug. The joy I feel for her comes out in laughter as I tighten my arms around her. "Oh, Sabina, I'm so happy for you. You couldn't have shared any more wonderful news."

As she pulls away, Nerissa, who is now standing next to us, also gives Sabina a hug. "Have you told Twila?"

"No. Not yet. I've . . . I've just wanted time alone, with God. But I will tell her."

"Thank you for sharing your news, Sabina."

Sabina's face shines with a new radiance. "Thank you, both, for your warmth and acceptance. Now, I'll let you get on with your lunch."

As I turn to sit back down, Sabina stops and turns back toward me. "By the way, do you play golf?"

I chuckle. "I play as often as I can pick up a partner or join a foursome. Why?"

"My husband, Antwone, is taking some time off to come be with me. He's an avid golfer and would enjoy finding someone to play with."

"Great. There's a course in Little River and with our temperate weather, we can play year-round unless it's raining or too windy. I'd enjoy the company."

"Good. Nerissa, it was nice to see you."

"You too, Sabina."

I sit back down. "God is so good. He used something I said to impact Sabina, and He's provided a golf partner. At least temporarily."

"I don't think you realize, Miles, how often God uses you to touch others' lives. You're His faithful friend."

I look at Nerissa and swallow the emotions suddenly clogging my throat. "You could pay me no higher compliment."

"It isn't a compliment. It's truth."

Ellyn

By the time the owner and I finish our conversation, Sabina is waiting for me by the front door. I glance back at Miles and then follow Sabina out of the café. I stand at the curb with her and chat a few more minutes and then give her a hug.

"Come by for dinner sometime over the weekend. Things are slowing down with the holidays approaching."

"I will. You know I'm not going to cook for myself, girl." She gets into her car and I wave good-bye, and then turn to walk the two blocks to my café, where I know Rosa and Paco are already well into the daily routine. But I know two blocks doesn't give me enough time to process all that took place during that lunch hour.

I stand still for a moment and raise my hand to my shoulder—the shoulder Miles rested his hand on. I'd startled at the feel of his hand, but now I'm still tingling from his touch.

I move my hand from my shoulder to my chest. I cover my heart. What is that feeling? I glance back at the restaurant, longing for another glance of Miles.

Longing? Is that what I'm feeling? *Oh Lord, You're the One who fills my emptiness, well, at least when I don't fill it with a crois-sant. So now I want to fill that void with a croissant and a man? I'm so sorry.*

I start down the block toward my café.

Ellyn, I am the only One who can satisfy you fully. But I also express My love for you through the love of others.

My steps slow as I consider the whisper in my soul.

One thing is certain, it isn't Earl's blabbering.

Lord, are You saying You might express Your love for me through a . . . man?

Hey, Chubs! Are you kidding me?

I pick up my pace. Rather than trying to make sense of the voices in my head, I shift my focus to the conversation over lunch with Sabina. That I understand. *Oh, Lord, thank You for opening her eyes—for revealing Yourself to Sabina.*

I look across the street to the waves breaking in the cove and feel the same peace that Sabina radiated. I may not get what's going on in my head, or my heart, but I do know Who is in control.

Miles

When I get back to my office after lunch, I still have an hour before my next patient is scheduled. I sit at my desk, intending to use the time to catch up on e-mail and paperwork. When I open my e-mail, I see something from Alex. Just what I need today—to connect with my son. I smile and open the message.

> *Hey, Dad, Kimberli and I were talking about Christmas this morning. What's the plan? We can have it here, but we'd love to come there. I talked to Will and he agrees. We could all stay through the New Year. We'll all pitch in with the decorating and cooking. What do you think?*

Christmas. I hadn't given any thought to Christmas yet and it's just five weeks away. Last year, I went south and spent the holiday with Alex and Kimberli. Will joined us for Christmas Eve and Christmas Day. I stayed through New Year's. It was too soon for all of us to have Christmas here, where Sarah's absence would pierce us at every turn. But now, maybe we've all healed enough. Maybe we can remember her with joy rather than grief.

I shoot my thoughts back to Alex and then block out the time on my calendar. I also send an e-mail to Nerissa and invite her and Twila to join us for Christmas Day. The boys know Nerissa. She's like family now.

That's when the thought hits me . . .

Who does Ellyn spend holidays with? Her mother, in the city? Funny, I know so little about her past. Our conversations, for the most part, have centered on the present. She mentioned a close relationship with her father before he died, but beyond that, I know little.

But then, I don't need to know more. We're just friends.

I turn from the computer screen and attempt to put Ellyn out of my mind.

Ellyn

It's a quiet evening at the café. Thursdays and Sundays are slow during the winter months, which is often a nice reprieve, as long as they're not too slow. We had a decent crowd between 6:00 and 7:30 and then it began to taper off. But tonight, I'm not sure I want a reprieve.

"Hey, Bella, do you mind if I take off early? Maria called and two of the little niños have the flu. She could use a hand."

"Oh." I look around the kitchen, although I already know he's taken care of all he needs to. "Of course, go ahead. I can handle it from here."

After he's gone, I go to the swinging doors and look out at the dining room. Rosa is chatting with a couple of regulars, and my two servers are taking care of the other customers. I turn back to the kitchen and try to busy my mind.

It's no use. With the quiet come thoughts of Miles again, but this time they're accompanied by what I believe the Spirit whispered to my soul this afternoon.

Is it really possible that God wants to express His love to me through a man?

Through . . . Miles?

Odd, but the thought isn't accompanied by the usual quiver of fear that comes with the thought of an intimate relationship with a man.

Who are you kidding? God expressing His love through a man? Men are all the same. You know that.

I only know that because that's what you've told me. And you know what, Earl? I think you're a lia—

"Ellyn, you come say hello to the Reynolds. They going to Arizona for the rest of winter. They not come back until summer."

I stare at Rosa.

"Ellyn? *Hola?* You in there?" Rosa waves her hand in my face.

"Fine." I take off my apron, hang it on the hook by the door, smooth my black chef's coat over my hips, and then go out to the dining room and fulfill my role—just as Rosa's demanded I do.

Who's the boss here again?

I DO MY DUTY and chat with the Reynolds, who frequent the café when they're at their home here. After saying good-bye, I go back to the kitchen, walk past the large table in the back, and go into the office and close the door.

I pick up the phone without giving myself time to think—or Earl time to reprimand—and punch in the number I now know by heart.

"Hello."

My heart flutters.

"Hi, Miles. It's Ellyn."

"Hey, gal. Is everything all right?"

"Yes, fine." My voice shakes and I pray he doesn't notice. "No rats or anything like that."

He chuckles. "Well, good. What can I do for you?"

"I . . . I was wondering if I could buy you a cup of coffee?"

He is quiet on the other end of the line for what feels like hours but is, I suppose, only seconds. Then I hear him clear his throat.

"Well, that's a hard offer to refuse."

It is?

Oh.

"Great. How about meeting me at the café again. I'll bake those cookies you liked." My fluttering heart spreads its wings and soars.

It is possible God is allowing me a *do-over?*

If so, I plan to do things right this time.

After I hang up the phone, having set a time with Miles, Earl's words come back to me: *Men are all the same.*

But those . . .

Those aren't just Earl's words, are they?

My eyes widen. No. No they aren't. I've heard them over and over. Because . . .

Those are my mother's words.

God grant to human minds to discern in a small thing universal
truths valid for both small and great matters.

SAINT AUGUSTINE

CHAPTER FORTY-NINE

Twila

I SQUINT AGAINST THE sun reflecting off the water
and then lean forward in the chair I'm sitting in on Ellyn's upper
deck. I take off the sweatshirt I have on over my sweater. "This
weather is, like, amazing."

"Isn't it? Sixty-eight degrees in December. Gorgeous." She takes
a sip of her herbal tea. "Thanks for coming over. I need to talk to you
about the whole vegan thing. It's not working for me."

"Okay. So what part isn't working?"

"Oh. The vegan part."

"Yeah, it doesn't work for everyone."

"I know you told me that in the beginning, but sometimes I'm
stubborn."

"That's okay. Now you know."

"I haven't lost any weight. Not even a pound. Doesn't that seem
strange to you?"

Ellyn shifts in her chair, like maybe she's uncomfortable talking
about not losing weight. "You can even gain weight eating a vegan

diet, it just depends on what you're eating. Maybe we need to talk through your motives. Like why did you want to change your eating habits in the first place? What positives have you experienced since you changed your diet. Things like that, you know?"

"Sure. Well, my motive should be obvious. I need to lose weight."

"Need to or want to?"

"You're kidding, right?"

She looks at me like I'm crazy. "No. If you're healthy and like, your numbers are good, blood pressure and things, then you don't need to lose weight. If the weight is bothering your joints or there are other issues, than you might need to lose weight. But if it's just because you think you'd look better, or whatever, then you *want* to lose weight. It's a desire, not a need."

She shakes her head and waves her hand in front of my face. "Honey, *look* at me."

"I am looking at you. But I told you that we don't always see ourselves the way others see us. Like, you look at me and see someone who's thin, but I look in the mirror and I still see someone who is overweight. I mean, logic tells me I'm not, but my mind plays tricks on me."

Ellyn looks out over the headlands, thinking. Then she looks back at me. "I understand your point, but there's a difference between us. I look in the mirror and I see reality. You don't."

I shrug. "You see what you're conditioned to believe is reality."

"What?"

I stand up and walk to the railing of Ellyn's deck, then motion for her to follow me. I put my hand up to shade my eyes and point out to the headlands and the water. "Describe what you see out there."

"Okay. I see the headlands, prairie grass, trails, the road, the cliffs, and the ocean."

"What else?"

She looks again. "Birds and rocks and a few trees. If I look to the north, I see the point and the rock outcroppings that form islands. And I can see the surf crashing against the rocks."

"What does it all say to you?"

She is quiet and then she takes a deep breath and her shoulders relax. "It speaks to me of God's power, of His magnificence. It reminds me that He is unfathomable. It fills me with awe."

"Cool. So when you look at God's creation, you see God, and you're filled with awe, right?"

She stands still looking out at the view from her deck. "Yes."

"Men go abroad to wonder at the heights of mountains, at the huge waves of the sea, at the long courses of the rivers, at the vast compass of the ocean, at the circular motions of the stars"—Ellyn looking at me now, listening—"And they pass by themselves without wondering."

I watch as her eyes fill with tears. "Where . . . where did you hear that?"

"It's another Augustine quote. I read his autobiography and some of his other stuff when I was in treatment. He lived in the 300s, but his writings are still relevant."

"Say it again."

Ellyn stares out at the sea as I repeat the quote. She echoes the words, but more to herself than to me.

"And they pass by themselves without wondering. In other words, if I see God—His power and majesty in His creation . . ." She motions to the headlands and water. "Then I should see Him in myself as well."

"Something like that. I mean, it isn't a *should*, like something you were supposed to do and didn't. So don't, like, get all down on yourself. It just means that we sometimes miss seeing Him in the most important thing He created. Us. We're so conditioned to buy into—and compare ourselves to—the image that American culture deems perfect. But that just messes us up. It isn't real. And that isn't what God looks at. That's not what's important to Him. He sees our inner beauty—the condition of our hearts, you know?"

"*Imago Dei.* Your tattoo. I knew what you meant when you first explained it, but I couldn't accept it for myself, somehow. I want to, but . . ."

"I know. I still struggle. I get it, but then I forget. I started to see that when I could, like, embrace the truth for myself, then I wasn't so hard on myself. How could I treat myself, one of God's creations—the one created most like Him—so bad? I didn't want to do that anymore. So the tattoo reminds me of that."

There's an intensity in Ellyn's expression, like she's processing what I'm saying.

"But it isn't just about how I treat myself. It's about how others treat me too. Like my dad"—I look out at the horizon and watch as a cloud drifts by—"He hasn't treated me with respect. He wanted to use me for his own purposes. He wasn't interested in what's best for me. I can forgive him for that, but I don't have to be in relationship with him. I don't want to let him treat me, one of God's creations, like that. I have to have as much respect for myself as God has for me. Or at least I want to try—"

Ellyn is silent.

"Sorry, I'm talking too much."

She's quiet a moment longer, looking out at the headlands. "Honey, you're teaching me. I'll listen to you all day long. You just keep talking." She turns and goes to sit down.

I join her. "So how do you feel since you changed the way you eat?"

"Since the issues I had the day I ended up in the hospital, I've felt fine. But I don't think that had anything to do with how I'm eating."

"Wow. Cool. Has the diet changed your perspective about, you know, the way you eat?"

She hesitates. "Yes, it helped me see that I've used my job as an excuse to eat whatever I want and that . . . well, sometimes I eat for the wrong reasons. I eat for comfort when I'm upset instead of turning to God for His comfort. I realized I was putting my trust in food rather than in God. I hope I can do that less often."

"It's good to know those things about ourselves."

"I got rid of my scale too. The number on the scale was starting to rule my emotions."

"Seems like veganism worked for you in a lot of ways."

Ellyn's eyes sparkle in the sun. "I guess you're right. Just not in the ways I expected."

"So now what?"

"What do you mean? What diet do I want to try next?"

"No, I mean what are you going to do now with the knowledge you've gained?"

"Oh." Ellyn leans her head back and looks up at the sky. She thinks for a minute. "I want to think and pray about what you said today. The Augustine quote. And I want to listen to God's voice rather than all the negative chatter I hear in my head all the time."

"That sounds pretty wise. Every time I have a negative thought about myself, I try to replace it with something positive—one of God's truths."

"That's a good idea. For me, I think it's easier said than done."

"I know. It takes practice."

"I bet you do know." She reaches over and puts her hand on my arm. "You are a gift to me, Twila."

I shrug. "Thanks. Hey, about the food part, if you want to, add some grass-fed beef back into your diet. Like about two ounces. It will help get your metabolism going. Have it with breakfast."

"Really?"

"Yeah, really."

"What about butter?"

"Add a little back in and see how you feel."

Her face is serious—almost like she might cry. Then she leans over and gives me a hug. A big, tight hug. As she hugs me she's mumbling something in my ear over and over. I finally make it out.

"Thank you, oh, thank you, thank you . . ."

I RIDE MY BIKE home from Ellyn's and enjoy the last of the day's sunshine on my face. With fewer tourists here now during the week, the streets are quiet. I like it this way—it's peaceful. After my dad left, I needed peace. He may not like Mendocino, but for him to think I'd like New York shows he doesn't even know me.

Sure, Mendocino's small, and I don't have a lot of friends my own age here anymore, but God has put good people in my life. I think again of how different my dad and Miles are—and what a difference Miles's relationship with God makes. I pray my dad will turn back to God someday. He says he's a Christian, but, like, something's missing. With Miles, you see it—you see Jesus in the way he acts and the way he cares about people.

When I reach my street, I get off my bike and turn to look back at the ocean. This is the last place I can see it before turning down my street. As I stand there and watch the deep blue water turn to darker shades of gray in the late afternoon light, I recall what Ellyn said about how the ocean speaks to her of God's power and His magnificence.

I open my mind and heart to God and let Him, like, search me. I wait and listen and then pray just three words: *Ellyn and Miles.*

God knows the rest.

Then I get on my bike and ride the last block home.

> I was wholly ignorant of what it is in ourselves which
> gives us being, and how scripture is correct in saying that
> we are "in God's image."
>
> SAINT AUGUSTINE

CHAPTER FIFTY

Ellyn

"I THINK THIS WAS a bad idea." I stand in front of The Great Put On—a boutique on the corner of Lansing and Albion—looking at a dress in the window that appears no wider than the zipper running down its back. "Who wears that kind of thing? Are you sure she carries my size?"

"Yes, I'm sure. And this was a great idea. Let's go."

I stay rooted to the sidewalk until Sabina gives me a push toward the door. "Oh, fine!"

My first thought upon entering is that my mother would shop here. That tempts me to turn and run, but I know Sabina would chase me down. The glass cases next to the register are filled with bracelets, earrings, necklaces, and hair clips. These I can do. They'll fit. I stand in front of one of the cases looking at a bronze cuff brace-let until Sabina pulls me deeper into the store.

"May I help you?"

I look at the young woman—long blond waves, chocolate colored eyes—and not an ounce over ninety-eight pounds. I mumble something about just looking.

"Yes, my friend here is looking for a few things."

Superhero Sabina to the rescue.

Great. Thanks.

"You probably don't even carry my size, so we'll just look around."

"Sure, we have lots of things that will fit you. What are you looking for?"

"Oh. Well, um . . ." I look at Sabina, eyebrows raised.

"Casual chic in colors that will set off her gorgeous hair and eyes."

At this point, I'm certain both Sabina and the clerk can hear Earl laughing.

I'm ushered to a dressing room, where the clerk and Sabina bring me outfits to try on. At first, it's an excruciating experience, but then I try on a pair of wide-legged, flowing, brown pants, with a long, forest-green, cotton-knit sweater. The outfit feels good. I make a slow turn toward the mirror and catch my breath. I turn to the right and then to the left and then I turn around and look into the mirror over my shoulder.

You look like a giant sequoia.

I turn away from the mirror and start to take the sweater off, but then I recall Twila's suggestion. I stand for a moment with my back to the mirror, then I pull the sweater into place and turn to the mirror again.

I look . . .

I swallow.

Then I take in my red curls, cascading over my shoulders, and I notice the way my light green eyes shine against my milky complexion.

I look like a beautiful child of God. Created in His image.

Somewhere in the background of my mind, Earl still mumbles, but my mind is elsewhere. "Thank You, Lord . . ." The prayer whispers out of me as I stare at the image reflected in the mirror. I'm not sure what I'm thanking Him for, but it is the first time I've ever looked into a mirror and responded with gratitude.

"How's it going in there?" Sabina stands outside the dressing room. "Ready for a few more things?"

My reflection smiles at me. "It's actually not going too horrible. Sure, give me a few more things."

WE LEAVE THE BOUTIQUE with bags full of clothes and accessories. The only shopping I've done in years has been ordering chef's pants, smocks, and clogs online, along with an occasional pair of sweats. Today I spent more than I've ever spent in one store. But I have the money, so why not use it?

"Where am I going to wear all these clothes?"

"Well, your first event is coffee with Miles tomorrow."

My stomach does a somersault. "Oh. Right." I stop at my car parked along the street. "Do you have time to go over to Thanksgiving's?"

"I have all the time in the world, girl."

"Okay, let me put these in the trunk and then . . . I want to . . . I want to talk to you about . . . Earl."

Sabina just nods. "Sure."

I appreciate her subtle reaction.

WE SETTLE INTO A table at Thanksgiving's, Sabina with her café au lait and me with a nonfat latte.

"Look, real milk."

"You're no longer a vegan?"

"No, it didn't really suit me."

Sabina laughs. "How could a diet void of butter ever suit you?"

"I don't know what I was thinking." I take a sip of the latte. "Mmm . . . even though the milk is nonfat, it's wonderful."

We sit in silence for a few minutes, each sipping our coffee.

"So . . . Earl. Who is he?"

I start to answer, but nothing comes out. Because the answer isn't what I expected. It takes a moment, but I finally say it out loud. "She."

"She who?"

"Earl."

"Earl is a woman?"

I'm as surprised as Sabina. I take a deep breath . . . and know. Absolutely. Earl is a woman. And in my heart, I think I've known it all along. "Yes, her name is actually . . ."

Am I really about to say this? *Can* I say it?

"Ellyn?"

I hold up one hand. "Just . . . just give me a minute."

"You can do this. And somehow, I know freedom resides on the other side of this conversation."

Freedom. The meaning of the word washes over me. Am I really bound? Yes. And freedom is possible? "How can you know that?"

"Maybe Twila's wearing off on me." Her tone is soft. "Or maybe God is speaking to me—through me, to you." She shakes her head. "Can you imagine?"

Can I imagine? "Yes, I can." I take a deep breath. "Okay . . . *Her* name is . . . Earleen."

"Who is Earleen?"

"Earleen, or Earl for short, is the voice I hear in my head. My accuser. The one who makes certain I never get a big head by reminding me how big my backend is, among other things."

"I see. But why Earl or Earleen? Where did you come up with the name?

Don't you dare, big girl.

I wipe my palms on my pants and then clasp my hands in my lap to keep them from shaking. Oh yes. I dare. You bet I dare. It's time. Long past time. "Earleen Amelia DeMoss."

"DeMoss?"

"Yep."

Understanding dawns on Sabina's features. The same understanding that just dawned in my heart.

"Earl is your mother."

It's a statement, not a question. I angle a look at her. "You're not surprised?"

"Not really. A mother is a powerful force in a child's life, even when that child becomes an adult. That impact can be positive or negative—most often it's a combination of both. But mothers don't have to determine who we ultimately become."

If only that were true! "Even now, at forty-six? I think it's too late, I *became* a long time ago."

"We're always becoming, Ellyn. Always growing and changing, unless we're stuck, the way I've been. The way I think you may be too. But no, it's never too late to change—to become—it's a lifetime process. I'm a living example of that. So what's her role in your life?"

"My mother?" I shrug. "After my father died, I ran away—from her, I think. I was an only child and I felt . . . I don't know, sort of suffocated by her, I guess. I think she meant well and loved me, in her own way, but"—I shrug again—"now, I keep distance between us. It feels better that way, at least to me. And yet . . . she's always with me. In Earl."

Even as I say these things, I marvel at them. So this is how it feels to have an epiphany. "I guess I've always known, on some level, that Earl was my mother, or at least born of my relationship with her. It's sort of like Earl is the evil spawn of my mother." I raise my eyebrows and smile.

"Which would make your mother an alien or a fish?"

"Well, not exactly, but I'm not sure she's human, either. Unless a human can survive without a heart."

"Oh, Ellyn. I'm sorry."

Sabina's response carries none of the levity I'm trying to maintain. I try to laugh, but the laughter catches against the lump forming in my throat.

"Oh." I look away from Sabina and try to put what I'm feeling into words. "I . . . I've never let myself . . . I've never really thought about this, or analyzed it. It just is and always has been. I try to ignore what Earl says in my head, but I've heard those accusations for so long . . ."

"How much of what Earl says are things your mother actually said or says to you?"

I turn away from her. "Oh. No . . . she didn't . . . I mean, maybe . . . but . . ." This conversation is sitting on my chest like a circus elephant. I turn back to Sabina and shake my head. "I thought I wanted to talk about this, but . . ."

"We don't have to talk about it. But I think talking about it with someone, a counselor, is important."

"Oh great, we're back to me seeing a shrink?"

"Ellyn, it sounds like you've listened to that voice for most of your life. It might be good to have support, someone who can help you change something so woven into your being."

She has a point. I don't know that I've ever *not* heard Earl. Or my mother. Or . . . I can't believe all those accusations, all those condemnations, are the voice of my mother. But for the first time, I'm certain that is who they began with.

It is my own mother's voice the enemy has used against me.

"Of course, that is *if* you want to change."

What? "If? Why wouldn't I want to?"

"Change, even good change, can be frightening. It leads to an unfamiliar emotional landscape. A place where things are new, different, unknown. Sometimes we prefer the known to the unknown."

A twitch, just above my eye, nags as Sabina talks. "Look at me, I'm a nervous wreck just at the thought of it. Maybe I'll ask Twila who she sees."

"Now that"—her warm smile spreads across her features—"is a great idea."

AFTER SABINA AND I part ways, I head to the café, but her comment plays on my mind: *Of course, that is if you want to change.* Figuring out how much of Earl is really Earleen could prove . . . healing.

For me.

And for my relationship with my mom.

Oh.

Is a healthy relationship with my mom even possible? If so, do I want that?

No.

Nope.

Not even a little bit.

I sigh. What's *wrong* with me that I wouldn't want a better relationship with my mom? Haven't I forgiven her? Yes, I have. Over and over and over again!

The circus elephant is now tap-dancing on my chest.

I set my purse on the desk in the office and then go to the kitchen to take care of a few things.

Forgiven me? For what? You're the one who let me down. Over and over and over again, I might add.

I walk into the refrigerator, the cold air a slap on my hot face. I stand for a moment and stare at the trays filled with ramekins of cooling crème brûlée. One of our most popular desserts. I developed the recipe myself. The secret is the lavender steeped in the boiling milk and cream.

But as much as I want to concentrate on that, I can't. Earl's accusation demands my attention.

Okay. Yes, I did and do let my mother down on a regular basis. Earl speaks truth. As a child and through my teen years, I was a daddy's girl. My mother always pointed that out, and never in a good way. Always as though it was a bad thing. Almost as though . . .

My eyes widen.

It almost seemed as though my mother was jealous of my relationship with my dad.

But that's ridiculous.

I shake my head. Whatever the case, I was a disappointment to her as a daughter.

I turn and walk out of the refrigerator, cross the kitchen, and take a spoon from the trays of flatware. I am, and always have been, everything my mother isn't. She's a tall, slender, beautiful brunette.

Hair coiffed and nails manicured at all times. I, her only child, got my father's red curls and green eyes. As for manicures?

Never in my life had one.

If I hadn't given birth to you myself, I'd think you belonged to someone else.

"Come on, Earl. Like I haven't heard that from you a million times."

Not just from Earl, though. I can hear my mother saying it. See her expression, as though she's taken a bite of something bitter.

Standing back in the refrigerator, I take a ramekin off the tray and dip the spoon into the cool custard. Later, one of the staff will use a small torch to burn sugar into a caramelized crust on top of each crème brûlée. But now, it's just the creamy custard base. I put a bite in my mouth and savor the sweet concoction.

I take another bite.

Enjoy it. In fact, when you finish that one, help yourself to another.

No. One is enough. I am made in the image of God. Made in the image of God. Made in the image . . .

I take the last bite and then scrape the spoon around the edge of the ramekin to get any of the remaining custard.

I lick the spoon clean.

You're made in the image of your father, who betrayed me, just like you're going to betray me. Who are you kidding, Ellyn?

I frown at that. Dad betrayed you, Earl? What do you mean?

You know what I mean. He was just like all the others, Ellyn. Just like all men. You know that. I've told you so. They all want just one thing and once they get it, they'll toss you aside. It happened over and over again. Men will ruin you. Have another crème brûlée.

I reach for another ramekin and dip the spoon into the custard. I lift it to my mouth—

And stop.

My father wouldn't have betrayed my mother. He wouldn't. He was a man of God. I know he was. But . . .

I lift the spoon to my lips.

"*No!*"

I hurl the spoon across the refrigerator and it clangs against one of the metal shelves and then falls to the ground. "No! No! No! I'm done with your lies!" I lift my arm—and the ramekin of crème brûlée over my head—ready to smash it too. But again—

I stop.

I walk out of the refrigerator, go to the sink, turn on the hot water, and rinse the custard from the cup. I watch as it goes down the drain. Why smash it and make a big mess for myself to clean up?

I lean against the countertop and wipe away the tears I didn't even realize I'd shed. Somehow, my mother's pain, her dysfunction, is wound around my soul, suffocating who I am . . . or who I was meant to be. It's not her fault.

My eyes widen again.

It's not her fault.

All those things she said . . . they came from hurt. Deep, piercing pain. And I was never strong enough to stand against the power of that pain when it came out in her words.

But that is all changing now.

Now that I know who I am.

I am a woman created in the image of God. And that image fills me with awe.

I go get the flying spoon from the refrigerator, put it in the sink, and then go to the office. I sit down at the desk and pick up the phone.

"Hi, Twila. Honey, I'd like to get a name and phone number from you."

May your mercy illuminate me . . .

CHAPTER FIFTY-ONE

Miles

I PULL THE PLASTIC dry cleaner's wrap off a blue oxford shirt in my closet. As I button the shirt, Ellyn's words come back to me: *"I wondered if I could buy you a cup of coffee sometime."* The same words I used when asking her out for coffee. Her phrasing had been intentional. But what did it mean? Is she asking if we can start over? Or is that hopeful thinking on my part? And if it's "hopeful thinking," then why am I dreading the time with her?

Lord?

I sit on the bench at the end of the bed and slip on my loafers. Then, with my elbows on my knees, I put my head in my hands.

Lord . . . I want Your will, but I'm not sure what that is when it comes to Ellyn. Maybe it's still too soon for me to think of getting involved with someone—maybe that's why the rejection from Ellyn hurt so much. I want to reflect You to her, Father, if that's Your call for me. But if there's another way, I pray You'll show me. Your will be done on earth as it is in heaven.

I get up from the bench, walk back into my closet—the one I shared with Sarah—and reach for my wool blazer. It's one of those gray, December days, where the fog feels like it goes right through you. You never know what you'll wake to here.

As I put the jacket on, something Sarah used to say runs through my mind: *"Remember, Miles, you're not the savior, that's Jesus' role."* She'd point her finger at me in mock exasperation and I'd get her meaning. I don't have to be all things to all people. I'm not the only person God will use in someone's life.

I haven't thought of that in ages.

Lord, is that Your answer? I know You don't need me—You can do all things and use anyone. Are You freeing me from the responsibility I feel to represent You to Ellyn?

A sense of peace settles over me and remains with me as I drive to meet Ellyn at the café.

"I LIKE THOSE COOKIES." I look at the plate on the table—the table set just as it was the first time we met at her café for coffee.

"Thank you."

"That's one of the things I miss"—I hesitate—"Sorry. I was going to say that's one of the things I miss about Sarah—homemade cookies."

"You don't ever have to apologize for missing your wife. Or her cookies."

Her voice is tender and I see compassion in her eyes.

"Thanks."

"Have a seat, I'll get our coffee."

Ellyn disappears into the kitchen, giving me a couple of minutes to collect my thoughts . . . and emotions. When she returns, she sets a cup in front of me and then sits across from me.

"Thanks for coming, Miles."

"Sure. You look great." For the first time since I've known her, Ellyn is wearing makeup . . . or at least more makeup. Whatever she's done makes her clear green eyes stand out. And she's wearing something different. She's taken time with her appearance, which makes me wonder again why she's asked me here.

I reach for a cookie and put it on the small plate in front of me.

"The cookies are a small thank-you for taking care of the rat." She brushes a crumb off the table. "I made enough for you to take some home too."

"Thank you, but you didn't need to do that."

"I wanted to."

We make small talk for a few minutes and then land on the subject of Sabina. Ellyn tells me more about her friend's decision to reengage in her relationship with God.

"It's amazing the way God works." I smile. "Not only that, but I'm getting a golf partner when her husband comes."

"She mentioned that." Ellyn looks down at the table and then back at me. She fidgets with her spoon. "Miles, I know I've already apologized for the way I"—her face colors—"I treated you. But again, I'm so sorry."

I don't say anything. It seems safer that way.

"I'm learning some things about myself. I think God used our . . . friendship to show me some areas in my life where He . . . wants to heal me." She looks down at the table again. "I told you that I don't date, but I didn't tell you that . . ." She takes a deep breath. "I've never dated. In fact"—she blushes again—"you were my . . ."

She stops, then she peeks up at me through those long eyelashes. "Well, never mind, I just wanted you to know that I—"

"Ellyn, I was your what?" I keep the question gentle, but I want her to finish what she was going to say. I watch as tears come to her eyes, and understanding hits me. She's embarrassed by what she's sharing with me.

I want to put my arms around her and tell her it's okay.

"You were my first . . . kiss."

She whispers the word *kiss*. In fact, her voice is so soft I wouldn't be sure of what she'd said if I hadn't been able to also read her lips. She looks away from me again.

It takes me a minute to assimilate the information she's just imparted. *Lord, how do I respond?* Then it comes to me. "Ellyn, look at me . . . please." She looks up again and I read the pain in her eyes. "I'm honored. I really am. And, by the way"—I chuckle—"it was great." Now *I'm* the one blushing.

"Oh."

I'm not certain if she's going to giggle or cry. "So now what?"

She rolls the spoon between her fingers. "Well, I wondered if we could start over with our . . . friendship? And maybe, later, we . . . you know, could just see what happens?"

I can see how much it's cost her to ask—to make herself vulnerable. I hesitate—Do I really want to do this? Does God want me to do it?—but then I remember my earlier sense of peace. I run my hand through my hair. "Ellyn, I appreciate your honesty. I want to match your honesty with my own." I pick up my spoon and stir my coffee. Now I'm the one fidgeting. "I can't do that—I can't put myself in that position."

"Oh. Okay. I understand." She looks away.

"I want to make sure you do understand. Ellyn?" She looks back at me and I see her shoulders slump, just a bit. I know I'm hurting her, but I fear I'll hurt her more by leading her to believe I'm content with friendship. "I care about you. I care deeply. I want more—"

I clear my throat. "More than just a friendship with you. If you reach a point where you'd also like more, let me know. I know I'm taking a risk here. You may never want anything from me but friendship, but I . . ."

What? How do I tell her all I'm feeling? Maybe I've said enough.

I shrug and then stand. "I'm sorry . . . Listen, thank you. For the cookies and coffee. But mostly, thank you for your honesty."

Ellyn stands. She says nothing more.

As I head to the door, I put my hand on her shoulder. "You're a very special woman, Ellyn."

Then I make my way through the kitchen, out the back door, and to my car. I just want to go home.

> I did not relapse into my original condition, but stood my ground
> very close to the point of deciding and recovered my breath.
>
> SAINT AUGUSTINE

CHAPTER FIFTY-TWO

Ellyn

I GO BACK TO the kitchen and look at the plate of cookies I'd made for Miles to take home. How could I be so *stupid?* To think he'd still want to be friends? Or want anything to do with me, for that matter. I felt his discomfort the moment he arrived. I felt it the day I offered to make him breakfast, and invited him to stay for lunch at the café. And again, at the restaurant when we ran into him. He'd said he wanted to remain friends, but I knew.

Something had changed.

So what did I do? I set myself up for disappointment.

Rejection.

I told you he was only after one thing. When a man says he wants more, what do you think he's referring to. Don't be naïve. Have a cookie, you'll feel better.

I look at the plate of cookies, but they don't even tempt me. My stomach is tied in knots. I slump against the kitchen counter and let the tears fall. They come as much from humiliation as disappointment. I stand up straight again and reach for a paper towel to wipe my eyes and nose. When I do, I see the cookies again.

Go ahead, have one. I made them for you. They'll make you feel better.

I look at the plate and a memory, long buried, digs its way to my consciousness.

I'd just come home from school—my freshman year of high school. My dream had come true: Eric Neilson had asked me to the Homecoming Dance. Eric Neilson, a junior, had asked me, a freshman, to the dance! I burst through the front door.

"Mom, I'm home!"

"In the library, Ellyn."

I ran into the room off the large foyer, where my mother took her afternoon tea. She isn't English, but she adopted the custom after vacationing in London with my father. "Guess *what?*"

"What? Goodness, Ellyn, your face is beet-red. Slow down."

"Eric Neilson asked me to Homecoming! I have to get a dress. Can we go shopping? Can we go today?"

I remember her taking a sip of her tea and then setting the cup on its saucer. "Ellyn, sit down. I have something to tell you."

"But can we go shopping?" I went to the sofa and sat down.

"No, we're not going shopping."

"But—"

She held up her hand. "We're not going shopping because you're not going to the dance. I'm so sorry to have to tell you this, but . . . Eric Neilson is making a joke of you. His invitation wasn't serious. Some of his schoolmates dared him to ask you. The vice principal called me today and informed me of this unfortunate scheme."

I just stared at her. It wasn't true, *couldn't* be true. Eric was so kind—we'd become friends. I shook my head. "I don't believe it."

"It is true. I'm sure you're humiliated, but you're better off this way. Boys . . . men . . . rarely have a woman's best interest at heart. It is better that you learn this lesson early."

I continued to shake my head, wanting to deny what she'd said.

"Really, dear, are you that surprised? Look at you—that hair of yours alone would scare off most boys. You must have suspected something."

That's when it happened.

She reached for the plate of cookies next to her teacup, then held it out toward me. "Go ahead, have one. I made them for you. They'll make you feel better."

When I returned to school the next day, I found Eric. I wanted to ask him if it was true, but when he saw me, he turned and walked the other way. It was clear he was ignoring me.

He never spoke to me again.

I look now at the plate of cookies on the counter, the cookies I baked for Miles, and the same sick feeling that cloaked me that day so long ago, the day I ate not just one or two of the cookies my mother made for me, but—at her encouraging—the whole plate of cookies, settles over me.

I ate that day until I was sick.

Why would she encourage me to eat like that?

That was the first time I remember her doing it, but not the last. No. There were many such occasions when she encouraged me to stuff myself. Did she *want* me to get fat?

No. That's ridiculous. Isn't it?

She was always the one pointing out my weight—admonishing me.

Condemning me.

I pick up the plate of cookies and carry them back to the office to jot a note on a sticky pad. I put the note on the covered plate, and then take it to the kitchen and leave it on the counter for Paco to take home to his little ones.

Then I go back to the office and reach for the phone number Twila gave me when I called her.

It's time to schedule an appointment.

Nothing can restore hope to us except your mercy,
known since you began to transform us.

SAINT AUGUSTINE

CHAPTER FIFTY-THREE

Twila

ON CHRISTMAS MORNING, I wake to the sound of rain
beating against the house. The wind howls and the windows rattle.
I pull the covers up and snuggle down into the bed, where I think
about what this day means. As a kid, I woke up thinking about what
I wanted and what I'd get. Now, those things don't matter to me.

I close my eyes and sort of just hang out with God. We don't
talk, or anything—we're just together, listening to the storm.

When I do get up, I go to my closet to decide what to wear. My
clothes are pretty standard—jeans, sweaters, and hoodies. But we're
spending the day at Miles's house, and I'm meeting his family for the
first time. My mom knows them, but I was never around when they
were. Plus, it's Christmas, and I want to wear something special to
celebrate Jesus.

There's not much to choose from.

I slide clothes back and forth on the rod in my closet and come
across a long, straight, black skirt that I'd forgotten about. I pull it
out and pair it with a long, pewter knit sweater. Perfect. I can wear

my Dr. Martens boots with the skirt. They're my only pair and they cost a lot. Mine are a dark green background covered in a print of tiny flowers. I save them for special occasions.

I lay the clothes on my bed and then go downstairs to make a cup of tea.

"Merry Christmas, love."

My mom is in the kitchen fixing a dish she's taking for Christmas dinner.

"Merry Christmas." I walk over and give her a hug and then set the teapot to boil. "Today will be fun, right?"

"Yes. I think you'll enjoy Miles's sons and his daughter-in-law."

"Yeah, me too." I don't say this to my mom, but it will be nice to hang out with a few people closer to my age.

"What's Ellyn doing today? She isn't alone, is she?"

I shake my head. "No, she spent last night with Sabina and her husband. This morning she's driving to San Francisco to spend the day with her mom."

"Oh, I didn't realize she had family in the city."

"Yeah. Maybe you could pray for her today. I think it might be kind of an intense relationship."

"Oh, thanks for sharing that with me. I will pray."

I take my tea and go back upstairs to take a shower and get dressed. I don't usually do much to my hair, but after I pull the sweater over my head, I pull it up in a loose, sort of messy bun. I look at it sideways in the mirror.

Cool. I like it.

Then I put on a little makeup. I look at the effect in the mirror. Not bad.

After I put my boots on, I do something I rarely allow myself to do anymore. I go and stand in front of the full-length mirror. Before looking at my image, I close my eyes and prepare myself to see something other than reality. But when I open my eyes—I'm surprised.

I look . . . okay.

Not too fat.

Even with the bulky sweater.

I turn and view my profile. I pat my tummy and smooth out the sweater. Then I turn and look over my shoulder so I can see the back view. I stand in front of the mirror for a long time, trying to find the fat girl I've always seen there.

But this morning, I can't find her.

"Thank You, Father."

It's going to be a good day. I feel it.

WHEN WE GET TO Miles's house around 11:00, everyone is in the kitchen drinking hot cocoa. Kimberli, Miles's daughter-in-law, made stir-sticks out of peppermint sticks with marshmallows stuck on the ends. Christmas music plays in the background, and a fire crackles in the fireplace in the family room, off the big kitchen.

It's like a Christmas card, come to life.

Miles pats me on the back. "Don't worry, gal. We have herbal tea for you. You can float a marshmallow in it if you like." His eyes shine with fun.

We're greeted with warmth and hugs. They're, like, such a kind family. Then introductions are made.

"Alex and Kimberli, this is Twila—Nerissa's daughter."

Alex puts out his hand. "Twila, nice to finally meet you."

Alex looks a lot like Miles probably looked when he was younger.

Kimberli gives me a hug. "Hi, hey it's nice to have another female around. I'm so glad you came."

"Thanks. It's good to meet you both."

Then Sabina comes and gives me a hug. "I'm so glad you're here. I want you to meet Antwone." She looks around the kitchen until she sees Antwone. "Twon, come meet Twila. This is the special young woman I've told you about."

Antwone towers over me. "Twila, I'm so grateful for your relationship with Sabina. Thank you for befriending her." His big hand weighs on my shoulder.

I shrug. "No problem. She's great."

Then I meet Will.

My mom told me he's twenty-five—just a year younger than I am—and just graduated with his masters in . . . something. She couldn't remember his major.

Will looks more like his mother. He has Miles's dark hair, only Will's is longer and his complexion is fair and his eyes are hazel, rather than blue. He's tall, lanky, and, like, really easy on the eyes.

Like Alex, he holds out his hand to shake mine as we're introduced. As he does, the cuff of the flannel shirt he's wearing pulls up to reveal a tattoo on the upper part of his right wrist—a fish symbol.

I shake Will's hand. "Hi, nice to meet you."

"Yeah, you too. Great tat. What's it mean?" He nods toward the thorns on my cheek.

"It's a sign of solidarity with those who suffer." I shrug. "Every time I look in the mirror it reminds me to pray for those in need."

"Wow. That's deep."

Something inside me, like, quivers. "I noticed you have one too." I point to his wrist.

"I do." He pulls back his sleeve and shows me the tattoo. "Pretty basic. But do you know the history behind it?"

"No."

"You see them everywhere—on the back of cars, hanging from necklaces, whatever—it's sort of the universal, evangelical symbol of Christianity now, right? But in the early church—around AD 54 through 68, during the reign of Nero, Christians were persecuted and, therefore, hesitant to speak of their faith. So they used the symbol of the fish, or ichthus, as it's now known, to identify themselves to other believers. They'd draw the symbol in the dirt or on the wall of a cave as a means of letting others know it was safe to talk about their belief in Jesus."

And he thought my tat was deep? That's amazing.

"So it reminds me to pray for the persecuted church in other countries. There are so many who suffer for their faith." Pain or sorrow seems to settle over him.

I look him in the eyes. "Okay, that's deep too."

"Yeah. Hey, it's nice to not be the only one with ink, for once."

I pull up the right sleeve of my sweater and turn my hand and wrist over so he can see my other tattoo.

He looks at it, and then looks back at me. His stare is intense.

"You're created in the image of God."

"Yes! You get it, right?"

He nods. "Not many people, especially in our culture, understand the significance of who we, as humans, really are. I bet it's especially hard as a woman. Women are oppressed in so many ways, including American women who are oppressed by the over-sexualization of their gender."

"Exactly." This is just . . . amazing! "You really get it. So my mom said you just finished your masters. What's your degree?"

"A Masters of Non-profit Administration. I'm interviewing now. I'd like to work with a non-profit organization that provides micro-loans for individuals, particularly women, in developing countries. What about you?"

"Really, that's what you want to do? That's amazing." I know I've thought it a bunch of times already, but it's the truth.

Just.

Amazing.

He shrugs. "We have so much. It seems natural to want to help others."

"Cool." Then I tell him about my schooling and what I do now. "I've taken it kind of slow. I've had some . . . health problems to deal with too."

"Really? Wow, you wouldn't know it. You look great."

My face gets warm. "Thanks."

We stand in the kitchen and talk until Will looks around. "Hey, where'd everybody go?"

He's right. The kitchen is empty except for us. "I didn't even notice they'd left."

"Me either. Too bad we didn't hit it off, right?"

His humor reminds me of Miles. "Yeah, too bad."

"Hey, I'm here through New Years. Would you want to hang out? Maybe get dinner or something one night?"

"Sure, I'd like that."

"Great. What are you doing tomorrow night?"

I laugh. "Um . . . having dinner with you?"

"Yes!"

In your gift we find our rest.

SAINT AUGUSTINE

CHAPTER FIFTY-FOUR

Sabina

I'VE BEEN LOOKING FOR a phone for several minutes, to no avail. So I go to the source. "Miles, is there somewhere I could make a phone call?"

"Sure. Use the den." He points to a set of French doors. "Just through there. Close the doors so you can hear yourself talk."

"Thank you, I'll do that."

I walk into the den, close the doors against the joyful clamor coming from the family room, and then sit in a leather chair situated in the corner of the room. I look around. This is Miles's space. I punch Ellyn's number into the phone. If I don't catch her, I at least want to leave a message.

"Sabina?"

"Oh, good, I caught you. Are you at your mother's?"

"I just crossed the bridge so I have about ten more minutes of peace."

"Good. Listen, it feels odd to say this, but . . . I'm praying for you." I sit back in Miles's chair.

"Thank you. I'm going to need divine intervention to get through this. How are things there?"

I hear a wistfulness in her question. "They're good. There's even a little romance in the air. Girl, you should be here."

"Romance? Um . . . Miles?"

I sit up straight. "Miles? Oh, no. No. It's Twila and Miles's son, Will. They haven't taken their eyes off each other since Nerissa and Twila arrived."

"Oh. Really? That's great. Oh, that's so great."

"Well, who knows? It may not go anywhere, but they sure seem taken with each other. I'd say it was love at first sight."

"Good. And how is Miles?"

"He's fine, Ellyn. He is such a delight, but you know what I think of him. I wish you were here though, and not just because I miss you. I think he misses you too."

"Thanks, Sabina. But . . . I can't think about that right now. I have to confront the situation with my mom. I need to . . . you know."

"Yes, I do. You're doing the right thing, Ellyn. I'm so impressed with your courage. You're making some good, wise choices."

"It's time."

"Yes. Call if you need anything. And Ellyn, Merry Christmas."

"You too, Sabina. Give everyone my love."

I hang up and then decide now is also a good time to call the twins, who are celebrating Christmas back East with Antwone's parents. The holidays have always been an event in our home, but when the girls suggested staying back East rather than traveling home this year, I knew it was the right choice. It freed me to be here through the holidays and beyond. At least, that's how long I used to think I'd stay.

Of course, now, with Antwone here, I realize I want to be with him. Need to be with him. We are building a new relationship on a new foundation. But we agreed not to make a decision on timing until the new year.

He is loving the time here as much as I am.

And I have lost time to make up for.

Where I discovered the truth there I found my God, truth itself, which from the time I learnt it, I have not forgotten. And so, since the time I learnt of you, you remain in my consciousness, and there I find you when I recall you and delight in you.

SAINT AUGUSTINE

CHAPTER FIFTY-FIVE

Ellyn

BY THE TIME I pull into the driveway of the home I grew up in, my hands ache from gripping the steering wheel all the way down Highway 1, and my stomach is knotted at the idea of a day spent with my mother—

And the conversation I know I must initiate.

While Christmas Day may not seem the best time to confront the past, this is, I believe, God's timing. Confused memories continue to surface as I work through some of my issues in counseling. The primary issue being Earl—or Earleen—and my fear or reluctance toward men.

Turns out, Rosa was right all along.

I'm terrified.

Or I was.

Some of that is subsiding as I work through my history. What's more, my weight is no longer the issue it was.

Wow, Ellyn, roll that one around in your mind for a moment . . . *My weight is no longer the issue it was.* That doesn't mean I've lost weight. No, that would take an act of God—He seems to have given me the economy metabolism, whereas others sport a racecar metabolism. Oh, well.

Instead, the act God deemed important was that I accept myself as one created in *His* image. I, Ellyn DeMoss, am created in the image of the most holy, majestic, and awesome God. Not in a physical sense, although Jesus did come in bodily form, but rather in a *spiritual* sense. And that is what's important. I am, I'm coming to believe, beautiful from the inside out. As I accept that fact, I'm also seeing myself as beautiful from the outside in.

Somehow that knowledge empowers me for what I need to do today.

Too much remains either unknown or misunderstood between me and my mom. The time has come to sort it out.

I reach to the passenger seat of the car and pick up the cyclamen plant I brought for my mother, along with a gift bag containing a silk, hand-painted scarf made by a Mendocino artist.

She'll hate it.

Which, at the moment, gives me great satisfaction.

I've learned I can't win with her, so I gave up trying, at least in the gift-giving department, long ago.

Oh Lord, remind me that this confrontation is an act of love and respect for both myself, and my mom. It is not retaliation for years of pain.

I take a deep breath, get out of the car, and then climb the front steps of the home in the Marina District of San Francisco, where my mother has lived since before I was born. I stand at the grand front door and ring the bell. I'm no longer free to walk in. When she answers, I'm struck again by her beauty and the care she takes, even at seventy-five, with her looks. Her hair is lighter now—dyed and highlighted, I'd guess, to cover the gray, and her skin is still smooth.

Her nails are perfect, as are her black wool pants and cranberry silk blouse.

"Ellyn, so good to see you. How long has it been? A year or more?"

"Hello, Mother. Merry Christmas. These are for you." I hand her the plant and the gift bag, which saves me from one of her faux hugs and air kisses.

"Well, come in, don't just stand out there."

I step into the large foyer which jettisons me back thirty-five years. Nothing much has changed in the house since then.

She sets the plant and bag down on the round entry table in the middle of the foyer. Well, one thing has changed. The flowers in the vase on the table are fresh. A florist replaces the arrangement each week. This one is made up of what look like redwood boughs, pinecones, and poinsettias.

"Let me look at you." My mother lifts her head, just a bit, and looks down her nose at me. The typical inspection. "Why, Ellyn, is that a new outfit?"

"Yes."

"It's lovely. I didn't know they made such nice things in your size. Come dear, I've waited so long for you, I fear the food is cold."

I look at my watch. "I thought we weren't eating until 4:00."

"We're not. But we have appetizers, of course."

I follow her into the library, where I find a spread fit for a party. "Who else is coming? I thought it was just us."

"It is just us, Christmas is a family day. You know that."

"But Mother, there's enough food here for a dozen people."

"Nonsense. Here, take a plate, and help yourself. I'm sure you're starved after your long drive."

Anger, a simmering pot, is ready to boil over. But I put a lid on it and turn down the heat. *Oh Lord, help me.* I look at the spread of hors d'oeuvres and for the first time wonder how my mother keeps her trim figure. Genetics, I'm certain. I'm built like my father. But still, there's no way she could eat all she prepares and not gain weight.

I take the plate she hands me and choose a few samplings.

"Oh, Ellyn, try the stuffed mushrooms. It's a new recipe."

Habits are hard to break, and I bow to her wishes, even though I don't want a stuffed mushroom. But it's easier than saying no.

As is always the case with her.

WHEN WE SIT DOWN for dinner, I'm already stuffed, but she's made a traditional Christmas dinner: prime rib, Yorkshire pudding, and the works.

"Mom, how do you expect me to eat so much?"

"You have a large appetite, Ellyn. You always have."

The pot simmers again.

I put the linen napkin on my lap. "Evidently my appetite isn't as large as you think. I'm already stuffed. I can't eat all this."

"Can't or won't? Are you dieting?"

"No, I'm not dieting. And both—I can't *and* I won't eat any more. I'm sorry you went to all this work, but . . . you'll have to save it for leftovers."

Just like that, I'm breaking away. From the expected. From the old habit.

"Don't be ridiculous. Here, have a slice of meat—rare, just the way you like it." She hands me the platter of prime rib.

"Mom . . ." My tone is tender though I was going for firm. Tears prick my eyes. *Oh, great.* I am *never* vulnerable with my mother. In fact, I don't think I've allowed her to see me cry since that afternoon when I was a freshman and she told me about Eric Neilson. I clear my throat. "Please, listen to me."

"Fine, don't eat the meat. You don't need the calories, that's for sure."

"Mom, why do you do that? Why do you press me to eat and then condemn my weight? Why?"

"I just want you to be happy, and food has always made you happy."

I get up from the table, leave the dining room, cross the foyer, and go into the library to collect my thoughts for a minute.

Oh Lord, I feel crazy. I don't know how to do this with her. I don't know what to say.

I hear my mother's heels tapping across the travertine floor of the foyer. By the time she enters the library a few seconds later, God's answered my plea for help.

I don't know what to say, but I know how to say it. God is asking me to trust Him by offering my vulnerability to my mother. It isn't *her* response I count on—it's His.

"Ellyn, it's Christmas. I can see you're upset about something, but can't we just enjoy our day together? I have a few gifts for you— let's go sit by the tree and you can open them."

She says all this to my back. When I turn to look at her, tears are leaving tracks on my cheeks. "Mom, sit down. I . . . want to talk. I need help understanding a few things."

"Ellyn, you're crying. Let me get you some tissue. You know if you cry that fair skin of yours will blotch something fierce."

"It doesn't matter, please, just sit for a minute."

"Oh, fine." She drops into one of the damask-upholstered wing-back chairs. "What is it?"

"This isn't about food, Mother. It's about . . . men."

"Men? Oh, Ellyn, you don't need a man. You have a fine career and someday this house and all I have will go to you—"

"Stop. Just stop! Listen to me." My plea comes out with a sob. *"Please . . ."*

She crosses one leg over the other and leans back in the chair. "I'm listening."

I take a deep breath and ask a question that's nagged for some time. "Did . . . Dad betray you? Did he have an affair?"

She stiffens. "If you're asking if I have proof, no. But I didn't need proof to know the truth. Your father, as much as you loved him, was just a man, Ellyn."

"But just because he was a man doesn't mean he was unfaithful. Daddy was a man of God, you know that."

She looks away from me. But when she looks back, I see pain etched in her features, which now look aged. "First and foremost, he . . . was . . . a . . . *man*."

I'm quiet for a moment, not sure what to say, but then it comes to me. "Mom, what, or who, turned you against men? Who hurt you?"

She sucks in her breath. "Plenty of men hurt me. I'm not going through my sordid history with you. There is no need to dredge up the past. But trust me, they only have one thing on their minds and they will use you!"

She spits her words like a cobra spewing venom.

Already exhausted, I sit on the sofa across from her. "Just one more question." I hesitate, but the question has pounded at me since the memory surfaced. "Did Eric Neilson really just . . . make a joke of me?"

"Who?"

"Eric Neilson. High school. He asked me to the Homecoming Dance."

She waves me off as though it doesn't matter.

"Mother, you told me he asked me to the dance on a dare, that it was a joke."

"Ellyn, that was more than thirty years ago, how do you expect me to remember that?"

"I think you remember." I watch as her features become set— and then I know. "You lied to me, didn't you?"

Stony silence is all she offers.

"Mother, did you lie to me?"

In a sudden movement, she stands. "No, Ellyn. I *protected* you! That's all I've ever done is protect you! I wanted the best for you. And . . . and this is what I get? Your accusations?"

Now she is the one crying. She turns and leaves the library.

I lean back against the sofa, my emotions spent. Protected me? Yes, I see it now, in her mind, she thinks that's what she did. I sigh, pull myself up from the sofa, and follow her. I find her in the kitchen standing at the sink. I watch her for a minute and then walk up behind her. I put my hand on her back. "Mom, I'm seeing a counselor and she's helping me. Maybe . . . you could do the same and we could both get healthy, you know?"

She turns and faces me. "Healthy? Ellyn, I'm the picture of health."

"I mean emotionally healthy."

She searches my face. *Oh Lord, let her lay down her fears. Let her follow You to health.*

"Some man has finally gotten his claws into you, hasn't he? Has he defiled you? Have you given him the one precious gift you should have saved?"

"Mother—"

"Emotional health, Ellyn? Don't be ridiculous. There's nothing wrong with my emotional health. I know the truth and I live by it. Just as I taught you to do. But now, clearly, you've turned on me and on that truth. What is it? Do you fancy yourself in love with him? Let me tell you, it will only end in heartbreak. Heartbreak, Ellyn, do you hear me? The very thing I worked so hard to keep you from."

Her face crumples as she talks. Deep lines form around her eyes and mouth as bitterness seeps from her.

She straightens, then turns to leave the kitchen. But she looks over her shoulder at me. "I have a headache. I'm going to bed. I expect you to be gone when I get up. *Merry Christmas.*"

With that, she stalks out of the kitchen and her heels tap through the foyer and up the stairs.

I just stand there.

What happened?

You spoke truth, My daughter, and the truth will set you free.

The voice of the Spirit—gentle, tender, and loving—whispers to my soul.

I go to the dining room and begin clearing the table. My movements are slow and my heart is heavy. Yet, with the grief also comes a sense of peace.

Only in the realm of God do the two comingle.

I put food in containers and put them in her refrigerator and then I do up the dishes. I wipe her counters clean. And before I leave, I go to the desk in the kitchen, take a notepad out of the drawer, and leave her a note on the center island.

I love you.

I sign my name and tuck the note under a decorative plate on the island.

The words for my mother are not my own, because, believe me, I'm not feeling love right now. Instead, I know they are God's words for my mother, written through me. Part of being created in the image of God is reflecting Him to others. That is difficult to do when you're mired in bitterness or focused on your own pain. God, through my counselor and friends, is teaching me.

And freeing me.

I get my purse and my coat.

And I leave.

But I do so weighing less than I did when I arrived.

My entire hope is exclusively in your very great mercy.
Grant what you command, and command what you will.

SAINT AUGUSTINE

CHAPTER FIFTY-SIX

Ellyn

 "HOW DID IT GO?"

I'm sitting next to Sabina at the dining-room table in her rental. The blinds are up, and we're both sitting on the side of the table that affords the view of the surf crashing in the cove. The day is every shade of gray and gorgeous in its own way.

I take a sip of my coffee and then answer. "It was hard, like having your gallbladder removed without anesthesia hard."

"That painful?"

I laugh. "Well, maybe I'm exaggerating, but only a little bit." Then I grow serious as I recall the conversation with my mother. "But yes, it was hard. She believes, really believes, that she's protected me from evil all these years. That by filling my mind with what she believes to be true in her mind, that she's somehow protected me."

"Wow. I'm so sorry, Ellyn."

"All I can do now is pray for her. But, for me, I think it was a huge breakthrough. I'm not saying it was a miraculous healing and I don't have any more work to do, but when I left her house yesterday, I left Earl—and years of shame—behind."

Sabina lifts her hand in the air. "High five, girl."

I put my palm against hers.

She wraps her hand around mine. "You are amazing. I am so proud of you."

I shake my head. "I'm not amazing. God is amazing. He led me every step of the way."

"Good."

"Do you mind if we talk about something else. I'm still sort of emotionally exhausted. I can tell you more in a day or two."

"No problem."

"So, you enjoyed yesterday?" I look out at the view as Sabina answers.

"We really did. It was a rich time with incredible people."

I look back at her. "I'm so glad. So what's up for New Year's?"

Sabina's face is radiant. "Well, I'm spending New Year's Eve with my man. We're going to ring in a new season of life together."

"Oh, Sabina, I'm so happy for you. By the way, where is Antwone?"

"He and Miles and the boys went to hit buckets of balls this morning."

"It sounds like Antwone and Miles have really hit it off."

"How does the saying go? 'Necessity is the mother of invention.' They both needed a golf partner, and that foundation seems enough to build a lasting friendship on. Oh, and speaking of New Year's, this is so sweet. Will and Twila were making plans last night to ring in the New Year together. They're spending the evening with Alex and Kimberli. I wish you could have seen Twila—she was glowing."

"Oh, that's so great. I'll give her a call today and get the scoop." Twila is so deserving of love. My heart swells for her. Sure, they just met yesterday so it's too soon to know whether or not they're in love. But if Will isn't the one for Twila, there will be someone else. Of that I'm certain. She is so full of courage. And she's leading the way for me.

If Miles isn't the one for me, then I can believe now that there will be someone else. But, oh. It will take me a while to get Miles out of my mind.

And heart.

Sabina's brow furrows. "What will you do on New Year's Eve?"

"Oh, don't worry about me. I have a standing date with a stack of old movies and a bowl of popcorn . . . with butter." I raise my eyebrows. "Don't deny me a date with butter. There's nothing better." I mean what I say, too. I'm content . . .

Sort of.

As I make the short drive from Sabina's rental to my house, an idea begins to take shape.

Really? Is it ridiculous? Wistful thinking? *Lord? But what if* . . .

I weigh the pros and cons with God as I walk into the house. By the time I reach the phone in the kitchen, there's only one thing I can see standing in the way of the idea. Well, two things . . . and one of them I have no control over.

I'll leave the unknown in God's hands.

I call Twila. She shares the details of her Christmas with Will, and I hear a new lilt in her voice. When she's done, I ask her the question that will give me either the red or green light on my plan.

I'm given a green light.

Oh Lord, I think this is from You . . .

When I hang up the phone, excitement has me trembling . . . and, okay, a touch of uncertainty, too. I grab a pencil, a lined pad of paper from a drawer in the kitchen, and sit at the table in the nook to jot down ideas.

As the ideas shape up, one truth hits me: I can't do this alone.

Back to the phone.

I hear the humor in Sabina's voice when she answers. "Miss me already?"

"No. I mean, yes. But, no. Never mind. I have an idea and I need your help."

DECEMBER 31 BLOWS IN clear and cold. The forecast earlier in the week prepared me for a high of fifty-two degrees. The wind of early morning gives way to a chilly, but still, afternoon. I'll take it.

At 4:30, as the winter sun is dipping on the horizon, I'm rushing between the upstairs deck and the kitchen downstairs—making sure everything is in place. I stop at my bedroom during one of my trips back and forth and change my clothes. Makeup done, I pull the band out of my ponytail and brush my hair until it shines. I leave it loose, hanging over my shoulders and down my back. Then, before heading back down to the kitchen, I reach for a new bottle of fragrance and spray a bit on my neck.

I stand back and look at the image reflected in the mirror. "Beautiful."

At 6:00 p.m. on the dot, there's a knock on my front door. That's when my knees begin knocking too. I take a deep breath and go to the door. I stand there for just a moment.

Lord, this is Your evening. I trust You.

I open the door, knowing who waits on the other side. "Hi."

"Hello."

I can't tell if he's irritated or just confused.

"I believe I was just kidnapped by my buddy Antwone, who then pulled into your driveway, told me to get out of the car, and then . . . left me."

"Well, then, I'm glad I'm home."

"Ellyn?"

"I'm sorry, Miles. The kidnapping was by design. Please, come in and I'll explain."

He steps inside. "You're all dressed up. You . . . look . . . great, Ellyn."

"Thank you. If you don't mind, just follow me and then I'll explain. Okay?"

"Well, it's either that or I walk home, I guess." He chuckles.

I'm so grateful for his sense of humor and willingness to go along with me, at least for the moment. I walk to the stairs and begin to make the ascent. For just a second, I'm aware that he's behind me, and might be watching my least favorable asset make its way up the stairs. But then I choose a different mind-set. What he's seeing is, in fact, my *biggest* asset. A giggle escapes.

"Are you laughing at my predicament?"

I turn and look over my shoulder. "No, I'm just cracking myself up. C'mon, we're almost there." I lead him up to the guest room, cross the room, and open the door to the small outside balcony. Then I head up the last set of stairs to the upper deck. The evening is dark, the moon still hidden. I lead Miles to the balcony overlooking the headlands. The sound of the surf breaks in the distance. "Wait here just a second."

I go grab the gift bag I planted nearby, and then come back and hand it to him. "Here, this will explain things."

I reach for his hand and put the handles of the bag around his fingers.

"I can't see it."

"Oh, right. I turn and reach for the candle and lighter I left on the railing. Everything is planned to perfection and in its place. The only unknown is how Miles will respond. But I won't worry about that. It's in God's hands.

I light the candle and hold it between us. "Okay, go ahead."

"The bag looks familiar." He reaches inside, pulls out a small box, and takes off the lid. He takes a smooth piece of sea glass out of the box. He rubs his thumb over the word etched into the glass. "Here, hold the candle closer, Ellyn. I can't read it."

I move the candle closer to the piece of glass he holds. My breath catches and my hands tremble. The flame sways back and forth with my shaking.

He looks at the piece of glass and reads the word inscribed on it. He stares at it for a moment and then rubs his thumb across the word again.

"Miles . . ." My voice is hoarse. "You told me to let you know if I was ever ready for more."

He looks up at me.

"If you're still . . . interested, I'm . . . ready."

He stares at me for what feels like forever and then he looks back down at the piece of glass he holds. "You're ready for this?" He holds up the sea glass. "Ready for *Love*?"

I nod. "Yes, I am. Miles, I . . . love you and I'd like to date you. In a romantic sort of way."

His face is shadowed, but the flame flickering between us catches the glimmer in his eyes. He reaches out and takes the candle from me and sets it on the railing. Then he takes me in his arms and pulls me close.

I snuggle into the warmth of his embrace.

"Oh, Ellyn . . ."

"Hmm?"

He shudders against me. "It's . . . *freezing* out here."

I pull back. "Yes, I know. Stay here." I go over to where a power strip with multiple cords plugged into it sits beneath an outlet. I reach for the plug and push it into the socket. As I do, the upper deck comes to life with hundreds of white, fairy lights. They hang from the railing encircling the balcony, and they outline the frame of the white rental tent that is set up in the middle of the deck.

"Wow . . ."

There is awe in Miles's voice.

I go back to him. "I hope you'll stay for dinner."

"Dinner?"

"Yes." I walk to the tent and pull back the two front flaps, revealing a table for two set inside. Next to the table stands my outdoor heater, along with candelabras standing on either side. I tie the flaps back, pick up the lighter I left on the table, and light the propane heater and the twelve tapered candles. On a small buffet on the side of the tent are covered serving dishes with flickering pots of Sterno under each. I light candles I've set on the table, along with a small votive in the center of the table. I turn back to Miles. "Please, come in, it's cold out there."

He walks into the tent, where the heater already warms the interior. He turns and looks back out the open flaps at the stars twinkling overhead. Then he turns to me—he stands so close that I feel his breath on my cheek as he whispers, "Ellyn, would you give me the honor of your second kiss?"

I stand on my toes and tilt my face up to meet his.

His lips are warm. His kiss tender.

He pulls back from me. "And your third kiss?" Then he kisses me again.

His voice is husky. "And your four—"

I reach for his face and pull it toward me. My kiss is more demanding than his. When I need to catch my breath, I lean back just a bit. "Miles Becker, you were my first kiss, and I hope you'll be my last kiss, and every kiss in between." As I watch his face, tears glisten in his eyes . . . as they do in mine.

"That, Ellyn, would be my great pleasure."

And he proves it.

You called and cried out loud and shattered my deafness. You were radiant and resplendent, you put to flight my blindness. You were fragrant, and I drew in my breath and now pant after you. I tasted you, and I feel but hunger and thirst for you. You touched me, and I am set on fire to attain the peace which is yours.

SAINT AUGUSTINE

CHAPTER FIFTY-SEVEN

Sabina

ON THE FOURTH SATURDAY in May, Antwone and I sit side by side, along with fifty or so of Miles's and Ellyn's closest friends and family. As we wait, I look up and see blue sky peeking through the top of the cathedral—the canopy of cypress branches. The branches sway in the spring breeze and sunlight dapples the cathedral floor, reminding me of the day not so long ago that God met me here and called me unto Himself.

Sitting here now, I'm staggered by the changes that have taken place since that day. When the bonds of shame are broken, freedom soars.

I reach over and grasp Antwone's hand, then lean in and kiss him on the cheek. "I love you, baby."

He gives my hand a gentle squeeze. We are not the only ones soaring today—nor are we the only ones wooed by romance.

Twila sits in front of me, her hand clasped in Will's—they lean, heads together, and whisper to one another. There is, as of last night, a thin platinum band with a small diamond on Twila's left ring finger. They announced their engagement, at the urging of Miles and Ellyn, at the rehearsal dinner last night. The dinner was a formality, as there was little to rehearse for this simple ceremony. Rather, it was a time for those closest to Miles and Ellyn to affirm and celebrate their love.

Nerissa sits on Twila's other side. Her left arm drapes around Twila's shoulders. The ring Nerissa wears on her left hand also speaks of love and commitment. She's committed her life to her eternal Bridegroom. I notice her eyes are closed and I imagine she is enjoying this moment with Him.

My thoughts are interrupted by the singing of violin strings signaling the beginning of the ceremony. Miles and his pastor walk down the middle aisle and take their places.

Then Ellyn appears.

She walks into the grove and stands at the back.

The friends and family gathered all stand and turn to watch her. Before I turn, I wait to see the look on Miles's face. I see such joy there . . . and maybe even a hint of awe.

As I stood with Ellyn just a couple of hours ago and fastened the dozens of small, pearl buttons up the back of her dress, we talked of nothing.

And of everything.

Once the dress was buttoned, Ellyn turned toward me. "How do I look?"

Her face glowed—a hint of peach touched her cheeks and lips. Her sea-glass green eyes shone beneath thick lashes touched with dark brown mascara.

"You're breathtaking."

She smoothed the antique white dress over her ample hips and then turned to look into the full-length mirror in the room. She adjusted the bodice of the dress. "Too much cleavage?"

"No. You know just how to take advantage of your curves. It's lovely and appropriate. Though, it might distract Miles a bit."

Ellyn blushed. "Well, let's hope so."

I gave her a hug then. "Oh, my friend, we've come a long way, haven't we?"

"Yes, we have."

"You were and are God's gift to me, Ellyn—my dearest friend."

"Likewise. All of this . . . I don't think it would ever have happened if it weren't for you."

"Oh, no. I'm not taking the credit for any of this. This is about you—your willingness to follow God and do the hard work He called you to do. This is His doing . . . and yours."

Tears of joy glistened in her eyes.

"Oh, no, you don't. You don't cry. You cry and you ruin your makeup. You hear me?"

Rosa walked in and took over. Someone needed to be in charge. She reprimanded Ellyn and then she stood on her toes, reached up and put her hands on Ellyn's cheeks, and kissed her forehead. "He's a good man. But if he don't take good care of you, he has me to deal with. And you know I told him that. He knows." As she talked she fussed with Ellyn's dress and her bouquet.

I stood back and watched. How like God to provide a mother hen for Ellyn, especially today, when her own mother, who refused the invitation to the wedding, won't be here.

"Now, go. Go! De photographer is waiting . . ."

Ellyn

I stand at the back of the cathedral and wait for the music signaling me to walk down the aisle between our guests. Though the cathedral is full, all I see is Miles. While I know he is surrounded by the beauty of creation—the grand cypress trees and the view of the ocean beyond—it is invisible to me today.

Instead, my gaze is drawn to Miles's face—he is the creation of God I see. And soon, he'll be my husband.

My husband. Words I thought I'd never utter.

When Miles sees me, I watch emotions cross his face. What I see in him, through him, is the reflection of God.

Is the reflection perfect? No.

But it is splendid, nonetheless.

Lord, let Miles see the same in me. Let him see Your image, in and through me. Now and always.

As the music plays, I feel as though I float down the aisle.

The bonds of shame are loosed, and I soar.

When I reach Miles, I see tears in his eyes. He takes my arm and leans down to whisper in my ear. "You are beautiful, Ellyn. I love you." His voice is thick with emotion.

The pastor opens his Bible and reads the passage I chose from Ezekiel:

"'When I looked at you and saw that you were old enough for love, I spread the corner of my garment over you and covered your nakedness. I gave you my solemn oath and entered into a covenant with you, declares the Sovereign Lord, and you became mine.'

"'I bathed you with water and washed the blood from you and put ointments on you. I clothed you with an embroidered dress and put leather sandals on you. I dressed you in fine linen and covered you with costly garments. I adorned you with jewelry . . . you were adorned with gold and silver . . . Your food, fine flour, honey, and . . .'"

The pastor pauses. ". . . butter."

Our guests erupt in applause.

"This is the Ellyn DeMoss version we're reading from today."

Miles looks at me, his delight and love so evident. My breath catches, and tears well. I mouth *I love you* to him and hold his hand tight.

The pastor continues. "'You became very beautiful . . . because the splendor I had given you made your beauty perfect, declares the Sovereign Lord.'"

Miles

With Ellyn's hand in mine, I listen to the words the pastor reads. So appropriate. God has made Ellyn's beauty perfect, inside and out. I look down into her sea-green eyes and wink. She squeezes my hand in response.

Lord, thank You. Thank You. Several years ago, just after losing Sarah, I thought a moment like this was impossible. I knew I'd never love again. The ache of loss was all I could feel. Yet, here I stand today, my heart full with a rich and mature love for the woman by my side. A woman, I smile to myself, *who I find irresistible.*

The pastor closes his Bible. "We are gathered here today to celebrate the love between Ellyn and Miles, who will now share their vows with one another."

Ellyn takes a step closer and gives me her other hand. We stand facing one another now. I hear her take a breath and then listen in awe at God's goodness.

"Miles, I am created in the image of God and I am made beautiful by His splendor. Today, I vow to embrace my splendor and share it with you for all of my days . . ."

Sabina

As Ellyn continues her vows, I look beyond her to the opening at the end of the grove, where that picnic table seems to sit on the edge of the world. The water in the distance is a deep, dark blue today, broken by the pure white of the foaming surf. The view is framed by the cypress trees, leaning in, branches stretched in a protective embrace over this ceremony.

The grandeur, the splendor of His creation, is nothing compared to that of those gathered here. Those who walk by themselves without wonder. And those, like Ellyn and Twila, who understand and claim their God-given splendor.

I'm roused from my revelry by the sound of clapping and laughter as Miles leans down and kisses his new wife for the first time.

His beautiful wife.

Created in the image of Almighty God.

Ellyn

As Miles vows his love and commitment to me, I stand in wonder. Through this man, I've seen a side of God I never knew existed. And tonight, as we become one, not only will my intimacy with Miles deepen, but so will my intimacy with God. I will know Him not only as Father, Savior, Friend, Provider, and Protector. But I will also know Him as Husband and Lover.

Through Miles, God will love me and continue to reveal Himself to me in new ways.

After we exchange rings, we are finally given the go-ahead to seal our vows with a kiss. Miles bends to me and I reach and put my arms around his neck. The scent of the cypress trees and the salt of the surf mix with the warmth of his cologne making for a heady, enticing scent.

His lips on mine are soft, warm, and tender, as always. We linger for just a moment and then pull back from one another, though our eyes remain locked in an intimate gaze. Then I reach for him and kiss him again.

And again.

Because, honey, this man's kisses are better than anything I've ever tasted.

Even butter.

Dear Readers,

"Don't edit your life."

I pondered the words spoken to me by my life coach and spiritual mentor after I'd lamented about the struggle I was having writing this story.

"But this isn't *my* story. It's fiction."

Again came his encouragement. "Don't edit your life, especially with this book."

How could he say that? He knew nothing of the book I was writing—only that it was another novel. He didn't know the characters, the plot, or even the title. Yet, his words cut to the core of my struggle. I was living a piece of the story I was writing, but I wished I wasn't.

However, it was the story God was giving me.

I wasn't to edit it to suit my own desires.

Instead, I was to live it.

And write it.

I've struggled with my body image since my early teen years. I didn't and I don't share the iconic female shape of our culture—tall, long waist, long legs, and thin. Oh, so thin. With each passing year and each pound gained, that image taunted me more.

For many years, I woke each morning with accusations running through my mind: *You're fat. You're worthless. You're lazy. You'll never change.* My own personal *Earl*, the Accuser, hurled lies at me, and I began each day defeated.

So I hid. Not literally, but metaphorically. I hid behind a wall of competence. If I could do everything well, then the real me, the one weighed down not by the pounds I carried, but by the shame I embraced, would be invisible to others.

Invisibility has been my persistent desire—my besetting sin.

331

I unknowingly carried that desire with me into my forty-ninth year of life and into the writing of this, my third novel. Then one afternoon, I happened upon this quote from Saint Augustine:

Men go abroad to wonder at the heights of mountains, at the huge waves of the sea, at the long courses of the rivers, at the vast compass of the ocean, at the circular motions of the stars, and they pass by themselves without wondering.

The quote led me back to a familiar verse—one so familiar to many of us that we, perhaps, take it for granted:

> *So God created mankind in his own image, in the image of God he created them; male and female he created them.*
> (Gen. 1:27)

I was stunned. As one who sees God in every glorious twig created, I had never seen Him when looking into a mirror. Instead, I saw brokenness. I saw shame. And I wanted to hide.

I'm not alone. Neither are you. In fact, this desire has followed us through history.

We've longed for invisibility and hidden in shame since that fateful day in the garden when Adam and Eve recognized their nakedness and hid from God.

But just as He called to them, "Where are you?" He's calling to us, "Where are you?" And just as He, in His great mercy, covered Adam and Eve in garments of skin, He covered us in the blood of His son—Jesus Christ.

Please don't mistake *Invisible* for a story about weight—too much or too little. Nor is it a story about health, or food, or sedentary versus active lifestyles. Neither is it a story about competence or self-reliance, loss or grief.

This is not a self-help book written as a means of condoning or judging any of the above-mentioned states of being or practices.

No.

This is a story of freedom from the bondage of shame. Freedom found through believing the truth of God's Word.

Saint Augustine, who lived between 354–430 CE found this same freedom through the truth of God's Word. His autobiography, *Confessions*, chronicles much of his journey. He was a man bound by sexual immorality, gluttony, and grief, and imprisoned by the untruths He believed. But when He accepted the truth of God's Word, he was set free. His story, written so long ago, is startling in its relevance today.

Truth remains forever relevant.

Do shackles of shame still bind you? The shame of abuse, addiction, pornography, promiscuity, weight, whatever . . .

Are you hiding?

The merciful voice of the Father is calling you out of hiding. He's wooing you to Himself. He longs to erase your shame and replace it with the truth of His love and mercy.

Will you come out of hiding and walk with Him?

Will you accept yourself as one created in His image?

Will you look into a mirror and smile at His glory reflected there?

Oh, how I pray those are choices you'll make. Because in doing so, you'll walk in freedom! I know, because as this story drew to completion, those are choices I made.

With love,

Ginny L. Yttrup
www.ginnyyttrup.com
ginny@ginnyyttrup.com

DISCUSSION QUESTIONS

1. Have you ever wished you were invisible or wanted to hide? If so, why?

2. The characters in *Invisible* each display attributes of Saint Augustine whose struggles thousands of years ago are similar to many of our struggles today. Was there one character you most related to? Or did you see parts of yourself in each character? Explain.

3. Did reading *Invisible* change your view of Genesis 1:27? If so, how?

4. What does it mean to you to be made in the image of God?

5. How did believing God's Word set both Ellyn and Sabina free?

6. Have you ever felt angry with God? Did you express that anger? Why or why not?

7. Sabina blamed herself for the deaths of two people close to her. Have you ever assumed responsibility for something you had no control over? If so, why?

8. Earl's lies were woven into Ellyn's being, affecting her beliefs about herself and about men. Have you believed lies about yourself that kept you from recognizing the truth about yourself or others?

9. What was the difference between the way Miles and Sabina handled their grief? Did you learn anything from Miles that might help you look at your own loss, grief, or frustrations in a new way?

10. Ellyn and Twila both struggled with body image issues and food choices, though in different ways. Why did Twila seem to grasp emotional health and freedom sooner than Ellyn?

11. What shift took place in Ellyn's thinking that led her to finally pursue a romantic relationship with Miles?

12. *Invisible* is a story of being set free from the bonds of shame. Has shame bound you in any way? How might you, like the characters in *Invisible*, ultimately enjoy freedom?

WORDS

continues to make an impact.

2012 DOUBLE-CHRISTY AWARD FINALIST
Best Debut Novel, Best Contemporary Stand Alone

2012 CHRISTY AWARD WINNER
Best Debut Novel

2012 *FOREWORD REVIEWS'* BOOK OF THE YEAR
Religious Fiction

"Yttrup writes a riveting, emotionally charged story."
—Publishers Weekly

★★★★
—RT Book Reviews

ALSO AVAILABLE
Lost and Found